The
RADIANCE
of a
THOUSAND
SUNS

Manreet Sodhi Someshwar is an award-winning writer of four books, including the critically-acclaimed *The Long Walk Home*.

The
RADIANCE
of a
THOUSAND
SUNS

MANREET SODHI SOMESHWAR

HarperCollins *Publishers* India

First published in India in 2019 by
HarperCollins *Publishers*
A-75, Sector 57, Noida, Uttar Pradesh 201301, India
www.harpercollins.co.in

2 4 6 8 10 9 7 5 3 1

P ISBN: 978-93-5302-965-4
E ISBN: 978-93-5302-966-1

Typeset in 11.5/15.2 Adobe Caslon Pro at
Manipal Digital Systems, Manipal

Printed and bound at
Thomson Press (India) Ltd

MIX
Paper
FSC FSC® C010615

A Hundred Million
and more

For my parents
Haripal Kaur Sodhi and Gurbax Singh Sodhi

and
Malvika, Prasanna and Nyx

Prologue

TALL STRAPPING MEN, wrapped in wool blankets for warmth, huddled on the mist-laden lawn, still as trees, dewdrops gathering on their turbans. The Punjab Police had plucked out their sons in the night, like thieves in the darkness. Niki peered out from behind curtained windows as her lawyer father was hurriedly summoned outside.

The boys had been trussed up like chickens, the waiting men recounted, their voices muffled. Then they had been thrown into white Maruti Suzuki Gypsys which had roared off, dust devils dancing in their wake. Their boys would be incarcerated in some jail without bail, the men hoped, for it was also possible that the Gypsys would head straight for the Indo-Pak border. The Punjab government was battling terror and, patrolling the alluvial banks of the Sutlej, policemen routinely encountered militants fleeing to the other side. The river sundered India from Pakistan, and even buffaloes were known to swim across – the police had no choice but to open fire.

Which was why the men had come to find a lawyer who could file habeas corpus petitions on behalf of their sons. A lawyer foolhardy enough to appear for these missing men, for while it was a time of terror, none knew exactly who the terrorists were: the militants demanding a separate Sikh state or the police quelling them.

Ten-year-old Niki watched Papa disappear into the night.

Upon his return a day (or several) later, Papa took off his turban, his forehead a suntanned arch, and soaked his feet in a basin of hot water, which slowly greyed. His face was drawn with what even she, young as she was, could understand was more than fatigue. Still, he answered all of Niki's questions. He had to rush because the window to file the petition was capricious. Habeas corpus, the writ with the Latin name, mandated the body in custody be produced. But the police might delay, finally producing a bullet-riddled dead body instead. Yes, they were all Punjabis, many of them Sikhs, several of whom wore turbans. No, there were no bad guys, just one brother fighting another—

The thunder of an express train roused Niki back to the present. She was at the 42nd Street station, waiting for the B train that would take her home at the end of a long day. In the subterranean belly of the New York City subway, three decades later, the past had intruded into the present: in her mind, the turbaned men from the lawn huddled on the platform with her. What had caused them to emerge from the fog of memory?

That day at SAYA, the South Asian Centre for Youth and Adults, the non-profit where she volunteered, men had gathered in the spare office, still as the leafless branches of the oak outside the window. Despite the large population of undocumented South Asian workers in New York, most Americans assumed all illegal immigrants were Mexican. Just as they assumed all turbaned men were Muslim or Arab. As she helped them fill out applications for the NYC identification card, free for all residents, Niki had learnt about the men who fried pakoras, shovelled snow, made beds in Midtown hotels, flew bicycles to make food deliveries.

They had not shown up for work that day, afraid of being deported for robbing citizens of jobs. They were afraid to return to their homes in case immigration agents were waiting with handcuffs. Their wives' voices had whispered over secret phone calls that uniformed men outside their doors were commanding them to 'open up!' They had deposited their children overnight with relatives who were resident aliens. Despite the heating, they had kept their winter coats on, pockets bulging, eyes darting, ready to run with whatever meagre possessions they had on them.

With great zeal, the new government had begun executing its campaign promise to rid the country of undocumented immigrants. Using a printout from the American Civil Liberties Union website, Niki had advised the men about what to do if immigration agents showed up at their door.

At the clang of an approaching train, people moved forward and Niki joined the surge. Squeezing through the crush, she located a spot on the nearest pole to latch on before the train sped up. As she put on the mute act of the subway commuter, eyes averted, a gasp made Niki swivel. Beside her, a woman was staring at something, her mouth open. Niki followed her gaze and her eyes popped. And widened as she scanned the subway car. Swastikas in black ink were scrawled on glass windows, framed posters and advertisements.

'Anyone got hand sanitizer?' The woman's voice rang out, her extended arm indicating the graffiti. A susurrus of indignation built up through the car, heads swivelled, and a young woman held up a bottle of Purell. Niki dug into her bag for tissues. The woman began to erase the 'Heil Hitler' and swastika on the nearest MTA map. A sudden awareness dawned inside the car as commuters pulled out tissues and bottles of sanitizer and began attacking the graffiti. Several minutes later, the car was smelling like an alcoholic, wiped clean, and commuters resumed averting their gazes.

Swastikas, Niki snorted. An auspicious Indian symbol which a fascist had appropriated, giving legions of Nazis and neo-Nazis a ready symbol of hate. Discreetly, she studied the woman who had led the clean-up operation. Tall, chestnut skin, hooped earrings, grey braided hair gathered at the nape of her neck. With a bittersweet spasm, her heart recalled Nooran. And Jyot. Two women bound by similar tragedies – of fate and faith, patriarchy and prejudice. Nooran had raised Niki on stories while it was Jyot's fiercely-guarded story that Niki had learned. Nooran had raised Papa as her baby brother, and Jyot was the missing sister who had haunted him.

With determination and dignity, the woman had righted in a few minutes the graffiti many had noticed but chosen to ignore. It wasn't that people didn't know right from wrong. They almost always did. Doing the right thing was what snared them. The right thing was tiresome, boring, too much work... Even that would be okay, if the objections were limited to life's tedium. But what kept people silent was the knowledge that resided in them like marrow in their bones. If you made a habit of doing what was right, one day, it would kill you...

Book 1

I
(1977–1984)
Us and Them

Long long ago in India, a fraternal war was fought over a kingdom. The story of the warring princes, the Kauravas and the Pandavas, is the central spine of the Mahabharata. But like any epic, it has stories within stories, and the narrative resembles an ancient banyan, its primary trunk propped by motley aerial roots like scripture, philosophy, folklore, side stories and legends. The Mahabharata claims: 'Whatever is here is found elsewhere. But whatever is not here is nowhere else.' Blame the bombast on Vyasa, the immodest writer of the epic, who is also a central character, and, indeed, the progenitor of all the princes. Only remember, in this epic, the past is forever intruding into the present.

1
(1977)

❊

THE PRICE FOR children was wrong.

Nooran narrowed her eyes as the rippling banner caught her attention.

> **Incentives for Sterilization**
> 2 Children: Rs 100/-, 3 Children: Rs 50/-
> 4 or more Children

The limp wind rippled the thin fabric. She returned to ministering Roop, whose head was in her lap. As Roop cradled her swollen belly, she moaned. In the driver's seat, Biji hunched forward and clutched the steering wheel harder, trying to avoid the tonga that careened where the road narrowed ahead due to repair work. The clacking of the horse's hooves rang above the screech of the scooters weaving about like impudent mosquitoes amongst the stalling four-wheelers.

Roop's water had broken ahead of schedule, and the young mother-to-be had panicked, assuming another miscarriage. Biji had

3

prayed for Guru Nanak's mercy as they guided Roop to the car. With
Roop supine in the backseat, cushioned by Nooran, Biji had shoved
the hospital bag in the front seat before releasing the clutch and
sliding the car onto the road. She was an occasional driver, delegating
the navigation of chaotic roads to her son. But Jinder was away, the
road was dug up for repair, the passenger was pregnant and terrified,
and they had to reach the hospital quickly but safely. So Biji drove
like she had commandeered a military vehicle in the cantonment
town – at a precise and steady pace amidst civilian mayhem.

The car stalled again. They were within spitting distance of the
hospital ground. Nooran dabbed Roop's perspiring brow, the banner
drawing her attention again. It was strung across the arch of the
gateway leading to the hospital.

Ferozepur Civil Hospital
Sterilization Is Best Method Of
Family Planning

The price of four plus children, she noted, was even lower, averaging
Rs 10 per child. Tch, Nooran clucked under her breath at this bad
omen. A Punjab Police jeep and an empty passenger bus were parked
at the entrance where policemen idled.

'What are the police doing here?' Biji muttered. As the traffic
coughed to life, she turned right to the hospital. The gate was open.
The car moved forward. A policeman detached from the group and
held up an imperious arm. Just then, Roop groaned aloud, writhing
in the sweat that had dampened the rexine seat. Biji pressed the
accelerator, the car roared and shot forward. The startled policeman
skittered out of its path.

Inside the hospital, a long line of men was strung through the arid
lawn like overused hospital laundry. Nooran pursed her lips. Roused
out of their homes by police, no doubt, they had been bundled into
the passenger bus and dumped at the sterilization camp to be leached

of their manhood. Now, with stitched-up scrotums, they must be waiting for compensation. At the far end where the colonial-era building curved was a colourful huddle of squatting women who had been brought to the camp. Biji slowed down to navigate past the winding queue. The policeman whom she had startled was chasing them, brandishing a lathi. When he caught up with the car, he rapped it on the side. Peering through the window, he yelled, 'Where you going?'

'To a doctor! Can't you see?' Biji tossed her head towards the backseat.

The cop leaned forward, saw the pregnant Roop cradled by Nooran, rolled saliva in his mouth, and then asked them to wait.

'What's there to wai—' Biji protested. But he was already going back to the gate. She cast a worried glance at her daughter-in-law in the backseat before studying the disappearing cop in the rear-view mirror. The car grumbled.

In the line of waiting men ahead, a group had formed. A constable strutted towards them, his belly leading the way. With an alacrity that was at odds with the rest of his body, he brought his bamboo staff crashing down upon the clustered men. The sound of wood meeting flesh cracked the dry air, followed by yowls and shuffles. The men scattered, rearranging their injured selves in line. The constable brought his left index finger up to his mouth and held it there for several theatrical seconds as the men watched him ruefully.

'SILENCE is golden!'

Nooran clucked her annoyance but softly. For the past twenty months, that slogan had been repeated on TV, repeated on the streets, repeated in newspapers, repeated on people's lips. The work of nation-building was on, the government had a twenty-point program, the countrywide state of Emergency was for their benefit, and all they had to do was keep their mouths shut and play their part. 'Silence is golden! Work hard! Produce more! Maintain discipline!' The 'produce more' exhortation was not extended to family, though. India's population was at a bursting point, Nehru's daughter

Prime Minister Durga had warned the country. Sterilization was necessary to help India progress and camps had spread through the country faster than a drought. Like the annihilating goddess of her namesake, Durga was charging through the country, rendering its press, politicians and public sterile.

The constable, pleased with the effect he had had on the men, sauntered down the dusty walkway, straight into their path, tapping his staff and flouting his own dictum of silence. As Roop moaned again, Biji had finally had enough. She pressed on the pedal, her hand hit the horn, the car shrieked forward. Its shrillness caught the constable mid-swagger. The queueing men swivelled synchronously like sugarcane stalks tossing their heads in the wind. The car sailed up the driveway, sending stray dogs and the constable flying out of its way. Its urgent journey came to an end near the porch in the centre of the building where steps led up to the outpatient department. Flinging the car door open, Biji hopped out. She then yanked the rear door and bent to retrieve Roop.

'Oye!' an angry voice hailed. 'What's the ruckus for, haan? Disturbing public peace—'

Biji straightened, her arms attempting to hold Roop upright, whose own two hands cradled her ballooned-up belly. Nooran was right behind, her tall frame the scaffolding against which Roop crumpled.

Free from propping up Roop, Biji hurried up the steps to the OPD. The constable hovered nearby, as if in a quandary. A quick scan later, Biji reappeared, shaking her head. From the porch, she questioned the constable, 'The doctors? Nurses? Where are they? Why is no one on duty?'

The constable found his voice. 'Camp,' he said. 'Sterilization camp. Staff is busy.'

'The entire staff? Who is on emergency duty?'

The constable pulled himself upright. 'The camp is priority, madam. Direct orders from up. 300 is the target. Guess how many doctors that needs?'

Roop moaned and looked set to sink to her knees.

'Biji!' Nooran hissed.

'You,' Biji pointed to the constable. 'Go find Dr Bajwa. Tell him Zohra Nalwa is looking for him – urgently! If you don't find him, get another doctor.'

The constable stood rooted.

'Do you want this to be an open-air delivery? Hurry!'

It was Nooran's first time in an emergency room and nothing about it indicated immediacy or care. A metal bed was arranged against one wall, partially screened by a limp green curtain. Across the room from the bed was a grimy stone shelf with a gas burner, some steel trays and implements. The third wall had a desk, beside which was a stack of wooden shelves with files, plastic trays and instruments under dusty covers. Instead of antiseptic, the room reeked of blood and sweat.

Biji rummaged through the shelves for clean sheets. Finding some, she spread them out swiftly, patting the covers over the metal railings. Then she helped Roop unpeel herself from the scaffolding of Nooran's body, and they eased her onto the bed. Biji glanced at her wrist. Nooran knew what she was thinking: it was one hour since Roop's water had broken. Retrieving a towel from the hospital bag, she handed it to Biji, who wiped her daughter-in-law's forehead which broke into fresh perspiration. It was not looking good.

A head burst into the room, peering from behind the curtains in the doorway. 'No doctor available,' he said, 'thanedar told me to tell you,' and vanished.

'Stop!' Biji rushed to the door.

A head reappeared, this time with the body of a young man. He was dressed in the blue uniform of a hospital orderly.

'Wait.' Biji hastened to the desk where she had deposited her bag, and retrieved a crisp 100 rupee note. She let the man see the money, then folded it and put it in his shirt pocket. 'Double when you return. Within five minutes. With a doctor, nurse, technician – anyone you can find to assist with a delivery. Understood?'

The man gulped. For that amount, a busload of men outside were losing their manhood. No wonder his eyes bulged.

'Go,' Biji urged, 'and return quickly.'

He nodded and left.

Meanwhile, the moaning from the bed had intensified. Roop's water had broken six weeks before her due date. A premature baby and no doctor for the delivery.

'Biji,' Nooran said from in front of the gas stove where she had set a pan of water to boil. 'We should prepare to birth the baby.'

'*What*? By ourselves? How?'

Nooran was inspecting the instruments in the steel tray. She took a couple of knives and examined them. 'Biji, have you forgotten? My mother was a midwife; there isn't a child in our village that she didn't help birth – Hindu, Sikh or Mussalman.'

'That doesn't make you a midwife, Nooran!'

The water was bubbling and Nooran dropped the implements into the pan. 'I helped deliver calves and kid goats at home.'

'No, no, no!' Roop moaned. 'Find a doctor … *aah*!'

Biji pressed the sides of her forehead with her hands and closed her eyes. 'Nooran, that was thirty years ago, and you were – what – nine–ten? Besides, delivering a human child is a little different from delivering a calf.'

'No difference.' Nooran glanced at Roop, whose eyes were scrunched as contractions convulsed her. 'You help her with the breathing and I'll see to the delivery. A woman's body knows how to give birth.'

'You are not a doctor.' Biji wrung her hands. 'You don't understand the implements, what to use… What if the baby doesn't come out, or if there is infection, if—'

Nooran held Biji by her forearms. She was a foot taller and her round face gazed evenly at her mistress. 'All we need is a basin of hot water, a sharp knife to cut the umbilical cord and,' she held up her palms, fleshy, stout, 'capable hands.'

Roop cried out. Biji hurried to her bedside and began massaging her hands, casting anxious glances at the door. Nooran stood by the stone shelf, dipping implements into the bubbling water. She was faking it well, but someone had to hold it together – at least until Jinder arrived. Maybe Biji's son could rustle up a doctor? The driver had hurried to the police station where Jinder Nalwa, lawyer, was interned for protesting the imposition of Emergency.

Nooran was not the praying sort and she had never seen a cow or doe need much assistance when giving birth. And didn't Bulleh Shah, the great bard of Punjab, say: 'I only know myself, I cannot know any other. Who, then, could be wiser than I?'

Through the haze of the rising steam, Nooran recalled those distant years when she was apprentice to her mother. Once, they were called to attend a cow who was different: nervous, lying down, getting up, flicking her tail, before she eventually got down to the business of pushing the calf out. Nooran stole a sideways glance at Roop, whose face was as white as freshly churned butter. Roop had lost two babies before, each miscarried in the last few months of the pregnancy. This was the first one she had carried full term, which meant the baby was ready to arrive. 'Niki or Nika, little girl or little boy. I don't care about gender. All I want is a healthy baby,' she had said. As a nursery school teacher, her lap was filled with children, but she wanted one of her own.

Nooran remembered Ammi, a bucket of warm water, clean soap and rope beside her. She had helped the heifer calve over seventy-two hours of labour, soothing her with words, massaging her flank, feeding her, watching the vulva for that first sign of the calf's feet and nose. But, most of all, she saw Ammi's hooped gold earring swing as she said, 'We have to trust a mother's body, Nooran – it has prepared for birth over months, and we must let its rhythms guide us.'

As Roop's labour progressed and no assistance arrived, Biji and Nooran discovered their hitherto unknown skills at midwifery. It would be a primal birth, only the baby would not be born of the dust or spring from the body of its creator father. Without the assistance of science or scripture, the two women listened to the rhythms of Roop's body, followed their instincts, and through the contractions and dilation, they stayed with the mother, mopping her brow, reminding her to breathe, massaging her feet, singing to her, feeding her. Biji's greying hair came loose from her usually neat bun. Nooran's polyester kameez shone in drenched patches. Time melted away as the women engaged with the hard work of labour and birth.

When Nooran finally took a break, she stepped outside for some air. The sky wore a grey pall, and underneath it, men snaked through the grounds of the Civil Hospital in an unending line. The medical staff was wholly engaged with the obstruction of birth, briskly snipping male tubes and tying up female ones. The family planning officers, seated at tables at the far end of the ground, recorded the mounting numbers of achieved sterilizations. A mass murder of potential lives was going according to plan, indifferent to the miracle in progress in the emergency room.

And a thirty-year old memory, of corpses rotting in the stifling sun, of a sky dark with vultures, of droning flies supervising a mass murder, assailed Nooran. She clenched her fists.

A live birth in the midst of mass sterilization was a transgression. In a nation that had been told to shut up and follow orders, this was neither silent nor orderly: a birth was a messy, bloody affair conducted with ululation – much like life itself. A great unease seized Nooran. She inhaled deeply, before hurrying back.

Thirty hours after they began, a baby girl was born. 'Niki,' Roop breathed with a teary smile, too exhausted to sit up. Nooran once again became the scaffold against which the new mother leaned as she held her infant in her arms and gazed at her. Niki held a fist up to her mother and Roop rubbed her nose against it. Nooran beamed at the new arrival; a new story had begun. But a story that was beginning when other stories around it were being snuffed to death was one that would pay the price for its advantages. As she swaddled

Niki, Nooran could not quell the disquiet within her. The world was not fair, and mothers knew this for they dared to bring life into a world which, as the Incentives-for-Sterilization banner broadcasted, apportioned diminishing zeroes when enumerating lives.

By the time Jinder arrived, the baby had attached to her mother's breast. Jinder had spent hours coaxing the officer on duty at the police station to release him on account of the extenuating circumstances, dropping names of influential colleagues. As the day progressed and the baby smacked her lips, Roop started to twitch like a leaf in a storm. Jinder scurried about until he was able to inveigle a doctor into the room. He examined Roop, his expression dour, the stethoscope perfunctory. Injecting her with an antibiotic, he left, promising to return in an hour. Chills seized Roop even as she bathed in her own sweat and mumbled incoherently. Nooran cradled Niki by Roop's bedside, singing lullabies as she soothed the mewling infant and the cramping mother. Biji massaged Roop's limbs, trying to coax life into them. 'Niki, Ni-ki, Ni-ki...' Roop mumbled as she faded.

When Jinder managed to retrieve the doctor, he shook his head wordlessly. Roop's body was succumbing to an infection. The hospital, prioritizing murder over birth for the last twenty months, had accordingly neglected sanitation. Tears streaming into his unkempt beard, Jinder pleaded with the doctor to do something. 'Too late, too late,' the doctor sighed. The multiple pans of water that Biji and Nooran had boiled could not tackle the germs in the air, and Roop's eyes started to glaze over.

Later that day, election results were announced, and the whole nation spoke in one voice. PM Durga was lassoed; the Emergency lifted. Outside, a babble arose as people rediscovered their tongues, road repair was abandoned, traffic went berserk and horns erupted with pent-up rage. Inside the emergency room, Biji clutched her head in her hands, Nooran still cradled the day-old Niki, and Jinder clung to his wife's hand as she faded into silence.

2
(1982)

❋

NOORAN HATED FLIES and God. In that order.

In 1947, returning from the field of death at the age of nine, she had carried two things with her: the stench of carrion and the drone of flies. This was why Nooran always walked on a whiff of attar, a plastic swatter dangling from one corner of her dupatta. Even in the most immaculate Punjabi household, a fly or two was inevitable, as elemental as summer heat. But not in the house of her Biji Nalwa. The swatter wore out every two summers and was the only item Nooran required replacing on a regular basis, not the steel colander or the plastic buckets or the ceramic jars. The only time the swatter was not on Nooran's person was when she stepped out of home.

In every way, though, Nooran was an anomaly. Punjab prized fairness, but she was dark as the underside of a griddle and nonchalant about it. Punjabi women tiptoed around their menfolk, but Nooran strode about like an unapologetic peacock. In a land where multiple gods were invoked in one breath, non-belief was deviant behaviour in need of correction. But Nooran would wrinkle her nose and declare, 'I encountered God long ago; he stinks.'

12

Now, Nooran took off her dupatta-with-the-swatter, picked a floral one – red and white flowers emblazoned on the long wide scarf – bolted the door of the house and stepped out. Niki's bus would arrive any minute at the end of the lane on which their house stood. At 1 p.m., the five-year-old would be drowsy and would need to be carried home. Niki had begun big school, which meant six hours of study and time enough to tire an adult. A bumblebee buzzed in the shade of the guava tree, its fruit ripening in the autumn sun. A bus pulled up. Laughter spilled out of its open windows and door. Nooran mounted the steps and scanned the seated children, the older ones chatting and the younger ones in various stages of slumber. Niki was slumped against a window, her schoolbag slack by her side. Nooran hoisted Niki upon one shoulder, the bag on the other, and exited the bus.

Niki was getting bigger, her feet now dangling down Nooran's thighs. She smiled at the observation as she strolled down the lane. The next instant, her breast was groped, the schoolbag slid from her shoulder, and a bicycle sailed by, the man on it looking back at her, twisting his mouth in a lurid kiss.

Nooran was incandescent with rage. She steadied herself, aware that Niki had been jolted awake, the schoolbag was on the ground, while the man was pedalling leisurely on. Helping Niki stand up, Nooran bent, plucked something from the gravel and hurled it in the direction of the bicycle. An 'aayeee' rang out, the cycle wobbled and the man hunched in pain as the stone found its mark. He cast a wary look behind and Nooran pretended to bend again. He pedalled as if chased by a rabid dog.

'Coward!' Nooran spat.

'What happened?' Niki asked, wide-eyed.

Nooran grabbed the schoolbag and with Niki's hand clutched in hers, they marched down the lane.

'I taught him a lesson.'

'What lesson?' Niki skipped as she walked.

'When a man is violent, not every woman will remain silent.'

Sighting their gate, Niki ran ahead, stood on its bottom railing, reached for the latch and swung backwards with the opening gate. Her red-ribboned plaits danced as she raced down the path to the front door on her chubby legs. Nooran, meanwhile, watching her progress with affection, absentmindedly reached for the air with both her hands, curling them as she tucked them to the sides of her head. Shorthand for drawing towards herself any evil that might befall Niki. In a land where violence could surface unexpectedly, mothers had learnt to ransom themselves for their children.

3
(1982)

❋

IN THE NALWA household, the study was where everyone congregated. Niki sat cross-legged on the floor, the tip of her tongue poking out of her mouth as she concentrated on sharpening pencils. The shavings fell in her lap, which Nooran would need to rescue fairly soon unless she wanted to sweep the floor. Biji sat in an armchair rereading one of her books, a glass of whisky by her side. Jinder was at his desk, which was overrun by files and papers, the light from the lamp turning his grey hair white. It was five years since Roop's death, he was barely thirty-five and yet, he was acquiring the look of an old man. He blamed himself for her death, Nooran knew. If he hadn't been imprisoned, he would have been by his wife's side arranging medical care. Perhaps. Since then, Jinder had reduced his political activism, focusing instead on Niki.

The doorbell rang. Nooran peered through the French windows that looked onto the porch. The curtains were drawn but she saw a shadow, restless. At nearly 9 p.m. on an autumn night, it could only be one of Jinder's clients. The bell rang again, more persistent this time. As Nooran made towards the door, Jinder walked out of his study, one hand raised for her to wait.

15

A tall turbaned man, a blanket draped around him in the manner of country folk and his feet in worn leather juttis, stood at the door. The men conferred in the doorway. Meanwhile, Niki looked like she was tired of sitting on the floor. Nooran hurried to her with a plate. 'Here,' she scooped the contents of Niki's lap into it, brushing the flannel frock free of lead particles.

'Ouchie,' Niki said.

Nooran massaged the cramped leg and then hoisted the five-year-old up. Niki held up six pencils, sharpened to tips, whirled around and ran. 'I am going to show Papa!'

Biji and Nooran exchanged a glance before Nooran followed her to the living room. Niki was on her father's arm.

'...you don't come now, Nalwa saab, it will be too late. By morning, I will have lost both my sons. You know I have no idea where the older one is. He left home six months ago, and the police insist he's gone over to the other side.'

Jinder stroked his beard. 'The other side, eh? The Punjab Police will have us believe Pakistan is an in-laws' home!'

'The police are spreading such terror in our village, plucking boys out of homes in the middle of the night. Torturing them. My neighbour's son came back after a fortnight, his legs all bent. Please, Nalwa saab, my younger son is only sixteen—' the man broke off, sinking his face into the folds of his blanket.

Jinder placed a hand on his shoulder and guided the man inside. Nooran took Niki in her arms and headed to the kitchen as Jinder began to talk to Biji in the study.

'Papa didn't look at them, Nooran,' Niki's lower lip trembled as she held up her fist, where a bouquet of pencils bloomed.

'You arrange them on his desk before going to bed. In the morning, he will be so happy to see them.' Nooran handed her a whole-wheat pinni from the fresh batch she had made that morning. Fragrant with ghee and roasted atta, it was Niki's favourite winter sweet, guaranteed to distract her. If only Nooran could quell her disquiet with the same ease.

Trouble had started again. Men were asking for a separate state for the Sikhs now, Khalistan. Assisting them in that cause was the separate state that had been carved out for the Muslims in 1947. News and rumours flowed as swift as the Sutlej River: boys were crossing the border to train as terrorists in Pakistan. Upon their return, they targeted Hindus, forcing them to flee from Punjab because if Punjab was emptied of Hindus, Sikhs would get their state. The Sharma family, who had lived down the road for forever, had already left, their house boarded up since the summer. Biji said the Guptas who owned the flour mill had received threatening letters. They had two policemen posted behind sandbags at their gate, which was always locked now. Nooran walked out of the kitchen with a tumbler of water, Niki at her legs. She served Jinder's client and then went to the study to clear up.

'I don't want to leave this late at night,' Jinder said. 'It gets more dangerous with each passing day. Nobody knows who is on which side—'

Biji watched her son.

'—but if I delay going, Fauja Singh might never see his son again. It is likely that the boy is still in a jail cell, and we can get to him before...'

Nooran knew what was left unsaid. The Punjab Police had had many recent successes with 'encounter killings', the tally of dead terrorists mounting. The police wanted the Punjabis to know it was winning the war on terror. But stories had also begun to filter through of boys being plucked from villages, taken to the border, ordered to run in the direction of Pakistan and then shot in the back; another terrorist killed in an encounter while fleeing to Pakistan for training.

'Go, puttar,' Biji patted him on the back. 'We'll be fine.'

Niki arranged the pencils on her papa's desk where a half-finished glass of whisky sat.

'Come, Niki,' Biji urged with her arms open. 'Bedtime.'

'Story time!' Niki ran to grab her picture book. A hardback, the front cover had an archer taking aim in the direction indicated by his blue-skinned charioteer as a fierce battle raged around them, horses and soldiers tumbling onto the back cover.

Biji took the illustrated Mahabharata, held Niki's hand and glanced in Nooran's direction.

'I'll get her milk.' Nooran tidied up the study, switching the lights off on her way out. Fauja Singh sat by the door, hands cupped in helplessness. She looked away, gripping the plate with the pencil shavings. In the kitchen, she emptied it into the bin. A pencil had drawn the border in 1947, partitioned a homeland and made enemies of brothers. That same line went through Nooran's home such that the front door opened into India and the rear door into Pakistan. Having fled that home, Nooran became aware of that singularity much later when Jinder brought it to her notice. Apparently, the house that split down the middle between the two newly-formed nations was listed amongst the absurdities of Radcliffe Line, the border between India and Pakistan.

Nooran entered Niki's room with a glass of hot milk. Biji and Niki were in bed, the book open in front of them as Biji read, 'All wars are wars between brothers…'

It didn't help that in homes on the border, the Radcliffe Line had partitioned even doors.

4
(1983)

❋

SIX-YEAR-OLD NIKI WAS in Class 2 and, unusually for a child, unhappy to miss school. They had awoken to a curfew and shoot-at-sight orders. Vans with mounted loudspeakers patrolled the streets, alerting residents to stay indoors until further notice. Jinder was in Chandigarh for an appeal at the High Court. Biji turned to BBC Radio. The previous night, a Punjab Roadways bus had been stopped by Sikh militants, and Hindu passengers had been dragged out and shot. The Ferozepur district was a hotbed of militancy, and the government had assigned the paramilitary Central Reserve Police Force, the CRPF, to assist the Punjab Police.

The morning had passed peering from behind curtained windows and looking at their neighbours across the street doing the same thing. By afternoon, the novelty had worn off; milk was getting over – the milkman hadn't made his rounds; there was no newspaper to read; and folks were sick of tuning into the radio. The TV wouldn't be airing anything worthwhile until late evening. For an aberrant day, it was turning out to be staid, the hush broken by the barking of stray dogs.

Nooran was clearing the lunch table when a gunshot sounded. They raced to the window. A stray lay bleeding on the road, gasping for breath. A one-ton truck of the CRPF disappeared up the road, rifle mouths sticking out of its open maw.

'Rabba! What sin is this?' Biji exclaimed, a hand to her heart. She made towards the door but Nooran grabbed her elbow. As the death anniversary of her husband approached, Biji's nerves usually acted up. It was almost twelve years since the Indo-Pak War of 1971 when Brigadier Nalwa had died on the battlefield.

'Why don't you go lie down?'

Niki, who had missed the action due to a toilet break, which mostly synchronized with meal times, came racing up to where they stood at the windows. As she clambered up to join them, Nooran grabbed her. 'Finish your food, will you?'

Niki shook her head.

'Okay then, I'll keep all the pinnis for myself.'

A reluctant Niki dragged her feet to the dining table as Nooran urged Biji to rest.

Crouched on Nooran's bed, Niki solved her jigsaw puzzle. Across from her, Nooran hummed as she embroidered. It was a deliberate attempt at cheer for she took to the unfinished embroidery whenever the past forced its way into the present. In '47, when Partition was announced, Nooran had been at a relative's place in Malerkotla and survived. Her family, though, caught in the quicksand of Ferozepur – a Muslim majority town but granted to India – was killed. When news arrived that the police were requesting assistance with identifying and burying the dead, nine-year-old Nooran went forth with her relatives. There was no family; just corpses guarded by vultures, in heaps, like broken dolls, clothing rendered indistinguishable by blood-dust-flies. Eventually, Nooran reached her one-room home. All that could be looted was gone. Inside an upturned canister, she found a piece of cloth. It was a work-in-progress bagh, phulkari embroidery on red cotton fabric that her mother had begun. The two motifs, woven in silk thread, were a peacock and a couple of mangoes dangling from a brown stem with a green leaf. It would have been completed in time for Nooran's eldest sister's marriage, the base cloth disappearing under bright silk threads and a tapestry of happy motifs that signalled prosperity and fertility. Nooran had carried it back with her.

With time, she had added motifs of her own. One square was densely embroidered in black thread; a closer inspection yielded a swarm of black flies. Another motif marked Niki's birth: an infant cupped in several palms. Nooran was selective about the motifs she put on it, and there were still two rows remaining in the bagh, but it was always on display. When not being worked upon, the embroidery was a coverlet on Nooran's bed.

At 9 p.m. that evening, the vans returned announcing the end of curfew. People tumbled out of their homes to reclaim the roads and rant about the government and its inefficiency: couldn't they have ended the curfew an hour earlier so that people could buy essential groceries? Postprandial walks continued late into the night, as if to make up for the lost daytime as gossip and bemusement reigned.

'All border area districts were under curfew!'

'This is the result of Nehru's daughter playing with fire in Punjab! She can't handle any other party apart from Congress in power.'

'First Pakistan, now Khalistan!'

And in the midst of it all, they discovered the bloody bodies of stray dogs throughout the main street, sprawled on the side or stiffening into the middle. Their blood had crusted, flies buzzed about. Nooran gagged into her dupatta and walked straight back home. Apparently, a bored soldier in a CRPF truck, fed up with no militant sighting, had shot all the strays he had come across. Some men dug a hole at the rear of the colony where the fields ranged. Others piled the carcasses onto a cart and tossed them into the pit.

'Such madness,' Nooran clucked. 'It's '47 all over again.'

5
(1984)

✵

IN JANUARY, THE cold settled in like a guest that never intended to leave. The sunshine that sieved through vast blankets of muddy clouds was the colour of weak tea. The rivers that gave the land its name exhaled mist, which mingled with moist fields readying for the rabi crop. Sharp bitter rain arrived. Fog as tall as men invaded the plains, and Niki discovered the childish delight of extending her arm into the fog and watching it vanish. The mist was sitting in their garden and had inched to the windows as Nooran spread the folding bed in Biji's bedroom for the night. In the study, Niki was busily organizing Jinder's desk under Biji's supervision.

Jinder was at his farm overseeing the wheat crop. If the police and newspapers were to be believed, terrorists were sneaking across the border under the cover of mist and night. The increased police patrolling at the border meant that the fields that edged it routinely suffered from police highhandedness. Which meant that Jinder, a gentleman farmer, was spending more time at the farm as the freshly sown wheat was tilled. On those nights, the women huddled in the room for warmth and stories as they cracked groundnuts and chatted. As Niki snuggled into her, Biji confirmed with Nooran that she had secured the front gate and all doors.

'Not this today, Dadima,' Niki said, thrusting the illustrated Mahabharata aside. 'Tell me another story.'

'Shall I tell you a story about when I was a girl?'

Niki's eyes widened. 'You were a *girl*? But you are so old!'

Biji chuckled. 'In Lahore, I was a girl – Zohra.'

'Zo-hra!' Niki cupped Biji's cheeks.

'That's my name,' Biji grinned. 'And my best friend Ameena lived down the road, and we would meet every day after school to play together, and then after college to chat and study, at her house or mine. Though, I preferred her home.'

'Why?'

'Nihari.'

'What's that?'

'Heaven on a plate. Or hell – depends on who's talking about it.'

'Dadima, tell na!'

'Ameena's ammi made this dish called nihari, a thick, spicy gravy with tender meat in it. But I wasn't allowed to eat at Ameena's home. We could play and study and swap secrets and lie in each other's beds, but food was a no-no.'

'Why?'

'Because that would make me Muslim.'

Niki frowned.

'See,' Biji said, taking Niki's hands in hers. 'There were once two boys who were neighbours. They were alike.' She waved Niki's hands. 'But over time, they started to believe they were so different, they even stopped talking. Then a guru came and made them shake hands. That handshake is a Sikh. I am Sikh, you are Sikh—'

'And Nooran is?'

Both Niki and Biji turned to look at Nooran. She paused in the middle of cracking a groundnut. 'People say I am Muslim, but Nooran is Nooran.'

Niki swung her head back to Biji. 'Go on,' she urged.

Biji patted Niki's head. 'I was okay with not eating. Who cares about food anyway! But the day Ameena's ammi made nihari, I would know as soon as I walked up their garden. My mouth would water, I would make loud sucking sounds, which made Ameena accuse me of eating the tamarind toffees we usually shared. That damn nihari was trouble. It wafted out of the kitchen, filling the whole house with its aroma. So, whether we chatted inside the house or on the rooftop or studied in the garden, there was no escaping it. Ameena was immune to the charms of nihari, I wasn't, and her Ammi soon found out.'

'How?'

'A mother's eyes trail her children everywhere. And Ameena's ammi devised a simple plan, which I put into action promptly. I flew back home and started to walk to Ameena's place once again. Only this time, I recited the kalma as I walked.'

'Kalma?'

'It is a prayer that when you recite you become Muslim. So I recited the kalma, became Muslim and ate nihari at Ameena's. It was every bit as delicious as I had imagined. When it was time to return home, I recited the mool mantar, which you know, on the way back.'

'Wah, Biji!' Nooran flicked an appreciative hand. 'You solved the problem of religion.'

'Shhh…' Niki admonished, a finger on her mouth.

'So, from that day on,' Biji popped a groundnut in Niki's mouth, 'I had a simple formula: while going to Ameena's, I recited the kalma and became Muslim and on my return, I recited the mool mantar and became Sikh again. And I ate whatever I felt like at Ameena's. It was no different from when we played with our dolls, Ameena and I. We could make our doll a teacher, an air hostess, a memsahib, get her married, make her have a baby – it was all up to our imagination really. And I had realized that grownups played at religion too. Eat beef, you become Muslim. Eat pork, you can't be Muslim. Grow a beard and you become Sikh. Wear a thread and you are Brahmin. In fact, the adults had developed a rather funny system of games and rules. Ameena and I kept it simple. She did the same in reverse when she came to my home and Maji, my mother, who always cooked vegetarian food, had no problem with us sharing meals.'

Biji sighed and gazed into the distance. Her nose pin set off her elegant profile: high forehead, slim nose, full mouth. With her right hand, Niki angled Biji's chin back. 'So, where is your friend Ameena?'

'In Lahore. It's a long story—'

'Tell me, tell me, please tell me!'

Lowering her head, Biji rubbed noses with Niki, which set her off giggling. 'Ameena and I were friends for a long time, ten years or so, before things began to change. A fence and a gate appeared at the lane to our colony and people began to take turns guarding it. Bapuji, my father, grew more worried each day. Ameena's brother and Veerji, my brother, started to take turns dropping us to Kinnaird College. That didn't bother me; I had a terrible crush on Ameena's brother by then!'

Niki's mouth was agape, one front tooth missing. Nooran grinned.

'Our neighbours began to change. Hindu and Sikh families started to move out of the colony. Some relocated to Amritsar. We would get independence soon people said, and Pakistan would be created.'

In her mind, Nooran saw corpses guarded by vultures, lying in heaps like clay cups, crowned by blood-dust-flies. She sighed.

'The adults were at their religious games again. Pakistan would be home for Muslims. So, the Hindus and Sikhs had to move to what would be their home, India. Bapuji didn't know what to do. His farms were just outside Lahore, and it was land that had belonged to our family for years. But the rumours grew and we kept waiting. Until one day a rock came flying through our living room window and landed on the glass centre table, shattering it to bits. That night, Ameena's father arrived at our rear door like a thief. Bapuji and he were talking in whispers for a long time. Hooligans, bad men, were roaming our colony, targeting specific houses, armed with paraffin bombs. They were men from outside the colony; Ameena's father had never seen them before, not even in Anarkali Bazaar where he had his wholesale textile shop. We should leave for some time, he said. Get away until the madness died down. Maji hurriedly packed clothes and food.'

Nooran could see that Biji's mind had journeyed to Lahore of '47.

'We slunk out of the rear door, huddled in the alley until Ameena's father could get his car. Our house was dark; unfamiliar sounds breached the night air – shrill, urgent – as if an action movie was playing in the open. The car rolled down quietly and stopped. It was a narrow lane, bordered by fields on the rear, fenced by wire. Quietly, we trooped towards it. Maji lost her footing and cried out. She had twisted her ankle. Bapuji helped her into the car and we followed, Veerji and I occupying the remaining space as Ameena's father and brother sat in the front.

"'Ah!" my mother gasped. She clasped one palm over her mouth, choking. I followed her gaze. The car's headlights picked up our rear-facing living-room windows. Something shone on the window sills, red, livid, leaking trails that ran down the white wall. "Ah!" my mother gasped again and bolted out of the car. She hobbled to the gate in a frenzy, fumbled in her bag for the keys, threw it open and marched towards the window, Bapuji close behind. My brother and I looked at each other. Maji howled then, a piteous cry like someone had wounded her physically. We saw Bapuji console her, before grabbing the offending red mass and arcing it across the lane. It landed with a thud in the grass. A ripe smell hung in the air. Maji shook her head repeatedly, ignoring Bapuji's entreaties until he returned to the car. Lowering his head, he conferred with Ameena's abba. The clamour in the air was intensifying.'

Niki climbed into Biji's lap.

'It was meat, fresh bloody hunks of meat, that someone had deposited on all the window sills, their bloody trails weeping over the walls. My mother wouldn't leave until the meat was removed, the walls wiped clean of blood, her home purified.'

Nooran did not know how much Niki was comprehending. But responding to Biji's anguish, Niki had wrapped her arms around her Dadima's neck.

'What followed was a very scary half an hour. My mother brought out a pail of water from within the house and got down to scrubbing the walls as the men collected the meat and bagged it. Ameena's abba walked deep into the fields to discard it. A roar was filling the air. The smell of barbecue rode the night breeze. My eyes stung from smoke and fear. Veerji had sweat on his forehead and Ameena's brother clutched the steering wheel as if it was threatening to run away. As they took away the meat and fetched water, Bapuji and Ameena's abba cast furtive glances but Maji was as focused on the scrubbing as she would have been if she were cleaning the gurdwara floor. Then, suddenly, shots rang out. Bapuji grabbed Maji and bounded to the car. Ameena's abba slid into the front seat. Not a word was spoken as the car revved up and slid its ghostly way down the lane to where it connected with the main road.'

Niki snuggled into Biji, fingering her earring as she listened intently.

'We reached the banks of the River Ravi near our fields. There, a boatman was waiting to take us across. "Across where?" I asked. But nobody answered as everyone scrambled in. The two fathers had a hushed exchange and we set off down the river. I remember it as if it was yesterday. Dark and quiet, the waves were lapping our boat, and the oars were soundless as they sliced the water. All the way, Maji clutched two things tightly – me and her bag. She was a gentle person, occupied with housework, needlework, and reading the Guru Granth Sahib, with little time for the outside world. She had given birth to five children and lost three. I had never seen her agitated, except on that night. Fresh bloody meat had defiled the purity of her home. You see, Bapuji ate meat, as most men did, but he always ate it outside the house. I wondered what she would say if she knew I had enjoyed the nihari at Ameena's. Would that make me Muslim or a man?'

'Then?' Niki whispered.

'The ride across the Ravi deposited us on the outskirts of Amritsar. My mother never went back to Lahore or our home. In her bag, she had carried her jewellery, most of which was sold so that Bapuji could buy land once again – except for one item. And at my wedding, she gave it to me. It was the one link to our past, she said, to a place and time that was forever lost.'

'What? What was it?'

Biji turned to the side table, where a framed picture of a woman with a dimpled smile dressed in bridal finery rested. She tapped the pendant on Roop's forehead. 'This mang tikka.'

'Mama!' Niki leaned forward, grabbed the picture and cradled it in her lap.

'And Biji gave it to your ma,' Nooran added.

Biji cupped Niki's face in her hands. 'And one day, it'll be yours.'

6
(1984)

❋

THE FIERCE WINTER had yielded to the fierce summer of 1984. People were dropping dead, in the manner of flies in the Nalwa household. Those the heat had spared, the terrorists didn't. Nor did the Punjab Police, who were 'mopping up' militants in border areas. Violence was everywhere. Nooran saw a fly alight on the teak wood dining table, the one she had wiped clean after dinner. A stench of carrion and the drone of flies assailed Nooran, reducing her to a nine-year-old girl. She placed the tray with Niki's sherbet-sweetened milk on the crockery cabinet, minced forward, drew the dupatta-with-the-swatter forward slowly and thwacked the fly dead. Then, she swept it off the table and rinsed her hands in the kitchen sink.

In the study, Niki scowled at the sight of milk, her dimples deepening. 'I am working,' she said, arms folded across her chest. Her seventh birthday had been last month. She had started Class 3, but had seen few days of school; curfew had become another day in the week, erratic and whimsical. No wonder she had the energy to be up late and 'work' with Jinder, who was cleaning his desk. Nooran was permitted to dust the surface, but the files, folders, loose sheets were to be left alone.

'Can I help?' Nooran asked.

'No, you can sit with Dadima and watch.'

Jinder handed her a sheet marked with green ink and Niki placed it carefully atop a column of paper on the floor.

'Gupta is on a hit list,' Biji said, 'and the whole family stays indoors. In this heat, that's understandable, but nobody ventures out for a walk even after dinner.'

'Who doesn't value their lives, Biji?' Nooran settled on the cane stool.

'The hit list grows daily. Bearded boys enter shops, demand cash or threaten to add the shopkeeper to the dreaded list,' Jinder snorted. 'The militant saint who wants to command the Sikhs is behaving no better than a petty thief!'

Indeed. Stories of Sant Bhindranwale were all she heard whenever she stepped out – to buy groceries, take Niki to the park, ferry her to-and-from the school bus. 'Yesterday, when I picked Niki up from the school bus, do you know what the older boys were singing? "Our Bapu has swords and arrows, and their Bapu has a stick!" The Hindu boys looked out the windows, pretending to ignore them, but...' Nooran clucked.

'Us and them again,' Biji said. 'Mahatma Gandhi is not the father of the nation any more, only of the Hindus—'

'The Sikhs have chosen a rustic demagogue as their father – hear, hear! – one who never poses for pictures without a sword in hand.' Jinder sipped his scotch, then looked up with distaste. 'Any mention of him makes my single malt bitter.'

The three adults sighed variously. Niki was righting the paper columns growing on the floor. For a late Saturday evening in the summer, it was very quiet. No honking buses, no trails of laughter, no film songs echoing off a radio – only the hum of the air cooler. The border between curfew and life had blurred; everything was uncertain. Like Mr Mehra who had started to wear a turban when he stepped out of his home, his unshaven chin accreting a respectable beard daily. Or Kohli sahib, whose beard was glued to his chin with lashings of Fixo, which locked his jaw and made him sound like Niki's walkie-talkie doll. Recently, he had let his beard loose, trailing to his chest. Apparently, the sant had decreed that the length of a Sikh's beard was a good measure of him.

Jinder's fingers drummed on the table. 'The news is not good. I spoke with a senior policeman at the court yesterday. He was visiting from Amritsar. Apparently, militants have taken sanctuary inside the Golden Temple, where they are getting weapons training. He said the shopkeepers in the surrounding bazaar have heard gunshots from within the temple complex.'

'Tauba!' Biji touched her ears. 'Defiling the house of god. Is this Sikhi?'

Niki, having finished stacking the sheets into columns, bounded into her father's lap. She smiled up at him and stroked his face with both palms, smoothing his scruffy beard. Jinder had tied it with a thread that morning and trimmed the hairs that were protruding. The sant would regard him an apostate. Niki giggled as her father pretended to eat her palms. Matter-of-factly, he said, 'It might be a good idea to move to Chandigarh. Niki's schooling is suffering. I am gaining notoriety for handling cases for "terrorists". Curfews day in and day out...'

'Another migration, another dislocation,' Biji said grimly. 'I know nobody in Chandigarh.'

It was a modern city, so clean and green that when Nooran visited, she felt it was like the London she had heard of. Lights on the streets told cars when to stop and when to go. In Ferozepur, even the police couldn't manage that. Jinder had studied there and claimed it was the one spot of sanity in all of Punjab.

Jinder shrugged. 'The border is cursed.'

The border had marked them all, Nooran sighed. Biji had married into a landed family in Ferozepur whose farms bordered the Sutlej River. Nooran's parents had lived on the border such that it had barrelled right through their home in '47, sundering it between India and Pakistan. Jinder had been born in the town, as had Niki. Now, the border was birthing curfews and hit lists and militants. And regular Sikhs were suspect because they were not hirsute enough or had Hindu friends. Was Biji Nalwa's household doubly suspect because of its Muslim resident?

Jinder interrupted her thoughts. 'What do you think, Nooran?' he asked.

Biji and Jinder seldom took a decision without asking her opinion. Nooran knew she was fortunate. Soon after the Partition riots, she was brought to Biji's father by a Muslim worker on his farm. Though they were only nine years apart, Nooran had always addressed her as Biji, as 'mother'. She had started with helping take care of six-month-old Jinder. From straddling him on her waist to braiding his hair into a top knot to tying the sehra at his wedding, Nooran had raised her baby brother. In 1947, Biji had come across another orphaned refugee girl in a camp overseen by her husband. She had considered adopting six-year-old Jyot but, in the end, how many refugees could one take home?

'Biji is right to be reluctant, but perhaps we can put a distance between the border and us—'

A roar sounded in the lane outside, followed by the crunching of gravel and the abrupt braking of vehicles. Like the eruption of noise in a school at the end-of-school bell, the whole neighbourhood sprang alive. Lights came on in houses, faces popped up between curtains, bolts sprung open. Jinder and Biji were at the windows of the study, peering out. Niki ran to Nooran and hid in her lap. The telephone sounded shrilly in the living room.

Jinder returned at midnight. Niki was asleep, but Biji and Nooran had waited and watched anxiously from behind the curtains. A CRPF van and a jeep from the Punjab Police were parked near the Gupta house. Men in uniform strode about, talking on their handheld devices or with each other. Jinder and a few men from the colony had been summoned.

Terrorists had broken into the Gupta home and killed Mr Gupta and his son, sparing the women and children. The policemen on guard at the gate had dozed off; the terrorists had gagged them, tied their hands and feet, and stuck a note on a sandbag saying: FIGHT ON THE RIGHT SIDE. Both guards were Sikh. How had they fallen asleep? It was so deadly quiet, not even the barking of a stray dog sounded, and they had never realized when fatigue had overwhelmed them.

'Where have all the stray dogs vanished to?' the CRPF commander asked.

'One of your bored soldiers killed them, sir.'

7
(1984)

✳

CHANDIGARH WAS UNFETTERED by the past. It was birthed by Nehru, who had wanted a fresh new capital for East Punjab since Lahore had gone to Pakistan with West Punjab during Partition. Independent India's first prime minister had wanted to build a city of the future to compensate for the loss of a historic city. An orderly grid instead of an acculturating hodgepodge. Thus, Jinder raved about the 'city beautiful'. 'Not even twenty-five years old, Ma!' he declared, arms spread wide.

Biji looked as if those arms held a bushel of sour gooseberries. Since the Gupta killings, Jinder had acted quickly on his decision to relocate. A bungalow in Chandigarh's Sector 8 was up for sale, the owner immigrating to Kuhnayda. 'Ca-nuh-da,' Jinder corrected repeatedly. It was much smaller than the sprawling bungalow they lived in now, which had been in the late Brigadier Nalwa's family since the turn of the century. When it was first built, there had been orchards all around it. Now, it was surrounded by a mishmash of houses like flies settling on something sweet.

34

'Ma,' Jinder pleaded as he approached her and massaged her shoulders tenderly. The farmers of Punjab had sold their land to the government so that Nehru could realize his dream. Now Jinder had sold most of his land to follow his Chandigarh dream where real estate, sheltered from the border, was expensive.

'You know what this house means to me.' Biji was forlorn at the thought of leaving. In October 1946, she had arrived as a young bride at the Nalwa House in Ferozepur, a Muslim-majority town. As Independence approached, in the prevailing game of where-will-the-border-be, the town was expected to be in Pakistan, but Lieutenant Nalwa had assured her the cantonment would be safe either way. And on the night of 15 August, as the Radcliffe Line marked the new border, baby Jinder was born and Ferozepur spared. As an Army wife, Biji moved from one cantonment to another with a new posting every three years; but with Ferozepur being the biggest one, they kept coming back. Until the winter of 1971. The war was over in thirteen days and India won, but men on both sides of the border had paid the price, Brigadier Nalwa amongst them.

'No one's selling the house, Ma.' Nalwa House would stay in the family with an old farmhand assigned to guard duty. For Biji, the house was sacred, but Jinder didn't see it that way. Or like Chandigarh, he was newfangled and practical.

To cheer his mother up, Jinder suggested a visit to the Sufi shrine of Sher Shah Wali, followed by a visit to the Hussainiwala border to see the retreat ceremony. In the strange fashion of the subcontinent, where religious purity made it difficult to eat with or marry outside your faith, the Sufi dargah was one place where religious identities came together. The shrine was a favourite with all the residents of the border. Legend had it that during the '71 war, when the Pakistan Air Force combat aircraft prowled the sky above Ferozepur, pilots reported a haze that made it difficult to pinpoint targets, resulting in multiple failed missions. After the war was won, it was unanimously understood that the saint of Sher Shah Wali had kept Ferozepur safe.

They arrived at the shrine in the early evening. A green awning covered the courtyard under which Nooran sat while Biji, Jinder and Niki proceeded to the saint's tomb. Devotees trooped in and out as hawkers of incense, rose petals and embroidered cloths tried to snare their attention. Nooran enjoyed the cool marble floor against her bare feet as sweat lined her back. Sparrows chirruped in the shade of a neem tree, and traffic roared in the background. The somnolent air lilted as a voice rose in a familiar rendition.

Glancing around, she saw a man reclining against the far wall of the courtyard. His hand caressed the air as he hummed 'Heer', that tragic ode to Punjab's favourite lovelorn heroine. With no musical instrument to accompany him, he sang untrammelled, a few people surging to his side, adding a word now and then, lending their appreciation to his melody. The next instant, Niki bounded out of the sanctum and bounced into her lap. She played with the golden tassels of the parandi braided in Nooran's hair. A breeze stirred the neem leaves and the tune took Nooran back to mornings when she would wake to her mother humming as she milked the family buffalo, her bangles singing.

Heer tells the monk: You lie!
Who unites lovers separated?
None have I found, I tried,
Who brings back the departed...

Along with the gift of the border, the Angrej had left behind this circus of 'beating retreat'. Jinder said when the Angrej had first started it, the ceremony was used to recall patrol units to their fort. Now, it was a cockfight. From their concrete seats in the stands, they watched the Indian BSF men in khakis on this side, the Pakistan Rangers in olive green Pathan suits on that side, a border of steel fencing in between. As one man from each side advanced, the ground trembled with such ferocity as if each step was stamping the enemy's head. They stopped just short of the border gate, puffed up like cockerels, hands on hips, eyes glaring, nostrils flaring – set for the Mahabharata.

'Bharat Mata di jai! Victory to Mother India!'
'Pakistan Paindabad! Long live Pakistan!'
Slogans bounced back and forth, each side trying to outdo the other, Niki clapping in mounting excitement. The soldiers marched down the length of the Hussainiwala border checkpoint, flinging their legs as if bent on dislocating them. The energy in the air was of people readying for either a war or a wedding. The buglers drowned in the din. One jawan marched towards the Indian gate, leg lifted with each step as if in a vertical yoga asana. He threw it open with great anger. The Pakistani gate swung out with no less aggression. In the next instant, a man raced across from the Indian side. So fast that he was a blur, he squeezed through the open gate and dropped on the sliver of ground called no man's land. Both the jawans and rangers froze, as did the entire audience, their breath suspended, in an incredible stillness, like the moment before the baby's head pops out of its mother. Was this the birth of the next Indo-Pak war?

As if the same realization shot through everyone, frenetic activity resumed: men on both sides straightened, postured, cocked their guns. People rose in the stands, their fists aloft, while others dashed for cover. Jinder draped one arm around Biji and Nooran while the other clasped Niki. The man on the ground was still as death. In the rising shrillness, Nooran grabbed Biji's hand. An Indian officer sped to the gate, gesturing with flicking fingers. A Pakistani answered his call. They spoke briefly. Then, each turned back to their own side and said something to the soldiers.

Some jawans and rangers peeled off towards the frantic crowds, beating the air with extended arms. 'SIT! SIT!' they urged. The soldiers with cocked guns eased up, as if a children's game of Statues had been called off. Now, the two officers examined the man on the ground. The Indian officer flicked his right wrist and a tall jawan appeared at his side. Bending, he hoisted the prone figure off the ground, draped it over one shoulder, even as the man thrashed his limbs in protest, and jogged in the direction of the guard's cabin at the entrance of the viewing stand. An exhalation, like air escaping a distended balloon, followed.

In the car, they pieced together what had happened.

'For a second, I thought: *War!*' Jinder whistled his relief.

'Did the man die, Papa?' Niki asked.

Jinder stroked his daughter's cheek with the knuckles of one hand. 'He's fine, just unwell.'

'Was he looking for a doctor?'

The three adults tittered. 'He was seeking a cure for sure,' Nooran said. Green fields whizzed past, barbed wire fences looming in the distance as the car raced away from the Indo-Pak border, the sun sinking into the Sutlej.

'His name is Beli Ram,' Jinder said. He had managed a quick word with his BSF friend as they were leaving the border.

'"Laur, I want to go back to Laur," he moaned,' Biji clucked, regurgitating the information her son had gleaned. 'How unfortunate! Poor man must have fled Lahore during Partition.'

'A fine time he's found to hurl himself at the border!' Nooran snorted. 'He was spared only because he had an audience. Otherwise, the police would gladly have notched up another encounter killing.'

Didn't Heer die lamenting that time didn't reverse? What was taken once, finished. Lahore too. End of story. Didn't this Beli Ram know that, ultimately, all stories drowned in the river of life? Only a few, like Heer's, made their own tributary.

II
(1947)
Jyot

8
(1947)

THEY FEARED IT was the time of pralaya – just as the Mahabharata had foretold. Such devastation would take place that the world would unravel, it would be the end of an epoch. I did not understand any of it; I was six. With my parents, an older brother, two older sisters, some hens and a moody buffalo, I lived in a mud house with a courtyard that edged along the reeds of a river in Punjab. But I rolled that word around my mouth several times – pralaya, pralaya – until mother sharply tugged my braid and forbade me from saying it.

It was jamun season and the sweet-tart berries fell from the giant jamun tree nearby like blessings from the gods. All I needed to do was gather them, rinse them in the flowing Sutlej, sprinkle salt and the tastiest snack was ready. I ate so much jamun so often that there were constantly stains on my tongue – my siblings called me 'black tongue'. But Mother objected to that name; it was bad luck to have a black tongue.

'Why?' I asked.

'When people with black tongues say mean things, those things *always* happen.'

The summer of 1947 was exceptionally hot, or so the adults complained. The entire country was burning. The hens agreed as they walked to the riverbank with their wings stretched. One hen made neon green shit, which worried Mother. The sun bleached everything except the gulmohar flowers, which were scarlet. We played in the shade of the trees and when it became hot, we slipped into the river with our clothes on and ran out dripping wet.

'Such heat,' my mother complained, wiping her brow with the edge of her mulmul dupatta as she started the tandoor for dinner.

'God alone knows what is going to happen,' my father added from the jute cot where he sat, bathed in sweat, his lungi hitched to his knees. 'No rain and all this hot air about freedom and division!' A fly settled on his nose. He smacked it away, beads of sweat leaping off his hairy arm.

'We are all going to fall dead like flies,' I said.

Mother gasped, hand to her mouth. Rushing forward, she shook me by my shoulders. 'Unsay it!'

I didn't mean it. I had only parroted what I had heard the adults say. But Mother looked terrified, and so, I took it back.

A few days later, a man arrived, claiming to be Cheema Chacha, Father's younger brother. Mother screamed when she saw him and none of us children recognized him. The Chacha we knew was bearded and turbaned. Instead, this man had no moustache, only a trimmed beard, and he wore a skull cap. He looked exactly like the maulvi at the mosque. Father and he had a big fight.

'Brother, haven't you heard? Hussainiwala is going to Pakistan! How can it not? The village has a majority of Muslims; it is named after their pir baba. By the rule of division, Muslim-majority areas go to Pakistan, the rest stay with India.'

'So you become a Muslim?' Father prodded Chacha's chest with an index finger.

'What option do we have? We are poor people. I can't afford a house in India and in Pakistan; I have to make a choice. And if I want to stay here,' he jabbed the ground with his hand, 'I have to convert.'

'Says who?'

Chacha shook his head. 'The Muslims.'

'No, not a single one of my neighbours says that.'

'It's not the neighbours,' Chacha hissed, 'you know that. It is the Muslim militia that has the run of Hussainiwala. And not just our village, all the hamlets all the way from Ferozepur to Lahore are under their sway! They have guns, ammunition and their command is clear: convert and stay, or lose life and land.'

'The gurus made us Sikhs a bridge between Hindus and Muslims. If we do not hold, Punjab will be torn asunder.'

'Forget Punjab, think of your family!' Cheema Chacha shook his head. 'Brother, you know, the English have announced their pack-up and the partition of India. Punjab is to be carved up between Hindus and Muslims—'

'But we Sikhs are spread throughout the state—'

'Which is why the English cannot give us our own state!' Chacha clucked. 'We Sikhs fought two world wars for them, but now they have washed their hands off us.'

'I won't leave the land my forefathers have tilled with their blood.'

'Good,' Chacha leaned in, his voice lowered. 'No one knows how the new border will snake through people's homes and farms. Convert today, and tomorrow when the madness settles, grow your hair and go back to being a Sikh. I've done it,' he waved a hand over his shorn hair. 'Wasn't I a Sikh?'

Father snorted. 'You forget what the tenth guru said. A brave man fights to defend his faith; even the prospect of being cut to pieces does not make him flee the battlefield. You,' he waved a dismissive hand, 'were never a Sikh.'

Chacha stood there, chest heaving, hands on his waist. 'I was sent here to advise you, but you don't want to listen. Then hear this: they're coming – tonight.'

After he left, Father and Mother conferred urgently. After that, my brother joined Father, and Mother resumed cooking. As I washed the buffalo's trough, the evening breeze fanned the leaves of the gulmohar tree. Thick bulbous eyes watched me as I kept a safe distance from those curving saber horns. She was placid, when not being menacing.

Dinner was early, and special, because Mother fed each of us sisters the first morsels of food. We sat on the packed mud floor of the courtyard in a row, eldest to youngest. No dal or vegetables that day, just choori, crushed rotis with ghee and jaggery. Her smile was thin and pained, as if I had said something wrong again with my cursed tongue. She fed me last, which was also unusual.

But her eyes were moist, and I saw myself in them. 'Jyot,' she said, 'Jyot,' patting my head insistently. The choori tasted of incense and flowers. It reminded me of a black pellet I had once bitten into, thinking it was candy. Mother had extracted it from my mouth with an index finger, instructing me to never touch it again.

Father and my brother did not eat. They stood in the far corner of the courtyard, keeping vigil. Each held a weapon. My brother held a gandasa, the curved blade mounted on a wooden stick to slash sugarcane. Father had a broadsword in his hand.

I started to feel sleepy, which was strange because I was still eating. The world around me slowed. It took forever for my father to walk towards us, holding the sword aloft. In the dusk, its blade shone like fire and he walked in giant steps. But I was floating. I glanced at my sister. Her head was resting on her shoulder, already asleep. With a great effort, I looked beyond to my eldest sister; her neck was sunk on her chest. Mother, meanwhile, was sitting upright, hands folded, eyes closed, as she murmured a prayer. Birds twittered in the trees as they set up their evening chorus. The breeze carried the smell of woodsmoke and the rumbling of a din, as if a herd of buffaloes was rampaging down.

Father's leather jutti rustled as it cracked a twig. He stopped in front of Mother, and lifted his sword high above her head. She did not move or open her eyes. The sword descended, Mother's head rolled to the floor. She stayed upright, hands still folded in prayer. Blood bubbled from her neck like a fountain. My eyelids were stones.

They descended. Blood dripped from Father's sword as he turned to my eldest sister.

I smelt woodsmoke again. It was in my throat. Fire crackled in my ear. I was hot, so hot, my skin stinging. I opened my eyes and bolted upright. I was sitting atop a mountain. The mountain was made of limbs and hair and clothes and dried blood. Below me was a pile of wood logs. Another such mountain was adjacent to me – it was already ablaze. A man holding a burning log in his hand had set it aflame. He turned.

It was Cheema Chacha. He approached my mountain with a glum face that glowed in the light of the flames. His eyes were bloodshot. As he neared, he looked up. The torch tumbled from his hand. He cried aloud. He started to clamber up the mountain. Rough hands grabbed me, and I was flying in the air. There were shouts, hurried footsteps and the stench of burning flesh.

The question of why I did not die made people nervous. They speculated that Father had not beheaded me because I was the youngest and had eaten enough opium to kill me anyway. But it had not killed me. Had my black tongue kept me alive while others died?

Having plucked me alive from the pyre, Cheema Chacha could have kept me as another member of his newly-Muslim family. But his brother had martyred his womenfolk and died resisting like the Sikh gurus. I was the reminder of one brother's cowardice and the remainder from another's heroism. I had to go.

People were fleeing, taking with them what they could carry. Who would want another's child? They would take a buffalo: four legs for transport in a time of exodus. Chacha, though, cut a one-plus-one deal.

Our buffalo – placid when not being menacing – and I joined a family fleeing in the direction of safety. Bullock carts piled with people and possessions, children riding buffaloes, women with babies astride donkeys, adults trudging along with children on their waists or shoulders, or with older adults on their backs – we could be

THE RADIANCE OF A THOUSAND SUNS ✍ 45

a throng headed to the annual festival of a pir baba but for the sullen silence, only broken by the clanging of utensils dangling from carts and cycles, and the downcast eyes as people walked, as if counting each step. The clothes grew stiffer as dust, churned by shuffling feet, starched them.

The sun shone like a brass plate in the cloudless sky. There was no space for me in the bullock cart, which was covered by a sheet strung on four poles in the corners. Inside, there was a woman with a baby suckling at her breast, an old man who reclined with his mouth open, an old woman who fanned him with a handheld cloth fan, and several children who lay strewn around.

The buffalo was my saviour. She wouldn't let anyone ride her, so I got that perch. The sun warmed her black skin, and I sizzled upon it like roti on a griddle. But at least I didn't have to walk.

At night, we rested on a dry riverbed. Small fires were lit, a little food was cooked, and I got a half roti. In the scrub, people passed watery shit. Then, they washed their hands and face in a puddle and drank its water.

There were people ahead, people behind, people alongside, people everywhere, but there were no parents, no sisters, no brother for me. We were a kafila, a caravan, sad strangers who had fled their homes and were journeying together to a new home. A home without my family? That question made my eyes burn, and when I wiped them, my eyes burnt more. Dust weighed my eyelashes even. What little water we had was for sipping. I stopped licking my lips – first, I tasted dust, then blood as my mouth chapped and cracked.

The baby in the cart was dying because the mother's milk had dried. The old man had died of cholera. Cholera, cholera, I rolled the new word on my tongue. Vultures watched us from treetops. Were they afraid of the buffalo's curving sabre horns?

Soon there was another kafila. As if a mirror was reflecting us: everybody was coated with dust, churning more dust, abandoning the dead and dying in the dust. Only, it was headed in the direction of our old home.

Soon, people started to drop off. One instant, they were upright, the next, their knees buckled, they pitched into the dust. A child tugged at her dead mother's hand, begging to be carried. The people who hunkered down to pass a watery stool sometimes did not get up thereafter. A woman with a sickly baby clasped to her chest watched with vacant eyes as we moved on. A commotion every now and then meant that one man had leapt on another from the other kafila, or that a woman had been grabbed. Nobody stopped, the kafila slouched on.

Exhaustion. Dehydration. Diarrhoea. Death.

I was flat on the buffalo's back, limbs limp around its sweating flanks, my eyes rolling in my head, my mother-father-brother-sisters beckoning me. My hair stiff as stalks, my body dry as wood, I was tinder for lighting.

I could be my own pyre.

Above me, a dirty ceiling. Around me, pitiful cries. Within me, a pipe sucking me dry. I had died and gone to hell. The buffalo was Yama's mount. She had brought me to his kingdom. I would never meet my family. I moaned and shut my eyes. A figure hovered over me.

When I came to, I was not covered in dust, there was no grit in my eyes, my hands were clean, my lips not swollen. A bottle slung from a pole fed my body. A nurse patted my head and spoke to me gently. I had survived cholera. My dehydrated body had been brought to a makeshift hospital by some good soul. Where was the buffalo? Probably dead. She had had nothing to eat or drink in the several days of our journey. A woman checked on me several times during the day. She fed me orange segments by hand. Her name was Zohra and she reminded me of Mother.

One day, I heard excited shouts. I raised myself on one elbow and saw a peacock walking between the hospital beds. The nurses hugged each other. Somebody shouted, 'Now we'll have proper rain!' A peacock is a good omen, Mother would say. If she found a peacock feather, she would keep it. I missed Mother so much. Zohra came and asked me why I was crying. The next day, she brought me a wooden peacock toy. Its long neck was purple, its folded wings red and golden, its tail green and dotted with eyes. I never let go of my peacock after that, making sure to clutch it in one hand or the other.

It came with me to Machhiwara, where I was sent to a gurdwara providing shelter to orphans like me. Machhi-wara, the fishing village. Yet, there was no fish around. Bapuji, the head priest, and Maji, his wife, had so many children like me. They assigned simple errands to each of us. I was to fetch water from the well. Each child got one bucket for bathing and a set of clean cotton clothes. Early to bed, early to rise. The day started with singing japji, the morning prayers, and ended with rehras, the evening prayers. Maji needed help with milking the cows and preparing meals. Bapuji taught us under the banyan tree in the vast courtyard. There was a swing in the yard, and other orphans and stray dogs for us to play with.

The day was okay, but the night scared me. I was terrified I would wake up and know nothing and nobody. Maji's rhythmic patting helped me sleep and I woke up every day to the sonorous recitation of the holy book, which reminded me of the Sutlej flowing behind our home.

The river was fifteen kilometres away. People said it had shifted course. How did it do that? And why didn't it move its massive body such that my home, on its bank, stayed within India and safe?

III
1984
Men and Masks

Making our way through the thicket of the banyan, let us trail the blind king Dhritarashtra, father to the hundred Kauravas, husband to Gandhari, who wears a blindfold in spousal solidarity. In the royal palace also reside his nephews, the five Pandavas, with their mother Kunti. But the true head of the household is the white-robed elder, Bhishma, renowned for his pledge of celibacy. As the boys scramble in the gardens, focus on Duryodhana, the eldest Kaurava. A serpent is coiled tightly around his heart for he envies the Pandavas their good looks and popularity, indeed, their very breath. So he plots, again and again, to destroy them, especially Bheema, the second Pandava, who is strapping and strong. Duryodhana proves an incompetent assassin, but a mother's sixth sense bedevils Kunti as an undercurrent of violence ripples through the palace...

9
(1984)

✵

THE NALWA HOUSEHOLD had not even wiped its feet at the threshold of Nehru's city when Nehru's daughter shook Punjab. On the night of 2 June 1984, she appeared on TV, remarked on the militants holed up in the Golden Temple, appealed for peace and ended with the words: 'Don't shed blood, shed hatred.' To a people suckled on stories of the Mahabharata, this late mission of peace reminded them of Krishna's failed attempt to avert war between brothers. Two days later, the Indian army entered the Golden Temple to wage war against its Sikh brothers under the code name Operation Blue Star.

The searing summer air crackled with non-stop transmission from BBC Radio; people knew better than to trust the state-run media. A state-wide curfew muzzled their voices. Information arrived like reluctant rain, rumours raged like the infernal summer heat.

'Punjab was under Army rule.'

'Some Sikh units in the Army had mutinied.'

'The sant had escaped and would address people on Pakistan TV.'

'Police had arrested 5000 boys from villages claiming that they were terrorists.'

Sullen, people stewed inside their homes, regurgitating scraps of information like the pious rotated their prayer beads.

=

To break the interminable passage of the summer – school vacations, the court in recess, frequent curfews – Jinder invited their next-door neighbour, Tiny Maini, to drinks and dinner. When the doorbell rang, Nooran opened the door to a man so tall that he had to stoop to enter. He wore a printed turban, complete with a turla, pleated and unfurled like a peacock's tail in the fashion of men from a previous generation but he looked younger. In his white kurta-pyjama, he was either a politician or a feudal landlord.

When Nooran returned from the kitchen with a platter of pakoras, the adults were in conversation, drinks in hand, the TV playing on mute in the background. Niki was on the carpet sketching, copying the picture from a round glass bottle. It was Roop's perfume, the only fancy cosmetic on her dresser. With a complexion like full-cream milk, Roop had needed little adornment.

'From what it appears, you didn't leave Ferozepur a minute too early,' Maini said. 'Not that Chandigarh doesn't see any action but because of its special status, it has immunity from the general violence of Punjab.'

'What special status?' Niki asked.

'It's a UT, union territory,' Maini said. 'Which means it gets to be the capital city of Punjab *and* get special treatment.' Turning to Biji, he asked, 'Have you had the chance to meet any of the other neighbours?'

'I met Mrs Mehta and her daughter-in-law, Suman, who is pregnant.'

'Permanently pregnant,' Maini said, as he helped himself to mint chutney. To the furrowed brows in the room, he elaborated, 'Mr Mehta has several daughters and one son, born last. The daughters are all married off. Now, he's on the quest for an heir, a grandson via the sole son.'

'You mean—'

'Mr Mehta understands the wonderful confluence of science and commerce. The business he gives to ultrasound clinics for sex-determination tests, he might as well open a clinic in his house.'

'The curse of Punjab,' Jinder scowled.

Biji looked as if she had swallowed a spoonful of vinegar.

'So what do you do, Tiny?' Jinder asked as he sipped his scotch.

'Nothing.'

As Biji looked confused, he said, 'Before you judge me harshly and banish me, let me state that I am a man of means who likes the simple pleasures of life.'

'A bon vivant,' Biji said. She still had the pinched look of having tasted something bitter on her tongue.

Tiny Maini's eyes twinkled. 'I couldn't have described it better. I do,' he said, between bites of a pakora, 'write freelance. And pen a poem or so when it comes to me.'

'Convenient.'

'Oh yes! My father, you see, came from Pakistan in '47, penniless, with just the rags he was wearing. But his wits were intact as was his memory. He made his money in the Delhi construction boom. All those refugees pouring into the city needed homes, right? He attached himself to the right folks and made his way up. Quintessential Punjabi: work hard, don't look back.' He paused, then wiped his hand on a napkin that he folded again and put on the side table. 'My two older brothers run the family business now. And I was always the odd one out. So my father, God bless him, figured that leaving my fate in the hands of my brothers would ruin me. He set me up with this house and enough cash to ensure I don't have to ask my brothers for anything.'

'Did he name you as well?' Jinder grinned.

'He had a sense of humour, I guess, or just love. I was Tiny because I was the last. You should see my brother when he comes to visit me next: Lovely is likely the ugliest Punjabi you'd ever meet! And Shinty, the second? That's baby talk for Squinty.'

Jinder and Tiny laughed together. Nooran had finished laying the dining table. The food was ready in the kitchen, except for the last-minute tempering and topping with chopped coriander.

'Tiny,' Biji said, 'you mentioned something which made me curious. Would you mind if I ask about it?'

'Anything, Aunty,' Tiny said, in the dutiful manner of good Punjabi boys.

'You said your father had his wits and his memory intact. What did you mean by the latter?'

Tiny leaned forward, hands interlaced. 'I asked him once why he worked so hard, as if he were punishing himself. He said it was the only way he could keep the ghost at bay. He wanted the sleep of a labourer because only that kind of sleep could drown out the images that haunted him even in the daytime.' Tiny brought his hands together to his lips and a meditative silence followed. The only sound was the scratching of Niki's crayons on paper.

'He was an orphan, you see. So he left for India in a train in the company of strangers. It was one of those ghost trains that pulled into Delhi, full of non-Muslim corpses. He survived because he jumped off the train into a canal below. When he reached Delhi, he started working on a construction site lifting bricks. At night, the men would sleep on lengths of burlap amongst the cliffs of stacked bricks. One evening, a prosperous looking bania passed by. An older boy said the man was actually Muslim; he was only dressed as a Hindu trader. My father pooh-poohed him and proposed a bet. "Let's strip him and check if he's circumcised," he said. "The winner decides the loser's penalty."'

Nooran had pulled up a chair and was sitting by the dining table, listening. Niki, finding the three adults engrossed, clutched her sketchbook and perfume bottle, and padded to her. It was a non-curfew day, yet the neighbourhood lay quiet, as if it was still to reacquaint itself with the outdoors.

'The man was stripped, and they found he was Muslim. The boy wrestled the man to the ground and several men pinned him down. "Kill him! Kill him!" they shouted, but my father hesitated. The men jeered. He grabbed a brick and pulped the Muslim's brain.'

Niki stood between Nooran's legs, biting a corner of her sketchbook, watching the storyteller. Nooran caressed her head.

'The ghost of that Muslim? My father never shook him off.' Tiny Maini settled back into the sofa and sipped some more scotch.

Over dinner, they were enjoying Nooran's ma ki dal, simmered over the stove for hours, and criticizing Doordarshan, the government TV channel that was showing another programme to justify the military action in the gurdwara. This showed the major general who had led the operation: erect bearing, grey hair, he spoke gitter-mitter Angreji.

'A Sardar at that!' Biji said with disdain.

'One with shorn hair,' Jinder interjected. 'You have to hand it to Indira. She used one Sikh to fight another.'

'There is not a trick the Bahmani doesn't know. Poor Nehru!' The crest of Tiny's turban bobbed as he chewed. 'All those splendid letters wasted on this daughter.'

Suddenly, the doorbell rang, and Nooran opened the door. Fauja Singh stood there like a guilty dog. It had taken him nine hours by bus to reach Chandigarh, twice the usual time because of the multiple security checkpoints. His son had been picked up by the police during last night's curfew. 'It's become easy for them to arrest anybody. The curfew is like a snare.'

Nooran hurried to bring Fauja Singh some food and water. Jinder urged the others to finish dinner as he pulled up a stool and the two men talked.

Biji filled in Tiny Maini on the details of the case of Fauja Singh's son. 'Poor boy has still to recover from his earlier incarceration. They beat him so much, he lost sensation in his spine.'

'This is only the beginning, Aunty. Police excesses are only going to grow. You should take his case to the Human Rights Watch. Or, better still, take them to PUCL.'

Biji frowned.

'People's Union for Civil Liberties. I know the person in charge of the Chandigarh chapter. I can take you to meet them.'

Jinder came back to finish his meal. He waved off Nooran's offer to reheat his food as Fauja Singh sat eating slowly. The TV had lost transmission and a blue spectral light bathed the living area.

'I'll leave with Fauja in the morning. We have a lucky break in curfew,' Jinder snorted. 'Perhaps my contacts can still yield something? Ferozepur is officially a "disturbed" area now, and the police have special powers.'

Nooran switched off the TV. Niki had fallen asleep on the sofa. All those stories of violence – what were they doing to the child's mind? Nooran sighed. They were all children of violence; Niki's case was no different. Jinder had done right by her in relocating to Chandigarh. Except that they had fled the border to escape violence, but violence had still followed them home.

10
(1984)

❋

NOORAN LOOKED AT the wall clock; Niki would be home in ten minutes. School had finally reopened after a week-long break, because ten days ago, the Sikh bodyguards of the prime minster had shot her.

In the Mahabharata, when Draupadi was humiliated in open court, she swore not to tie her long hair until she had washed it in her tormentor's blood, which, sure enough, she did when Bheema killed Dushasana and offered Draupadi his blood. Like Draupadi, Punjab was humiliated when Nehru's daughter invaded the gurdwara, curfewed the state and sent people to jail. Punjabi men were roosters, the Sikhs, the cockiest of the lot. Now, their long tails had been plucked – by a woman at that! So what if she was the prime minister and called Durga after the fiery Hindu mother goddess? No virtue was higher than honour. To keep it intact, men killed as a matter of duty, something Punjabi women knew, but perhaps PM Indira Gandhi didn't?

Nooran switched the dupatta-with-swatter for another dupatta and smoothed her hair. Did the Mahabharata end after Draupadi had finished washing her hair in her enemy's blood? Did the camps of opposing brothers say, 'Okay, we've killed men on both sides, now let's say bye, call an end to the war, go back to our homes?' One humiliation had led to another; war became a mounting mound of tangled corpses and piled humiliations. If the men of Punjab thought Durga's death would restore their honour, the problem, once again, was with their memories.

In the days following the PM's death, Punjab became a safe state as Dilli found its battle worthiness. Bearded, turbaned Sikhs become the object of revenge killings. Their womenfolk – wives, daughters, mothers, grandmothers – became the object of humiliation. The public disrobing of Draupadi all those years ago had given all honourable men a template: honour was vested in a woman, and to dishonour her was to humiliate the man.

Once again, news was restricted and rumours raged. Swathes of Delhi had become funeral pyres, its gutters choked with the shorn hair of Sikh men, the skies clogged with smoke from fires still smouldering...

PUCL Delhi needed volunteers to record the mounting terror because the police had become bystanders as government-led mobs invaded Sikh homes, torching men, raping women, ripping foetuses. Biji had returned home ashen-faced after five days in Delhi. All the horrors of '47 that Biji had fled from had finally caught up with her in '84.

≡

'Why won't he talk?'

Niki pointed at the man who sat on their porch, still as a sage. Jinder had brought his grandfather, Biji's father, to stay with them. All day he sat outside, as if on guard duty. Despite the November chill, he insisted on sitting on the porch or in the garden with its view of the street.

'Maybe he has too many stories buried in him?'

Nooran patted Niki's head as she glanced at the elderly man. He had brought her to Biji's door in '47 and saved her. Otherwise, what life would a nine-year-old orphan Muslim girl have had? She tended to him, fetching him milk and tea and meals, anticipating his needs.

'Niki, help me,' Nooran said as she helped the old man out of the chair. When he was upright, she handed him his cane, and clasped Niki's right hand around his free arm. She moved his chair such that it was in the sun, then Niki and she walked him to it. His eyes remained glued to the horizon. If only he would talk. Nooran sighed. And now, his daughter had taken to bed quietly.

Niki turned the handle on Biji's door and peered into the darkness. Not even a smidgen of light. Nooran had draped dark sheets atop the curtains to help Biji sleep. Now, with a finger to her lips, she motioned Niki away.

'Why won't Dadima wake up?'

'She needs rest.'

'Is she sick?'

Nooran clucked. 'People say their lentils won't soften, and I have seen stones dissolve often.'

'I don't like your riddles, Nooran!'

'You will know when you know,' saying which, Nooran led Niki to the bathroom to wash up.

In the kitchen, Niki climbed on the countertop as Nooran crumbled thick, wholewheat rotis with ghee and jaggery in a steel bowl. She handed Niki her favourite after-school snack and watched her mouth glisten as she munched on choori.

'Will Dadima get up for dinner?'

'If her migraine is better.' Nooran put a pan of water to boil for tea.

'What is a migraine?'

'It is a headache you get from seeing terrible things.'

'Nooran, I don't want to see terrible things.'

Sweeping the air around Niki with both hands, Nooran tucked them to the sides of her forehead. 'A pox on terrible things!'

Niki balanced the bowl in her lap and mimicked Nooran, who promptly grabbed Niki's fists. 'Na! Only adults can do this.'

'Why?'

Nooran pounded cardamom and shrugged. 'To keep their children safe.'

Niki licked a piece of jaggery off the corner of her mouth. 'So what do children do for grown-ups?'

'Try not to forget them?'

'Like you do old man Bullah? And Heer and Draupadi?'

Nooran laughed. 'Yes! In songs and stories. Like we remember Roop.'

'Nooran, tell me that story about Mama again!'

'Which one?'

'When Papa saw her the first time!'

'Ah!' She added tea leaves to the boiling water and let it simmer. 'Jinder had already said to Biji, "I don't want to marry." But to keep her happy, he came along with us to see the girl. So we are drinking Coca-Cola when Roop enters. It is early summer, and she has just cycled back from college. The heat has made her bloom like a red rose.'

Niki listened, wide-eyed, almost bouncing in anticipation of her favourite part of the story that Nooran was just about to get to.

'She is perspiring, but her face looks moist as if she has just finished bathing, pearls dangling from her tresses and,' Nooran leant in and her index fingers alighted on Niki's dimpled cheeks, 'nestling in those dimples.'

'She looks just like a pari!' Niki completed with glee.

'Jinder saw her face, just like an angel's, and promptly fell in love. Then he couldn't wait to get married!'

Niki swung her legs happily as she declared, 'This is my favourite story, Nooran!'

'As it should be,' she tapped Niki's nose before opening the fridge. She looked through the vegetable tray. Jinder was travelling, and Biji showed no appetite – perhaps she should make khichdi? The mushy dal and rice would be light on Biji's stomach and nutritious for Niki—

'Nooran! Can I have some tea too?'

Nooran shook her head. 'When you're older.'

'How old?'

'Old enough.'

Clutching the bowl in one hand, Niki made a fist of the other, bent her back, pretended to dodder and croaked, 'As old as ooo-ld man Bullah?'

Nooran grinned, brought her palms together and bowed to Niki. 'Bullah says, "I am your slave, my master."' She turned off the gas and strained tea as Niki sang in the background: 'Bullah says, Bullah says, O what does Bullah say?'

Nooran shook her head in tune to the familiar ditty, Niki's usual response to her frequent referencing of the ancient Sufi poet. But it wasn't just Nooran; all of Punjab agreed on one thing: whatever they wanted to say, Bulleh Shah had already said it better!

Niki jumped down from the countertop and declared, 'I'll drink tea when I am as old as you, Nooran!'

'When you are as old as me, I'll be older.'

Niki waved a dismissive hand. 'You are not growing old, Nooran.'

11
(1984)

❋

BIJI STAYED LISTLESS for days after returning from Delhi, and Tiny
Maini proposed a change of scenery. Perhaps some live theatre? He
had passes to an open-air performance of Yakshagana, a folk art
from South India, and he came in his chauffeured car to drive them
to Tagore Theatre. So Biji, Niki, Nooran and Tiny took their seats to
watch an enactment of a scene from the Mahabharata.

'Yakshagana,' Tiny read aloud from a brochure, 'is traditionally
enacted by an all-male cast—'

Nooran snorted. 'As if there aren't enough heroes in the story!
Now the men want the heroines' roles too!'

'I'd like my Draupadi to be a woman, please,' Niki added. She
smelt of roses and cloves, having insisted on putting on a dab of
Roop's perfume before leaving.

Tiny leaned across and saluted, 'As you command, Your
Highness,' which made Niki giggle. The lights dimmed. Throats
were cleared, seats adjusted, voices muffled as people settled down
for the performance.

Bheema spins in a slow circle. Around him the air is resonant with shrieks, war cries, the slash of swords, the slap of fleeing feet. He will drink Duryodhana's blood, he declares. It will taste better than mother's milk. Or any wine. He thumps his chest. He knows this with the intimacy of a boy who has wrestled with his brother in childhood, rolling in dust as they lunged at each other, hands slick with sweat, his own and the other's. Bloody scrapes, best resolved with a dash of spit. A cut finger popped into the mouth and sucked until the other's bleeding stopped. This time, though, he will tear him open and feast on his blood!

Dust shrouds the air, masking the frenzied feet and the whirling wheels that are spinning it off the ground and into the air, denser than rain clouds, wiping out even the sun. Bheema squints, eyelashes heavy, grit leaking at the corners of his eyes, a fist clenched tight on the weapon.

He had raced his brother down the lane to school, Bheema tells the audience, danced in front of his caparisoned mount on his wedding day. Their concerns were alike, their joys similar. That was then, and this is now. Now Bheema's eyes have been opened to the treasonous nature of his 'brother'. Who wants a greater share of everything? Who will covet his home, his land, his wife even? Who will breed enough children that they will overrun his land? Who will defile whatever he regards holy? Who needs to be taught a lesson? That viper. That entire viperous clan. Kill him. Kill all the hatchlings.

Nooran's forearm was being strangled as Niki gripped it tight.

Now Bheema sights his quarry. With a roar that ripples through the clouding dust, he barrels towards Duryodhana and a fierce battle of maces erupts. Finally, smashing his mace into Duryodhana's thigh, Bheema brings him down. Then he rips Duryodhana's stomach open with his bare hands, flicking his tongue out to catch the squirting blood.

Fear made Niki's back rigid. Nooran stroked her grasping fingers, easing out the terror.

Bheema thrusts his face into Duryodhana's abdomen, his bloody hands holding up dripping entrails. Bheema sings his delight aloud. The blood is sweeter than honey, he tells the warriors who have paused to watch the spectacle. No milk, no buttermilk, can match its texture. The men around him are engaged in a similar pursuit, bent on killing and looting and maiming and destroying. But they pause to watch him, and watching, start to slowly step back. Their hands are covered with blood too, but they know what they are witnessing has raised the bar. In the future, in a war, people will recount this incident and this man, and hold him up as the gold standard. The one to be emulated. For in his hatred, he has transcended his natural state—

A shriek tore through the theatre.

Niki dug her face into Dadima. The drumbeats picked up as the performance reached a frenzy, the character of Bheema rampaging across the stage, a red silk ribbon hanging from his mouth. As Niki clung tight, Dadima whispered to Tiny, gripped Niki's hand and quietly started to step through the row, apologizing softly to those seated as they shuffled their knees and feet to accommodate them.

In the foyer, Dadima asked, 'Shall we walk?'

As Niki nodded, the door behind them opened and Nooran exited. 'Biji, you can go back. I'll sit with Niki.'

'Na,' Biji waved a hand. 'Enough violence for one evening. Let's get some fresh air.'

They stepped out into the open. The sky was an indigo coloured dupatta with stars embroidered on it like silver mukaish. The fragrance of the night queen flower wafted in the air as the two women ambled towards the lawns, Niki gripping their arms to hop ahead, her discomfort forgotten. What a blessing to have a child's memory! Biji had wrapped her wool shawl tightly around her and was inhaling deeply. In the distance, a horn blared.

They must have reached the rear of the theatre, near the stage, for the dying sounds of the Yakshagana reached them, an occasional jubilant cheer breaking through. A door opened onto a porch where a stray dog was curled up. A shuffle from the corner drew her attention and Nooran watched an actor step out. In the shadows, his costume looked impressive, his headgear rising a foot into the air at least, ankle bells jangling as he strode down the porch to settle on the platform edge.

'Bheema,' Biji nodded.

'Even he needs a break from his fearsome character!' Nooran snorted. She glanced from Niki, who was gathering fallen chrysanthemums, to him, and wondered how Niki would react if she saw him now. At this distance, in repose, Bheema looked severe in his elaborate make-up of thickened eyebrows, kohl-lined eyes and bushy whiskers. The fear he engendered came from those manic gestures, the high-octane voice, the smacking sounds as he pretended to drink blood. In his hands lay the incriminating evidence, the spool of red ribbon that he had clutched in his jaw and showcased as his enemy's bloody entrails. As they passed him, the women nodded in acknowledgement.

'You watched the performance?' His voice surprised Nooran. It was a regular male voice.

'Until you scared our child!' Biji pointed towards Niki, who was squatting beside a flower bed.

'Ah! I have that effect. This make-up,' he drew a hand along his face, an elegant movement that resembled a downward spiral, 'is the main culprit.'

Curious, the women halted.

'How many hours does it take?' Biji asked.

'Four or five.'

'That long!'

'Yes. Every day. Back home, all of us actors work during the day, and after an early dinner, we lie down and get our make-up done. After which, the night-long performance begins.'

Biji hadn't known this aspect of the Yakshagana, assuming the actors were full-time professionals. 'So, what work do you do?'

'I am an electrician.'

Mighty Bheema, who ripped his enemies apart, repaired wires and fuses for a living.

'You get to choose your part?'

'I grew up watching Yakshagana. As a teenager, I started practising with the village group that performed every year. I slowly evolved into this role. I have been performing for twenty-odd years now. My height,' he soared a hand in accompaniment, 'makes me eligible for the role of Bheema, eh – the strongest Pandava.'

Nooran nodded as she leaned against the porch. Inside, another crescendo was rising, the celebration of another slaying by another hero. Niki ran towards them, palms full of plump white flowers. Seeing Bheema, she gasped and edged towards Biji.

He grinned. 'But yes,' he rolled up the ribbon neatly, 'I scare children. My own daughter, when she was small, would refuse to come near me when I changed into Bheema. But there's nothing to be scared of. Here!' He took off his peacock-feathered crown and leaning forward, plonked it on Niki's head. 'There, you are the mighty Bheema now!' Niki giggled, her shoulders hunching in merriment.

'But something happens…' Bheema said.

As the women looked puzzled, he continued, '…when I wear this make-up and costume. The behaviour of others around me changes. Neighbours, friends, my children even – I sense an awe in their faces. As if by playing Bheema and undergoing this transformation, I have temporarily discarded my electrician self and now, I am one to be feared. Even the man who does my make-up treats me differently when he has finished. You see, I feel it too. My voice changes, I walk taller, I feel powerful.'

As he spoke, his voice became robust, he sat upright, his chest thrust forward, and he casually flung the ball of red ribbon outwards. For a few seconds, it trembled in the air, bloody enemy entrails again.

He glowered at the darkness, his fearsome painted facade shiny in the porch's dim light. The transition from electrician to Bheema had been swift, compelled as it was by the fiery persona he was enacting, consumed by vengeance, propelled on the wings of an ageless myth, an epic bloody battle between brothers which, several thousand years on, was still being re-enacted in this land.

═

In the car ride back, the dam Biji had built to hold back her emotions burst.

She had spent five days in Trilokpuri picking her way through the aftermath of anti-Sikh riots. Yet, there was not a single surviving resident who had witnessed the massacre in their neighbourhood. *They were away during that time. Hadn't heard anything either.* But the corpses rotting in their lanes? The gutters clogged with blood and ligament and hair? The smoke still being emitted from charred homes like dying gasps? *No, they shook their heads – they had seen nothing.* The few people that trembled forward as witnesses recanted their testimonies soon after. But they had participated in identifying the houses of Sikhs, marking them with large Xs, led mobs to their doorsteps, joined in the killing. How had neighbours morphed into murderers? *No. Na. Nahin. Nothing. They knew nothing.* Indeed. Because to kill the men and women who lived next to them, they had donned a mask. A mask that changed them from feeble men to mighty killers. That was all it took to change men, to unleash the monster within – a mask.

Niki wiped Biji's wet cheeks with her small hands and Nooran draped an arm around her back. From where he sat beside the driver, a concerned Tiny watched them in the rear-view mirror, his plan having gone woefully wrong. The car sped past the mighty oak trees of the City Beautiful.

IV
(1947–1984)
Jyot

12
(1947–1984)

I SOON LEARNT THAT there was comfort in small things. In the swish of a reed broom as it accompanied the recitation of the morning prayer; in the squirrels that scampered about, their tails flying; in mustard flowers in a sea of fields; in pink skies before dawn; in the breeze whispering in the banyan trees.

With no river, no fish, a lie for a name, Machhiwara was another dusty little village, but one with history. And therefore, people came to Machhiwara. To accommodate them, the village had four gurdwaras. The pilgrims wanted to visit the place where the guru had sung his heart out to his beloved friend, in the woods along the bank of the Sutlej, the Machhiwara of history, of lore, of the guru.

Mittar pyaare nu, haal mureedan da kehna, to my beloved friend, of my plight do tell.

Maji was partial to that particular shabad. The tenth guru, wandering in the woods of Machhiwara, after having sacrificed his four sons, alone and surrounded by the enemy, had addressed God. I found the story daunting. How could a man who had lost everything still turn to God and believe him to be a beloved friend? Haunting, piercing, lyrical – it always made me well up.

As the days passed, I fell into a routine. Every day, before dawn, I drew water from the well to clean the gurdwara. I was quick with my lessons. If I finished them early, I helped Maji in the kitchen. People dropped in through the day and the kitchen was always warm. I learnt to roll out rotis by the dozens, cook ten types of lentils, use every seasonal vegetable to stuff parathas, spot the freshest mustard greens in the market, churn hillocks of white butter, pickle a cart of green mangoes in earthen jars to last a year. Maji said, if the Indian army were to be fed on the march, I would manage to feed them on my own.

My mango pickle was savoury enough to substitute an entire meal, and rotis flew off my fingers. In mango season, the entire neighbourhood would turn up at the gurdwara with sacks of green mangoes and earthenware jars, and requests for pickles that were either less salty, hotter than usual, more tart. Everyone wondered how I tailored each order with such finesse – including me. All I knew was that my tongue could parse each ingredient as if on a measuring scale. Perhaps it was my black tongue: I wished upon a specific pickle and it just happened. Of course, I never spoke about my tongue or its alleged abilities.

Bapuji said that helping others came easily to me: comforting a sick child, changing bandages, giving medicine, easing bedpans, checking temperature, mourning the dead. He consulted with some city folks and I was enrolled at a nursing school. I commuted by bus to nearby Ludhiana to study. Dr Batra, the senior-most doctor at the school, said I had empathy, a big word that meant I understood the suffering of others.

Bapuji and Maji were also on the lookout for a suitable groom for me. I didn't mind the idea of marriage if I could continue living in the gurdwara where I grew up, in Machhiwara, the dusty village of no river, no fish, but of the guru, which had given me refuge. In my final year of nursing school, they found Jeet, a bus driver from east Delhi. And I was married upon graduation.

In 1970, the year of my wedding, a Hindi film had become very popular. Jeet looked like the hero, Ranjha, with his thin moustache and skin the colour of golden wheat. When I told him that, he said it was because I was his beloved Heer. But we were no star-crossed lovers, he declared. That was just the way he was, unfazed by man or fate. Like the sun on a winter day. But I knew I was no Heer; I was more like a doe startled by her own good fortune.

After our wedding, Jeet brought me to his tiny rented one-room place in Jangpura. The congested snarl of matchbox houses stacked against one another was a shock after the serenity and sprawl of the gurdwara. It was a refugee colony, where those who fled after Partition had settled and rebuilt their lives. Like the Punjabis around us, Jeet and I set down to working hard and working our way up. And then, I became a mother.

I massaged my Niki with mustard oil, gave her warm baths, suckled her at my breast, and watched her sleep in my lap. I fed her choori by hand, watched her dimples deepen with happiness. I oiled her hair and braided colourful ribbons into them. I stitched frocks for her, and knitted sweaters and mittens. I watched her take baby steps as, in one hand, she clutched the wooden peacock, my companion from the hospital that saved me. In each of my actions, I mimicked my mother. And I recalled the child I used to be. It was strange to be a mother and a child at the same time in the same body – to be so alive.

The only thing I didn't do was ask Niki to unsay anything. No child of mine would have a black tongue or be accused of having one. Maji had taught me that there was no such thing. Kirat karo, vand chakho, naam japo – work hard, share with others, contemplate God – these were the three pillars of Sikhism, and they were the pillars I built my life on.

In time, three more children arrived. At eighteen months, Laali was my youngest. His hair fell in curls and I let them hang loose. His top knot could wait. He was my doll, and when he giggled, his eyes vanished in his chubby cheeks. Soni was my six-year-old monkey. There was not a height she could not scale or jump from. A fresh wound at the beginning of a fresh week: a knee scraped, a finger cut, a toenail broken, an ankle sprained – as a nurse, I always had a full-time patient! Ten-year-old Veer looked like his father, but he reminded me of mine with his intensity, his uprightness, his refusal to be cowed. Niki, my firstborn, was most like me. People said: 'A gentle soul like her mother'. Quick to help, good with her hands, popular.

One day, when I was returning from hospital, I saw a slum being demolished. The Emergency was in effect, Indira Gandhi wanted a clean Delhi, and no one was allowed to complain. Jeet heard from a colleague that a new colony was being set up across the Yamuna for people left homeless after this slum-cleaning drive. Prices were cheap and we could afford a bigger house if we moved. It seemed like a good idea. So Jeet spoke to some people who guided him to a real-estate agent, who helped us buy a two-room house in Trilokpuri. Our savings were cleaned out, but we now had space for our children.

That was 1976. Our neighbours were poor and disadvantaged, which was not the problem. But because they were poor and disadvantaged, nobody paid any attention to the new resettlement colony. Delhi was still growing and people kept pouring in. The colony grew like a baby without supervision. Since there was no planning, the narrow lanes ran into each other, dingy houses sprouted, drains overflowed, electricity wires hung overhead.

In 1982, Jeet brought home a colour television. The children whooped in delight, and even Laali was entranced by the pigmented screen. And I realized, with a shock, that my life before this marriage had been black and white. In twelve years, my world had filled with colour: the sunflower yellow of Jeet's turban, the coal black of his eyes, the rose pink of Niki's tongue, the red-purple of Soni's bruised skin, the sparkle of Veer's cat-like eyes, the white of Laali's buttery cheeks! The only thing that remained of my previous life was that I couldn't eat jamun. When monsoon arrived, and I walked by handcarts laden with those berries, my jaw locked and I had to remind myself to breathe.

Every payday, I would stop by a bakery shop on my way home and pick a dozen vanilla pastries. As I rounded the corner to our house, Soni and Veer would be scouting the lane like monkeys atop the banyan tree in the bazaar. Niki would take the box and apportion the pastries, forsaking a few of hers and Laali's for the other two. That night, Jeet would cook his special butter chicken. Because I didn't eat meat, he would toss some fried paneer into my gravy. Dinner would be in front of the TV. The children would watch actors fight and dance and I would watch them, their eyes alight, their faces awash in the TV's light. If Jeet caught me looking, he would wink at me.

One day, the *Indian Express* reported that in Punjab, Sikh militants had ordered Hindu passengers out of a night bus and shot them dead. That night, rioters wielding iron rods and flaming torches surrounded a bus making its way down a deserted road. Smoke rose from the piles of wreckage that littered the ground, and shrieks rent the air again and again. Blood for blood! The bus halted and the rioters jumped on. They pounced on the women cowering inside and dragged them out by their hair. Multiple men lunged at each woman, stripping her, taking turns at raping her while others held her down. After they were done, the men relieved themselves on the fallen women. From inside the bus, male passengers watched, petrified. Until Father strode into the crowd, sword in hand, and lopped off the heads of the rioters as Jeet, the bus driver, looked on.

I awoke from my nightmare, convinced that my head was missing. I felt for my neck, nose, ears – all there. To calm myself, I watched the chests of my children, rising and falling as they slept. Beside me, Jeet snored. I was alive, I had my family with me. I lay down but could not sleep. I realized that I was now older than Mother and Father had been, and it felt strange to have outlived them.

In the early winter of 1984, I smelt woodsmoke and froze, until Niki informed me that the neighbour, having run out of kerosene, was burning wooden blocks for fire. That evening, I got delayed at work. As I hurried through our darkening colony at dusk, a black buffalo waded into my path. Stray cows were normal, but a buffalo? With majestic sabre horns fit for the mount of Yama himself? She watched me with bulbous eyes. I stumbled out of her way and clung to the brick wall that bordered the lane.

Who was the lord of death seeking?

V
(1987–1992)
Partitioned Women

Refusing to learn from the past, Duryodhana invites his cousins to a palace of wax and sets it afire in the night. The Pandavas, forewarned by their spies, create decoys and escape to a forest where they spend their days in disguise. Meanwhile, Duryodhana sheds crocodile tears even as the serpent around his heart frolics. When King Drupada invites suitors to a contest for the hand of his daughter Draupadi, the Pandavas realize that winning her hand will grant them a major alliance. The assembly of contesting noblemen is no match for Arjuna, the third Pandava and the greatest archer who ever lived. Having won Draupadi, the five brothers return home to their mother and exclaim, 'Surprise! Look at what we have brought home.' Without looking, Kunti asks them to share whatever they have equally amongst themselves. Thus, Draupadi, the dusky beauty born of fire, finds herself partitioned into five...

13
(1987)

❋

NIKI AND HER school friend, Aruna, were in the garden sailing paper boats. The downpour had made canals of the flower beds, and Niki fancied herself a Venetian boatman as she crooned in the manner she'd seen in a Hindi film about a great gambler. The sky was inky still, which meant more rain. Next to her, Aruna was prodding the water with a twig, shoulders hunched in concentration. Niki sank her fingers into the water and flicked it at her. As Aruna recoiled, Niki bounded down the walkway.

'Cheater!' Aruna ran after her, high-jumping through the puddled walkway. Niki laughed as she darted behind a chair on the porch, jogging on the spot, darting to one side, then another, anticipating the direction from which her friend would approach. Aruna made a feint to Niki's left, then rounded to her right, which sent Niki shrieking around the porch. Slippers sliding, arms flailing, screeching-racing-braking, the girls dashed about the porch as if in a game of musical chairs, until Aruna crashed into a chair, said 'sorry, sorry!' and backed away guiltily.

Niki followed her to the walkway, feet squelching. Aruna was rubbing her hand where it had hit the chair and its occupant. 'He didn't scold me.'

'Oh,' Niki tossed her head in the direction of the porch, 'he doesn't speak.'

'Never?'

Niki shook her head.

'Who is he?'

'Bapuji. My dadima's father. I don't even know if he can see.'

'Is he blind?'

'No, but he never looks around.' Niki shrugged. 'I'm hungry. Want something to eat?' Aruna assented. Niki led her to a tap set in a brick pit by the far end of the porch where the garden extended. 'Let's clean up. Nooran won't let us inside the house like this.' She opened the tap and started to rub her muddy feet and legs, one foot atop another. Suman Aunty, supporting her big belly with both hands, passed by the front gate, a servant holding her umbrella.

'Niki, have you finished the Delhi essay?'

'Almost.'

Aruna crumpled her shoulders. 'Ahh … what a bore, you and the essay!'

Niki grinned. 'You enjoyed it too.'

'The school trip, yes; the essay…' Aruna stuck her tongue out.

Niki stepped out and Aruna took her place. Last week, the ten-year-olds had been on a two-day school trip to Delhi, accompanied by their social studies teacher. En route, 100 kilometres from Chandigarh, they had passed the university town of Kurukshetra. 'Dharamkshetre, Kurukshetre, the field of dharma, the field of the Kurus' – words that opened the Mahabharata had sprung to her mind. In Delhi, they visited Aibak's Qutub Minar of the twelfth century, Shah Jahan's Red Fort of the seventeenth, Lutyens' Delhi of the twentieth, and the teacher had declared at day's end: 'Children, we haven't even begun scraping the surface of Delhi!'

Delhi had gobsmacked her. History was as alive there as it was dead in her trite textbooks. How alive, she had learnt the following day. After walking through the spidery lanes of Chandni Chowk, one of Delhi's oldest neighbourhoods, festooned with overhung wires and trapeze monkeys, the teacher presented them with what he called 'a religious trifecta': Digambar Jain temple, Jama Masjid and the Sisganj Gurdwara. As they were about to enter the Sikh temple, her classmate Karan Bansal sneaked up and hissed, 'Sardar toh gaddar hain!'

Niki had ignored the idiot but the rallying cry of the '84 riots – Sikhs are traitors – had made the history of Delhi up close and personal. Dadima and PUCL were still working with the '84-ers, chaurasiye, the survivors, to get them justice. But India had elected a new prime minister, Indira Gandhi's son, and he had dismissed the riots as mere tremors caused when the felling of a tree shook the earth.

'Okay!' Aruna shook the excess water off her slippered feet. 'Will you help me with the essay after we eat? Please, please, na? You're good at it, but at least admit it – history's a real pain.'

14
(1988)

✳

'TELL ME, BIJI, why does a woman need God?' Nooran asked from where she sat cross-legged on a mat on the floor, shelling a mound of peas with astonishing dexterity. Across from her, Niki sat atop an old newspaper, polishing her school shoes. Slathering the Kiwi black polish on the scuffed toe of her shoe, Niki paused to watch them. Dadima and Nooran were vastly different from any other women she had encountered: school teachers, mothers of friends, women on TV and in the movies. Their conversations made eleven-year-old Niki feel like she was being let into a secret sorority of dangerous ideas. With a ringside view, she came away mostly enlightened, if occasionally mystified.

Dadima sat curled up in her favourite armchair, reading, the light from the floor lamp lighting her up in a halo. She looked up from the newspaper and, from behind her reading glasses, studied the two squatters at her feet.

Now that she had her attention, Nooran did not wait for an answer but ventured one of her own. 'What is it that God does exactly? Why do people worship him in so many different ways? Wearing out their slippers with daily treks to temples and mosques, fasting some days and feasting on others, flogging themselves in remembrance and flogging others in riots, blaring prayers over loudspeakers and blowing conch shells … why? And whether they eat pigs or cows or grass, all of them agree on one thing – that *he* created this world. But how is he different from a woman who has the power of creation right here?' A pea pod in Nooran's right hand was pointed at her abdomen in a fine illustration of her point. 'A woman has a womb, and she creates a baby. We have proof of her powers. Where is the proof of this God anyway?'

'Like Brahma, the creator in the Hindu trinity,' Niki added knowledgeably. 'But he doesn't have a womb, I think.'

Nooran nodded. 'Men were plain jealous, which is why they felt the need to create this fantastic creature,' her hands created a canopy in the air. 'God. Then another man said, "Why, I fancy my own god." And because he wanted to be different, he gave his god wings, or blue skin, or a crown of thorns. And then it spread like disease, squabbling men building personal gods. Next, like a king needs a kingdom, each god needed an army of followers. And that's how they had religion.'

Dadima folded the daily and took off her glasses. 'Women certainly don't need religion.'

'Why, Dadima?'

'Look at this article.' She indicated the newspaper with a disdainful hand. 'It says that in Khalistan, the proposed "pure" state of the Sikhs, women will be required to keep their hair long, their heads covered and wear salwar kameezes only. In effect, this is another version of Pakistan, the original land of the pure!' she snorted.

Seeing the puzzlement on Niki's face, she clarified, 'Who is issuing these diktats? Men. Whom are they issuing them for? Women? Why, I ask? If you are so interested in rehat-maryada, cultural traditions, observe them yourself. Why does religion always boil down to a rule book on how to control women?' She paused and looked at her granddaughter pointedly.

'Because men are scared of women?'

'And why are they scared of women?' Dadima prompted.

'Because women can do one thing men can't?'

'Yes! A woman's religion is motherhood, which is why men are forever trying to dictate to them which "religion",' Dadima made quote marks in the air with her fingers, 'they belong to. When they stamp a woman – Hindu, Muslim, Sikh – they automatically stamp their children as well. And that's how they assume the command and control of the tribe, when, in reality, as Nooran said, the command should lie, if at all, with the original creator.'

Nooran clucked in agreement. 'Women create babies, men create God. So they can kill in his name. Then they'll wash their sins in a temple or mosque. But going to Mecca solves nothing, no?'

Old man Bullah, Niki pondered. Didn't Nooran know he was a man too?

'I'll tell you what,' Nooran said, 'give men one condition – just one condition – then watch them straighten up like bamboos.'

'What condition?' Niki asked.

'A man has to give birth, physical birth, like a woman does. After which, he can go kill one person. Five children? Here, take five licenses to kill. See how quickly all killing stops. Remember that story from the Mahabharata, the birth of the Kauravas?'

Nooran pronounced Mahabharata such that it sounded like 'Ma-Bharat' – Mother India. You couldn't tell if it was her accent or a deliberate attempt to mispronounce.

'Gandhari was given a boon by Vyasa, and she asked for 100 sons. Though, why any woman would need so many babies beats me,' Nooran shook her head as she ran her fingers through the mound of peas looking for bad ones. 'She carried her pregnancy for two years. Now imagine if her husband, the king, had to have a mountain of a swollen belly for that time?'

'But Nooran,' Niki protested, 'a man doesn't have the organs to give birth!'

'Precisely. The apparatus required for birth is not just a womb. You think a man has the fortitude to carry a baby in his body for nine months? Then take care of it for years? The Mahabharata tells us that Gandhari birthed 100 Kaurava sons. There's no mention of how she raised those 100 mewling babies. Fed them, bathed them, loved them, taught them, is there?'

'She was a queen; she had help!'

'Sure, but a mother has to break up squabbles, sing lullabies at bedtime, cook 100 different favourite meals! Now, imagine the king caring for his 100 sons while his wife lolled about issuing orders?'

Niki imagined a bejewelled king holding an infant in his arms, watching with horror as piss trickled over his silk garments, while ninety-nine other babies besieged him.

'Instead, the blind king was keenest on the battle,' Dadima waded in. 'Which makes you wonder what he was thinking. That, with a hundred, he had sons to spare?'

'There is more than one way to be blind, Biji.'

Outside, dusk was turning to night quickly, as it did in the winter and the room had acquired a hushed glow. The women sat in a circle in the living room, the lit lamp like a fire around which they were gathered, absorbed in their individual tasks, shelling peas, polishing shoes, reading newspapers, conversing, occasionally illustrating a point for the benefit of the child in their midst, sharing stories to bind them together.

'Men,' Nooran offered, 'you place an infant in their arms, and they start playing passing the parcel!' She burst into raucous laughter, her belly jiggling beneath the shiny floral kameez she wore.

Niki paused in her polishing as a thought struck her. 'But Nooran, what about a woman who doesn't have children?'

'Someone like me, you mean? Why, she is still a god – make her another avatar if you like. These male gods have multiple avatars, no? Anyway,' Nooran plucked out the bad peas, 'why do I need a certificate from anybody? I am my own certificate.' She popped a few peas in her mouth, chewed and nodded to Dadima. 'Sweet.'

'But what Nooran said is so true,' Dadima resumed an earlier thread. 'If a man could give birth, he would find it hard to kill.'

'I wonder what Papa would say to that?'

Dadima uncrossed her legs and stood up. She crossed the room and switched on some more lights. 'He'd agree.'

Light shone off her polished shoes; she had done a good job of buffing it. She could do Papa's black leather shoes next. He was travelling to Punjab on field work, which meant that he would return with sneakers that Nooran would soak in a plastic tub for a full day to loosen the dirt. He would also bring loose sheets of paper filled with his handwritten notes, which Niki would be entrusted with filing. Lately, she had been doing it often. The police in Punjab had a new weapon: TADA. The image it conjured was of a giant policeman who squashed detainees under his ample ass. However, TADA was a special act of law that allowed people to be detained without being produced before a magistrate. And this was where Papa came in. Frantic parents hoped to use his skills and connections to get through to their sons. Papa would return after a couple of days, bearing soil and sun and stories. Stories that stayed with Niki; such as that of a mother who cooked rotis for her son daily, even after his body had been located and the corpse cremated.

Dadima's voice brought Niki back. 'You know what he said when I told him the story of Ameena's mum and how she taught me the kalma to recite on the way to their home, so I could become a temporary Muslim and eat nihari without guilt? He said that if Ameena's mum, an illiterate woman, could solve the conundrum of religion with such ease, would the violence of Partition have occurred if the leaders were mothers?'

'Like Nooran said, if only the king had given birth to 100 sons! But,' Niki frowned, 'the Mahabharata was fought over a kingdom.'

'Religion and real estate go together – like pus and a boil,' Nooran laughed.

'What is religion but the kingdom of God? And what does every kingdom need?'

To Dadima's questioning gaze, Niki replied, 'Land and people?'

'And sacrifice. The Mahabharata gave this land its name, which is important to remember, for that was what the story was about.'

'Not dharma?'

'That too, but the heart of the story is about land, its hold on men, and what men will do for it. Real estate, really.'

Dadima would know. She had lost her husband and her home to that story.

'Maybe, like Nooran said, women, like God, have no country, and the whole world is theirs. Or none.' Dadima sighed, 'Women are like train bogeys – shunted here, shunted there as borders are switched, old ones erased, new ones built. From parents' house to in-laws' house, from India to Pakistan, Pakistan to India…'

Nooran gathered the steel plate piled high with green peas and got up. In her salwar kameez of amber satin, gold earrings swinging in her ears, black hair braided with red thread, the tassels draped over one shoulder, she was brighter than any sun. As she stood in the centre of the room, she appeared majestic and playful.

'Biji, they can be Heer.'

Heer again. Hmm. It was a popular poem. About the heroine of the Heer-Ranjha couple, the Indian Juliet who had fallen in love with a man from the opposite camp, or something like that. The poem that was popularly sung was a composition by Waris Shah, Dadima had informed her. For a long-dead person, Heer was recalled often, almost as if she were alive…

'And be poisoned by their own family?' Dadima asked.

…and unfortunate, Niki completed the thought.

'How is that fate any different?' Dadima asked.

'She left her name on every Punjabi's lips,' Nooran swept out of the room, her long braid sliding from her shoulder to her ample hips, the tasselled bells tinkling as she walked.

15
(1990)

❋

A HALF MOON WAS entangled in the branches of the mango tree, nestling in its leaves. The night air felt cool and Niki tugged at Dadima's shawl, pulling it over her bare feet propped against the edge of Dadima's wicker chair. 'Why so quiet, Dadima?'

The amber light of the porch lamp, positioned in a corner behind her, shot Dadima's silvery-grey hair with gold and, as she smiled, she looked like an Indian version of a fairy godmother: bright, beatific, benign. 'I was thinking...' Dadima said.

'About?'

'Of shoes and ships and sealing wax, of cabbages and kings...'

'Huh?'

Dadima smiled. The gaps between her teeth were growing as she grew older. 'You should read that book.'

'I gave it up halfway. Alice's adventures sound so ... I don't know ... silly.'

'Hmm. Maybe you'll get to it at some point. The point where Tweedle Dee and Tweedle Dum are telling Alice a story about a walrus and a carpenter who encounter some oysters on a beach. They sweet talk them, lead them astray, then gobble them up.'

Niki sat up. 'Seriously?'

'Un-huh. It is a parable. Which is?'

'A story with a message. Apparently, the entire book is.'

Dadima smiled, as if to herself. 'Bless our teacher, Mr Howard. He made us memorize large sections of the text, the poems especially, and to this day, they just pop up in my memory.' She had studied *Alice in Wonderland* during Standard IX at Kinnaird College in Lahore. Effortlessly, she began to recite.

> The time has come, the walrus said,
> To talk of many things:
> Of shoes and ships and sealing wax,
> Of cabbages and kings,
> And why the sea is boiling hot,
> And whether pigs have wings.

Niki clapped. 'But why does the walrus talk such nonsense?'

'It's Carroll's way of illustrating the nonsense that religion passes off as sense. You would expect people to know better, that they would learn from the past and be wary of falling prey again...' Dadima looked off in the distance. 'The *Tribune*,' her hand indicated the newspaper on the table, 'is running a series on interfaith marriages because people need to be reminded that such things exist in our society – they are not alien. Barely forty-three years after the horror of Partition, and we have another demand for another partition. Khalistan now! Another land of the pure. All they have to do is open their eyes and take one good look at Pakistan – exactly how pure does it look? Where does it all end?' Her right hand spun the air in question.

The netting door swung open and Nooran stood in the doorway, the bright floral polyester kameez straining against her ample frame. 'Shall I get you milk? If there's no more work, I'll go to bed.' She surveyed the garden, the brick boundary wall and the iron gate at the entrance. 'Locked it, have you, Biji?'

'Yes, Nooran, fetch the milk, I won't keep you from your beauty sleep,' Dadima said.

Nooran was humming a popular song, white teeth that won't stop grinning, and Niki watched her saunter off, the net door creaking shut in her wake. Nooran possessed a set of pearly whites that would be the envy of any toothpaste marketer. It was unlikely, however, that Nooran would ever be on TV: her radiant complexion was the colour of a thundercloud, and atop that moon-shaped face sat several fleshy moles like a sprinkling of peppercorns.

Aruna, who had come over to play and for homework, was in the kitchen for a drink when she saw Nooran, and exclaimed, 'Oh, she's so, so – ugly!' The pressure cooker was bustling, but it was not that Nooran would have cared. Niki, though, was taken aback, as perhaps was Aruna, for she had searched for a suitable adjective before settling on the lame 'ugly'. There was a splendour to Nooran, that ample girth, the radiant complexion, the dulcet singing voice, the thick hair that she tied in a tight bun or braid which, when open, was Medusa's envy.

Niki turned to Dadima. 'Her boyfriend is visiting?'

'Perhaps,' Dadima shrugged.

That Nooran had a boyfriend was a well-kept secret, for Niki had only discovered it by chance a year back. Tall, turbaned, dressed in lungi and long kurta, he looked like one of Papa's rural clients: a farmer in a perennial tangle with his neighbour over well or crop or pump. Niki had paid him no heed until one night, when she ventured into the garden to locate a pen she had misplaced. Hearing what sounded like a scuffle from the outhouse, where Nooran had her own room-and-attached-bath quarters, she headed to investigate. All was dark inside, the window curtains tightly drawn. The narrow side window, though, allowed a sliver of visibility via a footlight. Niki narrowed her eyes to amorphous scuffling shapes: muscle, sinew, slipping, slapping, flesh against moist flesh, the motions of coitus on limited display. Then Dadima's voice had sounded. Niki had been torn. What she was witnessing was beyond her imagination. The summons came again, more urgent this time. Niki tore herself away, but she went to bed with the knowledge that a woman who could love thus could never be ugly. So when she returned her friend's ignorant remark with a superior look, poor Aruna was even more befuddled.

Meanwhile, Dadima had that faraway look on her face, which meant she was reminiscing. She had a way with stories, which Niki loved. Tugging at her shawl, she said, 'Tell me, Dadima.'

'Where do I start?'

'When you first learnt that you would have to leave your home.'

'1947, the new year had barely begun. I was already at the Nalwa House in Ferozepur, married. Bapuji kept going back to Lahore, returning with fresh stories. Apparently, the task of partitioning the nation was already underway. Everything was getting divided – library books, table lamps, steel cupboards, rugs even – into two piles: India and Pakistan.

'When Bapuji recounted this, people said, "Yes, of course, material can be divided, but people? In Punjab, Hindus, Muslims, Sikhs, we all live like spices inside a masala box, tossed together for flavoursome food."' Dadima sighed. 'Maji, my mother, worried constantly. I was also pregnant, you see, but Bapuji kept returning to Lahore... Soon it was 15 August, and we were all free. And that very night, your father arrived – midnight's child.'

'Your tryst with destiny,' Niki beamed, quoting from Prime Minister Nehru's first speech to independent India. 'Then?'

'17 August 1947, two days after freedom, we heard of Radcliffe's boundary line. Where was this mysterious line? At first, people assumed they were within it and safe. But not for long. The majority community started to turn upon the others, and, as if the boundary was actually a mirror, the same atrocities were reflected across it. Soon, people were streaming across that imaginary line, searching for it, but never finding it. No one knew its coordinates but when the attacks stopped, they knew they had crossed it and were safe.

'We fled by boat to Amritsar, as you know. But Bapuji kept slipping into Lahore, by train, by road, by boat. Maji cautioned him against going, but when he persisted, she suggested he bring some items back with him, essentials that would be handy as they lived off their relatives. But Bapuji never came back with anything of value, Maji complained.'

'What did he come back with?' Niki whispered.

'Stories. Of how Lahore was burning, of how he sneaked into our boarded-up home like a thief, how he visited his fields, but only at night for fear of being seen. The sight of a turbaned Sikh in the burning Lahore was like tinder. The few who stayed behind had shaved their beards, cut their hair and converted to Islam. His stories found eager listeners back in Amritsar, and warnings not to venture back. Still, Bapuji went back to Lahore.'

Dadima fell silent. The night air resounded with the staccato chirping of crickets. Niki knew what Dadima was remembering. The months of quiet desperation in which there had been no news of Bapuji. He had been on his promised 'final' visit to Lahore. Her mother had pawned her jewellery for daily expenses. The price of food and essentials had skyrocketed and Maji was a continuing burden on the relatives she was with. Days had churned into months until one winter morning, Bapuji finally appeared at the door. Only, he wouldn't talk. Over time, a disjointed picture emerged of what he might have experienced. He had been trying to water his fields, which lay parched because of the fires raging all around. A mob had chased him with spears and swords. Familiar with the riverbank, he had hidden among the reeds. That encounter, though, forced him to face his new reality: that the ground beneath his feet had tilted. In time, other people regained their balance, started lives afresh, but Bapuji's compass remained off-kilter. Every waking moment thereafter, his eyes sought the street.

Now that Niki was thirteen, she wished she had made some attempt to know the ancient man who sat silently on this very porch.

'What are you waiting for?' everyone asked him, first with puzzlement, increasingly with exasperation, and when he didn't answer, they stopped enquiring. Only once, Dadima said, as she sat cradling his hand, he had mumbled, 'Who knows who might turn up from vatan?'

Vatan. Homeland. He suffered from dementia.

'They took Laur from him,' Dadima sighed, using the vernacular for the great city of pre-Partition Punjab, 'but could not take his fields.'

On his deathbed, he pleaded with them to water his fields.

The great-grandfather Niki had never known belonged to that legion of men whose labour and sinew had changed the course of the rivers of Punjab to create fertile land out of scrub land. Land which they had guarded, repeatedly, with their lives from marauders like the Afghan Abdali. Land which they had sowed with their sweat and harvested with their hearts. Land which was never just coordinates on the ground but a member of the family, for every season, it had to be watched over in the manner of a newborn. Land which they celebrated in ritual. And Niki saw that lost, ancient patriarch gather those acres of swaying mustard, golden corn and ripening wheat, laced with water channels, fragrant with mango, fenced with eucalyptus, and cup them in the palms of his well-worn farmer's hands for safekeeping as the roiling dust storm of Partition plucked him up and tossed him into exile.

16
(1991)

✳

WHY DID MEN look at women as if they were still getting used to them? As if their anatomy was a circus exhibit? As if women didn't make up half the population of the second-most populous country in the world? Niki kicked a piece of gravel as she walked back with Nooran from the Sector 8 market. Dusk was settling with a hint of winter in its cool dark embrace. Or was it her sunglasses? She lowered her head to peer over.

'Do you intend to wear those even in the dark?' Nooran asked with an imperious nod.

Niki was getting accustomed to wearing shades. They made an effective barrier, casting ogling men into deep shadows, rendering them sepia like the sun did to the outdoors. She had recently started wearing a bra, and the manner in which men stared at her made her wonder if her underwear was breaking news in the local *Tribune*.

'Nooran, you should try them!'

'Na, I won't hide behind coloured glass.'

'But Nooran,' Niki squirmed, 'don't you feel uncomfortable when men look at you?'

'Men? The ones who scratch their balls in public with the same shamelessness with which they pick their noses? These men make me uncomfortable? Why?'

'Just … you know, the way they look at me. I hate it!'

'Niki, you're wearing a bra to support those mosquito bites on your chest. Wait till you grow fully into a woman. Will you wear a burqa then?'

Niki glared at Nooran, but it was useless behind those glasses. Nooran, with a pair of brass plates on her chest, could afford a size comparison. But how did she manage that confidence? Nooran didn't walk like a snake, the popular simile for women's gait. No, she walked like a peacock, sure-footed, deliberate, proud; a walk that said, 'Watch me. Do not touch me. Watch me, for I can kick your ass.'

'It is the nature of men to ogle. They will even lech at the bare ankle of a woman in a burqa. That is why in places like Iran or Iraq, lecherous old men, aware of similar tendencies in young men, forbid women from showing even an inch of skin or hair. Apparently, even nail polish is forbidden. Hain!'

A scooter whizzed close by and Nooran pulled Niki away from the edge of the footpath. 'Science says men, like women, have brains here,' she tapped her head. 'Now I didn't go to school, but I can tell you this: in the presence of women, men's brains descend to their groins.'

Niki started to laugh loudly and Nooran grinned. 'Niki, puttar, listen: each person comes into this world with only one thing – their physical body. The rest we acquire over the course of living, fooling ourselves that we are permanent residents on this earth. But all we really have is this body, with its brain and bosom and vagina and limbs. The only person with authority over your body is you. Know this, and never ever cede the authority of your body to another.'

The chirruping of the birds flying overhead rang clear. Niki linked her free arm in Nooran's as they turned the corner into their lane. Ahead, their neighbour's home was festooned with lights – the much-desired grandson had arrived and they were broadcasting it to the world.

'Kurimaar!' Nooran spat the word into a hedge. Daughter-killer.

'Noo-ran! That's rude!'

'Don't lecture me, Niki Madam. I didn't go to a convent school like you, so I have no manners and will gladly spit in his face!'

Music spilled out of the house in jubilation; a party was underway.

'Jinder says Chandigarh is a modern city. What kind of modernity is this where decrepit customs persist? Sometimes, I wonder if a modern city can even be built on these ancient plains.'

At home, Dadima had just returned from congratulating the neighbours on their good fortune. In a grey tanchoi salwar kameez with a pattern of white paisleys, silver-framed glasses and silver-grey hair, she looked so beautiful. Dadima had such dignity about her that Niki wondered if men dared stare at her.

'Well, I *am* glad for Suman,' she said, as she placed her clutch on the sideboard. 'Apparently, this was her last chance. Some women were gossiping that the abortions had rendered Suman sterile.'

Nooran tut-tutted as she retrieved items from the shopping bags. 'Did she look happy or relieved?'

'Don't know,' Dadima shrugged. 'I didn't see her.'

Niki and Nooran looked at her in surprise.

'The grandson was tucked into the grandmother's lap to be shown off. Suman was resting in her bedroom. Excessive bleeding during labour caused by multiple abortions, you see.'

Nooran's hand stilled, Dadima sat in the armchair like a grim godmother, and in the amber light of the living room, as night crept at the windows, a realization coalesced in Niki. The world was a terrible place for women. Niki needed to find a way to fight the odds.

17
(1992)

✻

IT WAS A glorious autumn day. The Shivalik mountains that ringed Chandigarh glowed in the mellow sun as the bus pulled out of the city. Inside, Niki sat at a window, dressed in her school uniform of white shirt, navy-blue skirt and blue blazer emblazoned with the crest of her convent school. Her tie flew in the breeze, which also puffed up Nooran's dupatta as she sat beside Niki. They were headed to Patiala, an hour-and-a-half's bus ride away, where Niki was to compete in the finals of a state-wide debating competition. In Class X, fifteen-year-old Niki was part of her school debating team. However, in the run-up to the final competition, she had fallen ill. The school had taken a substitute, leaving instructions for Niki to join them if she felt better.

That morning, Niki had woken up bright as Nooran, feeling as radiant as Nooran's proper name. Why not go to Patiala and compete? But Papa had left last night on an urgent summons. 'Just when I need the car!' Niki complained.

'It was an urgent case,' Dadima patted her arm.

Niki shrugged her off. 'All his cases are urgent.'

'Beli Ram is a border-vaulter—'

'Who cares?'

'Hear me out, then make up your mind, okay? The Punjab Police has jailed him on charge of terrorism. Your Papa was worried the opium addict would not be able to mount a defence.'

'Great! I am competing with an addict for my father's attention.'

'You know this man, Niki,' Dadima said quietly.

'No,' Niki's neck retracted, 'I don't.'

'From Ferozepur's Hussainiwala border. You know the burlesque both countries put on every evening? Well, some days, a man dashes across from the Indian side and somersaults onto the Pakistani side. He hugs the earth and doesn't move, lying spread-eagled in what is officially no-man's-land. The first time it happened, soldiers on both sides readied as if war had been declared. Now, they know the drill. A Pakistani soldier hoists the man on his shoulder and, at the border, hands over the limp body to the Indian soldier, who similarly hoists him and carries him to the shelter. Niki, you've witnessed it too – just before we left Ferozepur.'

Niki's eyes narrowed. 'Why?'

'He came from Lahore during Partition and wants to return.'

'Why now?' Niki said. 'It's 1992 – forty-five years after Partition!'

'I read once that when Indian sepoys were fighting in Europe during the Second World War, their biggest fear was not of dying; it was of dying and being buried in a foreign land.' Dadima sighed. 'Your Papa knows it is 1992. The situation in Punjab is improving. We have elected a new state government. But the police is unwilling to give up its special powers. To them, Beli Ram is another number in the terrorist tally.'

Niki nodded briefly.

'Nooran can accompany you on the bus. And both of you can return with the school van.'

Thus, Nooran and Niki had bought their tickets, boarded the bus and were on their way. They chatted about this and that and everything else in between because with Nooran there was never a dearth of stories. Halfway, the bus shuddered to a stop. The driver hopped down, as did sundry men, and after much examination announced he needed a mechanic and instructed them to board another bus.

They grabbed their bags and purses, and waited on the roadside with the other passengers. Buses were running to capacity with standees to boot. The more desperate ones clambered aboard. An hour later, Nooran and Niki were still standing on the roadside, and time was ticking.

'Nooran, we must board a bus if we are to reach in time to compete!'

As the next bus rolled down, Nooran ran to the middle of the road, flagging it down, grabbed Niki's wrist and hoisted her up the open door, following briskly. The bus was packed, and Niki slid her way through the thicket of bodies by the door. When she looked back, Nooran was separated from her by a wall of men but she could see the glint of her golden suit.

However, Niki was uncomfortable. She felt a pressure against her groin. A man squeezed into her even as he gazed into the distance as if he had no relation with his own body. She rearranged herself to face away from him. Next, she felt her bust being groped. Horrified, Niki smacked the offending hand, whirled around and shouted. But the thicket of men continued to serenely gaze ahead. Nooran, meanwhile, had forced her way through. As she joined Niki, she shouted at the men to behave. One of them turned to her and asked, 'If we don't, what will you do?'

'Aren't you ashamed? This is just a girl!'

'So should we touch you?'

'That's what you want? Try!'

The sudden aggression stunned Niki. As slander flew, she reached for Nooran's arm to stop her from engaging with the vicious men. But Nooran stood her ground, arguing volubly with them, loud enough for the entire bus to hear. The other passengers sat minding their own business, an ear cocked to the scrabble but no concern otherwise. And then the circle of men opened, an arm thrust towards Nooran, grabbed her, pulled her in and the circle closed.

'Nooran?'

Niki started to twitch. Suddenly, she was a child and all she wanted was the comfort of Nooran.

'Nooran?' Niki tried again but it sounded like a squeak.

Meanwhile, there was a scuffle from within the circle Nooran was in. Niki heard Nooran curse. A man swore. A slap. Shuffling of feet. There was a commotion within the circle. Then a thud sounded, like a bag had fallen from the luggage carrier mounted atop the bus.

But the bus continued to roll. Nobody shouted for it to stop.

Niki felt urine trickle down her thigh. Then she heard a voice cry, 'Nooran! Nooran! Stop! Stop! Stop the bus!' She realized she was screaming. Another passenger shouted for the bus to pull over. The circle of men parted. Niki raced to the open door and looked out. In the distance behind, yellow glinted on the road. She bounded down.

Nooran lay spread-eagled on the road. Her eyes were open but she didn't recognize Niki. 'Nooran! Nooran!' She didn't answer. Niki knelt down and lifted Nooran's head to place it in her lap. Her hands came away bloody.

'Nooran … Nooran … Nooran…'

Men gathered. Someone checked Nooran's pulse and clucked. Her arm fell limply down. The circle of men grew and gossiped and waved hands and shuffled feet and offered advice and summoned police and did what crowds did when they were an audience to an 'accident'.

At some point, Dadima arrived. Niki couldn't answer any of the police's questions. She could only hug Nooran's body and rock back and forth.

That was when violence, an essential character in all the stories she had grown up listening to from Dadima, Nooran, Papa, became a part of Niki's life. Casual violence towards women was in the blood of the Punjabi, ugly, ordinary, thoughtless violence, whether during the Partition, whether in the stories of the Mahabharata enacted to this day, during the Indo-Pak wars, in the '84 riots, or in daily life. Rapes, dowry deaths, female foeticide, bride burning, eve-teasing, acid attacks – it was a violence that sought to show women their place, to keep them in that place and if they dared resist, it would smack them back into place again, or take their lives. And a woman like Nooran, independent, fearless, agnostic, radical, was anathema to them. It was a miracle she had survived that long...

Nooran bled into Niki's school skirt, the blood crusted on her skin. Back at home, Niki refused to shower. Late in the night, Dadima bathed her, pouring mugs of water, letting Nooran's blood ease its way out of the crevices and folds of Niki's skin. It mingled with Niki's tears and Dadima's anguish down the drain.

Book 2

VI

(1984)

Jyot

18
(1984)

❋

OCTOBER 1984. IN the manner typical of a Delhi winter, evening turned to night abruptly, small fires erupted by the roadside, outside a hovel, beside a taxi stand – a common way to stay warm as people huddled over them in their woollens. Tiwari from the hospital where I worked was passing by our colony when the delivery van broke down. He could have it fixed, Jeet said. But it was evening, and Tiwari was reluctant to go hunting for a mechanic. So, he trundled the van down our narrow lane and asked if he could park there for the night. The van was in the lane, but Tiwari had unloaded some canisters of hospital supplies and stored them in the yard for fear of theft. But the very next day, trouble started.

Since the previous evening, I thought I saw my Hindu neighbours look at me differently. The prime minister had been killed by her Sikh bodyguards. They had wanted revenge because she'd sent the army into the Golden Temple.

When I had stepped out to fetch vegetables from the bania down the lane, a group of women huddled together had started to speak louder as I walked by.

'It's true, I tell you – my nephew works at Old Delhi railway station. He saw it with his own eyes: the train that pulled in from Amritsar – littered with corpses of massacred Hindus! Not even the babies were spared! Blood thick as a carpet lined the floor of the compartments.'

That morning, I pleaded with Jeet, 'Why do you have to go to work? Haven't you heard the rumours?'

But Jeet laughed me off. 'Some random outbursts of rage, that's all. The police have everything under control. Killing an old defenceless woman is no sign of bravery, hain?'

Jeet was acting as if it was a joke. 'You will get killed!' I shouted in panic. Then, I bit my black tongue, squeezed my eyes and unsaid it a thousand times.

He gripped my shoulder. 'This is Delhi, the national capital. What can go wrong here?' Sporting his yellow turban, he climbed atop his scooter and wove his way out of our lane, dodging the cows and pedestrians.

Jeet had been born in Delhi – it was his city, he knew it best, I assured myself. Yet, hadn't Jeet told me that Delhi was tied to Punjab like alluvium is to a river? The storm of Partition had spilled Punjab into Delhi. The capital city of independent India owed its progress to the industrious refugees who had poured out of Pakistan. Many of them lived in our neighbourhood, which was buffeted lately by every report of violence by the Sikhs in Punjab. How could Jeet be so unconcerned?

I fretted the whole day. The air swelled with rumours. I bolted the door. Jeet did not return at his usual time. Late evening, a knock sounded on our door. Hari Ram, the conductor of his bus. His slippers were caked red. Twitching, as if with epilepsy, he narrated the day's events.

The roads had been increasingly deserted as the day had progressed, bus passengers reduced to a trickle. Then they trundled into a barricade, a makeshift one, constructed from aluminium sheets, rubber tyres and tree branches. There was smoke everywhere.

A mob gathered. The few passengers fled, of which the turbaned ones were snared by the mob. Someone had lunged for the driver. Hari Ram, left behind in the bus, had cowered under a seat. When the horde had moved on, he had slunk out. Tiptoeing through glass shards and blood trails, he had reached our colony and stopped by to inform me.

After Hari Ram delivered the news, I left home with strict instructions to Niki to bolt the door and make no sound. I had to see the square where Hari Ram said they had stopped the bus, where my Jeet had been dragged out on the road. What if he was still there, his eyes seeking help, looking for me to come to his aid? Surely he would be waiting? A tall, strapping man with a burly laugh and burly good humour couldn't just disappear.

I wore a sari, wrapped it tightly around my shoulders such that it half covered my head, with my hair in a bun and not my customary long plait. That day, I needed to be visibly Hindu. Whatever. I could be Isai, Muslim, Parsi, Jain, or whatever it took to be with my Jeet.

Huddling against the funereal lanes of our colony, I reached the Ring Road. Traffic was minimal; a car or two streaked past. There was no police in sight. Even the police bunker with its sandbags was deserted. I hurried on, tripping over rocks strewn about like sand. Sweat lined my blouse and ran down my legs. The air was foggy because of either autumn or the fires, and smoke filled my lungs as I approached the chowk. Tree branches, tyres, rods, shattered glass, the tarmac streaked with diesel and blood. And limbs. One leg in striped pyjamas had its rubber slipper on. A ribbon of yellow cloth unfurled in front of the burnt shell of a bus. I collapsed on the tarmac.

Later, I scurried across like a hunted animal and gathered the cloth. I ferreted around, crept under the bus, clambered into its charred remains, but no. All I retrieved of Jeet was his striking yellow turban.

No, I cannot go on.

VII
(1995–2000)
Violence and Silence

Emboldened, the Pandavas claim their father's inheritance from their uncle and raise a splendid city. Their growing prosperity coils the serpent tighter around Duryodhana's scheming heart. Aware of Yudhishthira's weakness for gambling, he invites the Pandavas to a game of dice. Everything goes to plan as Yudhishthira loses his kingdom, himself, his brothers, Draupadi even. She resists, countering that as a slave himself, her husband had no right to stake her. Duryodhana dispatches his brother Dushasana to fetch her. Dragged to the assembly by her hair, Draupadi stands tall as she reiterates her argument. Incensed, Duryodhana orders that she be disrobed. Her stalwart husbands sit with sunken shoulders, the wise elders with bent heads, the blind king murmurs ineffectually, and Draupadi realizes that the cupidity and violence of men have made her body the battlefield. Frightened, she reminds herself that she was born of fire, and closing her flaming eyes, turns her thoughts to God. Will Krishna come to her aid?

19
(1995)

❋

FROM THE CAR window, Niki watched people crowding the corridors of the sessions court, spilling into the abutting packed-mud ground. Each visible door and window had men sprouting across it like mushrooms, since queuing was not part of the culture. It could well have been a bus terminus where, aware that a finite journey could take forever, folks hustled, haggled, pleaded, paid. Not that she had not been forewarned.

Filing a case in court was one thing and trying to get justice for Nooran was entirely another, Papa had cautioned. Three years after Nooran's death and several court visits later, Niki snorted her quiet agreement. Her show of disapproval failed to stir the heavy air in the car. Despite being parked in the shade of a large banyan – a privilege that lawyer Jinder Nalwa wrangled when accompanied by his daughter – the car was an oven. Niki refused air conditioning. With a waiting time of several hours, it was an exorbitant waste of fuel. Besides, if Papa could squeeze his way into thickets of supplicants, inveigle clerks for information, plead with judges and stay calm despite a sticky suit of sweat, all she needed to do was wait in the privacy of the car.

She rolled the window down further but there was no breeze. Using the end of her dupatta, she fanned herself. A passer-by bent and peered with the idle infringement of privacy that the Indian male was accustomed to making. A familiar momentary hollowing occurred within her, as if she was on a skywalk, standing atop glass which fell away abruptly. That was how every memory of Nooran reared inside her. Niki stilled.

'Maal,' the man drawled, withdrew his head and walked on.

Niki was eighteen years old, in the first year of her undergraduate course in women's studies, familiar with the crude words men used to commodify women and yet, every single time she froze. Nooran would have delivered the man a fine ass whopping. Oh, Nooran! To jolt herself into action, Niki wiped her forearms with the dupatta.

Jinder was walking towards her, the rim of his turban soaked. She stepped out of the car and hurried towards him. 'Is it time?'

He patted her shoulder and they walked forward in step.

=

Inside the courtroom, a ceiling fan spun, pirouetting cobwebs, churning heat. She was acquainted with the drill, and yet her palms were moist with more than sweat. A familiar hot-cold sensation assailed her, her throat dried up and a throbbing began in her forehead. She licked her lips. She wished she could wear her sunglasses. No. She would not panic. No. She opened her eyes wide and tried to focus on the courtroom, its bare furnishings and sundry men – why was it always men? – the tube light peppered with dust, the fat gecko above the door bracket. Trying to shut down the images from the video scrolling in her mind of the bus ride with Nooran, Niki stared hard at the tawny lizard. Why was that gecko so fat?

A shuffling sounded and people rose as the judge walked in. When he had settled down, the defence lawyer made a request to approach the bench. He handed over a sheet of paper to the judge. Niki glanced from the bent, bald pate of the judge to Papa, who was watching the proceedings with interest.

'Mr Nalwa,' the judge beckoned.

For several minutes, the three men were in hushed conversation. A tiny lizard darted on the wall behind the judge. Papers rustled and a soft susurrus from outside floated in. Jinder shook his head and withdrew.

Judge Khanna, who in three years had lost the battle of the comb-over to a glistening scalp, addressed the courtroom. 'The defendant has requested for adjournment since,' he glanced at the sheet on his desk, 'one of the accused, Mr Avtar Singh, lost his mother early this morning and has begged to be excused in order to attend her funeral. This will—'

Jinder's sigh was audible as he gathered his papers, his mouth stiff. His yellow turban, where it covered his forehead, was now mustard from being soaked in sweat.

The hearing over, Niki stood up and waited for Papa, who was conversing with the other lawyer. He must have cracked a joke, for Papa gave a small smile as the other leaned in. The Indian courtroom was a Byzantine venue where dates were set for future dates, actual meetings infrequent. As Papa often joked, in God's house there was some delay but eventual justice, but in the Indian courtroom, even God was clueless. Were they sharing that joke? Bonhomie, though, was furthest from her mind. Another hearing thrown out, the case stalled yet again. She clenched her fist, put on her sunglasses and walked to the door. Above her, the fat gecko darted out and gobbled up a tiny lizard.

20
(1996)

✳

'WAR AND PEACE,' Jinder said as he sorted the papers in his study, 'there is no such thing.'

Niki looked up from where she sat cross-legged in the capacious armchair, a notebook open in her lap. In the second year of her BA studies, her head was buried in textbooks most days, but she made time to help Papa out on Project '47, which he'd begun after Nooran's death. It was his attempt to gather the oral histories of survivors of Partition. With each passing year, survivors were dwindling, or their memories were failing. Unless this work was urgently undertaken, it was entirely possible that in a couple of decades all who had witnessed that cataclysmic event first-hand would have died, leaving few records behind. Like Nooran.

When Papa had begun work in 1992, a stumped Niki had asked, 'Why are there no records?'

'Because the authorities have not seen it fit to record much. Some individual attempts have been made ... we are all trying to gather an ocean with teaspoons.'

'But surely,' Niki had protested, 'history books, official records...'

106

'History books record the independence of India, not its twin, the Partition of India. They celebrate the victory of non-violence and how Gandhi forced the British to quit India. The Mahatma is remembered and rightly so, but the legions of fighters are forgotten. Bhagat Singh, Rajguru, Sukhdev, Bose ... and those who were butchered on both sides as Pakistan was carved out. For the survivors, there were refugee camps and the urgent task of rebuilding their lives in new cities. For the leaders, the priority was nation-building.'

'And the Sanghis,' Dadima had said about right-wing Hindus, 'would have us believe that "akhand Bharat", a pristine indivisible India, was what the British left behind, when what the British midwife delivered were premature twins, which countless women died giving birth to.'

Now, Niki waited for Papa to complete his train of thought.

'War and peace?' he repeated. 'Rather war and silence. Better still, violence and silence.'

'Rhymes even,' Dadima's voice floated into the study before she entered, bringing with her the stinging aroma of fried mustard; crisp pakoras, which she served to her, then Papa, who deposited the plate atop a hardbound journal. The sturdy rosewood table was overrun with tired brown case files, hardbound black books of criminal procedure law, stapled sheets, transcripts, a palm-sized tape recorder and a pen-pencil-sundries holder. Where the green felt table covered with a glass top peered its way through the jungle of bookish timber, a crystal glass with amber liquid rested.

Circling her right thumb and index finger, Niki signalled her approval of the pakoras to Dadima.

'Not as good as Nooran's,' Dadima sighed, 'but what is?' That Dadima missed Nooran – companion, confidante, daughter, sister – was like saying the fields missed the sun.

'Cheers to Nooran!' Jinder raised his whisky.

Dadima settled down on a cushioned cane stool. 'How many do we have now?'

'Seven done, and Niki is going to help me transcribe an interesting eighth,' he wiped his fingers, oily from the pakora, on his pants and reached forward for his glass of scotch. Jinder riffled through his diary. 'Let me give you a background on the case you have to write. Sawan Kumar, a right-winger, responsible for some of the most vicious sectarian bile in the last decade. He was eighteen during the Partition and recalls it vividly. But, as always, he's reluctant to talk. Prem, the clerk assisting me on Project '47, plied him with whisky. For three days, all he heard was how the motherland was hacked in 1947 by militant Muslims, and how the brave Hindus would not allow another carving up by separatist Sikhs. Prem was about to give up when on the third evening, after two pegs of whisky, Sawan Kumar started crying.'

'Ha!' Dadima sat up.

Niki slid forward in her chair.

'All the reminiscing about Partition had awakened memories of his hometown in Pakpattan, in Pakistan, where he had been born and brought up. Apparently, late at night, when the family was asleep, he would sneak out, meet his Muslim friends, and they would all go to the Sufi shrine of Baba Farid – to listen to Sufi music, which his family disapproved of. Even now, Sawan Kumar admitted, he could not listen to Sufi music without tears welling up in his eyes. In great detail, he described his life in Pakpattan, the friendships that were torn apart by the sectarian violence and how he still dreamt of his home.'

Papa paused and switched on the cassette player. A ghazal lilted into the room: Mirza Ghalib holding forth on the woes of his guileless heart. The ceiling fan spun softly, the worst of summer heat over.

'Home?' Niki asked.

Papa nodded. '*Exactly* what Prem asked him. To which Sawan Kumar said that in one lifetime, there could only be one home. But it was the homeland of the Muslims now, Prem insisted, to which the Hindu fundamentalist replied that all Muslims were not bad. In fact, it was time that was bad, time that had led them all to act in the way they did, both the Hindus and Muslims. It was the time of pralaya, as the Mahabharata says, when men will destroy.'

Papa sat back in the chair sipping his whisky. The room went quiet, the edges of the loose sheets stirring with the breeze of the fan.

'Some story,' Niki said, as she plucked up a paper napkin and wiped her fingers.

'And that's not all,' Papa said.

'More skeletons?' Dadima enquired as she was about to get up. 'My kadhi will have to wait.'

'Sawan Kumar sends a monthly money order to a woman in Pakpattan, an elderly Muslim who was his wet nurse. This man who has waged a hate campaign against Muslims for the last ten years has a surrogate Muslim mother whom he calls "Ammi" and supports to this day!'

'This gets weirder and weirder,' Niki snorted. 'Why the charade then, Papa?'

'Selective silence. No greys – only black and white. That is what happens when people indulge in sectarian politics.'

'I could share it in class, but we need more women's stories.'

'Women's stories, men's stories, enemies' stories, friends' stories – we need more stories. So that we can break the silence. So that we can remember, mourn, grapple with the violence within us, the violence that makes us kill our brothers, kill our women, kill our Nooran—'

Papa bowed his head. He cupped his face in his hands. Sobs shook his back.

21
(1996)

✻

NIKI MOVED HER palm over the embroidery, lingering over the silk threads of the bagh, her eyes closed. Nooran's room was her refuge, yet why didn't she see Nooran when she closed her eyes? Why couldn't her mind summon Nooran's image, as if out of a photo album? When she was sitting in class or riding to college, her mind would play incidents of Nooran unsummoned. She would hear Nooran's laughter, see her smile, watch her sashay down the hallway … but on demand, she couldn't conjure her up. Niki squeezed her eyes until they hurt.

When she opened them, Nooran's room was in soft focus, exactly like when Nooran was alive – Dadima hadn't changed a thing. Nooran would have laughed at the absurdity of keeping a perfectly good outhouse vacant: 'Who needs a shrine, Biji?' But Dadima was convinced: Nooran's room would not be violated. Even pragmatic people needed a totem of goodness to buoy them against life's tyrannies.

Niki let her eyes linger. The bagh remained as the coverlet on Nooran's bed; there was a painting of Heer by Sobha Singh on one wall and the Godrej steel almirah where her clothes lay folded amidst a collection of dupattas, all stained purple from the jamun berries Niki would gather. There was no memory where there was no Nooran. After her death, memories of Nooran had become Niki's companion, so they automatically inserted themselves into each present moment. Admittedly, it was a poor replacement. Niki crumpled onto the embroidery and bawled, tears pooling into her palms for she would not let them spoil the bagh.

Tomorrow was the day.

After endless dates, her turn to take the witness stand had arrived. Her testimony was crucial and Papa expected it to nail the case. Three-and-a-half years Niki had waited for this chance to send Nooran's killers to jail. But what if she failed? If her throat dried up like it did every time she was in the courtroom and no words came out? If her hands sweated and she shivered with cold and had to pee? What if she failed Nooran *again*?

If she had kept quiet on the bus that day, Nooran would still be alive. There would be no case or courtroom or travel to Patiala to depose before the judge. Nooran would be there to guide her and love her and teach her how to be... But she had killed Nooran. Just as she had killed Roop. She had killed both her mothers. Dadima said that was nonsensical, but it was true.

The door swung open behind her. Niki gulped and looked up. Putting an arm around her back, Papa sat down beside her. He patted her head. His palms were warm and fleshy and comforting, and she always marvelled how, for a man who worked so hard, his hands weren't sinewy but comfortably padded. The hands of a caregiver.

'Worried about tomorrow?' he asked.

Niki nodded tremulously.

'After we lost your mother, I didn't know what to do with myself. Nooran and Ma were taking care of you, so I could wallow in grief undisturbed. Some weeks later, Nooran sought me out. She talked, I listened. At the end of it, I was ready to rejoin the world.' Papa paused.

With twilight, birdcall sounded, and from the kitchen, Dadima's pressure cooker hooted.

'As you know, I lost my father, your grandfather, in the 1971 war. He was a soldier who laid down his life for his country. To me, he was the bravest of brave. But that day, after Nooran talked to me, I understood that there was another way to be brave.'

Papa bunched his mouth as he gazed at his past. Niki's cheeks were stiff with dried tears. In the garden, the crickets had begun their evening racket.

With a sigh, Papa returned to the present. 'You know Nooran's story: how her family was killed during Partition, how she came to your Dadima's attention, how she made her home with us. For someone who suffered so much at such a young age, Nooran should have become bitter, filled with hatred for the world. Yet, she chose love, and led her life like the sun, radiant, needing no one's permission to be. She was incredibly brave. I know that because I had lost your mother and I understood what courage it took to continue living, let alone living with love.'

The silk threads of the bagh were aglow in the gloaming. Niki squeezed Papa's hand.

'For tomorrow, ask yourself: if Nooran was here, what would she tell you?'

'You mean, what would Nooran do?'

'Hmm.'

The room had gone dark. Outside the window, a firefly lit up the dark moodily. Nooran tossed her thick braided plait over one shoulder, extended her hand and beamed. 'Niki, look the world in the eye, puttar!' Her voice was hoarse as Niki grinned at Papa. 'That's what Nooran would say.'

22
(1997)

✳

IN THE FINAL term of her BA programme, Niki was working on an essay. With the upcoming fiftieth anniversary of India's independence, the teacher had chosen a broad topic for them to write on in order to encourage diverse responses: 'Women in Independent India'. They could explore gender relations, revisit the Partition of India, probe sexual violence, examine the status of minority women. The gamut of things to focus on was wide but Niki knew the kernel she wanted to expand: Draupadi's daughters.

Draupadi was by far the most interesting character in the Mahabharata. Any woman who could put up with five husbands was admirable, but Draupadi also had a fine brain and a sharp tongue. It was dismaying how contemporary retellings of the story reduced her to a shrew responsible for the war or a Hindi-film-heroine type, praying to be saved as her sari unravelled speedily. Niki still bristled at her Class 8 conversation with a Hindi teacher about the validity of Yudhishthira as the embodiment of law and dharma when he could commit an act as immoral as staking his wife in a game of dice. The teacher had kept getting more and more furious as they had argued. Thankfully, Niki was born a feminist, or raised as one by three. Eventually, Niki was silenced with the remark that was the last resort of the clueless adult: 'You have a lot of growing up, and therefore, a lot of learning to do.'

'Here's your tea.'

The aroma of green cardamom floated up her nostrils as Dadima placed a fragrant mug on her desk. As she made to turn, Niki grabbed her hand and kissed it. 'Sit with me, na. I want to discuss my essay topic with you – Draupadi's daughters.'

Dadima sat in the armchair, cradling her chin in her left hand. 'What about them?'

'Where are they?'

'Elaborate?'

'Well, if the Mahabharata is the template of all storytelling in India, what is not in the Mahabharata is nowhere else, Vyasa being an immodest writer—'

'The template for India, indeed,' Dadima assented.

'Yes, for its cultural, social, ethical mores. And its primary heroine, Draupadi, is a feisty woman with a sharp mind—'

Dadima narrowed her eyes. 'What is the basis of your claim?'

Aha! Dadima was testing her. 'Well,' Niki sipped her tea, 'let me take you back to the gambling scene where Yudhishthira, the eldest Pandava brother, has gambled away everything, including the clothes on his back, and lost. Next, he stakes his wife and loses. A messenger is dispatched to fetch Draupadi to court. She refuses and sends back a question. However, she is dragged to the court by force, whereupon, she reiterates her question to the gathering: "Does a slave have the right to stake his wife?" A fine legalistic point, you'll agree?'

'Of course,' Dadima nodded.

'Okay,' Niki sipped more tea. 'Going back to my earlier point: if the Mahabharata is the template for India, Draupadi is the template for Indian women, right? Why then have successive retellers of the epic cast her in the mould of a vixen-wimp? Where has Draupadi gone missing? And where, indeed, are Draupadi's daughters?'

Dadima nodded. 'The silence is complicated.'

'I am listening,' Niki said.

'Make me a drink, and we'll talk.'

Niki walked to the sideboard to fetch Dadima's favourite drink. It was a cool January evening. They had rung in the new year of 1997 at Tiny Uncle's party a week ago, grateful to have won Nooran's court case. Ordinarily, Dadima would have gone to the gurdwara to thank God, but because Nooran had been an atheist, Dadima had prepared Nooran's favourite sweet to mark the occasion. Niki had taken her bowl of kheer to Nooran's room to eat. But the rice porridge tasted like sawdust, and Niki realized that no judgement would ever fill the Nooran-sized hole in her life. Now that college had reopened, everybody was back to business, including Papa who was focusing on getting new clients, his practice having been derailed by pro bono work for alleged terrorists and Nooran's demise.

As she opened the bottle of Remy Martin, Niki said, 'It is our epic, the story of India. And yet, how many women do we know, or have heard of, who are named Draupadi? The name of the one epic female character in India's greatest epic finds no takers, whereas Karan-Arjuna-Krishna sprout like weeds.' She padded across the room and handed Dadima her drink. 'Why are there no takers for women's stories? Why do we not want to talk about the violence that men have repeatedly inflicted on women? Why is there no song or drama or narrative around it? Why are women told to stuff their stories down their throats and stitch up their mouths?'

Dadima savoured her cognac. Light from the lamp lit up a rainbow in the crystal glass. Niki sat cross-legged and waited.

'Imagine – all the women around you being pregnant, visibly pregnant. All women, all girls, regardless of age, even infants. Imagine that each female has a swollen belly, like she has limbs and face and chest and other physical organs, as a part of her physical self,' Dadima paused and looked at her.

'Like Suman Aunty of yore – freaky.'

'Unnatural?'

'Yeee-s!'

'And what if I told you that this is true, that all females in this land have pregnant bellies, only these aren't visible?'

Niki frowned at Dadima, then glanced down at her flat abdomen. 'Erm, Dadima, some might accuse you of hallucination.'

'People believe in many things that aren't visible: God, ghosts, rumours, superheroes. Why then is this difficult to conceive?'

'Because there is no logic to it. See, each of these invisible things you mention serves some purpose: God gives people faith, ghosts help explain things they don't understand, superheroes rescue them, etcetera, etcetera. But women with swollen bellies? What purpose does that serve?'

Dadima flung her arms wide, smiling. 'There!' As Niki looked perplexed, she said, 'A state of permanent pregnancy means something has not been delivered. And therefore, it is not part of the public. Now, imagine that what the swollen bellies were carrying was not babies, but stories. Stories which women have not been allowed to tell, which they have not been permitted to mourn aloud, which they must keep hidden within themselves because talking about them would bring shame upon their menfolk and their families. Women who were raped during Partition and '84, whose flesh was branded with a trident or a crescent, whose breasts were chopped, whose foetuses were ripped out of their bellies, who were made sex slaves by men of enemy communities, who were massacred by their own fathers and brothers to prevent being defiled, who jumped into wells to escape the marauders – this violence unleashed on women by men cannot be talked about. Instead, women must store up this trauma in their bodies – silently. Contrast this with the violence that men unleash on men.'

'Agreed, Dadima. Men's stories become a society's narrative and our heritage; women's stories are forced underground, sealed and locked away. That we've read about in our course. But your metaphor, women pregnant with stories, is … striking!'

'The imperative is to birth these stories. Jinder is gathering the oral histories of Partition. My work with the survivors of '84 is yielding many stories. Eventually, we hope, they will enter public discourse.' Dadima wagged a finger as she remembered something. 'Did you write to that contact your Papa gave, Mr Malik in New York?'

Mr Malik was a Partition survivor who had relocated to New York. Papa and he had exchanged several letters in an attempt to gather his story. In one of those letters, Mr Malik had mentioned another survivor, Jyot Kaur, who had had the terrible luck to live through both '47 and '84. Jyot Kaur, however, was unwilling to be interviewed. Dadima had suggested Niki write to her via Mr Malik in the hope of getting greater insight for her women's studies programme. But the truth was that Dadima also felt guilty about Jyot Kaur.

Niki shook her head. 'Mr Malik could not convince Jyot Kaur to cooperate.'

Dadima sighed.

'You can't blame yourself for what happened to her.'

'No, not blame,' Dadima waved a hand distractedly. 'But if I had taken a different decision, her fate might have been different.'

Dadima was referring to the aftermath of 1947, when she had come across an orphaned refugee girl in a camp overseen by her husband. Dadima had been one of the women helping resettle these children. She had considered taking six-year-old Jyot in before she found a good home for her with a priest and his wife in Machhiwara. Jyot had grown up, trained as a nurse and settled in Delhi after marriage where, in 1984, she had lost everything – except her life.

'You couldn't have adopted every child from the camp surely!'

Dadima gazed into her eyes. 'You sound like Nooran.'

'How?' Niki laughed, secretly pleased.

'Nooran would cut my wishful thinking off, saying, "You can't be a universal mother, Biji. India has enough of those already!"'

Niki hooted. Dadima laughed.

'So, what happens next with your essay?'

'Right,' Niki sat up. 'I want to link the violence and silence of Mahabharata – the violence of a war fought by men, the subsequent silencing of the voices of women such as Draupadi – to the violence and silence of the Partition of India. "The Silence of D's Daughters".'

'D? When you were small, you used to say "Drop-D" instead of Draupadi,' Dadima grinned. 'Remember that telecast of the Mahabharata on TV? Buses were brought to a halt during its Sunday telecast time. To this day, two thousand years later, we still commemorate the battle between two sets of brothers. Bheema tears out Dushasana's entrails and feasts on his blood. Thousands are killed on the battlefields and epics are written on the great battle. The slain, the male victims of violence, are publicly mourned in elaborate siapa ceremonies. And this template of male violence has continued unbroken for two millennia. In the Mahabharata, Draupadi is publicly shamed in order to shame her husbands. During the Partition, during the wars we fought with Pakistan, during the sectarian riots in '84, men made women's bodies their battlefields.'

Dadima rubbed her chin. 'You can extend that thread to the subsequent silence from the government, the police, the public at large, and even some of the victims.'

'Absolutely! My teacher would love that. She might even recommend it for my final term research paper. And,' Niki's eyes lit up, 'Jyot Kaur would be the perfect story to tell with her encounters with both '47 and '84.'

Dadima rotated the cognac glass in her hand. 'Careful, Niki. One person's story is another's tragedy.'

'Sorry, Dadima,' Niki bit her lower lip. 'That … came out wrong.'

'Did I tell you about the last time I saw Jyot? In '84?' Dadima quaffed her cognac.

Niki bounded over to her. Curling up on the carpet, she rested her head against Dadima's knees as Dadima began recounting.

=

It was December '84. Nooran and I were in a car, going from Chandigarh to Machhiwara. A blanket of grey sky had put the sun to sleep. Mist hovered over the fields bordering the highway. Traffic on the road was scarce.

'Cha, Biji?' Nooran asked. She had made a thermos of ginger tea before we left.

I nodded. Nooran sat upright, and planting her feet on the car floor, poured steaming tea into a cup and handed it to me. Another cup for herself, the thermos was shut tight, and she settled back, pulling her legs up onto the seat.

I cradled the mug in both hands, the rising vapours steaming my glasses. While investigating the anti-Sikh riots in Delhi the month before, I had learnt about a woman. The lone survivor from her home, her husband and four children dead, she had been taken back to her maternal home in Machhiwara. As I pieced scraps of the story together, I figured out the woman was none other than Jyot Kaur, a six-year-old refugee girl I'd helped place in a new home during Partition. Thereafter, I spoke with her adopted parents on the phone, and now we were on our way to meet her.

I told Nooran: 'I was helping in the makeshift hospital set up for refugees in the summer of '47 when I first saw Jyot. Not just me, but the whole hospital staff came out to see as word spread. A sickly buffalo had strolled into the hospital, panting, eyes glazed, legs shivering. Stuck on its back, thin as a sheet of parchment, was a child, bare but for her dirty knickers. The child's limbs dangled lifeless, her hair was like matted jute, her skin like parched earth.'

Nooran sipped her tea and listened.

'Nurses prised the child away from the buffalo, which shuddered and collapsed to the ground. The child, a girl, had a faint pulse. The doctor attended to her immediately, and almost everyone pitched in with her care. She hovered in and out of consciousness as we watched over her, desperate for her to survive. No one said it, but we all felt like the farmer whose crop is dying in a drought but for one seedling that might make it.'

A horn hooted before a bus barrelled down the side of the car.
'Oye, you—' the driver rumbled a series of expletives as he eased the
car well to their side of the road.

'Need a break, Balram?' I asked.

'Na,' he shrugged. 'A mere two-hour journey, Biji. We'll be there
soon. Mind if I play songs?'

Soon, a hit Bollywood ditty rippled through the car; a woman
crooned about her fate and her lover's, and whether they were
destined to be together.

'And she survived, Biji,' Nooran said with deliberate perkiness.
'After which you found her a good home.'

'I could have done better,' I sighed. 'I did consider adopting her.'

Nooran took the empty mug from my hand. The singing woman
crooned about how we know not our fates and only God does, having
written them all.

Two hours later, at Jyot's maternal home in Machhiwara, Nooran
and I sat on string cots in the room adjoining the spacious kitchen. It
was the warmest place in their home because the kitchen, responsible
for feeding an army of children, volunteers and workers, bustled
through the day.

'She won't say a word,' Jyot's mother, the priest's wife said. 'Not
a word.' With her dupatta, she wiped her eyes, her hands trembling.
'To lose her children, four adorable young ones, two girls, two boys,
a … and her husband…'

We listened with moist eyes.

'I still remember when we got Jyot married,' she continued. 'Jeet,
so tall, so handsome – what a beautiful couple they made. I had
warded off the evil eye with salt and red chilli before seeing them off
… They were doing so well, their own house in Dilli, added another
floor for the growing girls … Jeet … Jeet … the men who dragged
him out of his bus forced a tyre around his neck and set it afire—'
An animal's cry pierced her mouth before she clamped it shut with
her hand. She buried her face into her dupatta, her frail back heaving
with muffled wails.

Nooran moved to her side, stroked her back, patting it with her capable hands. Kerosene-tyre: it was the new weapon of the '84 riots. So effective that it destroyed victim and weapon both. Jyot was left with no body to cremate, no body to bid farewell to, no body to mourn over...

Soon, Jyot's mother stopped sobbing, dabbed her eyes with her dupatta and rose from the string cot. She walked to another room and returned with a framed photograph. 'From the last time they were here, after Laali was born...' A man and a woman were seated on a bench. The woman cradled an infant, her head tilted as she smiled at the baby. The turbaned man with an open face gazed at the camera, with one arm around a little girl in his lap and the other wound around the waist of a lanky boy standing beside him. His top knot was the size of a cricket ball and leaned to one side. The woman was flanked by a pretty girl in a salwar kameez.

'Biji,' Nooran whispered to me as she tapped the photo of the dimple-cheeked girl, 'doesn't she remind you of our Niki?'

I nodded. Then Nooran clutched the air with both hands before pressing it to the sides of her head. She would not let even a stray luckless thought of her mind cast its evil shadow on our Niki.

Later, we entered Jyot's room, which was dark except for a single low-wattage bulb. Jyot lay on her side on a string cot, draped in a thin yellow muslin, the quilt rolled up by her feet. I pulled up a cane stool and sat beside her bed. Holding Jyot's limp hand in mine, I murmured to her. But for the gentlest rise and fall of her chest, Jyot could have been a clothed, adult version of the girl splayed lifeless on the buffalo's back. To lose one's entire family was a tragedy too large for one life. To lose one's family a second time? And in such grotesque conditions that people manufactured again and again: husband dragged out of a bus and set afire on the road, children dead when their house was burned down, and Jyot the lone survivor...

'To be the only survivor was to be terribly alone on earth. What kind of god allowed that?' Nooran clucked her dismay.

'But how did *she* survive, Dadima?' Niki interjected in a low voice.
'No one knows. And Jyot won't tell.'

'What then?' Niki whispered and Dadima went back to '84.

I handed over an envelope of cash and two suit pieces for Jyot with a promise to visit again. The priest's wife insisted we eat before setting off to Chandigarh. The three of us worked together: Nooran rolled out thick rotis, sprinkling salt and red chilli powder in the folds, Jyot's mother cooked them over the griddle, I sliced onions and squeezed fresh lemon over them. We tried to feed Jyot, who lay in her room, unmoving, eyes closed. In the kitchen, we stuffed food in our mouths, working it down our gullets, eyes moist, hands busy.

The hands must always be busy, Nooran always said. Even the mind followed the hands. As long as there was physical work – mending, sweeping, cutting, cooking, darning, stitching, washing, ironing – the mind could be tamed. Left to itself, it wandered like a mad person, banging head against walls, tearing clothes, sleeping in gutters—

'Rabba!'

A cry rang out from the courtyard. We bolted upright. Discarding our brass plates, we tumbled outside. A crowd was gathering around the well, a waving of arms, hurrying feet – Jyot had jumped in! Hearing that, her mother crumpled to the floor. Nooran and I hoisted her up and seated her on a string cot.

At the well, a man was descending on a rope that our driver Balram and a couple of other men secured around the trunk of an old oak. The water below was dark and still, until the man jumped in, paddled around, then disappeared from view. The circular well was deep, thirty feet, someone muttered. Jyot had wrapped the iron chain used to secure the bull around her waist before she jumped in, Balram informed us. He had been waiting by the car when he saw a woman stagger like a drunk towards the well, the chain weighing her down. As she clambered up to the edge of well, he shouted for her to stop and hurried over. But she had jumped.

A splash. A head emerged, then another. The man's arm lunged at the dangling rope. As the rope tugged, Balram and the assorted men were pulled forward. Hands, neck muscles and faces straining, they began to hoist. Sweat beaded their faces, their hands chafed and bloodied. The rope inched up, coiling on the brick floor, sluggish as kismet. As the rescuer neared the surface, arms were extended into the well. Nooran dashed back into the house. A limp Jyot was hoisted out, the yellow muslin a dripping garland around her neck. Nooran bundled her up in a quilt. She rubbed her feet and hands, and towelled her hair. The rescuer, a strapping bearded man, face red with exhaustion, went off to change. Someone hurried to fetch a doctor.

The men helped carry the quilted bundle of Jyot back to her room. From inside a steel trunk that sat along a wall upon bricks, I found a salwar kameez. With a pair of scissors, we cut away the wet clothes. Jyot was unconscious but my finger below her nose had felt a tremor of air. After drying her thoroughly, we pulled on the fresh clothes with effort. The doctor came, checked her, prescribed medication and left. Jyot would live.

Jyot's mother sat on the bed and cradled Jyot's head in her lap, murmuring. Jyot mumbled, 'Why, why, why?' She thrashed her head, a tear trickling down her face.

'Why save me when I'm dead already?'

23
(1997)

✳

NIKI SPED DOWN Madhya Marg, the spine of Chandigarh. Zipping down the oak-lined boulevard on her scooter was a routine joy, but not today. Her first year working as a researcher with Sakhi, a non-government organization dedicated to women's issues, was rewarding. Papa had been keen that she proceed to a master's programme directly, but Niki wanted some hands-on experience before returning to academia. But the new boss she'd just gotten might hasten her exit. She turned the corner into Sector 26, towards the red-brick building where her office was located on the ground floor. Her nemesis was just stepping out of a plush Honda City.

'Good morning, Ms Khurana,' Niki hailed as she parked her scooter.

'Call me Reshma, Niki.'

Niki nodded with what she hoped was not a plastic smile. Reshma Khurana, though, wouldn't have noticed as she strode ahead, her heels clacking. With a tilt of her head, she said, 'Meet me in my office in five? Need to discuss your project.'

The alarm bells in Niki's head, on a hum thus far, went into overdrive.

In her office, Reshma paced up and down. 'Look, I will be the first person to admit that this is a great project, and I'll give you full credit for the work you've done for the last, what—'

'Six months,' Niki filled in. Reshma was talking about the research paper she had produced.

'Yeah. Your paper, "Vignettes of 1947", was perfect. Perfectly timed for the fiftieth anniversary of our independence. Five survivor stories that exhibited a range of trauma. A fine documentation for which Sakhi, and you, got due credit. But, it's time to move on, don't you think?'

It had taken Niki four months to document five survivors. The vignettes had got such a positive response that her previous boss had commissioned Niki to extend the interviews in order to gather comprehensive case studies on each of the respondents. But Mr Arora was on extended leave due to ill health and his replacement, Reshma Khurana, MBA, new programme manager, who had previously sold carbonated drinks for a living, wanted weekly results.

'It takes time for a person who has lived with trauma for years to suddenly open up. It's like raising the dead. Often, they don't have the language because they have been silent for so long—'

Reshma patted the air with an extended arm, her outsized jewel-studded ring like a flapping butterfly. 'I agree hundred per cent. But we are an organization, not an agony aunt.'

Niki lifted one shoulder. 'We are a *not-for-profit* organization.'

'Which is no excuse for poor results. Much as I admire your grit, we just don't have the resources to dedicate months to one respondent. How many in-depth case studies do you have now?'

'One,' Niki chewed her cheek. It sounded woefully inadequate even to her own ears. But that was the nature of the beast.

Reshma smiled. 'My mandate is to move things along. It appears that we are extraordinarily slow in collating data, producing reports, publishing ... and I don't mean you specifically, no. It's the culture of Sakhi that needs an overhaul.'

With admirable ease, Reshma Khurana was diagnosing Sakhi and prescribing treatment. But the world of hushed conversations, moist eyes, trembling mouths, lingering silences was so far removed from this spiel. Niki kneaded her interlaced fingers in her lap as she heard the programme manager's way forward.

At home, Niki put on some water to boil and went into the living room where Dadima sat reading. 'She has no relevant experience, academic or work – zilch. And yet, she gets to sit on my head and dictate terms.'

'Well,' Dadima looked up, 'she's the one in charge.'

'But how?'

'She's got managerial skills. You said she is an MBA who worked with Pepsi. Clearly, she has been recruited to shake things up.'

'On a big fat salary!'

'Money is liberating.'

'Hmm,' Niki grunted and went back to the kitchen. She added tea leaves to the boiling water. Outside the window, she saw Karan, Suman Aunty's eight-year-old son, roaring down his garden with a toy plane aloft in one hand. Behind him trailed a servant girl holding a tray with a glass of milk.

'I love what I do, but I don't love what this woman plans,' Niki addressed Dadima from the doorway.

'Well, use this opportunity to pursue further studies then. Equip yourself to get a bigger job with more pay and say in matters.' Dadima returned to her magazine. 'Sakhi is not a paragon of excellence or efficiency, you know.'

Niki pursed her lips as she added milk. She had to admit it: what bothered her was not just the termination of her project but also that Reshma had the power to simply come in and set a forceful new direction for the NGO. If Niki had that power, there were so many initiatives she would undertake and complete. Dadima was right:

there were too many people at Sakhi who believed working at a not-for-profit meant endless cups of tea interrupted by work.

She leaned against the kitchen counter. Nooran had never allowed her tea, insisting she had to grow up first. 'I have grown up, Nooran,' she whispered, 'and I can make my own tea, but I don't know much else.' Outside, Karan sipped some milk and scooted away, the maid following. Niki shook her head.

What would Nooran do? Study hard, get a good job, be independent. Nooran would approve of Reshma, a woman who knew her mind. Reshma might not understand the nuance of breaking the silence of trauma victims, but that was not her job. Her job was to manage. And Niki wanted that kind of job, with its twin benefits of authority and money.

24
(1999)

✼

NIKI DIDN'T MAKE it to the top business school. But she did get admission into the prestigious Indian Institute of Management Calcutta, a thousand miles from home. Papa remarked on the coincidence of Niki journeying from one partitioned state to another: West Punjab and East Bengal had been carved through to form Pakistan when the British gave India independence and concomitant partition.

'Don't ask me to bring you survivor stories from Calcutta!' Niki said as she packed, excited and unsure. The school was famed for its emphasis on quantitative studies, not a core subject in women's studies, and she was worried about how she would manage.

'The workload is so intense students don't find time to shower, you know?'

'How French,' Papa said. 'We'll arm you with eau de toilette.'

'Pa-pa! Seriously, you think I'll survive?'

'You'll shine. We are sending Nooran with you.'

Niki took the package he handed her and opened it. 'Nooran's bagh?' She cradled the embroidery in her hands, a lump in her throat.

'Dadima okay with it?'

'It was her idea. So that you always have home with you.'

Niki recalled Nooran working on the embroidery as she scribbled or scrawled, both seated atop her bed. Faced with the prospect of IIM, what would Nooran do? When the world darkened, Nooran turned to the bagh. When it dazzled, she embroidered some more. Whatever it threw at her, she seized it and wrote her own narrative. Nooran would more than survive, she would thrive.

≡

'Wasn't the East India Company the first multinational in the world?' Niki asked as she sat with some of her new classmates in the deserted mess hall in the somnolent hours between lunch and tea. The group discussion on 'Globalization: Beneficial or Baneful', their project work for the upcoming marketing management class, was fractious.

'Your point being?' Arjun asked.

'You don't have to go too far back in your history to know what rampant globalization can bring. The East India Company was the first multinational in the world, and it transitioned from a corporate czar to the colonial master of India. There's a reason people are sceptical about global companies.'

'And we cannot forget Union Carbide,' Juhi said in her soft voice, her hands steepled under her chin. The tree hugger of the Indian Institute of Management Calcutta, class of 2000, wore her moniker with pride.

'Of course,' Arjun said, 'the 1984 Bhopal gas disaster cannot be forgotten, but surely a few rotten multinats don't wreck the concept of globalization?'

Arjun was so exasperating! Since their roll numbers were sequential, he usually ended up in the same projects as Niki.

'Even when it wrecked the lives of thousands? Union Carbide has avoided prosecution and failed to compensate the victims.'

'Okay, Juhi, so let's put Union Carbide aside as the one big villain. But there are companies which have been in India for years and are integral to its economy. Some of the biggest Indian brands are foreign in origin but Indians know them as their own: Lipton, Brooke Bond, Lux, Lifebuoy…'

Sam slapped Arjun's back. 'Rattling off names from your father's company!'

Arjun's father was a senior executive with Unilever, and his world view was framed by India's oldest multinational. That it had begun operations in India in 1888 with Sunlight soap, cartons of which had been unloaded in Calcutta harbour, seemed a source of personal pride to him.

'So,' Niki interjected, 'let's cast your dad's company as the hero for Union Carbide's villain and move on, shall we?'

'Guys,' Sam spread his hands between them, 'we need to get some *real* points written, so can we forget our personal biases and think, please?'

Arjun raised a hand, his fingers long and lean. 'The point I'd like to make is that the underlying premise behind globalization – that the transfer of wealth from developed to developing countries eventually benefits those at the bottom of the economic ladder – is correct. Since the Indian economy was liberalized in 1991, we have seen an average economic growth rate of seven per cent. And the trickle-down effect is visible all around us—'

'Yes, we can't be thankful enough for the McAloo Tikki burger, specially crafted to woo Indian hearts,' Juhi brought her hands together in gratitude.

Niki and Sam giggled, but Arjun wasn't amused. 'Look, if you want to be a naysayer, that's fine. If you want to debate the pros and cons, let's do it and get this project work finished. I don't think our personal beliefs are going to change because of this discussion, but our grades might.'

Sam applauded. 'Well said! You were saying, Arjun?'

'Well, the founder of one of India's most famous companies, Infosys, believes that when jobs are created for the educated, it benefits the entire ecosystem of support services for these employees: domestic help, drivers, cooks, cleaners...'

'Perhaps, but it's not a one-stop answer. A trickle-down theory never applies to women in wealthy Indian households where their voice is still restricted to the kitchen. They—'

'First history, now women's issues?' Arjun smacked the table with exasperation, 'Why don't you stick to economics?'

Niki had to frequently remind herself that she was in a business school to better understand how the *real* world functioned, brought up as she had been by feminists devoted to unpopular causes. 'Women's issues aren't about economics?' she frowned.

Arjun ran one hand through his thick hair and looked doubtful.

She could throttle Arjun! He knew exactly which buttons to press. Perhaps she could have a word with the professor, indicating her discomfort with her project mate – except that she kind of enjoyed his company, which was weird.

'Women are the world's largest minority. They do two-thirds of the world's work, receive ten per cent of the world's income and only own one per cent of the means of production.'

'Once again, Niki,' Arjun shook a puzzled head, 'your point is?'

Was his perspective so different because he was so antipodal to her: a South Indian Brahmin, the son of a hotshot corporate executive, to her North Indian Sikh, the daughter of radical feminists? The partition of north and east India had left the south so unaffected that Arjun could be from a foreign country altogether. 'That globalization, for all its vaunted aims of trickle-down bullshit, has done precious little for fifty per cent of the world's population. In India—'

'Globalization has created more job opportunities for women, making them more independent, which leads to greater gender equality. Right?'

'Women still have to come back home and cook and take care of children and families.'

'There we go again!' Arjun clasped his hair in his fists and sank his face on the table.

'Guys, guys – or, if you so prefer, Niki, gals and Arjun – the first year is almost over, after which we have three months of break when we won't have to suffer one another. Can we please get our shit together?'

Sam, always the referee. Without him, they would not have managed to submit a single complete project. They nodded.

'Good! Now that we are in agreement, let me summarize our high-octane discussion thus far. Arjun believes in trickle-down effect of globalization, Niki doesn't, and Juhi—'

Niki shook her head. 'It's not black and white—'

'Colour my world,' Arjun sang as his fingers played an imaginary keyboard, 'with hope of loving you-ooo…'

'As time goes on,' Juhi sang and jiggled her shoulders.

Arjun stood, and crooning, walked over to Juhi, arms outstretched. With a laugh, Juhi sprang up and the two began a slow dance on the dining hall floor, singing in unison.

Sam slapped his forehead with a palm. Niki felt a twinge of – what, envy? Did she really want that opinionated capitalist to ask her to dance? Okay, he was tall and could sing and dance and – oh hell!

As Niki pretended to share Sam's exasperation, a hand alighted on her shoulder and Arjun beckoned her with, 'And now, now that you're near…'

With a great show of reluctance, Niki joined him. She didn't know how long they danced. All she was aware of was her waist cupped in Arjun's hands, her hand in his, and of melting faster than ice cream on a summer day. When she got back on her chair facing the others, Sam was saying, '…there is bound to be a backlash to globalization after what happened two years ago in East Asia with the financial crisis, right?'

'People realize that while globalization creates opportunities for educated middle-class women like us,' Juhi said, 'rural and lower-class women are still getting marginalized. Right, Niki?'

Niki found her voice. 'The relocation of manufacturing bases for cheap labour is integral to globalization. Most of these bases are staffed by women, who are exploited – low wages, poor working environment—'

Arjun interrupted, 'What is a left-wing lemming doing in a business school, eh?' His transformation from charmer to offender was swift.

'Keeping capitalist pigs like you in check!'

Sam sank his head on the wooden table and groaned, 'We are going to fail – lemmings and pigs all.'

25
(2000)

✾

IN THE DARK, Niki watched the still water of the lake as music rippled out of the quadrangle. Laughter rode atop it when not drowned by the techno beats of the DJ. Carpe Diem, the annual cultural festival of IIM Calcutta, was rocking the campus of low-slung buildings and scattered ponds masquerading as lakes.

'Mind if I join you?' Arjun asked, a drink in his hand.

Niki shrugged. He settled down beside her and sipped some punch.

'That's an interesting perfume you have on, unless,' he glanced at the giant banyan above, 'this tree has sprouted roses and cloves.'

'You can smell it above that?' Niki indicated the glass of punch with her chin, which reeked of multiple beverages.

'This is weak as piss. They've added so much water over the evening, I might as well drink from the lake!' He upturned the punch onto the grass below. 'So, the perfume?'

Niki shrugged. 'It belonged to my mother.'

'Belong*ed*?'

'Hmm. My mother died giving birth to me.'

'Like Caesar's?'

'Aren't you supposed to say "I'm sorry" or something appropriate like that?'

'I could, but it would be a bit pointless. Besides, from what I can see, whoever raised you did a damn good job of it.'

'Meaning what exactly?'

'That you are a fine specimen of homo sapiens. You made it to one of the finest business schools in the country. Solid brain, tick. You are a fierce feminist who routinely massacres all the chauvinist men on campus. Ample brawn, tick!'

Niki narrowed her eyes before emitting a guttural 'Ha'.

Arjun grinned. 'Can I get you a drink? Not punch, some suitable liquor to loosen you up?'

'Do me a favour: get yourself something to shut you up. Anyway,' Niki got up and dusted her skirt, 'I'm hungry.'

'Let's get an egg roll outside the gate?' The egg roll cart usually stayed open late into the night on weekends for nocturnal students. And for the ongoing festival, Somakda, the cart owner, was running 24x7. 'My treat.'

Niki rolled her eyes. 'Please. I can pay for an egg roll.'

'Great. Pay for mine too. Gender equality and all.'

Niki shook her head. 'You're not all that endearing, you know...'

Arjun gave an extravagant bow, 'A charming mortal am I.'

He certainly was attractive, Niki had finally admitted to herself. *So what?*

The music faded as they walked down the leafy road. It being January, the night was cool, the lake overlaid with faint mist. Niki wrapped her arms around herself.

Arjun inhaled. 'I haven't smelt anything like your perfume before. It has a hint of the jasmine my mother puts in her hair but there is a whole other aroma too, something spicy...'

'You've got a good nose. Bal à Versailles, Ball at Versailles. It's a French perfume from the '60s. An aunt brought it as a gift for my mother from Paris. Apparently, my mother loved it. She left behind an opened bottle, almost three-quarters full. I use it occasionally.'

'Interesting how memory and smell are intertwined. Fresh laundry reminds me of home,' Arjun laughed. 'So entrenched is the smell of detergent in my mind.'

At the egg roll cart, a bunch of revellers waited their turn. Arjun and Niki sat on the concrete embankment that bordered the campus gate. The soulful notes of Rabindra sangeet floated from Somakda's radio. His elderly father, mouth ajar, perched in his usual spot on the wooden bench behind which the family lived in a low-roofed shanty. They discussed the upcoming summer placement, whether consulting paid better than I-Banking and how the entire class would willingly surrender its soul if it meant being hired by McKinsey.

'Considering there are no NGOs lining up, where do you plan to go, Niki?'

'I'll join a firm that provides me real corporate grounding. After all, you have to know the rules to break them, right?'

'Indeed you do!'

Somakda beckoned to them, and they walked up and placed their order.

'How's business, Somakda?' Niki asked.

'In "Carpedee" time,' he said, 'I get two assistants, one to knead and roll the dough, the other to serve.'

The massive griddle sizzled as he slapped a flour paratha upon it, smacked it with oil and flipped it over. With the other hand, he grabbed an egg from the tray, cracked it on the griddle's edge before pouring it over the bread. Stirring the yolk and egg white over the paratha, he added another splash of oil and tipped the contents over. The aroma of greasy egg and bread wafted up, and they grinned at each other.

'Nothing like the prospect of carbs to a stomach lined with alcohol!' Arjun said.

Somakda's father started to speak in his usual staccato manner, spitting words in Bengali, his eyes widening at what he was seeing. Fleeing from East Bengal during Partition, he kept seeing replays of the Great Calcutta Killings, when blood flowed in gutters and walking meant weaving your way through corpses. Niki understood – her work with survivors had acquainted her with the mind's relapse with senility.

As the first egg roll cooked, Somakda slid it aside and began the second. An empty bus rolled down the Diamond Harbour Road, its dust-specked wake garnishing the egg rolls.

'The not-so-secret secret of the famed Calcutta egg roll,' Arjun chuckled. Something irritated Niki's eye and she blinked repeatedly. It wasn't helping. She stepped away and opened her eyes wide.

A concerned Arjun towered over her. 'What's the matter?'

'Something in my right eye. From the bus likely.' She blinked again, her eye tearing up. 'It's got under my contacts…' She bent her head and tried rotating her eyeball. It hurt. 'Damn!' Looking up, she pulled the lower right eyelid down, probed her eye and plucked the lens out, as Arjun hurried away.

As she stood weeping, he returned with a glass of water. Niki splashed some in her eye gratefully. Behind them, Somakda's father's soliloquy had gathered steam.

'Better?' Arjun asked, taking the empty glass from her hand.

Niki felt disoriented: her left eye had its contact on, the right was blurry. A savoury smelling something popped up in front of her. She closed her right eye and confirmed the vision. Egg roll.

'Are you winking at me?' Arjun asked. 'I'm thrilled!'

'I am currently one-eyed and hungry. Don't mess with me.' Grabbing the egg roll, she bit into it. As it made its fiery descent down her throat, Niki wondered how she would walk back with her impaired vision.

Arjun stuck an elbow out. 'Go on,' he said, chomping on his egg roll, 'I am offering you my arm.'

'Thou art flirting,' Niki slid her arm into his.

Behind them, Somakda clanged the griddle, the radio spilled another lilting melody and her heart spun as they walked in step.

'Flirting with a one-eyed gluttonous Jhansi ki Rani? That would be love, no?'

VIII
(1985)
Jyot

26
(1985)

❋

IN THE END, Bapuji came to Delhi. He was so old, but he arrived by the Punjab Mail to take me home. I would not speak. I would not eat. I would not sleep. I lay with my eyes open; I sat with my eyes vacant. One day, I jumped into the well. But someone raised the alarm; I was rescued. Somebody mentioned a Punjabi lady doctor who needed help with children. In Amreeka. Bapuji thought it best to put some distance between me and what had happened. And so, in 1985, I went to Amreeka.

Flushing, Queens, New York City, New York. I was told to memorize the address, in case I ever got lost. My madam was a doctor with a husband and two children. She was always busy, her husband travelled a lot, and the children needed a nanny. She gave me detailed instructions, then repeated them. Because I spoke so little, she thought I was slow, which was okay because the new city was both familiar and strange. Like Delhi, it was dirty: overflowing garbage, littered pavements, dog turds, too many people. Unlike Delhi, it had too much choice: aisle after aisle stacked to the ceiling with food, so many different foods, so many varieties of one food; so many curious sizes – lb, oz, fl. oz; varied packaging even – polybag, bottle, carton. The supermarket struck terror within me. The first time I was inside on my own, my palms were sweating. I clutched the trolley and started to wheel it down. Accidentally, I bumped into a man who whirled around and started to complain loudly, blaming me for injuring his ankle, drowning the apologies that I kept mumbling. Then the man departed, as abruptly as he had begun. I felt every eye in the store upon me. Trembling, I abandoned the trolley and fled.

Slowly, I learnt to keep a safe distance from other shoppers, but the overflowing aisles threatened me every single time. My madam wrote down an exact list:

Danone low-fat yoghurt, 1 oz;
Stonybrook Milk, 5% fat;
Gala apples, 4

But it was like a hunting expedition in an unknown jungle: organic, free-range, cage-free, pasture-raised, omega-3, egg whites, large brown, low fat, no fat, no pulp, some pulp, pulp-free, with calcium, with calcium and vitamin D. They had nationalities even: Thai eggplant, Chinese eggplant, Italian eggplant. The United Nations of eggplants terrified me because I knew the oblong, purple vegetable as baingan in Hindi, brinjal in English, and I could cook it in five different ways. Would this exotic brinjal still yield to my hands? When I rubbed oil on its skin and slow-roasted it over a flame, would its juices ooze, its skin char, its flesh become soft and succulent? Or would it need some peculiar Chinese treatment, with chilli sauce and chopsticks? Was the Thai eggplant good only for cubing and boiling perhaps?

I took so long over one item that I barely managed to go beyond one product category in one visit. And so, it was dairy one day and vegetables the next. My madam, lips pursed, pruned the inefficiency by preparing a master list where each item had a biodata, the print out several pages long. All I had to do was locate that specific item, failing which I could move to the next. 'Lost cow,' my madam's husband had laughed. I was startled at that descriptor for me, but it was accurate. I had become that worthless. I, who was used to bargaining with the vegetable seller and getting the best vegetables at the lowest price, was now helpless in front of gleaming rows where polished vegetables sat like pieces of jewellery.

The abundance of the supermarket translated to an abundantly overstocked pantry at home, cascading with bottles, bags, jars, packets and cartons, some of which were discarded by their expiry date without ever being used. After opening a new packet, my madam did not tie it up with a rubber band to store the balance; it was just discarded. Abundant waste.

The sight of so much food – overflowing aisles, overflowing pantry, overflowing bins – filled me to the brim. When I sampled the food – muffin, bagel, pie – I found it gooey, sawdusty; it didn't satisfy my shrunk appetite. The sight of a hamburger, as tall as a brass tumbler of lassi, into which people bit, dripping juices and vegetables, made me cover my mouth with my dupatta.

My madam ate a version of Indian food, sliced bread, dals and vegetables; her children preferred pizza or pasta; and her husband travelled so much that his preferences didn't count. In the initial days, I nibbled at bread and salad with dal, some pie or pasta.

I was leaden and lost in an in-between world, neither awake nor asleep, where everything that was once familiar had become different somehow. Brinjal-eggplant. Queue-line. Dustbin-garbage can. Pavement-sidewalk. The sun was bright but not hot. One day was warm, the next cold. I wore my madam's hand-me-down pants and shirts and found a man looking back at me in the mirror. The children spoke English fast and in an accent I did not comprehend. My madam spoke Punjabi, but a busy doctor had no time. When I walked back from dropping the girl to her school, I would browse the Indian store where a group of turbaned old men hung around talking in Punjabi. I would linger and listen to the language.

About six months later, as I eavesdropped, a man placed a tall tiffin box upon a plastic stool, proclaiming his daughter-in-law had prepared a feast for his grandson's birthday. He removed the containers one by one, passing them to his mates to open and check. The men examined the contents and murmured appreciation, and a familiar aroma assailed me. The smell of warm wholewheat atta toasted on a griddle flooded my nostrils, filled my throat, flushed my lungs, and I started to drool. I ran out of the store.

At home, I grabbed the steel container in which the seldom-used wholewheat flour was stored. It had a rancid air. In a bowl, I added flour and some water, and began to knead. Leaden no more, my hands danced as I slapped and rolled the dough. I removed the griddle from under the oven where it sat unused, rinsed it thoroughly and placed it on the stove.

A short while later, I sat down on the parquet floor, a disused thali in front of me. On the rimmed steel plate were a couple of thick wholewheat rotis, a sprinkling of salt within their folds, a green chilli pepper, crushed garlic, some sliced onion. I feasted my eyes on the plate and inhaled the aromas.

I could now travel back in time, way back, when at a home with too many mouths to feed, love was a constant accompaniment to each spare meal. When a feast or celebration called for chholey to be cooked. When the meal was dictated by the season's harvest: saffron carrots, salty radishes, beetroot that bled to the undisguised joy of the children and became the agent of several scares on unsuspecting adults...

With my food, I could recall the person I used to be. Before everything changed.

I took an eager bite, then another; then a third and a fourth without chewing the previous bites, furiously tearing at the roti and stuffing it in my mouth. Willing my tongue. But no.

My mouth convulsed, my eyes stung, as I tasted sawdust over and over again.

IX
(2001–2004)
War Cloud

Dushasana tugs at Draupadi's garment which unravels endlessly. He sweats and frets and tires and tumbles. Outside the palace, black clouds darken the firmament, jackals howl, a storm erupts. The feckless blind king may not know justice, but he knows omens. Worrying for his sons' lives, he promises to grant Draupadi whatever she wishes. Her voice steely, her head held high, Draupadi demands the freedom of her husbands and the return of their weapons. And she declares that she will not tie her hair until she washes it in Dushasana's blood. Visions of corpse-strewn barren fields assail the blind king, who whimpers at the sight of bloated vultures refusing to eat more carrion...

27
(2001)

❋

IN 2001, AFTER business school, Niki was on a consulting assignment in the US. Very quickly she learnt that if you spoke English well but without an American accent, the standard question during introductions was, 'You're from England, right?'

Yeah, right. 'More Indians speak English than the English themselves,' Niki elucidated.

'Huh? You're native American?'

Christopher Columbus, in his quest for India, had seriously messed up the Americans, for whom India was in their backyard, while the *real* India was East India. That belief was rampant through the vast swathe of the US except for its coastal cities. Niki exhaled her relief as she slipped into a yellow cab – it was good to be back in New York. The road to Lincoln Tunnel, though, was a motoric beehive.

'Looks bad, huh?' Niki asked the taxi driver.

Mohammed Abuja, his medallion said, nodded. 'We're in for a long ride.'

Niki grabbed her laptop bag, unzipped it and flipped her computer open. Commuting time was precious in a consultant's road-warrior life. Her presentation was due tomorrow and she still had some excel sheets to crunch. Her second year of consulting, and Niki still didn't know what she was doing *exactly*. After completing an year-long assignment with a steel plant in Jamshedpur, she had been reassigned to a regional airline headquartered in Phoenix, Arizona. Since when had a graduate in women's studies become an authority on the steel and airline industries? When she was not crunching data, she was avoiding pointed enquiries from clients who wanted to probe her background to understand the source of expertise that their company had hired at tremendous expense. Niki felt like a fraud most days. To soothe her conscience, she bought a mug that showed some men in long white coats gathered around a misshapen rocket. The text read: 'Gentlemen, it's time we faced reality ... we are not exactly rocket scientists.'

The imagined glamour of world travel – one of the perks of consulting – had vaporized in the dust of India's Steel City and the heat of US's dust bowl. And the time away from Arjun meant that, despite being married, they were in a long-distance relationship. As she scrolled down the spreadsheet, she admitted the one benefit for which she was still around: the money. Back on campus, both Arjun and she had landed Day 1 jobs: banking and consulting respectively, located in India's financial city, Mumbai. She, though, was waitlisted initially because of mobility concerns: was a woman up to travelling in the hinterland where the newly-opened office of the global consulting firm had found its first domestic client? Niki finally got the job when the two male classmates ahead of her chose other offers. The firm hadn't joked about travel though – Arjun and she had just celebrated their first wedding anniversary apart.

When Papa called on her mobile to wish her, Niki was in Jamshedpur on work with her team. 'Not with Arjun?' Papa asked, the dismay evident in his voice.

'No, with five male colleagues though,' Niki harrumphed.

'You couldn't take a day off?'

'Flying to this end of India from Mumbai is like flying to Dubai! I would've needed three days off, and that's impossible since we are in the midst of final presentations.'

Papa had not commented further, but Niki knew he was not impressed with her choice of career. When she had announced that she was joining one of the world's top three consulting firms, Booz Allen Hamilton, he had asked, 'Isn't your priority women's issues?'

'It is. But I plan to build a nest egg before I can dive into a low-paying job.'

Papa remained unconvinced. Dadima, though, was happy for her. 'Money is liberating,' she reiterated her mantra.

The driver flung open the taxi door, stepped out and walked in the direction of a traffic cop who was being swallowed by the tide of traffic. Niki lowered the window for circulation. It was September, but the density of NYC amped up the temperature by a couple of degrees. The computer clock showed 2.30 p.m. She would be working late to get the presentation ready for tomorrow noon's discussion with the team leader.

Mohammed, the driver, entered the cab, thumbed at the cop and said, 'Accident inside the tunnel. No idea how long this will take, ah. You want a drink?'

'Drink?'

He pointed to a kiosk at the end of the road, across which a vending machine was under siege from commuters seeking hydration. 'No, thanks,' Niki smiled. 'I have water.' Another advantage of a consulting life: business-class travel and its perks. Niki retrieved a bottle of Perrier from her tote bag and sipped some sparkling water.

Mohammed swung a pointed index finger from him to the kiosk. 'I get some, ah.'

Niki nodded and returned to the computer screen. Her eyes were heavy from all the screen time. She tilted her head and settled back into the seat. Fatigue oozed out of her limbs. In the adjacent car, a woman cooed to her baby who grinned toothlessly. Niki found herself smiling, which surprised her. The snarl of traffic, conversation floating from sundry vehicles, the air dense with activity, the baby's gurgle... She snapped the laptop shut. Perhaps she would head downtown after the presentation, catch the Staten Island ferry to see Lady Liberty and the Manhattan skyline. Or go up to the Observation Deck at the World Trade Center... She mulled over the pleasures of sightseeing in a city where her past acquaintance had been limited to the corporate headquarters and the routes to and from airports. The prospect of a sunny fall day and some free time in the world's greatest city made her smile — before the guilt surfaced.

She ought to meet Mr Malik. She had his phone number and a Queens address. She had promised Papa she would try. But work had been so hectic, she had even ducked Papa's calls. He had finally begun writing his long-planned book, a diptych of stories of survivors of two cataclysms, the Partition of '47 and the anti-Sikh riots of '84. *The End of Silence* was his attempt to put forgotten people and their individual pain at the centre of epochal events. Except, he hadn't been able to break Jyot Kaur's silence; he hadn't managed to even reach her. In his last letter, Mr Malik had conveyed that she was categorical in her refusal to talk about her past.

When Niki opened her eyes, the car was moving and the sky had darkened. She realized she had taken a cat nap. Fierce black clouds were invading the previously blue sky. A fat drop splattered the window, followed by several more.

'Storm coming,' Mohammed drawled.

═══

A shrill sound penetrated through the fog of her mind. Bleary-eyed, Niki reached for her mobile vibrating on the nightstand.

'Are you safe?' Arjun sounded frantic. But why?

'Wha-at?' Niki yawned. The edge of the blind in her hotel room was alight, but Niki knew the sun in Manhattan blazed bright early morning. What time was it? She withdrew the mobile phone from her ear – 11 September, 9.04 a.m. – Arjun's garbled voice sounded, and she returned it to her ear. 'What? What did you say?'

'Niki, are you safe? Where are you? You sound dazed.'

'Of course I am dazed! You just woke me up! I had a late night finishing the presentation which has been postponed to the day after—'

'Oh god, Niki! Niki, I am so glad to hear that!'

'That I bust my ass slaving for a consulting firm?'

'Sweetheart, go to the bathroom now.'

'Now?'

'Yes. Take the phone with you. Just wash your eyes, okay?'

'What's going on—'

'Just do as I say, please.'

'Is Papa okay? Dadima? Ar-*JUN*!' Niki yelled.

'Everything's fine at home, with all of us, we're all good. Since you seem to be awake, listen. Switch on the TV, CNN, now.'

Niki grabbed her spectacles, thrust them on her nose, found the remote, switched on the TV and jabbed until she got CNN. A tower was smoking. To its left was … the Empire State Building? The camera panned. It was one of the Twin Towers, smoke curdling around its head. It was thirty streets from her hotel. Flinging the sheet aside, Niki scrambled to the window.

=

With no flights out of NYC, she was stranded between hotel and office. In the conference rooms, she watched the news on an endless loop with her colleagues. The phone connectivity was erratic. She called home when she could and exchanged emails with Arjun, who updated Dadima and Papa. Nooran was with her all through, rather the memory of her, as posters of missing people popped up; and Nooran's bagh, which travelled with Niki everywhere and was the first thing she retrieved in every strange new room. Niki wrapped herself in the bagh, the soft cotton and old silk a balm as she watched Manhattan grieving, blanketed in grey snow, streets ghostly, sirens wailing, air smouldering. After a couple of days, flights resumed, but the project she was consulting on was put on hold. Niki spent a few days in limbo. She tried Mr Malik's number unsuccessfully on several occasions. When she told Papa that she would go visit him, he objected.

'No. Stay in the safety of your hotel and office.'

'That's a one mile radius, max.'

'Stay put. Stay safe.'

'But Papa, the worst has already happened. I have so much time on hand, I might as well locate the mystery woman—'

'Niki, I forbid it!'

Forbid? Never before had Papa used that word with her. She did tell him that at Union Square, the closest you could get to the fallen towers, she had lit a candle at a makeshift memorial and hugged complete strangers. The day before, she had bolted when she saw others fleeing, reaching all the way to Central Park – the bomb scare had turned out to be a rumour. She was fearful, but it was a communal fear that cloaked the entire city.

'Nik-ki?'

'Yes, Papa. I hear you.'

After eight brittle days feasting on fear, Niki was on a flight back to Mumbai. Suspended in space, she was a newborn who had emerged from hard labour: sound sleep punctuated by feeding frenzies. The recent past seemed evanescent, yet its sediment was wedged within the loss she always carried with her.

Arjun came to the airport to pick her up. Arjun, dear Arjun. She collapsed in his arms in relief. 'Let's have a baby,' she said in greeting.

Arjun was taken aback. With his arm around her, he guided her out of the airport, treating her with a tenderness normally reserved for small children or trauma patients.

At home, Papa and Dadima, who had travelled from Chandigarh, engulfed her in their warmth. Later, when Niki announced her decision to become a mother, Papa asked in surprise, 'What's the hurry?'

But Dadima understood. A woman's answer to destruction was to create.

28
(2004)

✳

AUTUMN IN CHANDIGARH was Niki's favourite: mornings were nippy, afternoons bright, evenings lit up with Diwali candles. She had missed that in Hong Kong, where they had relocated in 2003 with Arjun's job. A growing China was ravenous for funds and the bank wanted to join the feeding frenzy. Moored to China, halfway between Tokyo and Sydney, the erstwhile colony continued to abide by British legal frameworks and be Asia's leading financial centre. Its history as an expat hub made it attractive to foreign companies, whose employees could send their children to English-language schools, hire affordable help and live in an international bubble within a territory that was ninety-five per cent Chinese.

'Ma-ma!'

Two-year-old Mehar toddled down the mosaic floor, dragging her stuffed elephant by its trunk. Niki scooped her daughter up and playfully dug her nose in her belly. Mehar let loose a series of cackles.

'Let's get you some milk, shall we?' They made their way towards the kitchen where Dadima was supervising the help. A tarty smell wafted in the air.

'Dima!' Mehar exclaimed, extending her chubby arms forward. Dadima smiled and took her in her arms. She seated her on the countertop, legs dangling, and handed her a wholewheat biscuit. Dadima's face was acquiring an Etch-a-Sketch elderly look: wrinkles were replacing laugh lines, liver spots freckled her face and her hair was mostly white because she refused to colour it. What bothered Niki were the plumb lines at the corners of Dadima's mouth weighing it down. The sorrow of the survivors she worked with had breached her heart and was rutting her face. The Dadima she knew and loved, she was losing, not in some dramatic disappearance but in bits and pieces eroded by life. When she visited them in Hong Kong, Dadima refused to take a trip down Victoria Harbour in a famed, red-masted Chinese junk or catch the ferry even. Niki had protested until Dadima admitted she was afraid.

'Afraid! Of what?'

'The water,' Dadima whispered.

'What about the boat rides on the Sukhna Lake?' Niki countered, recalling their frequent visits to Chandigarh's iconic lake.

'I was being brave for you,' Dadima admitted. That desperate flight from home on the Ravi as Lahore had burned in 1946 had marked her for life. Now, Niki closed the gap between them and hugged her fiercely.

'Hain,' Dadima said in surprise as Niki nestled her face on her shoulder. 'Mooli parathas for breakfast?'

Niki nodded. When had Dadima become so bony?

'Arjun likes them?'

'Arjun loves them!'

'My Appa Ar-jun,' Mehar sang, her mouth outlined in brown. The women laughed.

Niki wiped Mehar's fingers and mouth, and gave her water in a sipper bottle. 'What's the plan for today? Shall we go to Sector 17 market? Shopping and coffee?'

Dadima pinched some radish mixture from the plate that Lata, the maid, held up. 'Nice. Add half a spoon of the mango pickle masala and it's done. What?' she turned to Niki.

'Sector 17?'

Dadima waved a hand. 'Arjun and you go. I have to be at PUCL office.'

'What time? We'll drop you there and hang around until we can go together. Maybe pop into Rock Garden while you—'

'Ni-ki,' Dadima said, 'it'll be a long meeting. The twentieth anniversary of '84 is a month away, and we have so many things to discuss. Cases are pending in the courts but there has been no justice. What do we tell the survivors whose stories have filled my diaries and your Papa's files? That, like so many others, we failed them too?'

Dadima's mouth plumbed downward again. Government apathy, police inaction and lethargic courts had ensured that none accused of the pogrom were prosecuted, no victims compensated.

'Gaden, gaden.' Mehar begged to be lifted, dangling the elephant in the direction of the garden outside.

<hr />

Pre-dinner drinks in the garden were another autumn joy. Cane chairs were arranged in a circle and a coil of mosquito repellent burnt beside the centre table. Arjun and Papa prepared the drinks as Dadima fried onion pakoras and Niki tossed together a corn and pepper salad to accompany wafer-thin poppadums. A giddy Mehar ran in circles around the garden chasing fireflies, as mosquitoes trailed her. Niki had slathered her in Odomos, its noxious fumes a guaranteed repellent from her own childhood.

'Cheers!' Arjun toasted with his glass of scotch.

They responded. Papa bit into a pakora and sighed contentedly. 'Nothing like a good drink to lighten life. So, Arjun, how are the Chinese treating you?'

'Pretty well. They ensure I get a healthy compensation.'

'How does it work? They speak Mandarin, you don't. And the Chinese, I am told, are cannier than an Indian bania. How do you ensure they don't rob you and the bank?'

'I have an interpreter. I ask lots of questions, which gives me time to observe them without the distraction of words.' He paused. 'The body usually betrays a liar.'

Papa grinned. 'In the courts, it is the opposite. People will lie blatantly. Only the evidence speaks.'

'And don't we all know it,' Dadima said softly. 'You can slaughter people in public, but the police won't register a case. When they do, the judge won't pronounce guilt because there is no evidence. When you can't scare off witnesses, you wait for them to die.' She gave a bitter laugh. 'Maybe we should all speak Mandarin, Arjun – wait for the body to betray itself.'

Niki leaned across and squeezed Dadima's arm. They sipped their drinks as stars emerged in the deepening sky. The light from the living room windows cast their group in a cosy amber glow. Mehar snuggled up to Arjun, who hoisted her in his lap.

'How's the book coming along, Papa?' Niki asked.

Papa shrugged. 'Stalled, like the Indian justice system and traffic. In his latest letter, Mr Malik – remember him?'

'Of course, your New York respondent.'

'Right. He writes that Jyot Kaur is recovering from some accident. I think he suspects suicide.' He sipped some scotch. 'He doesn't want to push her, understandably. Neither do I.'

'Why don't you look for another respondent with a similar profile, whose story of '47 and '84 will be the spine for the two halves of your book?'

Papa and Dadima exchanged a look. 'You know Jyot's story.'

'That you guys go back a long way, from when Dadima encountered her in '47 in a refugee camp, etc. ...'

'Why don't you help me write the book?'

Niki was taken aback. Admittedly, Papa had alluded to needing Niki's assistance before. She could have pitched in, but being a mother was a full-time job. After delivery, there was despair instead of elation. She could not relate to images of angelic mothers breastfeeding their newborns. The suckling child was demanding and selfish. Dadima's soft ministrations and helping hands, cooing to Niki and Mehar, saw them through. Then came teething, walking, talking, socializing, potty-training, toddler music classes, baby Einstein videos and play groups. Dadima was perplexed at the frenetic pace of Niki's motherhood but science was scary: a child's brain developed eighty per cent in the first three years of life – while a new mother's career tanked.

'But Papa,' she protested, 'I want to resume my career after a two-year maternity break. And Hong Kong is not the easiest market considering I don't have language skills – knowledge of Cantonese or Mandarin is essential for a consumer insights professional.'

Papa laughed.

'What?' Niki asked as she swatted a mosquito.

'Thank you for the illustration: easier said than done.' He sipped from his glass, which was empty, and stood up. 'Another round, anyone?'

Mehar was asleep in Arjun's arms. Niki rose, extricated her and accompanied Papa indoors.

═

Dadima's migraine had forced her to lie down, curtains drawn tight, as the household tiptoed outside her room. She had returned from her meeting at PUCL and taken to her bed. For Niki, it was déjà vu. Autumn might be the best season for her but not for Dadima. For her, it brought the twin horrors of '84 and the loss of her husband in '71. In her selfishness, Niki had overlooked that.

Arjun and she walked in the garden, dew covering their bare feet. 'Do you want to go earlier to your parents'? The plan was to celebrate Diwali in Chandigarh and travel the next day to Bangalore to celebrate it with Arjun's family too. A reflection of India's diversity, Diwali fell on separate days in its northern and southern halves.

'Should we?' Arjun asked. 'Won't it help Dadima if we were together?'

'I don't think there's going to be much of a celebration. Dadima's migraine episodes last several days. And what the rest of the household does is carry on quietly. She refuses food even.' Niki sighed. 'I expect it'll be worse this time with the twentieth anniversary of the pogrom. I'll stay behind to see her through. I can't manage both Mehar and her though.'

'You're sure? We can be useful, you know.' He kissed her forehead as they walked on.

'You'll be more useful managing Mehar at your mother's.' She avoided a toadstool. Once, she had gathered them from the garden, tied a thread around their sticky stems and offered the bouquet to Nooran, who had snorted and made her wash her hands. 'Fart pies,' Nooran had said, 'you don't want to touch those!'

The roar of a motorcycle broke the morning quiet. It dashed down the road, screeched and sped down the walkway of the adjoining house before braking abruptly. The smell of burnt rubber floated in the air.

'Ass,' Niki mouthed as a young man pulled off his full-face helmet and waved to them. His hands were in fingerless leather gloves. 'He walks with all the privilege of manhood and none of its burdens,' Niki spat.

'Hey,' Arjun said, 'a trifle strong, no?'

'His mother suffered five abortions to birth this brat. Five dead girls for the price of one pompous boy.'

Arjun rubbed her upper arm as he acknowledged the neighbour's wave. Niki, meanwhile, examined the grass intently.

'People can't see reality, even when it stares them in the face. For every young man walking around, there are the ghosts of his dead sisters around him.'

'Come on, Niki, that's overly dramatic!'

'Really? Well, Mr Facts, according to Amartya Sen, Nobel prize-winning economist, India has a hundred million missing girls. *One hundred million.* Why have the girls gone missing? Because their parents killed them as foetuses. We're well aware of the Holocaust – six million Jews killed by the Nazis. But what about our own Nazis that appear in the avatar of son-seeking parents? Why the silence around the violence that India routinely inflicts on its women?'

Book 3

X
(2014)
Welcome to New York

Unnerved, the Kauravas grant the Pandavas one more game of dice to win back their kingdom. But the stakes are high, the dice are loaded and Yudhishthira is shockingly amnesiac. The Pandavas lose yet again and are banished to thirteen years of exile. In the wilderness, the brothers are stoic and stout, and Draupadi shares their hardships but she will not let them forget her humiliation. When the exile is over, the Kauravas refuse to return their kingdom to the Pandavas. Krishna tries to broker peace but Duryodhana is drunk on power. War is inevitable...

29
(2014)

✳

ON THE FLIGHT from Hong Kong to Chandigarh, a stewardess asked Niki with concern, 'Is everything all right?' Twelve-year-old Mehar cradled her mother's hand. Arjun got up and had a quiet word with the attendant, after which she left Niki alone.

All right? How was the world continuing to function as if everything was normal? The taxi from home to the airport sailed smoothly, they checked in without a glitch and security seemed negligent in its ease. The world was functioning with a rhythm and routine as if it hadn't tilted off its axis and was tumbling around, waters leaking, land askew.

Dadima had found Papa dead at his desk, pen in hand, a transcript in front of him, his whisky glass half finished. She'd got up in the morning as usual, made two cups of tea and had hers with the newspaper, wondering why he was late from his morning walk. Only then had she realized that a light was on in the study. The doctor said it was cardiac arrest. Papa's heart had suddenly stopped working.

Niki was aware that her daughter was wiping her face with a towelette, that her seat belt was buckled for her, that the plane was

159

in the air, closing the distance to Chandigarh where Dadima waited with Papa's body. Like Niki had waited for Dadima with Nooran's body. Niki shut her eyes tight and pursed her mouth. She could wail – oh she would wail, the pain within was a dam about to burst – but Mehar would be terrified. And other passengers would eye her with alarm or pity.

Niki straightened up, breathed through her mouth and reminded herself that she was the adult. Roles had reversed. Besides Mehar, she was responsible for Dadima, who had lived with the loss of her husband and must now live with the loss of her son.

═══

At the cremation ground, they placed Papa's body on a pyramid of wood blocks. The men, led by Tiny Uncle, had bathed and dressed him in a white kurta pyjama. His face, with its perpetually furrowed forehead, was relaxed, a corner of his mouth upturned, as if he was still a bit bemused by the world. Niki expected him to wake up any moment. Surely the man whose eyes twinkled at her when he shared his stories, whose glass of whisky was never left unfinished, who was there to steady her after every tumble, surely that man, that father, couldn't just go away? Even as they piled logs of wood upon him, covering his face last? Even as he disappeared in a tower of wood, garrisoned for no escape? Beside her, Dadima, dressed in white, stood stiffly. Niki's arm cradled her back. She was afraid the slightest pressure would shatter her. Her other arm was intertwined with Mehar's, as if her daughter was unsure whether she could trust her mother to stay upright.

'Should she go to the cremation?' Niki and Arjun had debated. At twelve, she was old enough, but was one ever old enough to witness the burning of a loved one?

Mehar had concluded the debate for them. 'I am coming to say goodbye,' she announced, her mouth set in a fierce line.

The priest had begun chanting as he doused the wood with gasoline from a canister. Really? Then he lit a log. When it was burning steadily, he beckoned Arjun. In the Sikh faith, as in Hindu, a son set fire to the father's pyre. *Careful, priest, Papa might just throw off the logs and emerge, apoplectic at this casual discrimination.* He hadn't devoted his life to ending discrimination to suffer this ultimate travesty. Dadima held a hand upright, prodded Niki forward, took Arjun's right hand and placed it on Niki's right arm. 'Go.'

Though a film of tears, Niki perambulated around the pyre, torching Papa's body.

Once home, Niki withdrew to Papa's study and shut the door. She sat in the cushioned armchair from where she had listened to Papa as he sat at his desk. The house was quiet. The mourners had departed and Dadima was lying down. The rain, which had threatened to ruin the cremation, had arrived, the monsoon weeping with her. After withholding its bounty for weeks, teasing farmers – weathermen, statisticians, students, all seeking reprieve from the scalding heat, it was thundering down. Now it would breach embankments, burst dams, drown homes, convert land to lakes. In India, people joked that God was like the monsoon in its late but unmitigated munificence. Niki agreed.

Earlier, the bank had made Arjun an offer to relocate to its head office in New York, a global job with significant compensation. Papa and Dadima had been enthusiastic. Arjun liked the offer and had accepted. Now Papa was gone. They were to move in a month. Dadima would be left alone.

Niki gulped and walked to the table, which lay untouched. It gave off a peaty whiff. The whisky in the glass was golden, the uncapped fountain pen positioned across a ruled textbook, a stack of folders teetered. She did not want to disturb it, aware that the last time each item had been touched was by Papa. She bent and read his cursive handwriting.

What connects the two sets of survivor stories? One is from the sectarian riots in the wake of the Partition of India in 1947, and the other is from anti-Sikh riots in the wake of the prime minister's assassination in 1984. The nature of the beast remains the same: us versus them, brother against brother, violence and silence. But for narrative purposes, the diptych requires a hinge that holds the two sets together. This is where Jyot Kaur comes in, marked by the twin violence of '47 and '84; alive yet shrouded in silence, th

The text finished mid-sentence, an ink blot indicating the pen had paused as Papa's hand stilled before it rolled off.

Niki chewed her inner lip and tried not to cry. Papa's work on his book had stalled because of Jyot. 'Why this obsession with her?' Niki had often asked him. 'Surely there are other survivor stories that link the two events?'

'Perhaps,' Papa had shrugged. 'But this is personal.'

'Because Dadima met her in '47 and found her a home?'

'Because Dadima considered adopting her,' Papa said softly. 'In which case, I would have had an elder sister.'

Niki hadn't really understood. All said and done, Jyot was still an acquaintance from history, a happenstance. But now that Papa's unfinished book stared at her, public history had become personal. Whenever Papa had indicated that he could do with her assistance with his book, too considerate to demand it, she had deferred: she was occupied with Mehar, she was beginning a new job, her career was too demanding, she had no time…

Now Papa was gone. He had given the book all his time and yet, it hadn't been enough. Niki moved her fingers against the stacked folders, feeling the swollen pages, the dog-eared edges. The book was hers to finish now.

=

A week later, Arjun was ready to return to work. Mehar's summer vacation had begun and she was proving the perfect companion for Dadima, making her tea, fetching her slippers, giving her company as people stopped by to offer condolences. But the relocation was nearing and they had a moving checklist to initiate. Niki was in a dilemma.

'Nothing changes,' Dadima insisted, shaking her head. 'This is what your Papa wanted as well.'

'But that was before, Dadima,' Niki wrung her hands.

'And life must go on. You have a life to lead, Niki. As do I.'

Niki looked into her eyes and Dadima looked right back. 'Besides, Tiny is right here.'

Tiny Uncle nodded. In the three decades that Niki had known him, he had gone from being a writer on the fringe to a public intellectual with a weekly column in Chandigarh's respected daily, the *Tribune*. His attire of pastel kurta-pyjama set off by a printed turban with a peacock-tail turla had become his trademark, and it was not unusual to see him holding court on Page 3. To them, though, he remained steadfast neighbour, Papa's scotch buddy, Dadima devotee.

'And who knows, you might end up meeting Jyot?' Dadima's eyes rested on her. She knew what was left unsaid. Papa's book was unfinished business. Not that Niki needed cajoling now. The one reason New York made sense was that she could locate the elusive story that Papa had seen as the hinge for his diptych of a book.

'What is the submission deadline, Uncle?' Niki asked.

Tiny Uncle was well-connected with the publishing industry headquartered out of New Delhi. He had introduced Papa to the editor at a reputable publishing house. Papa's proposal of a diptych of oral history was a fresh idea, and in an amnesiac nation, it had not been attempted before. The editor was enthused and they had inked the deal.

'We have until the end of the year, but considering the changed circumstance...' Tiny Uncle worked a tip of his moustache.

'Yes,' Niki nodded. 'Well, I have a fresh proposal for the editor.'

'Fresh ... proposal?'

'Building upon Papa's book...'

Dadima watched quietly, Tiny Uncle leaned forward. Niki stood up, walked to Papa's study where Arjun was on a telephone call with his colleagues in Hong Kong, entered quietly, and returned with a sheet of printed paper. 'Here,' she handed it to Dadima, who read it and passed it to Tiny Uncle.

Book Proposal

The End of Silence: Survivor Stories from the Partition of 1947 and the Pogrom of 1984

The independence of India from British rule in 1947 marked a concomitant event: the partition of the subcontinent to create the Muslim-majority nation of Pakistan. The latter was a cataclysmic event that saw the migration of ten million people, the world's largest mass migration, and caused the death of one million people. One hundred thousand women had been abducted and raped. The sundering of land led to the sundering of homes, families, communities. The resultant violence was of such ferocity that people recalled it as a time of 'pralaya', as foretold in the Mahabharata.

However, almost seventy years later, there are few memorials to Partition even as independence is commemorated. Not enough records exist of the trauma suffered by individuals at the centre of this epochal event; indeed, there seems to be a widespread silence around it. The story of India's independence is largely a story of the bravery of Indian men. The parallel story of Partition is the untold story of silent survivors. The dance of violence and silence of '47 played out again in '84 during the anti-Sikh pogrom. The horrific violence of the latter echoed that of the former, as if a template existed and was being copied.

India will celebrate seventy years of freedom in 2017, and yet violence against women is rising. Every day, horrific crimes are being reported, where the savagery towards women seems senseless. Is this spate of violence exceptional or has it always been there? Does the abiding silence following the violence of '47 and '84 have something to do with the sexual violence we see today?

Through in-depth interviews conducted by Jinder and Zohra Nalwa with 110 survivors over twenty years, this narrative will tell the story of people – men and women – who suffered through the cataclysms of '47 and '84. The writer will explore the reasons behind the silence, and illustrate how internalized silence, particularly that of women, is integral to the spiral of violence in the subcontinent. Survivor stories need a public airing so we can understand the reasons behind the violence – both sexual and sectarian – that surfaces frequently, and having understood that, we can begin to heal and progress.

About the Author

Niki Nalwa, a graduate in women's studies and management, worked as a consultant with Booz Allen Hamilton, one of the top three consulting firms worldwide. Her training as a writer started when she began transcribing her father Jinder Nalwa's notes from his interviews with survivors of the Partition. She will bring her intimate knowledge of the subject matter, education and training to the successful completion of her father's ambitious work.

Tiny Uncle sat up as he finished reading.

Niki watched him eagerly.

He worked the tip of his moustache. 'But Niki, you are not your father. Why would the editor buy your proposal?'

'Because ... I was my father's assistant as much as I was his daughter. When other children were playing with dolls and balls, my companions were pencils and files, audio cassettes and transcripts. Because,' Niki studied the carpet, her mouth wobbling, 'the project is my sibling.' When she looked up, her eyes glittered. 'And this will be our pitch to the editor: the narrative will be interwoven with personal stories from the Nalwa family to make it more marketable. To a public inured to violence, I'll make the political personal.'

'Good, very good!' Tiny Uncle brought his hands together in a resounding clap. 'This is a new book and we must get a new deal: more money and a new deadline.'

The door of the study opened. Arjun stepped out and stretched his arms overhead.

'I'll leave the money negotiation to you, Uncle, but the deadline is clear in my mind.'

'What?'

'A year.'

'A year?' Dadima frowned. 'How will you finish it so quickly, Niki? You have to relocate to a new city. Locate Jyot, gain her confidence. There will be a new school for Mehar to adjust to, new offices for Arjun and you...' She looked at Niki searchingly.

Arjun pulled up a chair and sat down next to Dadima. He looked from her to Niki. 'So she hasn't told you?'

'Told me what?'

Niki sat upright. 'I'm taking a sabbatical from work to finish the book. I spoke with my boss, and he's agreed to a year's leave. Hence the deadline.'

30
(2014)

✼

ARJUN WAS TICKING items off the moving checklist: notifying changes of address, contacting requisite departments for discontinuing utilities, liaising with the shipping company. He really could have used Niki's help in Hong Kong, but Papa's manuscript had gone missing.

Dadima, Mehar and Niki raked the study, sifting through bookshelves, emptying out drawers, sweeping the study table, for the hardcover spiral-bound folder which had grown with sheets of Papa's cursive handwriting over years. Niki repeatedly insisted that it was not so much missing as mislaid: Papa was not the most organized person, as they all knew? But a cavern had opened up within her, which was pooling with grief. What if they didn't, couldn't, locate it? They would have lost Papa's life's mission. Moreover, Niki worried about Dadima, who was seeking it with a doggedness as if its recovery would bring her son back. She sometimes forgot to eat, and chose not to wear her hearing aid, preferring monologues over conversation, muttering reminiscences as she padded about.

This was why Niki didn't want to relocate. Dadima would be alone, despite full-time help and Tiny Uncle's frequent visits. She needed companionship. Instead, she affected bravado. Watching Niki skulking around the house, she had snorted, 'You behave like you're being sent to exile!'

It did feel like a kind of exile, being sent to the other end of the world when you were needed at home. Even if they couldn't relocate to Chandigarh, Hong Kong was only a five-hour flight away and Dadima visited them every year for a month. Besides, it was still Asia – everything was different and yet familiar. The Chinese were the only people who outdid Indians at rituals and joss sticks. But America was so far off, it had its own 'Indians'. And in the time it took to cover that distance, day became night.

What they did recover in their hunt for the manuscript was Papa's field notes for his book. Interviews and transcripts filed in multiple folders, diary entries – both Dadima's and Papa's – from across the years, pictures in bulging envelopes, audio cassettes stored in drawers. As Dadima pottered about the house trying to locate the manuscript in rooms other than the study, Niki started to sort the field notes into a coherent order. Several interviews were missing but she recovered many more. A rough count showed in the upward of seventy stories. That was a solid, workable number. But without Papa's manuscript, she had no idea of how he had arranged the narrative, except that he had built it upon the twin pillars of '47 and '84. Still, she had something that she could start off with, in the hope of discovering the manuscript—

'Amma!' Mehar bounded to the door of the study, her face pale. 'Come quickly!'

Niki bolted from the chair, a pile of folders teetering as she hurried after her daughter. In the kitchen, Dadima was on the floor, besieged by canisters, jars, jute and cloth bags, bottles, utensils, pans, woks, plates, cutlery. The doors of all the cabinets were open, the shelves empty, the liners trailing limply in the air.

Mehar looked from Dadima to her mother, eyes wide as chrysanthemums. Niki's right hand had flown to her open mouth as she tried to comprehend the scene. Dadima, meanwhile, had not registered their presence and continued to open jars, look within, mumble. She was working through a clear plastic jar of green mung when Niki called out to her softly.

Dadima spun the lid off, peered inside, and thrust the jar in Niki's direction. 'Not here, either. Where could the manuscript be, Niki?'

They picked their way through the flotsam. As Niki hugged Dadima, Mehar stroked her head. Soon they were locked in a huddle, sobbing, tears and snot mingling. In time, they lifted Dadima off the floor and guided her to her bedroom.

≡

What would Nooran do?

Work, stay busy, keep the hands going, if not in the kitchen, then on the embroidery. When your hands were gainfully occupied, the mind was too. Niki co-opted Dadima into organizing Papa's field notes. They arranged the interviews, photographs and cassettes into three separate piles. They sorted the interviews by the epoch they belonged to, then matched photographs with the persons interviewed where possible. After that, they arranged the two sets of interviews chronologically. Mehar, meanwhile, listened to each cassette, identified the respondent, labelled the cassette and gave it to them to add to either of the two interview sets. In the end, of the hundred-plus interviews conducted, they had recovered eighty-eight.

Niki filed those pages, dog-eared, stained with whisky or tea or oil, in varying stages of sepia as they had accumulated over the years, into a new folder. Pushing a lump down her throat, she labelled it 'Papa's Interviews'. As they stored the catalogued field notes in separate drawers, Mehar, as if on cue, said, 'Dadima, can you make me karah parshad, please?' The roasted semolina halwa was her favourite. Dadima nodded. Mehar clapped and bounded to her. Holding hands, they walked out of the study. Mehar's voice floated back to Niki, who stood cradling the newly-created folder. 'I have a whole bunch of things I want to eat and only a week left...'

31
(2014)

❋

NIKI SHIFTED THE tote bag to her other shoulder. It was heavy, but she refused to put it on the trolley or let it out of sight. The field notes were in it. She had lost Papa and his manuscript; she couldn't lose Papa's interviews.

It had been an hour-and-a-half since they had landed at Newark Airport, and she squinted at her surroundings. It was a bright day, but she couldn't be bothered with retrieving her sunglasses from her bag. After a journey of twenty hours, all she wanted was a hot shower and a comfortable, and flat, bed. End of August; wasn't summer over yet? Then she remembered the recce visit in April when she had learnt from the relocation agent that New York, unlike London, got sun most days. Cloudless blue sky, radiant almost. The kind of light she associated with Punjab. When they had visited the south of France, famed for the light that drew painters, she had wondered what the fuss was all about. The lavender fields of Provence were extraordinary, but she'd seen light like that all the time while growing up. It was the kind Dadima preferred, when she could read without narrowing her eyes. She wasn't doing much reading lately, though. All this sorting papers, she offered as explanation, as she pottered about looking for the missing manuscript.

Niki sighed. Too audibly, because a head at her elbow turned to her and, with a roll of her big eyes, Mehar indicated her own disdain with the general scheme of things.

'Welcome to New York!' Niki injected enough enthusiasm into her voice to make Columbus proud. But Columbus was an ignoramus, stumbling into America, calling it India at a time when India had been in conversation with the world for two millennia.

'Yeah, right,' came the reply as Mehar swivelled away, weary with the weight of the world.

Did I birth this creature? Niki wondered as she studied the slumped form of her twelve-year-old daughter. Mehar was even madder than Niki at being exiled, a situation compounded by the fact that she was a pre-teen going on nineteen. No wonder all those stories of exile in the epics never had a child accompanying the parents. Where would they find the time to wage wars in the name of dharma if they had to manage a child's protestations: Nobody eats berries for lunch!; You want me to sleep on hay?; Wait, what – bathe in that pond? These were all existential questions crushed in the minutiae of being a parent. In exile in the Mahabharata, all Draupadi had to deal with was five husbands biding their time to wage the great war – still, five men to feed!

'Hong Kong was *so-oo* organized.' Mehar shook her head as she surveyed the line of passengers waiting for taxis.

'Ah, here are a few,' Niki watched a couple of yellow cabs roll up.

'A trickle.'

This was true. Why would an international airport have taxi trouble? In Hong Kong, in her eleven years in the city, she never recalled having to wait at the airport. Another sigh.

'Amma,' Mehar said, 'you are sighing like Dadima.'

Niki narrowed her eyes at her daughter and looked away. Arjun was crossing the road, an errant bag in his hand. It hadn't shown up on the carousel, and Arjun had suggested they join the taxi queue while he attempted to locate it. Niki watched her husband as he walked towards them, a smile on his face. At least someone was happy. She felt irritated at him for keeping them waiting in the sun. But it wasn't his fault! Wasn't it? If they had not taken the flight, the bag would never have gone missing. Oh, so we're back to the relocation again?

'How's my family doing?' Arjun deposited the bag on the floor and took both women in his arms. 'Thundercloud 1, Thundercloud 2, registered.'

Niki snorted. She was being a bitch and she knew it. She sighed again.

Mehar crossed her arms, her face fierce. 'Incorrect,' she said, as she wiggled an index finger over her face. 'It's Typhoon 10, Hong Kong-style, and you are advised to seek cover.'

'Yessir,' Arjun mock saluted. 'Looks like we're getting lucky.'

Yellow cars beelined to the stand and they had a taxi. Bags deposited, address given, bundled in, they slid out of the airport. Mehar studied an airplane coming in to land, her eyes scrunched. 'Boeing 777,' she declared. 'Virgin.'

The distant concrete was coalescing into the much-lauded New York City skyline. Arjun patted Mehar's shoulder. 'Impressive, isn't it?'

'Nowhere as impressive as Hong Kong!'

Niki had to agree. The Manhattan skyline, famed as it was, couldn't compare with Hong Kong's confluence of sea, skyscrapers and emerald mountains, a stunning backdrop to a triple-masted red junk floating in the harbour.

'Sure,' Arjun agreed. 'But on its own, it's not half bad.' His extended finger picked up buildings as he rattled off names: One57, the New York Times Building, the Chrysler Building, the Empire State Building—

'I know that one, Empire State. Mount Olympus is located above it; you have to take the elevator to the 600th floor.'

'Huh? Says who?'

'Says Percy Jackson,' Mehar grinned.

Around them, traffic roared as they watched their future homeland appear in front of them. It looked accomplished, remote, forbidding. Mehar sat sandwiched between her parents, her hands around her pet elephant who had travelled the world with her since she'd been one year old. 'Where did the Twin Towers used to be?'

Arjun and Niki exchanged a look. For a moment, Niki was in a hotel room, woken up to the shrill ringing of a telephone and the urgent command, 'Switch on the TV now!'

Arjun leaned in to pick out the under-construction Freedom Tower in the tangle of skyscrapers downtown.

That first week after 9/11, there was no stranger left in NYC, all united in bewildered grief. Until President Bush took to TV with his 'You're with us or against us' speech, and the breach in the NYC skyline divided the world. As with Common Era, 9/11 became another way to mark time, a before and after story built around the great rupture with a distinctly western protagonist and clichéd eastern antagonists. The first victim of a hate crime after 9/11 was a Punjabi Sikh immigrant in Arizona, mistaken for an Arab because of his beard and turban.

The taxi slowed down. A baked smell of diesel and fish made Niki wrinkle her nose, compounding her motion sickness. They approached the Lincoln Tunnel, and the NYC skyline, that pivot of the before and after story, was swallowed up. The cab entered, daylight disappeared, and they progressed into the canal cradled by the Hudson River, forging through the tube towards an opening which poured them into Manhattan, with its susurrus of traffic and huddling towers. Niki shivered and felt suddenly alone. She blinked at the bright light, and the taxi sped down an avenue. A pressure to her left, and Mehar was nuzzling into her. Niki had been her age when she began helping Papa transcribe his interviews for Project '47, and viscous grief pooled into her stomach. Niki moved the tote snug onto her lap, invoked Guru Nanak with her eyes closed and turned towards her family.

32
(2014)

✳

MR MALIK'S TRANSCRIPT was missing from Papa's interviews. He lived in Queens, she recalled from her earlier stint in NYC when she had attempted to meet him. She had lost his contact details, but he ran a non-profit organization that sounded like the word for shadow in Urdu … Chhaya … Saya … yes, SAYA!

Niki googled SAYA. South Asian Centre for Youth and Adults. A non-profit organization, it helped South Asian immigrants with legal counsel, job opportunities, and physical and mental health. She scrolled further. The 'About Us' section informed her that SAYA had been founded by Mr Malik. The brief note talked about the organization's humble beginnings, its work gaining momentum in the aftermath of 9/11, etc., but there was no more information about Mr Malik. For a founder, he was either very humble or very reclusive. More googling showed that SAYA was headed by Ms Vandana Dixit. She scrolled down the staff listing when a name made her hand stop: Jyot Kaur.

A thrill radiated out of Niki's stomach. Here, finally, was the elusive woman Papa had sought, whose untold story was the spine of

175

his book. She might finally have the chance to interview her... There was a trail of moisture from her fingertips on the keyboard; her hands were clammy with anticipation. Niki wiped them on her shorts.

SAYA was seeking pro bono services to assist with their initiatives, she read with interest. This could be her entry point. Under the cover of volunteering – of course, she would help out sincerely but that wasn't her goal – she could approach Jyot, who had eluded the Nalwa family for so long. Niki clicked the email button and wrote to Vandana Dixit, offering to volunteer at SAYA.

═

She read 'Good Luck Kitchen' in gold capital letters on a storefront with Hello Kitty in the window pumping her forearm like some golden hammer, a straight 'beam-me-back-to-Hong Kong' moment, but for the neon 'LAUNDROMAT' sign to the right. 'Himalayan Restaurant' glowed to its left, complete with a 2D imitation of a stupa to authenticate the eatery's provenance. A banner ran across the top of the building: 'Kareem's Karate, Kickboxing, Cardio Fitness', followed by two phone numbers and a website address. They were all housed in a narrow, two-story red-brick building, which was the address she had for 'South Asian Centre'.

It all seemed appropriate – the mishmash of nations, elbowing each other for space as if in a crammed commuter bus of the subcontinent. Mr Malik had passed away some years ago, Vandana Dixit, who headed SAYA now, had informed her on the phone earlier. The office was on the second floor. Niki located a stairwell and started to climb.

It was a mid-sized room with desks arranged in two parallel rows, the rear wall lined with shelves and cupboards, some women, a sprinkling of men. She approached the nearest desk, where a bespectacled woman sat studying some pages, and enquired where she could find Ms Dixit.

'She has stepped out to the bank. Can I help?'

Niki explained that Ms Dixit had asked her to come in to discuss volunteering opportunities.

'Oh, good! We always need volunteers. I'm Sheila, by the way.'

As they shook hands, Sheila said, 'Why don't I show you around?' She bustled ahead, her pants riding up at the ankles as she walked. Niki hurried and fell in step, Sheila indicating people as they walked. 'Mr Sharma handles our accounts, Shermeen is in charge of admin, Lata and Maya are volunteers who come in three or four days a week.' They all looked up in acknowledgement, and Niki dipped her head in greeting. At the end of the rows of desks, Sheila paused, looking around. 'Jyotji should be around somewhere. She is our most senior volunteer,' she turned to look at Niki, 'both in age and years of service here, and she is the one we turn to when we need to know anything. You could say she's been here forever.'

Niki nodded, not trusting herself to speak. She didn't want to blurt out that Jyot was precisely the person she had come seeking.

Sheila gave a quick smile, brisk and efficient like the rest of her. 'What volunteer work would you like to help us with?'

Niki shrugged. 'I meant to discuss it with Ms Dixit. I can teach young children, help with spoken English or work with any other initiatives you have. I understand there is a certain amount of civic engagement that SAYA does as well.'

'Oh yes,' Sheila assessed Niki, crinkly hair pinned at her neck and fanning out at her back. 'Tuition for children and women is in demand for sure, especially English lessons.'

Niki looked around. It was an airy room, bare except for some functional furniture, with light streaming in from the two windows along one wall which probably faced west. The sound of traffic filtered through, mixed with the fragrance of incense and some spices.

'There!' Sheila indicated with her chin towards a corner which seemed to be a kitchenette. 'That's Jyotji.'

Niki watched a woman walk towards them with a large folder in her arms. She was dressed in baggy grey pants, a long-sleeved baggy blouse and a stole around her neck worn with a single loop in a manner that reminded Niki of a dupatta. She walked slowly, feet apart, a gait strangely evocative of a pregnant woman's waddle, which was odd because the woman, with grey-white hair receding from a broad, high forehead, was seventyish. As she drew nearer, Niki noticed her deep-set eyes, her face etched in wrinkles, a prominent mole on her chin. The wrinkles seemed excessive, like yards of wet muslin sagging on a narrow scaffold.

'Jyotji,' Sheila said, 'meet our new volunteer, Miss…' she frowned, trying to remember her name.

'Niki,' she smiled at Jyot.

At close quarters, her skin seemed papery, her hands holding the folder capable, veined and dotted with liver spots. Jyot wore a puzzled look.

'Niki, Niki Nalwa.'

Jyot's mouth parted slightly, followed by a sound like a strangled sigh, her eyes fixed upon Niki. Had she recalled her connection to the Nalwa family?

Sheila's phone pinged and she bent her head to read it.

Jyot said something, rather she attempted to say something, because her lips moved but no sound came out.

'What?' Niki said, dipping her head.

A whispery sound, softer than a leaf falling to the ground, and Niki didn't catch what was said. As she narrowed her eyes, Jyot swallowed hard, her mouth opened as if coming up for air, and said, 'You came back?'

'Haanji,' Sheila looked up from her phone and flicked it shut. Matter-of-factly, she took the folder from Jyot's slack hands, opened it to a page and began discussing a case. She was speaking animatedly about a recent development, while Jyot had her face bent.

Had she heard correctly?

Sheila walked with the folder to the rear shelf-lined wall. Niki turned to Jyot, who was scrutinizing her. 'Came back from *where*?' Niki asked.

The woman studied her with a keenness that seemed to summon an old intimacy.

'Do you remember Mrs Nalwa? Zohra Nalwa?' Niki asked, summoning Dadima's full name.

'Hunh,' Jyot muttered.

'My Dadima. You met her last,' she licked her lips, 'in December '84. In Machhiwara. Where she visited you…' But Jyot continued staring at her face. Odd. Niki steadied her bag on her left shoulder, though it didn't need steadying. 'I am here to volunteer. Have you been with SAYA for long?'

'Too long. It's been too long.'

Jyot's eyes had a faraway look, as if she had discovered something of interest on the horizon that extended behind Niki.

'Jyotji!' Sheila called.

The summons brought Jyot back to the present. She focused again on Niki. 'So long, it was so long,' she mumbled as she walked away. Her gait was stiff and slow, as if the joints in her body needed oiling.

That searching gaze, the puzzling question … Was Jyot's mind getting feeble? She was seventy years old, if not older, and a victim of two terrible tragedies. Enough to make anyone lose their mind. The excitement that had radiated out of Niki's stomach deflated, leaving her feeling cold and hollow.

XI
(2014)
Jyot

33
(2014)

✳

I DESCENDED FROM THE bus and joined the rush of pedestrians in Jackson Heights. I wanted to put some distance between the SAYA office and myself. I left early, unable to sit down or stand up, going to the bathroom again and again where I unzipped my pants and checked my legs, patting my dry crone skin in shock. Where was the warm liquid I was feeling trickle down my thighs, as if my water had broken…?

Had Niki come back? My blood had run backwards—

'I hope you don't drive like that! It was too close.'

The white woman was admonishing me stiffly for encroaching her personal space. I blinked. I must have weaved into her path. Ordinarily, I would have apologized, but my mind was scrambling like eggs on simmer. I pressed on through the mass of people, one heavy foot after another, my eyes unseeing yet seeing. Because what I was seeing was from a long time ago. Back, back, back. I bumped into somebody who swore and scowled. I was a public nuisance – someone would call the cops on a blind woman stumbling about Franklin Avenue.

There was a Key Food store to my left. I veered in. There were few people inside because it was late afternoon. I wandered into an aisle. A crochet cardigan I had knitted for Niki was in alternating pink and blue hexagons. It stopped just above her knees. She paired it with her brown corduroy jeans and with her long black hair and big eyes, she looked like Parveen Babi, the actress—

'*Ex-cuse* me!' an impatient voice urged.

I was standing in front of a refrigerator stocked with ice cream in candy-coloured wrappers. Beside me was a harried woman with a child in a stroller, trying to reach for the door I was blocking. The child's chubby cheeks were framed by brown ringlets, and if I scooped him up, he could be my Laali. The woman was eyeing me strangely. I was almost bent over the stroller examining her baby. I nodded, swallowed hard and stepped away.

Outside, amidst the focused bustle, I tried to gather my thoughts, knead them into pliable dough that I could shape to my needs. And thus, I reached my apartment building. In my hallway, the neighbour's cat watched me approach with unblinking eyes. All I had to do was reach out a hand and she would nuzzle against it, but I never did. Despite this, the cat would circle me, touch me with her tail, make friendly overtures. How simple it would be to fondle that little creature for comfort. The cat would press her face into my palm—

No. I did not allow myself any comfort.

Home Sweet Home.

As I passed that board on the neighbour's door, I remembered Mr Malik. Every time he returned to Amreeka, he said he liked being told by the immigration officer, 'Welcome home!' It made me wonder what I would feel if I ever took a flight and returned to those words. Home. Was this home? Where was home? Where one was welcomed, where one was born but thrown out of, where one fled from?

I unlocked my door and felt the cat's tail brush my leg. Years ago, Mr Malik had walked into the hospital a stranger, had me discharged and brought me to SAYA. Sixteen years I had been working at SAYA, finding relief in Mr Malik's advice: sometimes, the way to help ourselves is by helping others. The practice of that advice had kept me functioning. But now, my carefully stitched self seemed set to come apart like a cloth doll at the seams. As if my Niki, my eldest, had come back, with her dimpled cheeks, warm smile, trusting face...

And the past was colliding with my present.

XII
(2014)
There Is No Other

Conch shells blare and drums roll as the two armies meet on the battlefield of Kurukshetra. From his chariot, Arjuna gazes at the enemy, composed of his teachers and cousins, led by his great-uncle Bhishma, and panics. How will he raise arms against them? Their foremost warrior having lost his nerve, the Pandavas look set to lose the war before it has even begun...

34
(2014)

✳

THE DEADLINE FOR the submission of the manuscript was eleven months and twenty days away. Without Papa's original manuscript to build upon, Niki had only a few pages written, and she was stuck. The relocation allowed her a one-year sabbatical, 365 days that she could devote to her writing 24x7. All right, 24x7 allowing time for housework, laundry, grocery shopping and such sundries – the cost of being in a First World nation where the well-to-do couldn't afford help. Much unlike Hong Kong, where she had full-time help, as per the expat norm. Thankfully, their apartment on Columbus Avenue was a five-minute walk to Mehar's school on Central Park West.

Their neighbourhood of the Upper West Side, with its abundant brownstones and wide sidewalks, was so different from the Upper East Side, where her childhood friend Aruna lived. Wealth had come to the Upper East Side earlier, Aruna said, accounting for the residential high-rises. The Upper West, a.k.a., Upper Breast – a wink at its stroller-pushing mums – was the new-age old world.

Niki stepped away from her desk. There were household chores to be done. Arjun had forwarded an email from the building manager about a 'moth-like smell' from their apartment reported by another resident on the floor. The offending mothballs, which she had purchased from Bed Bath & Beyond, were legit. Besides, how could they cause the said offence several yards away through doors and thick walls? 'It's the smell of Indian food,' Arjun had concluded.

Niki fluffed and straightened the sofa pillows, stacked the pile of the *New York Times* on the centre table's lower deck, drank a glass of water and started to vacuum. Getting through to Dadima on the phone was proving tougher than she had thought: connectivity was either poor or Dadima wouldn't wear her hearing aid. Niki often called Tiny Uncle, who then hopped across from his house to continue the conversation.

Her two follow-up visits to SAYA had yielded little. Giving English lessons required her to be available in the evening, which was her time with Mehar. Besides, she needed a pretext for working with Jyot, whose demeanour was so stiff that Niki felt like she was trying to prise open a walnut.

At the window, something caught her eye and she switched the vacuum off. A flag waved in the breeze. It must have been there all along, the falling leaves revealing it only now. It stood in the capacious playground of a public school she had recently discovered. The plaque informed her the school, P. S. 166, had changed its name to the Richard Rodgers School of the Arts and Technology after an alumnus, Richard Rodgers. Of Rodgers & Hammerstein fame, she recalled with a tiny thrill of serendipity. The one musical film she absolutely loved was *The Sound of Music*, and to stumble upon the school where one of them went, one street from where she lived – why, it seemed like an omen! Of what exactly, she didn't know yet. In that sense, even her book-in-progress seemed shrouded in a similar exciting yet perplexing veil of potential, seething with possibility, yet, unyielding.

Growing up, Niki was aware that the past had been a living presence in her home, kept alive through its stories. Along with myths, epics, fables and folktales, the past was another fount of stories. However, she could not locate that past in her textbooks, which were chronological records of dates and facts, leached of life, dull as the newsreels of the Films Division with their desultory take on the freedom movement or the Bengal Famine.

And yet, the past was present everywhere. In the way people invoked Old Man Bullah to comment on life's vagaries. The manner in which the Afghan plunderer Abdali would pop up in droll observations of corrupt politicians. In a classmate, Sikander Singh, named after Alexander who had come seeking India in 326 BCE, whose one legacy was generations of namesake Indians. One could not go far without being informed that Ram had hunted in that thicket or Sita had rested in this bower.

That was why Papa's book, with its attempt to put forgotten people and their individual pain at the centre of epochal events, was so important. History was alive and entangled in the everyday stories of India, and it needed to be coaxed onto the pages of a book. In that sense, history was a woman, substantial, vigorous, complex and always given the customary short shrift. Like the legendary Anarkali or Heer or Draupadi. Or Sita even – not the long-suffering consort of Lord Rama, but the single mother who brought up her sons in a forest, who refused to return to her husband when he finally called her back, choosing instead to return to Mother Earth. Or Jyot, who had lived through two cataclysms – to tell her tale? No, that story needed coaxing ... Niki sighed and powered the vacuum cleaner.

==

That evening, Niki asked her husband, 'Why do you think Indians are so uninterested in their history?'

'Too much of it?' Arjun quipped. 'Too dusty? Is there much historical fiction out of India done in an interesting way?'

'True,' Niki said. 'Look at how the Holocaust is a subject for reworking in the West. Every year, a novel with that theme appears on the Booker longlist. Or the Pulitzer. Or whatever. You can be in India or China or Australia but if you read novels, you will have made sufficient acquaintance with Nazi villainy in concentration camps which, three generations later, a grandchild of a Holocaust victim will travel from USA to Europe to learn about first-hand. I just wish we Indians had a modicum of that too.'

'To do what?' Arjun asked.

'To memorialize, to remember, to sear it in our hearts so we never go down that path again. You think the schizophrenic Indo-Pak dynamic of love-hate-war-peace has nothing to do with '47? That the past doesn't intrude upon the present all the time? Did we lay the ghosts to rest? Do we tell the stories? Talk about them with our children and grandchildren? Do we have memorials to honour the ten million who trudged across the Radcliffe Line or a memorial for the one million who died? No monument to the unknown soldier here either. Weren't these victims of the sectarian mayhem of '47 heroes too? No truth and reconciliation committee. Ireland had it. As did South Africa. Even Tunisia's got one. Do we not need accountability and fact-finding? We let the killers go scot-free then, and now we complain of a lack of accountability in our culture! We reap what we sow.'

'Great, so finish writing your Great Indian Book!' He turned to the Blackberry in his hand.

Niki felt miffed by his dismissal, but she did tend to lose control when the issue of Partition came up. 'It's not easy,' she said. She sounded lame even to herself.

Arjun looked at her with raised brows that implied 'what is?' and merely said, 'Got to take a few calls.' With the phone to his ear, he walked into the bedroom.

Arjun's work hours were separated only by sleep. Perhaps not. Like the erstwhile Raj, the sun never set upon his work which spanned from USA to Hong Kong. If Niki was working, it would be similarly crushing hours. And the clock was ticking.

She must find a way to make Jyot talk.

35
(2014)

✤

MEHAR WASN'T SLEEPING at night. It was daytime in Hong Kong, when her friends were awake and available to chat.

'But it's ten in the night!' Niki indicated the bedroom clock.

'Shhh, Amma,' Mehar frowned from her laptop. 'Yeah, well, they have to do everything their way ... the traffic signal's green light is white, you drive on the right side of the road, and you cain't, just cain't, cain't, cain't speak with anything but an American accent. Because guess what? America knows best! Pffft!' She thrust her tongue out.

Niki heard excited screams and chatter from the laptop. She walked to Mehar's bed and peered at the screen. Three excited heads of schoolgirls in uniform were bobbing on the screen.

'Hello Aunty!'

'Hi!'

Niki smiled and summoned enthusiasm. 'Isn't this school time?'

'Yes!' they chorused.

'Amma,' Mehar hissed, 'it's break time. Can I finish my conversation please?'

189

Niki waved to the girls and as she backed off, she tapped the clock on her way out.

Arjun walked out of their bedroom after a marathon call. Indicating Mehar's room with a thumb, he asked, 'Isn't that late?'

Niki raised a hand in irritated acknowledgement. Mehar was missing her friends, some of whom she had studied with since kindergarten. But school started at 8 a.m. and this was cutting into sleep time. She hovered in the hallway until the byes were issued.

'Why don't you speak with them over the weekend like we discussed?'

Mehar shook her head. 'Because they have things to do over the weekend. Swimmong, soccer, violin lessons – remember Hong Kong, Amma?'

Niki sighed. 'But you're late for bed. It's 10.30 p.m.!'

'Not the end of the world.' Mehar slid into bed.

'Don't speak to me in that tone, young lady.'

'Don't "young lady" me!'

Niki could hear her breath snorting through her nostrils. Babaji, she invoked Guru Nanak, grant me patience. 'Let's discuss it over the weekend, shall we?'

Mehar had pulled the blanket over her head. Her voice sounded thick. 'By which time I'll have no friends left.'

==

A plane sailed through the sky above as Niki made her way to SAYA, leaping over a puddle on the curb. Hello Kitty greeted her with the relentless waving of her golden arm as Niki stepped into the building. There was an elevator at the rear, but she preferred to take the steps to the second floor. She had offered to assist with SAYA's outreach activities. Ms Dixit thought her consulting background was a good fit. Of course, it helped Niki's cause that Jyot was in charge of the programme. Niki saw Sheila tucking into her lunch and listening to music as she checked a file.

'Hi! Come, sit,' Sheila called out. 'Lunch?'

'I had a late breakfast,' Niki said. 'Please go ahead – I don't mean to disturb you.'

'Oh no, no formality! We aren't American,' she scoffed. 'I am an American citizen, but you know what I mean. We Indians don't believe in needless formality.'

Niki concurred with a smile as she took a chair. The melodious music caught her attention with its soulful rendition of a Sufi song, but she couldn't place the singer. When she enquired, Sheila replied it was Mr Malik.

'The singer, I meant. Who is he?'

'Mr Malik, of course. He was a popular singer, didn't you know?'

Niki shrugged. She didn't know much about Mr Malik, except that he had founded SAYA in 1995.

'When I joined SAYA in 2005, Mr Malik didn't sing officially any more, but when he was coaxed to sing, at functions or celebrations, he would make people go into raptures! He was,' Sheila chewed a morsel in thought, 'probably eighty-five years old then. Yes, he died three years later at eighty-eight.'

'Was he a professional singer?' Papa had known this man with a mellifluous voice. Sufi music must have been one way for them to connect. She wished she had read the letters they had exchanged, that Dadima would find Mr Malik's transcript and Papa's missing manuscript...

'He used to be.' Sheila sipped water. 'But you should ask Jyotji, she knew him the longest.' As she capped the water bottle, Jyot appeared in the doorway and Sheila waved her over. Niki watched the elderly lady walk with a pregnant woman's waddle. Jyot ignored her as she stopped at Sheila's desk.

'I was telling Niki here that you knew Mr Malik the best.'

'No. People knew him as much as he wanted them to know.'

Sheila frowned. 'But you did know him the longest, right, out of all of us at SAYA?'

'Yes,' Jyot replied in what Niki was realizing was an audio version of her stiff demeanour. Sheila, though, was unfazed. 'Exactly.' She picked up a sheet of paper and passed it to Jyot. 'The details of our November event. Ms Dixit said Niki should be able to come up with ideas for flyers and a page for our website.' She beamed from Niki to Jyot, the sheet in her hand.

With Jyot making no attempt to accept the sheet, Niki took it. 'Shall we?' She nodded to her and walked to the oval desk, which was used by part-time volunteers.

Jyot pulled a chair and sat down, back upright, her eyes on the sheet on the table. For one who had acted strangely familiar at their first meeting, she was rather uptight now. She watched Jyot mouth the words silently, reading slowly as she went down the printed note, her right index finger sliding along the paper with each word read. Clearly, she had learnt English late in life. She spoke it with the colloquial manner of immigrants, her speech peppered with 'you knows' and 'yeahs' in an exaggerated American accent. Niki waited for her to finish reading.

'That was a beautiful kaafi I heard,' Niki started. 'Sheila said it was sung by Mr Malik.'

No response.

'Was he Indian or Pakistani?'

Jyot didn't look up. Her face was lined with perspiration, even though it was a pleasant day.

'Are you okay? Here,' Niki offered her a wipe. When she didn't take it, Niki tucked it in her hand. Startled, Jyot clutched it and wiped her face in a perfunctory manner.

'Okay. I'm okay,' Jyot hastened to say. 'What were you asking?'

'Mr Malik. Where did he come from?'

'Nobody knew. He was South Asian, yuno, male, but Indian or Pakistani? Hindu or Muslim? He never told, yuno.'

Yuno? U-no? You know. 'Ah!' Niki acknowledged. In the subcontinent, religion was one big identity marker, something that announced itself in a person's name certainly; appearance, on occasions; choice of profession, at times. A South Asian was a genealogy hobbyist, attempting to pin down every new acquaintance in a matrix of religion, region, caste, community.

Should she ask a few basic questions to break the recurring silence? 'When did he come to the US?'

Jyot shrugged. 'Early '80s. He opened SAYA in the '90s.'

'He had a lovely singing voice. Did he perform publicly?'

'He was the must-have guest at every South Asian wedding in Jackson Heights.'

'When immigrants organize an event, what they want after native food is native music, right?'

Jyot tossed her chin in agreement. 'His voice was … as if coated with jaggery. It made people dance in the beginning and tear up towards the end.'

'Wow!' This was going well. 'So when did you meet him first?'

Jyot stilled. 'When I was taken to the hospital by cops, they contacted Mr Malik upon learning I lived alone.' Jyot looked Niki in the eye.

Niki licked suddenly dry lips.

Jyot glanced at her. 'The cops knew that new arrivals in Jackson Heights found their way to Mr Malik. Hindu, Muslim, Indian, Pakistani, Nepali – no matter, yuno.'

'Sounds like he was truly Sufi.'

'Mr Malik said that many people are Sufi, though they may not know it themselves. Like Lincoln, yuno.'

'Lincoln?'

'Amreeki president. He has a famous quote, "Do I not destroy my enemy when I make him a friend?" Mr Malik said that proved Lincoln was a Sufi.'

'Ah!'

'But they killed him.'

Niki was taken aback. 'Lincoln, yes, he was assassinated.'

Jyot didn't respond; her shoulders seemed to have caved in. She appeared weighed down, an immense sadness emanating from her.

Her face, wreathed in wrinkles, was at her chest. There was something ancient, primitive, defenceless about Jyot, as if life had robbed her of her soul. Niki wanted to reach out. Her hand hovered over the sheet of paper, unsure.

'Tea?' Sheila's voice rang out. 'I am making some.'

Niki looked at Jyot, who hadn't stirred. 'Yes, please, for both of us.' Sheila nodded and bustled off to the pantry with the stove in the rear of the office.

Niki touched the sheet. 'This event,' she said softly and waited.

'Yes,' Jyot said and raised herself with such deliberation that Niki had a vision of a bent figure uncoiling one rib at a time until the spine was erect. 'The event was Mr Malik's idea. After 9/11. When men with turbans were attacked and called Osama, diaperhead, Bin Laden and other such abuses. Mr Malik said we needed an event where Americans could see us and learn about us. The first event had a mehndi stall and a food stall with samosas and ginger tea. A few people came, and got a henna tattoo and a cup of tea, and one newspaper person also came. Next year, we added bhangra and Mr Malik sang Sufi songs, especially the ones sung by Nusrat, whom the Amreeki know.' Jyot paused.

She had spoken at length for the first time without the ubiquitous 'yuno'. 'And the event has continued since then?'

'Yes. Every year. Now, more people come; we speak with them, they speak with us. Each year, we all get less ignorant. Mr Malik always said violence comes from ignorance. When we get to know someone, we find how alike we really are.'

'What a wonderful initiative, getting Americans and others together,' Niki said.

Jyot looked straight into Niki's eyes, shook her head slightly and said, 'No. I didn't explain it well. Let me try again. Mr Malik liked to say he was a human-in-training. Once, someone asked him when he would know he had finished his training and become fully human.'

Niki listened. When Jyot spoke thus, her voice shed that wooden quality.

'We are all one. When he fully imbibed that truth, he would know. That's what Mr Malik said. Ignorance was the reason for violence, he believed. The moment we realize that there *is* no other, then all violence towards others becomes violence at our own selves.'

At the subway station, Niki's phone pinged. It was an email from the head of the middle school, with the subject, 'What happens when children don't get enough sleep?'

Niki skimmed the email with alarm.

'It has come to our notice that some children in the class are not getting enough sleep ... National Sleep Foundation ... recommended sleep ... Sleep deprivation linked to risky behaviour and moodiness...'

She blew air out of her mouth and read it again. No specific mention of Mehar – yet. But this was a warning.

XIII
(2002)
Jyot

36
(2002)

✳

I HEARD A BIRD. It was somewhere in a tree, but I couldn't locate it even after I craned my neck and spent several minutes seeking it. A robin, I was told, is the herald for spring in Amreeka. Its song surprised me – it was too robust for such a tiny body. But there it was, clear loud whistles, like some summons: 'Come out and play, spring is in the air!'

I was to take the girl to the museum in Manhattan, the Metropolitan Museum of Art, the Met, and wait in Central Park for four hours before bringing her back. The girl had her spring break, and my madam had planned a museum series for her. The first week we were doing five museums over five days – well, the girl was, and I was to ferry her back and forth and shop for groceries in between. The boy had a soccer camp for which a bus took him and dropped him back. And he had a key to let himself in.

The thermostat said forty-one degrees Fahrenheit, which was about five degrees centigrade. So many years in Amreeka, and I still needed to convert the temperature to centigrade to assess it. It would be warmish, a day to wear a salwar kameez. After four months of

197

winter, all I wanted was to stuff the pants and shirts and jackets and coats and mufflers and gloves and hats out of sight, and wear a cotton Punjabi suit and breathe. But I had to go to Manhattan and if I wore Indian clothes, people would look at me. Only in Jackson Heights, at times, at the height of summer, when people dressed strangely as a custom, did I wear salwar kameez outdoors. But I would need a coat, which came up to my knees so that only the salwar would be visible... I opened the window. A cool breeze. And the robin whistled again. A salwar kameez, I decided.

After dropping the girl at the Met, I walked to Central Park. I bought coffee from a Bangladeshi vendor and picked my way carefully over the sidewalk – winters in Amreeka had taught me that the scariest thing was not snow, but black ice. My first winter's encounter with it was fresh in my mind. That day, the temperatures had been above freezing as I stepped out. Then, it began to rain. As water hit the sidewalk, the tarmac began to glisten, and the next step was a free slide, after which I was on the ground, my bum stinging from the fall. When I placed my hands on the ground, I found thin ice below. What black magic was this? Someone leaned over, a capable looking man who said he would help me get up. With his hands under my elbows, he propped me up and I thanked the gora gentleman. He said something about black ice, about how it formed quickly as rain fell, even if the temperature was in the forties because the asphalt – he stabbed the sidewalk with his toe – was still colder and the difference in temperature created thin ice. It was trickier because the black ice was transparent and there was no visible snow or ice around. Nice man, like a kind teacher. I never forgot that lesson. I fell a few more times, but each made me more cautious. Looking around the park, I saw a bench around a curve, good for a coffee stop.

The drone of machines filled the air as park workers hacked ice and trimmed trees. A few visitors with cameras roamed the park. Nearby, sparrows perched on a fence, plump with new down. The sun was spreading like honey through the sky, bathing tree trunks and the thinning ice with a golden glow. To my right was a bush

with no leaves but bunches of black berries that had withstood the
winter. Dew from last night's rain clung to the bare branches. The
swoosh of cars, a dog's bark, the flap of wings and the sound of
someone laughing carried over the wind to where I sat. I took a sip
of coffee and looked up. The leafless plane tree fanned like a skeleton
umbrella, and on a branch high up was a ball of fur. I narrowed my
eyes. A squirrel curled up. In that moment, it seemed that the earth
and sky and everything in between was just where it needed to be,
that everything was as it should be, and I felt something like joy
loosen within me. It had been so long it hurt—

Something jabbed at the side of my head. I reeled, the coffee
spilled, running down the folds of my salwar. A rough hand grabbed
my left shoulder, and there was another hard shove at the side of my
head. 'You think you can come here and kill us? Ha?'

The voice was shrill. It belonged to a man who wore blue jeans,
badly scuffed at the ankles and knees. I saw him from the corner of
my eyes.

'I'm gonna blow your brains out, bitch! If you don't go back where
you came from, I'm gonna send your brains back!' He jabbed again,
a pressing down motion for emphasis. There was a gun at my head.

'Go back to your country, bitch, where you birthed the crazies
who fly planes into our buildings.' He spat, the sputum flying in
volleys in the air, landing on my left cheek, and my hand which held
the coffee cup, and my coat.

The time had come. I felt nothing, not even relief. One trigger
and I would know peace. Or nothingness. If there was an afterlife, as
the gurus said, then I wanted nothing more than for the trigger to be
pulled now. In the afterlife, I would meet my Niki-Veer-Soni-Laali-
Jeet again. I closed my eyes.

'Get ready, bitch!' the man shouted and pulled the trigger.

A lull. I opened my eyes. My brains were not scattered all over
me, I was breathing still, the sparrows were perched on the fence still.
The gun had failed. I had not died. Again. A laugh bubbled through
me. It burst out of my mouth like an exuberant 'ha!' and I started to

laugh hysterically. The hand holding the gun slackened against my head. I was tittering now, snickering at this world and its absurdity. Every day, people who didn't want to die died and those who wished for death with every breath lived on. Life was cruel, but death was a tease, and the only word for people like me was 'mar jiware', the living dead.

'*Crayyy-zy* bitch!' the man hollered.

I turned to face him. He was young, his pimpled face flushed red as he waved his fake gun in my face. He turned and fled around the corner, vanishing from view.

'Go back to where you came from!' floated upon the air.

I looked at the cold coffee in my hand, the sputum drying on me, my wet, stained salwar above those ridiculous sports shoes I wore. My throat was hoarse from that laughing fit. A sparrow flitted near me, pecking at the ground. Only in this world did moments collide so violently. The sparrow was proof that I had been happy, just for a moment, suspended like a dew drop. And now it was gone. Life had trampled over it. I got up and dropped the coffee in a waste bin. From my bag, I retrieved a tissue paper and started to wipe my cheek and hand and jacket. My salwar clung to me like a weeping child.

XIV
(2014)
Yoga

When Arjuna is unable to raise his arms, his charioteer-cum-mentor Krishna walks him through the Bhagavad Gita as he counsels him on the yoga of a warrior: Arjuna must act fearlessly, without desire or hope of reward or glory or success even. Krishna reveals his divine form, which blazes on the battlefield. Enlightened, Arjuna reposes his faith in the almighty and picks up his bow to resume his duty. A fierce battle ensues. For eighteen days, blood flows like a river in spate, and the earth is stilled such that not even a blade of grass grows. Both sides are equally matched but white-robed Bhishma, whose locks are silver from decades of experience, is invincible. If the Pandavas are to win, Arjuna must find a way to kill his great-uncle...

37
(2014)

✳

NIKI DISCOVERED A yoga studio on 84th Street between Central Park West and Columbus Avenue and took a trial class one afternoon. It was after lunch and the class was relatively empty. Of course, relative in Manhattan was itself relative; she could confirm that during the asanas, no part of her body was elbowed and none of her chakras was interfered with. The 2 p.m. slot worked for her, allowing her to return home in time for Mehar. She needed yoga to bring down her stress levels.

Niki rooted herself to the ground, palms together in front of her chest as the teacher demonstrated the first posture of the twelve asanas that made up the Surya Namaskar, the sun salutation. Inhale. Exhale. She was in the stick pose when she became aware of a sotto voce recitation beside her. Since Niki did her asanas with her eyes closed, she could not confirm its source. As she returned to tadasana, the teacher announcing the completion of a cycle of sun salutation, a breathy 'baai jat sik' floated in the air. Niki turned to the woman standing upright to her left. Blonde hair in a high ponytail, complexion like low-fat milk. 'Wei?'

The woman turned. Freckles rode her cheeks like butterfly wings. 'Ni hao ma?'

'Wo hao, ni? And that's the extent of my Mandarin!' Niki grinned, ducking as the teacher's voice rose in consternation at the chatter and the class bent waist downwards. Her neighbour winked as they resumed their yoga poses. The sibilant chant resumed as they progressed to the warrior pose.

At the end of their lesson, Niki and her Mandarin-speaking classmate fell in step as they made their way out. 'Oonagh,' she said as they shook hands. 'I learnt yoga while in Beijing; that's why the Mandarin names of the poses.'

'Ah! I'm Niki. How long were you there?'

'Five years. Enough time to see the country and learn its language.'

'I spent eleven years in Hong Kong and cannot speak beyond two sentences,' Niki said ruefully. 'Though, in my defence, Hong Kong is Cantonese speaking.'

They had reached Columbus Avenue. The white man was alight in the direction of 85th Street. 'Coffee?' Niki jerked a thumb in the direction of Starbucks. She had an hour left to get to Mehar's extracurricular class.

'Sure,' Oonagh said. 'Care for better coffee though? I know a place on 79th between Broadway and Amsterdam.'

'Am still figuring out the neighbourhood. Great coffee recommendations are just what I need.' They crossed and walked south.

'Relocated from Hong Kong?'

'Yup. Husband's job. And my book.' Where had that come from? Niki felt insecure with a new acquaintance if she had to admit she wasn't working.

'You're a writer?' Oonagh's blue eyes were on her.

Niki shrugged. 'I am trying to complete a book.' A pooch on a long leash wound his way between them and the owner, and they wove around the sidewalk attempting to untangle. Changing the topic, Niki ventured, 'Did you travel to India from Beijing?'

Oonagh shook her head. 'I wanted to, but I couldn't convince any of my girlfriends to accompany me. My boyfriend had left me by then.'

'Well, yes, it may be sensible not to travel by yourself as a woman. I hate to say this of my country, but it's unsafe in parts.'

'But that's true of any country. China. The US, even,' Oonagh shrugged one shoulder. 'Women are the world's largest minority, eh?'

They had arrived at a coffee shop tucked between two narrow brownstones. Niki had walked by it several times but never noticed the discreet storefront sign: Irving Farms.

'How do you like your coffee?' Oonagh asked as she led the way down a few steps.

'Strong, hot, a dash of milk.'

Oonagh winked. 'Let me introduce you to the city's best cortado!' Ten minutes later, Oonagh eyed the milky leaf pattern atop her coffee. 'I am a sucker for pretty food,' she said, and sipped appreciatively. 'How do you find living in New York City?'

Exciting. Similar to HK, yet different. You know how all big metropolises are the same? The regular clichés sprang to Niki's mouth. But there was no need to bullshit. 'Challenging,' she said.

Oonagh angled her head in acknowledgement. 'Every move takes time. How many months do you give yourself?'

'A year.'

'Practical. Why hurry?'

Well, there was a need to get going: a book to accomplish; a child to settle into school, city, life; a job to resume…

'It took me longer when I returned from China. And I am practically a native. Grew up in New Jersey. Went to NYU.'

'What did you study?'

'English literature. Except,' Oonagh swigged the last of her coffee, holding the cup above her mouth as the last foamy drops descended sluggishly, 'I left college midway – to go backpacking across China with my graduating boyfriend.'

Bold. 'Awesome,' Niki said, imitating the kind of response Americans seemed to throw in when encountering something unexpected.

'It was too. Though not how I expected. We travelled across the country, from Guangdong to Xian, from the coast to Tibet, by the end of which I had the rudiments of Mandarin and the dregs of a relationship. My boyfriend moved in with a Chinese girl in Shanghai.' She shrugged. 'Having forfeited my scholarship because of the unplanned break, I decided to stay on, learn Mandarin, see Asia ... There was a huge demand to teach English; a gweilo fit right in.' Oonagh raised her eyebrows.

Niki laughed at the Cantonese term for Westerners. 'Gweilo, yes.'

'So, tell me, how do I meet you in a Friday afternoon yoga class meant for tai-tais?' Oonagh angled her head at a group of moms chatting at a circular table.

Oonagh sure was up to date with her Cantonese slang for women of leisure. 'I am on an year's sabbatical from my job as a strategic advertising consultant – to complete a book.'

'A year to write a book! I love your life.'

'Finish it, actually. My father's book.'

'You threw me a curveball there!' Oonagh slid forward. 'You're completing your father's book because?'

'He passed away.' Niki's lower lip trembled, and she looked away.

'Oh, honey!' Oonagh's right hand enveloped Niki's free one.

Niki shrugged and sighed. 'And your tai-tainess is because?'

'Because I work shitty hours Monday to Thursday so that I can get Friday off to go to college, complete my assignments and squeeze in some fitness.'

'Which college?'

'City College, up in Harlem. Part-time but, fingers crossed and courses ticked off, I should have a master's in education in eighteen months. Then, I can expect to make more than a slave's wages. The

CVS pharmacist job pays barely enough to keep me in a railroad apartment.'

'Railroad?'

'Uh-huh. Like a train compartment? Where you need to go through one room to get to the next. No hallway. It's okay, there are two of us women and we suffer each other.' Oonagh snorted. 'I have learnt to sleep with the TV on full blast. I swear her boyfriend makes more noise than an express train in the subway!'

Niki started to giggle. Oonagh joined in and their laughter drew an irate glance from the woman at the next table, her hands flying off the laptop like a manic pianist's. A phone rang.

'Oh, heavens!' Niki shot up as Mehar's name lit up her iPhone. 'My daughter's school got over ten minutes back!'

38
(2014)

✳

'MANHATTAN IS SHIT,' Mehar declared as she packed her school bag. 'Brooklyn is nice.'

'*Whaa-t*?' Niki sputtered into her teacup.

Mehar grinned. 'Gotcha! We are learning geology in Science. Manhattan is built on a rock type called schist, which forms the island's spine. You see it in Central Park, Amma, in the rock that glitters? While Brooklyn is gneiss.'

Ah! Niki didn't want to show her evident relief. 'Now this is serious nerdy stuff you can teach Percy Jackson!' She pushed her chair back. 'Time to go.'

'One sec,' Mehar approached with her laptop. 'What do you think?'

A black cat with intense green eyes studied Niki from the screen. 'Nice.'

'She's beautiful,' Mehar sang as she swivelled the laptop away, shut it down and stuffed it in her backpack. 'Shall I book us an appointment this Sunday then?'

Whether her parents were ready or not, Mehar was going full-steam ahead at executing a cat adoption. They had promised her a dog on her twelfth birthday, but that was with Hong Kong in mind, live-in domestic help and reasonable weather aiding the promise. A dog in Manhattan would limit mobility, add sizeable dog-sitting costs to their monthly bills and create enough work without considering that a dog needed to be walked three to four times even in deep winter. The relocation agent had suggested a cat as a watered-down solution which, in a weak moment, Niki had disclosed. Since then, Mehar had begun educating herself on cats, and upon arrival in NYC, registered on the website of PetCo, which helped place rescue cats in loving homes. Now Mehar was shortlisting cats she'd identified as suitable for their home and emailing PetCo with her interest.

'Shouldn't we settle down first?' Niki avoided Mehar's eyes as she grabbed the keys.

Mehar crossed her arms over her chest, backpack slung over one shoulder. 'A pet was supposed to help me settle down, remember?'

Niki nodded and ushered her out of the door. The only glitch was that Arjun, having grown up with no animals, had no inclination to share a house with one. Meanwhile, Mehar had hinted darkly at kidnapping a pigeon from the sidewalk if her parents continued to dither.

As they walked to school, Mehar maintained a sullen silence. Niki tried to talk about school and friends, but she might as well have been conversing with the sidewalk upon which her daughter's eyes were glued. At the school steps, she was stiff as Niki embraced her and once inside, Mehar did not look back as usual.

In a quandary, Niki turned to Central Park West, straight in the face of passengers springing forth from the subway exit.

'Didi!' Sister. A South Asian man was hailing her. She stopped.

'Fifth Avenue. How do I go?'

'Cut across the park,' Niki pointed towards the entrance to Central Park from 86th Street.

A brisk nod, and he was off.

Since Jyot was not in office, Niki offered to assist Sheila with sorting and arranging files at SAYA, some of which dated back to the organization's beginning in 1995. Much as nature abhorred a vacuum, Sheila disdained silence, filling the spaces around her with her voice or music.

Leaning forward, Sheila passed Niki a cardboard sheet. A group photograph in fading colour. She tapped the middle, where a man stood, hands clasped in front of him. 'You were asking about Mr Malik. There he is.'

'He doesn't look very old.'

'This was,' she studied the photograph, 'soon after I joined – 2006.' The year was scribbled in the top right corner of the cardboard mount. 'Mr Malik would have been eighty-four or eighty-five. But you are right. He had a radiance about him. All that unmitigated goodness,' she smiled.

'Hmm.'

'That sounded bitchy, no?' Sheila laughed. 'But when people are so good, it makes me wonder what they are hiding.' She gave a slow, elephant-like nod. 'He made a perfect Santa though! The beard and the radiance. One forgot he had a useless leg.'

'Useless leg?'

'Uh-huh, he swivelled by the hip with every step forward.' Sheila stacked a folder onto an empty shelf. 'He was a sepoy in the Second World War. He didn't talk about it much, but I heard someone enquire and Mr Malik, as was his habit, didn't talk about his injury but wondered why it was still called "world war".'

'Meaning?'

Sheila shrugged. 'Mr Malik said it was Europe's war, one European nation fighting another for supremacy. Then why call it a world war?'

'Yeah,' Niki nodded. 'Like the War on Terror. It's essentially an American war, but what is good for America is good for the rest of the world, right?'

Sheila regarded Niki and gave her an elephant-like nod again. 'I guess you are right. Mr Malik and you would have got along well.'

He sounded like someone who questioned received wisdom. A true Sufi. Niki was brought up by one such woman, whose Old Man Bullah was Punjab's great Sufi mystic. Returning to the photograph, Niki said, 'I see you, Ms Sheila.'

She tapped the young sari-clad woman to the extreme left of the row of standees.

'My hair?' Sheila commented at the bountiful crinkly hair, which the cardboard seemed barely able to contain.

Niki nodded. 'You look lovely.'

'And slim.' Sheila slapped her wide girth. 'The Indian woman's hips had yet to emerge out of my nubile self.' Sheila shrieked with laughter, her set cynical face melting to reveal a softness. She studied the photograph. 'A lot of people have moved on, but Jyotji is still here.'

Niki saw her to the left of Mr Malik, looking as old as Mr Malik looked ageless. 'What was the occasion for this photograph?'

'Independence Day, Pakistan and India. It's handy that they follow each other: August 14 and 15. We'd have a skit by the children, a fancy-dress competition, and much singing, led by Mr Malik, of course.'

Niki handed the photograph back to Sheila.

'Jyotji looks glum, understandably – Partition orphan, you see.' She slid it within the plastic sheaf of a folder. 'So, how are you finding everything? Settled in now?'

'No, not at all. I've given myself a year, and it's been what, four weeks?'

'It's not easy,' Sheila nodded, 'moving from one end of the world. Personally, I found winter the worst, wading through all that snow. It all seemed so romantic, seeing heroines dance in chiffon saris on top of snowy Swiss mountains, but clearly Bollywood directors never tried living with that snow.' She tossed her head disdainfully.

'We are getting kitted up, buying snow boots and duvet coats. Mehar, my daughter, though, can't wait for it to start snowing.'

'Children,' Sheila smiled. She returned to her perusal of the folder before looking up and leaning closer. 'How is it working with Jyotji?'

'All right, I guess.'

'She can be difficult, but she has a good heart.' Sheila gave that brisk smile, which disappeared almost before it appeared, a curious illusion. 'Mr Malik's death was tough on her, but she doesn't show it.'

'What do you mean?'

'He was her only friend.'

'Only friend? She's been here for what, thirty years or so?'

'Yes, but I can tell you she's friendly with nobody at SAYA. And the few times I visited her home, I realized no one in the building knows her. She keeps to herself.'

'That must be awfully lonely.'

'She's a,' Sheila leaned so close her bosom spreadeagled across the accordion folder she was browsing, her breath on Niki's face – whatever she'd had for breakfast was tempered generously with asafoetida – 'chaurasiye. An '84-er, you understand?'

Chaurasiye.

Niki felt a stab of grief. One day after school, she had gone with a classmate to her home in one of the two satellite towns of Chandigarh. Mohali abutted the City Beautiful and lay within Punjab. Her friend lived in a bungalow in an area that was still developing. A large tract of land extended from the rear wall of the house, overgrown with weeds but plotted and sold, waiting to be built up. In the distance was a row of tenements that her friend dismissed as Chaurasiye Colony. Her father said the shabby, unregulated housing was affecting the market value of their property. As a wealthy businessman, he would know. Niki paid no more attention, until she was back home and telling Papa and Dadima over dinner.

'Chaurasiye Colony,' Papa repeated.

Something about his manner made Niki enquire further.

'What do you think the name means?' he said.

'A surname?' Like Hariprasad Chaurasia, the flautist, she thought, CDs of whose music were stacked amongst Nusrat Fateh Ali Khan qawwalis and Mehdi Hassan ghazals.

'The term "chaurasiye" refers to the victims of the anti-Sikh riots of '84. Quite a few Sikhs migrated from Delhi to Punjab in the aftermath. This, I believe, is a group of families that moved from Trilokpuri.'

'Is the government resettling them here?' A ten-year-old's naiveté equated government with governance.

Papa snorted. 'Nothing so benign or constructive. The cases against the rioters are pending in courts, in the rare instances where cases were registered by the police. These families, I guess, just decided they would be safer in Punjab than in our capital city.'

For the longest time for Niki, 1984 was the name of George Orwell's famous novel. After that conversation with Papa, and through observing his work as she grew up, she learnt that memory holes were not a fantasy. It was entirely possible for a modern-day event, reported by media, documented by human rights groups, and politicized by political opponents, to disappear down the chute of apathy and cover-ups, to be sidelined so skilfully that its victims were branded for life and yet had no admissible evidence of their victimhood. The areas where the pogrom occurred had no surviving residents to report the widespread massacre. No. Na. Nahin. Nothing. All sucked down the chute of the memory hole. Only the term remained – chaurasiye – to haunt the survivors. And the survivors were unpersons, their version of events did not count. A non-event that left unpersons in its wake. As a matter of fact, Orwell had not been writing fantasy – he had been uncommonly prescient.

'When did Jyotji come to America?' Niki asked.

'Some time after the '84 riots. I don't know when exactly, though. She doesn't talk about it.'

At the sound of approaching footsteps, Niki swivelled in her chair. Jyot was waddling up, a girl in her wake. She stopped at Sheila's table.

'This here,' she pointed to the girl who was now standing behind her, 'is Asha Singh. She will need to stay at the shelter for some days.'

Asha was dressed in faded jeans and a slouchy sweatshirt that sat on her like a gunny bag. Her dark hair fell straight as a cliff to her waist. With her smooth olive skin and prominent cheekbones, she could have been Native American, even Indian. She clutched a backpack tightly as she perched on the chair Niki had just vacated.

Sheila studied the new arrival.

'My new neighbour, next door,' Jyot said.

'Hmm,' Sheila acknowledged with a lift of her bushy brows. She reached for a folder, licked an index finger and flipped the pages.

'Her grandmother Juanita owns the apartment. Juanita had a Mexican mother and Sikh father. Her daughter, Asha's mother, doesn't know who Asha's father exactly is. Her boyfriend wants to pimp out Asha now. He thinks she's old enough at fourteen.'

Sheila sighed as she made an entry in the folder.

Niki, righteous anger furrowing her brow, said, 'Why doesn't her mother object?'

'Her boyfriend is her pimp too.'

'What about the cops? Won't they help?'

'The mother will get arrested for illegal possession of drugs. Perhaps Asha too. The man will just vanish.'

'I thought it was different here.'

'Different from?' Jyot asked. Sheila listened with one raised brow.

'Different from India, you know? Where you can't count on the cops?'

Jyot gave her a look of pity. 'It's all the same,' and the sweep of her hand took in Asha and herself, 'for people like us.'

In India, Niki would not approach the cops on her own, and definitely not the Punjab 'Pulce', as the police was deprecatingly called. What worked were either political connections or wealth or both. She had seen Papa, a well-regarded criminal lawyer, struggle with the police machinery and seldom win. But here, in NYC, she thought the rule of law operated. Perhaps it did, as Jyot implied, for people like her, a certain class – with that mix of status, job, income – which guaranteed security. In Manhattan, brown men were either cab drivers or Wall Street bankers, immigrants or expatriates, the gulf between them as wide as a skyscraper was tall.

39
(2014)

❋

AFTER DROPPING MEHAR at school, Niki had taken the B train to 42nd Street. In the Stephen A. Schwarzman Building, the New York Public Library's main building in Midtown, she browsed through books on Indian independence. She had begun transcribing the information she had gathered on Mr Malik from SAYA. Jyot, however, was proving less amenable; when not rebuffing her, she was taciturn. Slowly, Niki was discovering the canyon that lay between writing the synopsis and writing the book.

In a high-ceilinged room, Niki pored over images of Partition by Margaret Bourke-White. The gritty woman from New York had captured that horror for posterity: rotting skeletons as rails for voracious vultures, their bones tangled with strips of sundried skin, littered with brightly-painted horns, men and beasts indistinguishable…

After four hours in the library, Niki caught the subway and got off at 72nd Street to shop for groceries. It was early October and Halloween weeks away, but Fairway was dotted with pumpkins which, in true American fashion, were available in sizes from

215

XS to XXL. Requesting home delivery, she walked back along Broadway and warily eyed the skeletons that had become part of the community. Chalk-white, without a single blemish, wrapped in wisps of fabric on townhouse stoops, they contrasted with radiant orange pumpkins. An international enough phenomenon, Halloween was celebrated in Hong Kong too, but the aesthetic was toned down and it was more pumpkin than skull. Skeletal fingers crept out of street-level grilled windows and leery craniums goggled from banisters as dusk fell earlier each day.

Spurred by the extensive Halloween merchandise on display even at pharmacies, Mehar was canvassing for either a Halloween skeleton dog or a rotten haunted skull. Disgusted by both choices, Niki had bought a small painted pumpkin from Whole Foods which Mehar, with a roll of her eyes, had deigned to keep on her study table. Meanwhile, she had persistently been showing Niki real Halloween treasures on Amazon, the dangling skeleton garland being the last one Niki had refused to buy. Turning onto Columbus Avenue, she shook her head as Ricky's Halloween Superstore announced its presence with a mannequin dressed in a 'slutty cop mini dress'. The window displayed other delights like the Michael Jackson glove, Cher wig and creepy mask sequined suspenders.

She was being a killjoy but her recent readings in the library had ruined Halloween for her. What had happened during Partition hadn't ended there. '47 had had resonances. In '84, when Dadima visited Delhi to record the aftermath of the riots, her first diary entry read: 'Drains clogged with blood and hair, stray dogs gnawing at human corpses, the air is fetid with charred flesh and smoke.' To live in a society where skulls and bones could serve for annual jollity was a privilege indeed.

≡

Mehar gripped Niki's hand as an uncertain smile hovered on her lips. They pushed open the door to PetCo where, to the right, cats were arrayed in cages. Anjel Cat Rescue was hosting an adoption event.

'Go ahead,' Niki said. Arjun and she watched as Mehar identified the manager and introduced herself. The air was heavy with assorted smells. Arjun wrinkled his nose. Cats in the cages sat sphinx-like, no meowing, no movement. They were dressed up for display, the collars elaborate with studs, sequins, bows. Mehar was cooing to a black cat inside a cage as she talked animatedly to the manager. Niki felt a stab of envy; Mehar and she had been sparring too much of late.

'Guys!' Mehar waved them over. 'This is Tiger!'

A mass of compact black fur, tail, limbs, haunches tucked in, studied them with jade eyes.

'Panther might be more appropriate,' Arjun grinned.

'I'm Myra,' the manager extended her hand.

Niki greeted her and apologized for Mehar. 'She's too excited to remember her manners.'

'We see it all the time,' Myra laughed. Turning to Mehar, she asked, 'Would you like to play with Tiger a bit to help make up your mind?'

Mehar's head bobbed like a dashboard figure. As Myra removed Tiger from the cage for a secluded play area, Arjun let out an operatic sneeze. With a concerned look, Niki dug out a wad of tissues and was handing them to Arjun when he sneezed again.

'Looks like someone's allergy is acting up,' Myra remarked as Mehar and she stepped on the escalator down.

Arjun's nose was leaking and he sniffled. 'You go ahead. I'll get some fresh air.'

In the basement, Niki found Mehar in a corner room playing with Tiger.

'Your daughter's very diligent,' Myra said. 'I am impressed with her emails to me. They were so well written, I never realized I was communicating with a child.'

Niki smiled. 'Mehar is very keen on a pet.'

'It'd be great if Tiger finds a forever home with your family. She is a very sweet cat and has been in foster care for over six months now.'

Niki frowned. 'Isn't that a long time for a cat with a good temperament?'

Myra nodded, lips pursed. 'She's black, you see. And folks have their beliefs.'

Arjun joined them, his nose having grown into a pink onion. Inside the room, Tiger was curled up in Mehar's lap as she stroked her. 'How does a person with allergies manage?'

'Anti-allergy medication,' Myra said. 'It is not uncommon.'

Niki watched her daughter, in love with the cat, and turned to her husband, struggling with a leaky nose. 'We don't have to rush this,' she whispered.

'Looks like a done deal,' Arjun sniffed. 'She blames me for the relocation. I deny her this and I'll be Enemy Number 1.'

Myra popped her head in the door. 'Time up,' she sang.

'Oh!' Mehar sighed.

'Ah-choo!' Arjun signed off.

40
(2014)

✳

SEATED AT THE oval volunteers' table, Jyot mumbled as she read from the ruled college notebook lying open in her hands. They were scheduled to work on the flyer for the November event – was Jyot reading her notes? With that look of intense concentration, the black-framed reading glasses and singular absence of any jewellery, she seemed somehow vulnerable, very removed from the stiff disapproving woman Niki knew. She deposited her bag on the table and sat down. Jyot continued undisturbed.

Niki withdrew a notepad on which she had recorded their last flyer discussion. There was not much. She turned the page. Bullet points on the little she had learnt about Mr Malik. Studying it cursorily, she wondered about the best approach to get Jyot's story. In the distance, a shrill alarm peeled. Unceasing, it was getting louder. Looking around, Niki saw all heads in the office cocked to attention. Loud sirens were as distinctly New York as the white man at the traffic lights, and she was learning not to jump when an ambulance or fire truck blared down a street. But this noise would shatter her ears. Mr Sharma sprang up and rushed to the windows that looked onto

219

Roosevelt Avenue. Opening one, he craned his neck. The noise levels in the office surged and a foreign smell wafted in. Niki wrinkled her nose. Meanwhile, other colleagues were crowding Mr Sharma. Niki went to investigate.

Sheila spun around from the window, almost colliding into Niki. 'Fire in the adjacent building! FIRE!' she shouted in Niki's ear. 'We should walk down.'

'Oh!'

'They will want us to evacuate!' Shermeen added.

'Let's GO!' Mr Sharma's waving arms urged above the din of the fire truck. Shouts came from the street, where firefighters in heavy gear organized themselves. A dense crackle like wood splintering in a giant bonfire. 'Hurry, hurry!'

The smell outside was acrid, there was smoke in her eyes. Niki nodded and headed back for her bag. At the empty table, she plucked her notepad and bag and was moving away when something caught her eye. Jyot stood facing the wall, her arms pumping back and forth horizontally, hands clenched into fists. Then, she patted her hands, before lifting the right palm in an imaginary toss. Back to the pumping. Jyot was not really hearing the din from the street or the shuffle in the office, absorbed as she was in her task. That gesture was familiar to Niki – a rolling pin flattening a ball of dough before tossing the disc onto a griddle. Now Jyot used an imaginary cloth to press down the sides of the imaginary roti to coax it to puff. She plucked the cooked roti, plonked it on some plate, sprinkled flour on the rolling surface and returned to pumping. Roll the roti. Flip the roti. Tend to the roti on the griddle. Pat the roti between the palms. Pluck the puffed roti. Toss on the fresh disc.

Lifting an imaginary plate, Jyot turned and walked to the centre of the room where she sat down cross-legged. Tearing a roti, she made a bite and lifted a hand to feed the air. Next, another bite and the hand moved to feed another imaginary person seated beside the first. Thus, Jyot calmly went on feeding more mouths. She smiled and nodded encouragingly as she conversed with them softly. With her free hand, she appeared to caress one head, tuck a lock of hair on another, wipe the mouth of one with a thumb.

Niki's right hand was clasped around her mouth. She knew what she was witnessing. In her women's studies course, during the class on trauma, she had read cases of patients who had lost their families during a war or riots or some other horrific accident, and they would recreate the tragic scene under certain conditions which mimicked or evoked the original. The background clamour of sirens, shouts, fire crackling, coupled with the smell of smoke, had transported Jyot to the scene of her tragedy.

Somebody was hollering in the background as the sound of heavy boots on the building staircase filled the air. Niki should be dragging Jyot awake and out of the now-empty office – the others had all fled. This wasn't safe. But jolting Jyot out of this re-enactment might be dangerous too ... Niki inched forward, heart thudding in her ears.

Jyot was now putting somebody to bed, some bodies really, as she arranged their limbs, straightened their clothes and hair. Her face was full of tenderness as she bent over the imaginary bed on the floor and plumped the pillows. Then, she made to climb the bed and settled down on the floor, legs pulled up. With her left arm, she patted two bodies to her left. With her right, she patted two to the right. Next, she unlooped a dupatta-like scarf from around her neck and shook it open. She lay down, in the middle of the bodies, two on each side, and spread the dupatta like a sheet over them, tucking it in on either side. As Jyot closed her eyes, a convulsion shook her. Niki jolted. Her phone was vibrating.

'Y-yes?' she mumbled.

'Where *are* you?' Sheila said, her voice laboured amidst the persistent clamour outside.

Niki licked her lips. She should flee, but Jyot appeared comatose.

'... I don't see you.'

'I'm, umm, with Jyotji, in the office.'

'*O-ffice?*' A whoosh drowned out Sheila's voice.

Hadn't the cacophony grown? And her eyes were watering from the smoke surely, not the memory of Nooran? *Get the hell out, Niki!* a voice screamed from within as she glanced from Jyot to the exit.

'—that rundown building at the corner, where the taco truck is parked. A short circuit, somebody said, from using an electric plate. There is smoke pouring out of the third floor.'

Niki moved towards the exit, where the cell phone reception was better.

'—you escaped all this huffing and puffing! Listen, it's too noisy here. I'll come up soon.'

'*What*? Our building is safe?' Niki was yelling but Jyot lay still.

'The men are watching the drama. I don't see any flames but something definitely burned, and it was not a burrito,' Sheila laughed. 'I'm waiting for the elevator up.'

'Oh! Okay.' Niki exhaled and rotated her shoulders backwards. She tiptoed towards Jyot lying supine on the floor. She looked asleep. Niki glanced at her watch. The whole incident had lasted less than ten minutes, in which time Jyot had cooked rotis, fed her children – four children she remembered Dadima telling her – then lay down in their midst, folding her children into her. This re-enactment was from an earlier time, one which reflected today's noise, smoke, alarm. Chaurasi. The anti-Sikh riots. Niki had enough familiarity with PTSD to glean that she'd just witnessed some of what had transpired with Jyot in 1984. But what did *this* particular enactment mean? It was a peek into some secret that Jyot consciously refused to share, but which her body had automatically rendered…

41
(2014)

✳

NIKI GOT THROUGH on her fifth attempt.

'Yes, hello,' Dadima bellowed.

Niki distanced the iPhone from her ear. 'Hello Dadima! How are you?'

'Fine, fine! All fine!'

'Were you in the garden? It took me several tries to get through!'

'What guard?'

'Garden, *gaar-den*. Were you sitting in the garden?' An autumn dusk was perfect for a late tea or early drink. Again, her heart constricted as she imagined Papa and Dadima reclining in lawn chairs as she scampered about chasing fireflies, Nooran flitting in and out...

'No, I was in the study. Saw the phone light blink and went to put on the ear aids.'

Ah, that explained the multiple rings. Dadima had the same relationship with her hearing aids that Mehar did with her glass of milk: an essential nuisance.

'You couldn't hear the ring without the aids?'

'Too shrill with the aid. I keep the ringer low.'

Considering how she resisted wearing them, Dadima was solving for that rare occasion when she would be wearing the hearing aids and the ringer would be loud. But it was useless arguing with her. 'Tell me about Chandigarh, the neighbourhood, what's happening?'

'No, you tell me about Mehar – is she settling into Noo Yark?'

Trust Dadima to feign an American accent! She was clearly in good spirits. Niki told her about their lives in the city – Mehar's school, Arjun's office, her attempts at SAYA. 'Are you taking your medicines on time?'

'I have sifted through the whole study for your Papa's manuscript. He must have given it for typing.'

'Typing? Had he finished writing it then?' Papa wrote in longhand, with scribbles on the margins, annotations between lines like fish swimming in channels.

'Why else would he have given it for typing?'

'But you're assuming that, right?'

'That what?'

'That he had finished it.'

'I told you he had finished it! Listen to me and don't interrupt, otherwise I will forget what I was saying. He was at it for months, sleeping late, waking up early! I was serving him breakfast, lunch and dinner in the study, where he was marooned on an isle of transcripts. Once, Tiny came by and couldn't cross the threshold to the room, littered as the floor was with paper. So, he said to your Papa, "On such a full sea are we now afloat?"'

Niki giggled. 'Then?'

'Tiny pulled up a chair at the door and they chatted across the room.'

Dadima chortled. Niki laughed. The thousands of miles between them was sewn up by their shared laughter at the image.

'Ah!' Dadima sighed. 'I miss my son.'

Niki's heart was in her mouth. 'I miss him too,' she said, her mouth wobbling. 'So, who do you think he gave it to, to type out?'

'Hain?'

'Typing! To whom?' Niki yelled, though she knew she didn't have to. The sound of Dadima tapping her hearing aid hammered in her ear.

'Prem? Remember Prem?'

'Yes.' He was Papa's long-serving clerk who had assisted him on Project '47 as well, but he had retired years ago.

'Why him?'

'His son runs one of those photocopying shops, no? I called Prem, but he's visiting family in Canada. Which is why he didn't come for your Papa's funeral, remember?'

No, she didn't remember. She didn't remember much from the funeral, except suffocating in grief.

'I'll find it,' Dadima affirmed. 'The manuscript that took my son's life.'

'Dadima…' Niki struggled. 'Your medicine—'

'Wait, the doorbell.'

She heard the sound of the handset against wood, the shuffle of feet, an exchange between Dadima and the help, a shout – Tiny Uncle – and a rustle as the handset was retrieved. 'Okay, Niki, I am off for my walk with Tiny. Give my love to everyone. Call soon. Keep living.'

In a land that had been a gateway to famed Hindustan, where marauders surfaced with the ferocity of dust storms and littered the earth with corpses like grains of dust, people had developed an armour for daily living. So when death arrived, in war or peace, it was met with directly, without preamble. *She went to hospital to deliver her baby where she finished. She was travelling on the bus when she finished. He was at his desk, working, when he finished* … And Niki had learnt, you could run out of yourself. Finish. Just like that. Which was why the exhortation-as-blessing: Keep living.

42
(2014)

❊

'AND THE LORD said, let there be light,' Mehar rolled her eyes as she watched her mother.

Every day, Niki lit a lamp and incense before Arjun left for his office. Mehar would recite a couple of prayers, both Sikh and Hindu. Arjun would dip his right ring finger in the vial of prasad and dab it on each of their foreheads. Quick, efficient, easy, but Mehar had revolted. Niki reminded herself to be the adult in the relationship. 'Lordess?' she quipped.

Mehar puckered her mouth, 'Whatever.'

Mehar was used to Niki feminizing things, but she didn't care about gods or goddesses any more. Last night, at the dinner table, she had declared she had discovered during her Religion & Philosophy class that she was an atheist. And therefore, she would not be joining her parents at the altar every morning. Both Arjun and Niki were increasingly finding themselves agnostic, if not atheistic, and were casual about the ritual but the idea of abandoning it entirely had not occurred to them. For Arjun, it was a family tradition; pujas twice daily was what he had grown up with. For Niki, God was not an

226

abstraction – he was a friend she communicated with frequently. It was what she had picked up from Dadima, the image of Nanak as a dearly beloved friend, one who could be summoned in conversations as Baba Nanak, Babaji, a hoary sage, much like Nooran's Old Man Bullah. And thus, when they got married, Niki and Arjun had started their own family tradition: setting up an altar with twin pictures of the first and tenth Sikh gurus, another of the goddess Durga and a marble statuette of elephant-headed Ganesha. Now with Mehar declaring revolt, the easy harmony of that morning ritual looked set to be ruptured.

'Humour your parents,' Arjun said, 'join us anyway.'

'If you don't believe in God, then why not disband the tradition?' Mehar countered. She was practising what she had learnt in her critical thinking class, where they were taught to learn, observe and come up with their own conclusions. 'And all those stories of gods and goddesses, they are all mythology, you know.'

'Like Greek mythology, sure.' Niki smiled.

Mehar snorted. 'Okay, wait. It must be the whole family, right?' She stalked to her bedroom.

'Looks like she's deciding to humour us,' Niki winked at Arjun.

'Or Percy Jackson.'

Mehar returned with Tiger, who was now named Jade, snuggled into her arms and started to rattle off a prayer. With solemn green eyes, the cat followed the prancing flame and burning incense. Arjun, meanwhile, sucked in his stomach as if holding his breath. Niki could see a sneeze building up.

Of the fifteen allergens the doctor had tested Arjun for, he was positive to one: cats. Niki sat at her desk researching allergy management techniques – the writing could wait. Since Jade's arrival, Mehar was busy taking care of the cat, cleaning the litter box, feeding and grooming her. But Arjun's nose ran upon reaching home and as each evening progressed, he usually lay supine on the sofa, circled by a moat of used tissues. Returning the cat would create a rupture the family couldn't afford. So Niki set about looking to train the cat, which, she figured, was akin to the waves obeying King Canute. The doctor had prescribed anti-allergy medication. A friend had suggested some Ayurvedic medicine that strengthened the immune system. Niki was asking Baba Google for more ideas.

There was a slew of suggestions: buy a HEPA filter, run it continuously, reduce allergen levels; don't pet, hug or kiss the cat; wash hands with soap and water if you do. She would need to ensure that Mehar didn't go from cuddling Jade to touching Arjun—

A mail from Arjun popped up on the screen, forwarded from the building manager; it was a complaint about a moth-like smell from the apartment by a resident on the floor.

A-*gain*! What the F! Niki clenched her arms across her chest. In a world where profanity was a verbal tic, Niki was old-fashioned. Papa's advice was to always articulate better – the F word was for losers with limited vocabularies. In a region where language was punctuated by swear words with the abundance of spices, Papa was the sole Punjabi who didn't swear. His cheerful disdain for religion was another anomaly. And his passion for justice, which drew him into Punjab repeatedly as he struggled to save the lives of boys branded as terrorists, which made him take on pro bono cases as his practice suffered, which made him spend hours coaxing survivors who had forgotten their own stories to talk, which made him labour over a book that would record untold stories of a missing history, which was his life's work...

Niki felt like sobbing. Was it the memory of Papa, her concern over Arjun's health, the struggle to settle down, frustration with this unidentified, racist neighbour? She didn't know what it really was, but she felt like crumpling on the floor. *Niki, get a handle on yourself!* Nooran's face swam in front of her. Tall, assured Nooran, who walked like a peacock and looked the world in the eye...

Niki stood up, stepped away from her desk, and lifting her heels, stretched her arms above her head. If Nooran was here, she would read mothballs for the code it was and send the neighbour a dish of either stinky tofu or smelly durian.

What could explain this hypersensitivity to her cooking, which, yes, was seasoned with Indian spices but was mostly vegetarian, except for some fish which was cooked in the oven, Lebanese-Mediterranean style, sprinkled with salt and washed to remove the fishy odour first?

There were three other residents on the floor and the building management was not willing to say who the offended party was. Should she involve Mr Levy, the landlord? They had met him that first day when cartons were being unloaded and brought up. In the hustle of cartons being deposited in the right room and being checked for breakages, if any, which were to be noted separately for insurance purposes, Mr Levy was an inconvenience. He stood around for a while, a fixed smile on his face, as he dripped a few personal details and suggested they meet over dinner some time. He was no good at small talk, but he seemed amiable enough.

'Perhaps we should invite our neighbours to dinner,' Arjun had suggested. 'You know, "partake of an artisanal Indian meal, tuck into our food and flavours, and quit complaining."'

It was an idea, but really, the carping was getting to her. Perhaps she should call the women over for a cooking demonstration-cum-lunch? Or gift them a jar of homemade hummus?

The culture she'd grown up in, food was a marker for everything: joy, sorrow, love, friendship, so critical that it was offered to the gods during daily prayers. A repository of memories, which was why Dadima hadn't forgotten nihari to this day, the dish of her childhood love and loss.

As Niki was discovering, food could bind people together as deeply as it could other them.

43
(2014)

✳

'HOW ABOUT I treat you to a cuppa chai instead? For guiding me through the maze of Zabar's?' Niki smiled at Oonagh as they walked past Irving Farm in the direction of the grocery store on Broadway, famed for its coffee, salmon, bagels and cheese.

'Masala chai? The one with spices pounded into the brew? Count me in.'

The posters on the storefront announced the eighty-year provenance of Zabar's; a sepia picture of a young couple, the woman with a hand angled on her hip, looked back. Founded in 1934, Upper West Side's gourmet store was older than independent India.

Inside, they gravitated towards the cheese section. The French cheese board had samplings of French goat cheeses. Niki and Oonagh grabbed one each.

'How's the writing going?' Oonagh asked, as she savoured the crumbly cheese.

'Stalled.'

'Why?'

'Well, for one, it's my first book. Two, the theme, trauma and giving voice to the victims? It's complicated,' Niki shrugged.

'Sure.' Oonagh's hand on Niki's elbow guided her towards the smell of fresh baking. 'But you can consult books which deal with that topic. There's the famous South African Truth and Reconciliation Commission, which was widely reported. A writer came to NYU for a talk, a woman journalist who covered the hearings, and the hall was packed to the rafters.'

'Antjie Krog? *Country of My Skull.*'

'Yup, that's the one.' Oonagh inhaled deeply and sighed her pleasure. 'The homestyle rugelach,' she indicated the hillock of flaky pastry behind glass, 'is the best sin you'll ever commit.'

Niki grinned. The one skill Oonagh had acquired from her youthful Chinese misadventure was the ability to teach Mandarin. Cash earned from tutoring kids from posh households paid for her gourmet needs.

As they browsed the bakery, Niki returned to the earlier thread of their conversation. 'It's a wonderful confluence of reportage, memoir and meditation on guilt. But the Indian situation is different.'

A woman, holding her shopping basket as a shield, wove through them as Oonagh questioned with raised brows.

'The Holocaust and apartheid had clear villains. The Partition was a time when people who had coexisted as neighbours, friends even, turned against each other. Hindus and Sikhs against Muslims and vice versa. There were villains on both sides. So how do you apportion blame and culpability? The situation was further complicated by the Sikhs.'

'Sikhs?'

Mehar would like a panini for snack, Niki thought. She picked a baguette and asked for it to be sliced. 'Et tu?' she said to Oonagh. 'Ever taken a yellow cab? Seen a driver with a turban?'

Oonagh nodded.

'He was a Sikh.'

'Not Arab or Afghan?'

'Apparently, the most common surname for yellow cab drivers in the city is Singh. A Singh is a Sikh.' Niki took the sliced bread from the Hispanic employee.

'I am mortified by my ignorance.'

'Sikhism is the fifth largest religion in the world. And yet, people remain unaware of it. It had its beginnings in Punjab as a bridge between pluralistic Hinduism and monotheistic Islam.'

Oonagh dropped a rye bread in her basket. 'So how did Sikhs complicate the situation?'

They made their way to the cash registers, where lines were long and snaking. 'When the Partition of India was announced,' Niki turned back to face Oonagh, 'Punjab was to be divided between Hindus and Muslims. Sikhs were spread throughout the state. They toyed with the idea of a separate nation of Khalistan, but it didn't work out. So when the boundary line snaked through their homes and farms, violence erupted.'

'Are you Sikh?'

'Yes.'

'Next!'

Niki hurried up the vacant line. 'Hi,' she smiled at her cashier, a Hispanic woman named Maria.

'Does that complicate things for you?' Oonagh was right behind.

'Being a Sikh? Nah, I get mistaken for a Latina. It's the men wearing turbans who face racism. One such was the first victim of 9/11. But racism comes in subtle ways too.'

Oonagh frowned. 'With brown skin? But you live in a tony part of the Upper West Side!'

'Oonagh O'Brien, I present to you Exhibit 1: Racism in a mothball!'

'Wha-at?'

'One of the three neighbours on my floor has been complaining about a "mothball smell" emanating from my apartment. The odour from my kitchen, apparently,' Niki snorted.

'No! She's got her tits in a tangle over all those heavenly spices flowing down the hallway to her home?'

Behind them, billing was taking longer than usual as Maria trained a younger middle-eastern-looking man in the intricacies of ringing the register. Finally, Abdul handed Niki her printed receipt and smiled tentatively. As Maria looked on, he seemed to remember and hastened to add, 'Have a nice day, see you again.'

When Oonagh was done, the women headed to the exit with their orange and white bags. They shuffled behind an octogenarian, who pushed ahead with his walker.

'That, right there,' Oonagh angled her head at the cash registers behind them, 'was the United Nations in your neighbourhood grocery. Sensitive Nose needs to wake up and smell the coffee.'

Threading through the cluster of shoppers around Zabar's, they joined the pedestrians down Broadway. 'Remember, even the UN has Russia!' Niki winked at Oonagh.

44
(2014)

✳

THE APARTMENT FACED west and the sunlight that streamed in post noon was the same that had made Dadima draw thick curtains across the windows to encourage Niki's siesta during the long days of the summer vacation. In Manhattan, it was winter and a polar vortex was headed their way, but the sun was strangely disconnected from frigidity, burning brightly outside. Niki drew the blinds.

'Why, Amma?' Mehar asked from the dining table, where she was finishing her healthy snack. Their deal was that she could get a bowl of Kettle chips, provided she ate a balanced snack of either fruit, paratha or choori before.

'I can't see the screen properly,' Niki indicated her laptop as she sat across from Mehar. Having finished the choori, Mehar showed her the empty bowl glistening with ghee and scooted to get a packet of chips. She returned with her computer and put on her headphones as she listened to music while working on an assignment. She would be happy to play her music aloud – the American pop of the global teenager – but Niki needed what her Catholic school nuns called pin-drop silence.

234

When Mehar was born, Dadima had declared she slept best to the lull of Sufi music. Not surprising since that was Niki's music of choice on most days. She had fallen in love with her daughter the moment she saw the tiny bundle of flesh that had held a pumped fist up to her nose as they made each other's acquaintance. But she also felt strangely disconnected. Listless. Lost. Post-partum blues, yes. But she was missing something. As if someone had not turned up. The pregnancy had gone to plan, a healthy girl child had been born, delivered safely in her mother's hometown, cared for in her maternal home where Niki was swathed in love and linen as her body was allowed the luxury of time to mend. And yet, Niki felt something was amiss, often casting suspicious looks at her deflated belly. The doctor had never indicated it, but Niki was convinced that she had had twins to deliver.

'Amma,' Mehar said, 'you are sighing.' The Bose headphones did not cancel out human sounds.

'I am trying to exhale my story.' Niki sipped her fourth cup of tea since morning, her tea consumption index linked inversely to how much she wrote. She hammered at the keys, committed to stream-of-consciousness writing to unlock her creative juices. 'The story is within me, but it *has* to pop out in nine months; my submission deadline is counting down,' she declared.

'You're pregnant with a story!' Mehar guffawed.

Niki's fingers halted mid-air.

'What, Amma?'

'Dadima. She used that phrase while telling me the story of her return to Pakistan.'

'Tell me, tell me!' Mehar chanted.

'Dadima visited Lahore in 1998 after her visa came through. Pakistan was permitting tour groups on pilgrimages to Sikh holy sites. In Lahore, she met her childhood BFF, Ameena Aunty, after fifty years. They went to their old neighbourhood, and a commercial complex stood where Dadima's home used to be, which was a relief, she said.'

'She didn't want to see her old home?'

'It's a long story, and a different one.' But her daughter's eyes urged her on. 'Dadima's father died pining for his home. Now, the home didn't exist either. But in her memory, they existed together, her father and her home.'

'Like the parallel universe in *Lost*.' Mehar had taken to the TV series in a big way. After season one, her parents lost interest, but Mehar had finished watching the series and re-watched specific episodes.

'I guess so,' Niki shrugged.

'And then?'

'Through the evening and night, Dadima and her BFF swapped stories. They lost track of time, she said, eating dinner at 2 a.m., drinking endless cups of chai, which they made themselves as the cook had dozed off, and watching the sun rise over the old walled city of Lahore. Fifty years of catching up, she said, so many stories to tell.'

'Did she tell you any?'

'I remember one. The fascinating story of Ameena Aunty's cousin. She had come to Pakistan, her family migrating from India after Partition. The cousin got married off, was perennially pregnant but she never delivered a baby. Always, she miscarried. The doctors couldn't figure out why this was happening. Then, an old aunt spent several days talking to her. The next time she became pregnant, she delivered a baby after the full nine months. Everyone was happy. A mystified Ameena Aunty asked her cousin about what had changed. In the journey from India to Pakistan, the cousin said, she had seen so much. But no one wanted to hear her stories. We don't remember ghosts or snakes, she was told.'

'Why?' Mehar slid the headphones off.

'They were dark stories, terrible things that she had seen, for it was a time of great violence. But her father forbade her to ever talk about it. She was to stitch up her mouth and never mention that she had got separated from the family as they travelled towards Pakistan.

So, she sealed her lips. But she said she was pregnant with stories, so many of them competing for space in her womb that there was no space for the baby. It was only after the elderly aunt took her aside and they spent days whispering about the past that Ameena Aunty's cousin got the stories out. Finally, her womb was free.'

A shrill whistle sounded. Niki went to the stove to lower the flame, letting the kidney beans simmer in the pressure cooker.

'And Dadima joked that she and Ameena Aunty were pregnant with stories too, which they had to birth together.'

'So, how many story-babies do you have?' Mehar said.

'Just this one. And I am terrified that I might end up like Ameena Aunty's permanently pregnant cousin!'

45
(2014)

❋

A MAN WITH HIS left arm in a sling sat in Ms Dixit's office. As Niki placed her bag on the volunteer's table, Jyot waddled towards her. Pointing with her chin, she said, 'Vandana wants to see you.'

No preamble, no greeting. Oversight or intended rudeness?

Niki nodded. Inside, Ms Dixit introduced her to Mr Singh, a yellow cab driver and the victim of a hate crime in NYC. Three months ago, as he was taking a break late evening in Queens, he had been attacked by two men who called him a 'terrorist' and broke his collarbone and nose. She suggested they chat so Niki could record the incident as a case file to be submitted to the mayor's office.

Back at the volunteer table, Niki asked Mr Singh how he would like to begin. He patted his turban with the edge of his right palm as he appeared to think. It was neatly tied, not a pleat awry.

'In 1986, I came to Amreeka to escape the trouble in Punjab.' He narrowed his eyes. 'You know about that time?'

Oh yes! Perhaps he didn't see Niki's brief nod because he elaborated, 'You look young, so perhaps you don't know or don't remember. In the eighties, Sikh militants – now you would call

238

them terrorists, eh? – wanted to turn Punjab into a separate nation. And they started to kill people and spread terror. The police, in turn, started to spread its own terror. They began picking up boys, young men, from their homes or from the village square – a bit like how the NYPD picks black men for frisking. It was all random, or on the basis of some tip-off. And boys started to disappear. I was enrolled in a vocational training school at that time. The Punjab Police picked up my cousin from his home one night. A month later, we read his name in a news report about terrorists killed in a police "encounter". That's the euphemism they used for killing these men. Slowly, boys started to vanish. Parents learnt that when their sons were late getting home, it was time to hurry to the police station with a lawyer. I knew I had to run away.'

Mr Singh paused. He smoothed his neatly trimmed beard. Niki estimated he was in his late fifties or early sixties. She waited, drawing petals around the spot where her pen had stopped.

'I flew to Toronto, where I lived with a relative who drove cabs for a living. I first took on petty jobs, food delivery and such. But the US was where real opportunity lay. New York, everyone agreed, was Mecca! In those days, immigration was child's play. At the border, my relative declared of the passengers in his car, 'All Americans!', and we drove into the US, straight for New York. I began working with another relative in Queens as a cab driver – you know what they say about Punjabis and potatoes?'

'Anywhere in the world you dig, you're bound to find those two?' Niki smiled.

Mr Singh grinned. 'Those days, things were easy. In time, I got my citizenship, brought my family over – seventeen people in total, eh? Everyone was eager to get here for the promise of Amreeka. And the promise held. We sent money back to Punjab, built brick houses, bought tractors, the latest TVs ... and then 9/11 happened. Brown, bearded, turbaned became terrorist.' He shook a rueful head. 'Even the city changed.'

'How so?' Niki asked.

'You live in Manhattan?'

He'd gauged her correctly. Niki nodded.

'I'm talking about a time when Hell's Kitchen was truly hell's kitchen. Forget the ladies, even we didn't enter that area.'

'Why?'

'Gangs.'

Niki nodded in acknowledgement.

'When 9/11 happened, Giuliani used that excuse to clean up everything.' Mr Singh swept his hand to indicate a thorough sweeping. 'Spared no one. Gave the police extra powers. And now, I pick up high-class people, young people, who all want to go to Hell's Kitchen to eat at one of the restaurants opening there daily. Or I drop them home from there. Past midnight. No danger.'

Interesting. She'd repeatedly heard how New York had transformed post 9/11 to become a city with young families again. Mitali, who ran an art gallery tour Niki had attended, had recounted how Chelsea once used to be chancy. From posh Park Avenue, where her parents lived and where Mitali returned to every weekend to recover from her digs in the Village, the entire stretch from Chelsea to Hell's Kitchen had been a no-go zone when growing up.

'Where were you when 9/11 happened?'

'In the city. Ferrying passengers.'

'You didn't go back home?'

Mr Singh wrinkled his eyes in recollection. 'I was downtown, saw the clouds of smoke, so I drove towards the Twin Towers. It was like being on a battlefield. People were pouring out, covered with dust, there was dust everywhere. I took passengers, adding more as we drove, filling up the car, taking people away from the towers. Everyone was dazed. I dropped two at Central Park, went with one person to her husband's office in Gramercy, went back downtown with another whose wife had gone to the financial district that morning. It was a strange day.'

Niki would second that. 'Weren't there attacks on Sikhs who were mistaken for terrorists? Because of their turbans?'

'That happened later. That day, the dust covered us all. White, black, brown, turban, scarf, helmet – we were all dust. And everyone's need was the same – to get to safety, to find their loved ones, to get home.'

A tray with three tea cups appeared on the table, and Jyot sat down.

'Thank you, pehnji,' Mr Singh acknowledged.

'You weren't afraid?'

Mr Singh smoothed his beard with his right hand, the thick steel bangle of his faith worn proudly on his wrist. A slim version of it rested on Niki's wrist.

'When I came to New York, one of the first sights I remember was the Twin Towers. I sent letters back home with pictures of the towers, the tallest buildings in the world. Relatives who visited from India, I took them to see the towers. When I got my cab, I drove tourists there almost daily. I came in exile to New York but I made my home here, and though I lived in Jackson Heights with four other men in a small apartment, the towers were a part of my home, you understand? So, when they brought the towers down, I brought my meter down.'

Niki scribbled as she listened. 'It's been fourteen years.'

'You know, Amreeka used to be black and white. Now it is Muslim and white. And all brown, bearded and turbaned are Muslim.'

'And terrorist,' Jyot clucked. She had finished her tea and was cradling her cup in both hands, sitting upright, looking straight ahead.

'Did you ever think of going back?'

Mr Singh shook his head. 'After almost thirty years in this country, I am American now. I go back to my des, my India, every few years, but this is where I belong. When I first came here, all you had to do was arrive and you were American, you know? All the people here are like streams from across the world which have ended up in the Hudson or the East River, hmm? But in India, you have to be Indian to be Indian.' He paused.

'In my vocational school in Punjab, we had an elderly teacher, Mr Smith. He was Anglo-Indian, born in India, to an Indian mother and an English father. And yet, he was a pariah, an outsider. His circle was limited to the few other Anglo-Indians like him in nearby towns. I never saw him invited to any of our homes.'

'Yes,' Niki nodded. 'California and New York are the cosmopolitan centres of the US.'

Mr Singh shrugged. 'That's the US I know.'

'Did you ever, umm, think of getting rid of your turban?'

'Friends and relatives have done it, but they still get called Arab. With my turban, I am Osama.'

'Nappyhead, raghead,' Jyot interjected.

'Look, I can cut my hair, wait out the bad times and then get my turban back. But the time to wait on the platform is over. I am on the train, and my fellow passengers have stopped seeing me. They see my turban, my brown skin, but they don't see *me*.'

A silence descended as Mr Singh tapped the table, Jyot gazed in the distance and Niki darkened her doodles. Finally, a chair scraped and Mr Singh excused himself to use the toilet.

But most hate crimes that were reported were against men. What of women? 'Jyotji, did you … were you …' Niki licked her lips, 'ever witness to a hate crime?'

'Was I a target?'

That directness again. Niki nodded.

'Yes.'

Yes? Yes what? Say something, woman! 'Did you report it?'

'Why? How would that help? Would the police be interested in the case of an illegal woman immigrant? When the police in my own country didn't listen, why would white cops help me? Why? You think you'll do me a service by writing my story down? I have seen people like you in Delhi, human rights people, journalists, with their pens and notebooks…'

Niki stiffened against the back of her chair, unnerved by Jyot's metamorphosis.

'Ineffectual idiots or sentimental fools. They claimed their reports would bring us justice. Where? Where is the justice?' She leaned forward, spewing like an erupted volcano. 'Thirty years I've waited. Thirty years since the violence of '84. Can you show me one person who has got justice? Can you?'

Niki wanted to tell her to stop, that she was not the enemy, she was on the same side, her grandmother, her father had spent their lives trying to break the silence around that violence, to get the survivors justice, Papa had given his life to his work, to ... to...

But Jyot Kaur was marching away. Niki clamped her mouth shut and bent her head before tears spilled and proved her the sentimental fool Jyot accused her of being.

XV

(2004)

Jyot

46
(2004)

❋

I WORKED FOR FOURTEEN years with the doctor's family in New York. Then, my madam got a better position with a hospital in Chicago. The boy and the girl were in college, and they had no need for live-in help any longer. So I stayed behind in Queens, using my savings to buy a one-room apartment. SAYA advised me on my Green Card application. But after 9/11, things had changed. All illegal immigrants who had overstayed their visas were suspect, even elderly folks. I applied and waited. There was no hurry. Except in Delhi.

There, with the twentieth anniversary of the '84 riots approaching, a lawyer was filing a fresh petition to bring the guilty to justice. He had a new team of activists. He needed witnesses to step forward. They contacted me, my story was representative of the horrors of the anti-Sikh riots. I'd been out of India for eighteen years now, I had never once returned. I could not make up my mind.

A heaviness settled over me, dulling my senses. I lost sense of time. One day, I forgot to get out of bed. In my sleep, I smelt fresh roti kneaded with jaggery and ghee, acrid smoke, burning flesh. I saw dagger blades, glinting in the noon sun, gutters littered with torn limbs, choking with clumps of hair.

I woke up gasping. Thick streams of water hit my face, my clothes were as drenched as the bed I lay on. The window was open, through which fierce rain smashed in. I tried to get up and reach the latch, but I had no strength. The floor was flooded, littered with items the lashing rain had knocked over. My feet found the clock, and it was still working. 2 p.m., 31 October 2004. The twentieth anniversary of the riots had begun.

I changed into black pants and sweatshirt, looped Jeet's yellow turban around my neck like a scarf. By the time I reached the subway, it was 5.30 p.m. The platform was crowded with rush-hour commuters, which was perfect. The R train was arriving. I slipped from behind the pillar and walked on to the air above the thundering tracks. I hit metal and concrete and felt my body crunch. The train was bearing down, its heavy body would barrel over me, reducing me to rubble.

But arms grabbed me and hoisted me back up. I barely had time to register what was happening when I found myself being transferred from one set of arms to another. I moaned and flailed, but no one heard me over the commotion. Above me, faces huddled in a circle, concerned, angry, shocked. In the city where people had no time to give directions, to be saved from certain death by a good Samaritan was completely unexpected. Every year people died from jumping in front of trains, getting pushed onto train tracks, but not I. The circle parted to reveal the blue of uniformed cops. I could not bear to be saved. Not again.

It was Mr Malik who accompanied me home from the hospital and suggested I volunteer at SAYA. He had guessed, correctly, that I had had a life before this life. But I had had another life before that previous life. One person, multiple lives. But who was there to witness it for me? To gather all the strands of the messy, terrible, unforgiving life of Jyot Kaur?

XVI
(2014–2015)
911

The unconquerable Bhishma is honourable and scrupulous. Krishna knows his warrior code will not allow him to raise arms against a woman or one born as a woman. So he counsels Arjuna to fetch Shikhandi, who was born a woman and whom Bhishma had wronged in a previous birth, and take aim from behind her. Bhishma smiles as Arjuna's arrows rain down upon him, so many that when the great warrior topples, his body rises from the battlefield on a bed of arrows. Meanwhile, Abhimanyu, Arjuna's young son, gets caught in a battle formation called the chakravyuh from which there is no escape. In vengeance, Arjuna's arrows slash the air and fell warrior after warrior. Bheema kills the wicked Duryodhana in a duel of maces. The end is near. Night falls. As the weary warriors sleep, Ashwatthama enters the Pandava camp and slaughters everyone, including the five sons of Draupadi. Krishna and the Pandavas survive because they are (fortuitously?) away from the camp.

47
(2014)

❋

THE GRIDDLE WAS heated to just the right temperature. Niki tossed cumin seeds onto it, stirred briskly, heating without burning. Turning the stove off, she listened to the seeds crackle, inhaled the smoky aroma, watched the colour turn from brown to oak. She was late in making dinner, but the writing had taken forever. A smattering of words which, she knew, she would delete the next morning.

In the Mahabharata, Abhimanyu was the tragic hero who knew his way into a complex battle formation, the chakravyuh, but not out of it. Apparently, he had learnt the technique to enter as a foetus when his father Arjuna was narrating it to his wife, but she had fallen asleep, and so, the foetus never mastered the exit strategy. Blame Arjuna, for which pregnant woman would be regaled with tales of battle formations? Fearless, foolhardy Abhimanyu penetrated the chakravyuh singlehandedly and was trapped inside by an army of opposing warriors, with no option but to fight to death. On days such as this, the book she was writing was her chakravyuh. Because of Dadima and Nooran and Papa and their fount of stories, Niki knew the way in but without Jyot's story, there was no way out.

At the window, sunlight glinted at the edges of the drawn blinds, the blazing bright Manhattan sun outside. There were days when she woke up like that sun and wrote like the breeze of Central Park, accomplishing her daily quota of 1000 words in an hour. Then there were days when the sky continued to be bright blue and she couldn't write ten words all day.

Why couldn't she progress beyond these sixty pages? Like Ameena Aunty's pregnant cousin, she needed someone to take her aside and help her unblock ... but what did she need permission for?

She could see the eyes of acquaintances who enquired, as all good Indians do, where she worked, and hearing her answer, simply stare at her. Declaring you were a writer could do that to Indians who had forged their way through the academic jungle to reach Indian Ivy Leagues of IIT and IIM, started as foot soldiers in multinational banks and consumer companies, and resolutely worked their way up the corporate ladder as they amplified the zeroes to their bank balance, one eye permanently out for the opportunity to move abroad. Even Aruna, her school friend who she had met after years, was puzzled.

Niki could hear the inaudible reproach: Why would someone with an MBA from IIM quit a dollar salary to sit home and write? And write what? At least write for the *New York Times* or the *New Yorker* or something equally prestigious then! What was this about writing a book of survivor stories?' Every now and then, someone would slyly comment, 'Arundhati Roy-style, haan? Or are you aiming to go mass like Chetan Bhagat?' Clearly, an Indian corporate executive could quit the rat race but never the expectation of success and concomitant moolah. You may write but the expectation was the same: a Booker prize or money.

Arjun had advised that she state what was indeed a fact: she was on a sabbatical from work to write a book. She had worked in consulting, yet he came up with the best lines. She pitched that rehearsed line at the next get-together where they were still getting to know folks in New York. Sure enough, to the Wall Street types, it made total sense. A time to reset, to step back, re-evaluate and to come back with a fresher vision. The implicit understanding was that you would come back to the treadmill. Like Hotel California, you could check out but never leave.

Niki suspected a hint of envy as well. Even Arjun seemed to think she lolled about at home in her pyjamas, ran in Central Park when the fancy struck her, napped at noon and snuck in a TV show at lunch time. But the reality was dead-end research and an unwilling interviewee, the laundry load that waited, the dishwasher to be unloaded, the meal to be cooked. What she needed was a housewife.

As Niki sautéed onions, she turned the exhaust to full throttle. A raucousness akin to the thunder of a subway station sounded in the flat. Arjun had received yet another email, the third, from the building manager about a resident on the floor complaining yet again about the odour of mothballs. But by now, the offensive items were buried six feet under in a landfill. An open-plan kitchen was not conducive to Indian cooking, Arjun had pointed out when Niki had settled upon the apartment. And this was true. The aroma of spices cooked with onion and garlic settled in her hair. But the complaint was a double affront: her cooking flavours compared to the odour of a *mothball*?

Once again, Niki sighed at the thought of her home in Hong Kong. Was a culture of cooperation and tolerance an Asian thing? Why was it so difficult for this person to reconcile with an hour of cooking flavours that were understandably strong but still interesting, right? The pungency of asafoetida, the crackle of cumin, the tang of mustard, the sting of fried red chillies?

In their apartment block in Hong Kong some years back, there had been a knock on Niki's door. A tall, bristling American woman had been soliciting signatures for a petition to prevent a resident's son from practising his trombone in the evening. 'It interferes with my pregnancy,' she had shrugged. The trombone player resided on the floor directly beneath Niki's, but he always stopped before 7.30 p.m. and, while his musicality was suspect, she had dismissed it as the price of being a neighbour. Niki had dodged out of signing the petition. But the woman had been persistent.

One day, Niki had run into the building supervisor, a gentleman she had known for eleven years. He had told her that unless Niki signed the petition, the complainant didn't have a case because, as the resident directly above the trombone player, Niki was logically the party directly affected. Besides, according to the building's bylaws, the resident was perfectly within his legal rights to practice as long as he stopped by 7.30 p.m.

After that, Niki made sure to dodge behind pillars when she saw the pregnant American. At some point, her belly became flat even as the music continued. Perhaps the mother had discovered that her baby slept soundly to the music of its foetal days?

Pureed tomatoes sizzled as she added them to crisp onions. She was recreating Nooran's kaali dal. Perhaps she should go back to work, cut short the sabbatical, write over weekends, and get her dollar salary and her self-esteem back? There was a click, the door opened and Arjun stepped in.

'You're back early!'

He wiggled his fingers in front of his nose. 'I could smell this as soon as I got out of the elevator.'

Niki's mouth tightened. She turned to stir the pan, splashing tomato paste on the white-tiled panel behind the stove. As Arjun lingered, she glanced at him. His eyes were glassy, his nose pink.

'Dripped my way through a presentation,' he sniffled. 'So decided to leave right after.' He walked to the bin, dug into his jacket pocket and withdrew a wad of soiled tissues.

'I'll make you a cup of tea. Ginger?'

Arjun was nodding when a sneeze barrelled out of him. He doubled over, stuffed tissues up his nose and walked to the bathroom.

Niki had a pan of water on the stove. She grated ginger into it. This allergy was getting out of hand – none of her strategies was working. When she had asked Mehar to ensure that Jade didn't climb the living room sofa and chairs, she had scowled. 'She's a cat, Amma, you can't train them like dogs.' The HEPA filter – an expensive solution, but the Amazon reviews made it sound like a wonder product – was expected any day. A loud sneeze sounded in the hallway, followed by a syncopated series of exhalations. She mouthed a 'Bless you', and added tea leaves to the pan.

As she was straining tea, Arjun emerged wearing tracks and a hoodie. With the heating on, it was room temperature inside the house, but he was taking no chances. He accepted the tea gratefully.

'Bad, huh?' Niki sat across from him and sipped her tea. The food was on simmer, she could step away from the stove.

Arjun sipped and nodded sideways. 'The good news is that I have a work trip coming up. Ten days – the UK and Europe. It'll be like a retreat.'

Since they'd moved to New York, Arjun had enjoyed sitting put, a refreshing change from Hong Kong where he had been on the road most weeks. Niki lifted her brows in puzzled enquiry.

'It's time away from this cat-infested home, Niki! Who knows, I might get my health back!'

48
(2014)

✳

JYOT HAD NOT shown up at SAYA for six days in a row. She'd
not been in last Friday because of the blizzard, and the weekend –
when you could count on seeing her in – was accounted for by the
blizzard's fallout. It was Wednesday now. This absence was curious,
considering she was the centre's matriarch. When Niki entered the
date in the office ledger, 5 November 2014, the hissy fit of their last
encounter resonated. She made enquiries of Mr Sharma, Shermeen
and Lata, substituting for Sheila who was away to India on a month's
vacation. But no one knew. So, after looking up her address, Niki
decided to pay Jyot a visit.

Down Roosevelt Avenue and on 74th Street, the cab brought her
to a nondescript brick building. After a ride up in a clanking elevator
with a cockroach for company, she found herself at Jyot's door. There
was no nameplate but the unit was 6A. Niki rang the bell and waited,
feeling awkward. What would she say when Jyot asked what she was
doing at her doorstep? Wasn't a person allowed leave? Maybe she
was travelling. No answer. She rang the bell again, heard it pealing

inside, took her finger off the button and waited. From below, the sounds of traffic floated up. The cold was making her hop on her feet. The weather had turned frigid over the weekend because of a storm across the Atlantic seaboard.

She'd ring one last time and then she was out. She pressed a finger down on the doorbell, letting it ring for half a minute. Then, she raised her hand and rapped on the door, hard.

A door opened – the neighbour's. A face was framed in the ajar door. 'Asha?' The girl eyed her cautiously. 'Remember me? I am from the Centre? SAYA? You came with Jyot?'

Asha unfroze. 'Yes.' Indicating the next door, she asked, 'She's not answering?'

Niki shook her head. 'Have you seen her?'

'Not lately. My gran's away and it's she who really knows Jyot.'

'When did your gran leave?'

'A week now.'

'Do you have the key to Jyot's apartment?'

Asha shook her head.

'Are you sure? Your gran is a friend, right? Maybe she has a key, you know, for emergencies?'

'This is an emergency?'

'Let's hope not,' Niki said, 'but I'd like to be sure. If we open the door and find nothing wrong inside, we'll lock it and assume Jyot's gone visiting too – maybe with your granny, eh?'

'Okay.' Asha turned to go back inside. 'Come in.'

Niki entered and stood inside the doorway, taking in the apartment, clean but filled with Mexican curios, floor rugs and wall hangings, bursts of colour and patterns. Her gaze went from wall to wall, and she was taken aback to see a portrait of Guru Nanak amidst paintings of Mother Mary and vibrant sketches of fleshy yellow avocados and green palms. The kitchen was stacked like a chef's pantry. There was the sound of drawers being opened, searched, closed, a wardrobe squeaking, more drawers being opened, the sound of hurried sifting. Asha reappeared, shaking her head. 'Some residents keep a spare with the building super.'

The supervisor was not in his basement office and was off fixing someone's heat, the eastern European sounding cleaner informed them, and after asking Asha some questions, handed her the key.

Back at Jyot's door with Asha beside her, Niki fitted the key into the keyhole. The door clicked open to a dark refrigerator. An arctic blast enveloped them. Niki rubbed her upper arms. Asha probed the wall to her right and flipped on a switch. A yellow lamp lit the room, revealing a rattan sofa, a centre table and one chair. There was a kitchen to the left that appeared bare. The apartment was the exact opposite of its neighbour; Siberian stark against its tropical teeming. And quiet like death.

'Let's ch-ch-check the bedroom,' Niki's teeth chattered.

Asha led the way down the dark corridor to the area that lay beyond the living room. The door was ajar. Pushing it open, they stood at the threshold. Their eyes adjusted to the darkness before it became apparent that the bed was occupied. A body lay there. The cold wrapped Niki's heart in its fist.

'Stay here,' Niki whispered.

She took a few steps and found a switch. Lamp light picked up an old, a very old person, on the bed. In that terrible cold, the person lay without any cover or quilt, motionless, chest neither rising nor falling. Slowly, Niki approached the bed and gasped. The ancient person in the bed, her face wreathed in century-old wrinkles and jaw loose like a toothless granny's, was Jyot. Like Jyot would look a hundred years later. Niki put a finger below the aquiline nose and waited. No puff of breath, her finger stiffening in the cold. Quickly, she grasped the woman's wrist and waited. The skin felt like paper left outside on a winter night.

'911! Call 911!'

Asha stood paralysed. Niki turned, hustled her out of the room, dug her phone out of her bag and dialled. As she chewed on her inner lip, she saw a bowl of water with dentures sitting in them, Jyot's walking stick angled over the chair and the thin yellow muslin dupatta that Jyot was draped in.

'911. What is your emergency?'

⸺

The doctor at Mount Sinai Hospital said the situation was confounding – truly confounding. When Jyot was wheeled in, she had no pulse, she was not breathing and her body temperature was 71 degrees Fahrenheit. Her body had shut down. Ms Dixit's face pinched with worry as she listened.

The doctor rubbed his face with his palms and shrugged elaborately. 'This is rare, so rare,' he reiterated. 'The most probable explanation is that she fell into a hypothermic stage early on – you did say the apartment was freezing – and with no heating in the midst of blizzard-like conditions … It is a puzzle how this actually happened, but I can say that the patient went into a state of hibernation like bears do in the Arctic, and this protected her brain functions.'

'Will she recover?' Ms Dixit asked.

'We will keep her under observation. Five days without water with her metabolism at a standstill … but yes, I expect a full recovery.' As he walked off, his white coat flapping, he mumbled, 'Never thought I'd see a miracle…'

49
(2014)

✻

'DADIMA' THE SCREEN read, lighting up as Niki's phone vibrated across her desk. *Dadima*! This was a first. 'Is everything okay?' Niki hollered as she picked up.

'Stop shouting in my ear!'

'Oh!' Niki exhaled her relief. Dadima had her hearing aid on evidently.

'I found it! Your Papa's manuscript!'

Dadima was almost squealing in delight. 'Where? How?'

'Prem had it, just as I told you, no?'

'Well, why didn't he return it?'

'Listen, listen! Don't get ahead of the story. So, Jinder gave it to Prem just before he passed away to have it typed out, so he could share it with us. But Prem had to leave for Canada urgently since his brother had had a stroke. He returned last month, remembered the manuscript, had it typed out and came to see me. Oh Niki, I can't tell you how relieved I am! If we had lost it…' Dadima made a noise that was half-sniffle, half-sigh.

'But you found it, Dadima, you're brilliant!'

'Yes, I'd agree,' she laughed. 'So, it's on the way to you—'

'You didn't read it?'

'Na, I would rather you read it first. I don't trust my eyes – or my heart.'

'Hmm.' Niki gulped as a thought struck her. 'Did you make a copy?'

'Copy? No. Why?'

'No, nothing.' In her heart, Niki summoned Guru Nanak and entrusted him with the safe delivery of the manuscript. As Papa would joke, 'You've got to rely on God for *something*!'

'Tiny couriered it; we don't trust the post. It'll reach you within a week. You will be the first reader of your Papa's book, just as he wanted.'

50
(2014)

✻

FIVE DAYS LATER, Niki cradled Papa's manuscript in her arms. Nelson at her apartment building's front desk had handed it to her when she returned from her yoga class.

Sitting down to read, she could see that Papa had built his narrative upon the pillars of '47 and '84 through the oral histories of forty respondents, focusing at length on five principal characters. Of those five, Niki was aware of three: Beli Ram, the border vaulter; Mr Malik, the founder of SAYA; and Veervati, a woman she had interviewed while working at Sakhi. An appendix listed the names of each of the one hundred and ten respondents. Women made up sixty per cent of the total.

Reading his manuscript was like going back in time, back to Chandigarh, to his study, filled with conversation and laughter and whisky and stories. It seemed that Papa had finally spoken from beyond his ashes. And from that mother-of-all-stories, the Mahabharata, Niki recalled one – that of Nachiketa, the boy given by his father to Yama, the lord of Death, in a fit of anger. When Nachiketa reached his abode, Yama had ventured out. So he waited.

Upon his return, Yama found the boy at peace with his surroundings. Pleased, he blessed him with three boons. But the only thing Nachiketa was interested in was the one thing Yama did not wish to reveal: what happens after death? Yama parried, fed Nachiketa, fed his buffalo, watered his fields, offered him other boons, but the boy was insistent. Impressed, Yama relented. Upon death, the soul, atman, leaves the body to merge with the universal spirit, the Brahman, which was all around us.

Niki felt like sobbing. If Heer met the hoary writer of Mahabharata, she would cry out, 'Oh Vyasa, you lie; the departed never return!' What good was a soul when you couldn't converse with it?

But Papa *had* spoken, five months after he passed away, through his manuscript, which, Niki had to admit, needed work – a *lot* of work. The narrative was bare bones – case studies stacked together in a dreary read. But she knew what Papa had intended: to showcase, through the stories of the survivors, the cataclysmic violence of the Partition and how it was mimicked in the savagery of the pogrom of '84, and to examine how women's bodies became battlefields in both. Niki could see the personal story of the Nalwa family interweaving itself through the narrative, like a red thread that coursed through an intricate bagh's embroidery, starting with Zohra Nalwa and her family's flight from Lahore, to Papa's synchronous birth with India on the stroke of midnight in a border town cleaved by the Radcliffe Line, to Nooran's providential escape from killer mobs, to her own upbringing threaded with stories that others had snuffed...

Papa had constructed the diptych of India's violence and silence such that it needed a central spine along which the two leaves hinged. Jyot's story was that missing spine. Niki's education, her work with Sakhi and helping Papa with Project '47 had taught her that the other side of silence was not the untold story. Violence triangulated that relationship. There were cases when breaking a survivor's silence could risk reproducing the buried trauma, Niki knew from her studies and her first job at Sakhi. But Jyot had just attempted suicide, and it wasn't the first time, apparently. In which case, was it a cry for help to break her silence?

A thought struck her. What Papa's manuscript did have was the story of Mr Malik. A sepoy in the Second World War, he had returned to his hometown in Punjab with a medal, a holdall and one useless leg as his comrades lay buried in the foreign terrain of Europe. All he had wanted to do was to get married and put the past behind. But Punjab, and India, were fervid with azadi and vand, independence and partition. And the same brothers who had fought in Europe for the British had returned home and were fighting each other for their separate homelands. It helped that the British had previously armed them with weapons and taught them how to kill. But Sepoy Malik, cocooned in prospective matrimony, had steered clear of the sectarian madness, until a mob had set fire to the home of his betrothed. After that, the sepoy, with his cache of weapons and grenades brought home in a military green trunk, went about setting Lahore on fire.

Mr Malik, the genial founder of SAYA, had been another man altogether! It was a story that he had shared with no one, as he reiterated in his correspondence with Papa; his present self was an expiation of the past. Now Niki knew something that Jyot might value ... Jyot, who had known Mr Malik the longest and yet couldn't claim to really know him. If she heard Mr Malik's story, one that he had confided in only Papa, would Jyot be more willing to open up and share her story?

Either way, Niki's work was cut out for her.

═══

Niki sat in the sole cubicle in SAYA, which served as the director's office. Ms Dixit slid a plastic container across her desk, a honeyed aroma rising from it. 'From Jyotji – for saving her life.'

'Did she say that?' Niki asked.

Ms Dixit paused, lifted one shoulder. 'Why else?'

'Why not give it to me directly?'

'She is not one for displays now, is she?' With a bob and a fringe that framed her delicate features, Ms Dixit had a combined air of competence and daintiness. She was in her early sixties, though her sprightly manner was reminiscent of a sparrow.

'It is best to let her be after this ... episode. Though, I would like to ask a favour of you, Niki. Could you engage with her to get to know more about Mr Malik? It is a solid reason – the twentieth anniversary of SAYA's founding is approaching and a profile of its founder would be appropriate. As the oldest SAYA member and someone who knew Mr Malik, Jyotji is the ideal choice for illuminating his life, and, as a writer, you are the perfect person to compose it. This would be one way,' Ms Dixit tapped her steepled fingers, 'of giving her a chance to speak and, perhaps ... open up? Considering that you were the one who saved her life, she might feel less inclined to dismiss you?'

Would knowing about Mr Malik's sepoy avatar facilitate a headway? Niki wondered. As she nodded, Ms Dixit slid a folded sheet of paper across the table.

'Read it,' she urged.

'NAAMAARO.'

'The nurse on duty wrote it down. Jyotji's fevered mutterings were gibberish to her, but perhaps it meant something in a language she didn't know, she said.'

NAAMAARO was two words: Na maaro. 'Don't kill.' Niki gulped.

'The nurse said the patient had tears rolling down her cheeks as she thrashed and uttered that word with increasing hysteria.' The crow's feet near Ms Dixit's eyes dipped as she narrowed them. 'Man has reached outer space and yet, the distance between hearts remains the widest, no?'

'Shouldn't she see a therapist for her trauma?'

'A stranger will only compound her feeling of isolation. Before professional help, what she needs is an empathetic presence, an understanding other, who might propel her to share and heal. Forgive me for being personal,' Ms Dixit squirmed in her chair, 'but as a fellow Punjabi Sikh, Jyotji already gravitates towards you.'

Niki stepped out of Ms Dixit's office with the container in her hand, utterly mystified. Every culture had a dish which was shorthand for maternal love. In Punjab, it was choori, wholewheat flatbread minced with jaggery and ghee, a childhood staple. She walked to the rear of the hall where Jyot sat at her table.

Head bent over the folder in front of her, she was as still as a leafless London Plane in winter. There was no response to her approach, not even as Niki pulled a chair from across her, its legs scraping the floor. Jyot was intently studying the pages open in front of her – except that the folder was upside down.

'Jyotji,' Niki said. But Jyot continued with her hunched posture, vacant stare, questioning hands in her lap. Niki cleared her throat. The solitary confinement held. 'Jyotji,' she repeated and leaned in to straighten the folder. Jyot raised her head, her face a simulacrum of deep distress. Faraway eyes gazed blankly at her. Niki remembered her great-grandfather, the ancient kindly man on the porch of their Chandigarh home, his eyes forever seeking the street. Seconds ticked, as Jyot wound her way back to the present like a video that was buffering slowly.

Niki placed the container on the table, determined to look cheerful. 'Thank you,' she said. 'I haven't eaten choori in a long time.'

'I haven't made it,' Jyot said, her words coming out as if through a quagmire, 'in thirty years. Since '84. But I didn't make it for you to thank me.' As Niki made to shrug, Jyot continued, 'I am not thankful to you for saving my life. I wanted to die.'

Jyot spoke in an even lower voice and Niki had to lean in. Such dispassion about ending her life…

'I made it because you should not have had to go through … that … again.'

'Again?' Niki was confused.

Jyot waved a dismissive hand and lapsed into silence.

The air was fragrant with visions of Nooran kneading her after-school snack of choori as Niki prattled from her perch on the kitchen counter. A moat of food and love and stories protected her as violence buoyed the countryside, scudding now and then to suck Papa back into the fault lines he had fled from. What was the story of violence behind Jyot's tight lips and slumped back?

'Jyotji…' Niki began.

'I have nothing to say.'

51
(2014)

✻

'HMMM ... I don't need you to walk me to school any more,' Mehar said as she stuffed her bag, squeezing the PE kit inside.

'Why?' Niki asked.

'Because.'

'I am waiting.'

Mehar lifted one brow.

Niki envied her daughter that concise facial expression which conveyed exquisite disdain without wasting words. Roop Nalwa had done that as well, according to Dadima when Mehar had started to make that face. The mother she never knew had mysteriously manifested herself in her daughter. I had to go away, but I am here, see.

'I'm waiting for you to complete your sentence. Because what?'

'Just 'cause,' Mehar shrugged. 'It's an expression, Amma. It means for no particular reason. And please don't speak to me in Punjabi when we are outside!'

Huh! 'It's your mother tongue. And mine.' More precisely, it was Dadima-Nooran-Papa-Heer-Bullah-etcetera's tongue as well.

'Whatever.'

265

'Right. Well, your mother still needs a reason.'

Mehar snorted, crossed her arms and glared. 'Because it's uncool to be dropped off at school by your mother. Because I am not five years old any more. Because, guess what, I can walk home by myself! And you *did* forget to pick me up.'

Just once, just once, she had made Mehar wait. Calm is wisdom, Niki chanted the mantra silently and made herself as tall as her five-foot-two-inch frame allowed. It didn't help that Mehar was already five foot tall. 'Watch your tone, young lady. You're speaking to your mother.'

Mehar gave an odd laugh and swung her head. Jade wove around them, touching them with her tail. 'What was that?' Niki harrumphed.

'It's called a pity laugh, Am-ma!'

'Really? I don't think the man who got stabbed and mugged during the day on our street was laughing. Not when he was taken to hospital for his injuries; not when his wallet and e-reader were stolen. And remind me? How old was he? Thirty-three! A grown man.'

Mehar rolled her eyes.

'Try rolling your eyes at your principal.'

'Whatever,' Mehar turned to finish packing her bag. Jade was rubbing her face against a clasp. 'Go away!' she hissed.

Earlier that week, the school had emailed with the subject 'Neighbourhood Incident'. A teenaged male had approached a man from behind and mugged and stabbed him. The police believed it was an isolated incident, but the perpetrator was yet to be apprehended. All students were being reminded of the basic safety precautions they needed to take outside of school. The way Niki saw it, escorting her daughter to school was one safety precaution, considering one could get mugged in broad daylight even in the tony Upper West Side. But Mehar's face had a mutinous twist to it, and Niki set about repairing the situation. 'Did something happen?' she patted her daughter's bent head.

'Oh, Amma, all the other girls walk by themselves. They ask me why I need my mother to escort me.'

Niki sighed. 'How about you come back on your own?'

Mehar nodded. 'And going?' She paused in the midst of stuffing her sports shoes atop the books.

Niki grabbed a plastic bag from the laundry closet, took the shoes from Mehar's hands, packed them neatly and handed them back. Mehar clasped the backpack and hoisted it on her back. 'Well?'

Niki smiled and patted her belly. 'Tell your friends your fat mama needs to exercise and school is en route to the park.'

52
(2014)

❋

NIKI DECIDED TO bring Mehar along to SAYA for a day during the Christmas break. But Jyot was not in the office because she had a cold. So, they trooped to her apartment, with Niki hoping the company of a child would loosen Jyot up.

'Can we just show up unannounced?' Mehar asked.

Niki shrugged. It was a valid question, but it wasn't unusual for Indians to drop in at homes of friends and family without notice.

They found Jyot in her neighbour Juanita's apartment, where she met them with her customary detached air. As the adults sat in the living room, Asha took Mehar, who had come equipped with a book and her Nintendo DS expecting SAYA to be 'boring!', to her room.

A little while later, Mehar sailed into the living room, her hands spread out. 'Amma, look!' Her fingernails were painted neon green with golden highlights at the tips. 'See these?' she pointed to the gold flicks. 'You add them on top with glitter! Cool, right?'

Niki smiled. 'It is!'

'Asha showed me how. She has so many cool nail polish tricks!' Mehar beamed at Asha, who had crept up behind them and stood watching with a little smile. Now, she was showing her nails to Jyot, who patted her cheek.

'You don't have your mother's dimples?' she asked.

'No, but I have her mother's eyebrow!' Mehar said, raising one eyebrow sky high.

Jyot studied her, then lifted one eyebrow and held it for a few seconds.

'Cool!' Mehar lifted a hand, but when the expected high-five didn't happen, she brought Jyot's hand up and executed the action. 'And I smell like her.' She pinched her nose and sniffed audibly. She did smell of cloves and roses, having dabbed on some Bal à Versailles, which she had discovered in Niki's vanity. Laughing, she ran away, dragging Asha by the hand. Jyot's eyes followed them. Then, she got up and hurried out the main door. Niki was wondering what had happened when Jyot returned clutching a wooden peacock that she gifted Mehar. As her daughter looked hesitant, Niki nodded for her to take it. The hint of a smile parted the wrinkles on Jyot's face like a paddle.

'Your mother is in India?' Jyot asked as she sat down.

'No. She died in childbirth.'

'So you killed your mother?'

Whoa! Jyot had charged straight into battle. Niki had wrestled with that question, but Dadima and Papa had insisted it was the Emergency that had been responsible, the one wrought by Indira Gandhi's government and the ill-equipped government hospital. Nooran had swatted away Niki's misgivings like they were flies. So Niki didn't harbour guilt, but Jyot was talking, and it was worthwhile keeping her so.

Niki shrugged. 'I've had that thought.'

Jyot's eyes bore into her. 'And the guilt? How do you live with it?'

Niki felt heat rising up in her cheeks. Jyot clearly wasn't buying her act.

Juanita bustled out of the kitchen with a tray and beamed as she set down cups of steaming tea and a platter of jalapeño poppers. 'No conversation without tea mi Papā used to say. To which mi Mamā added, "And poppers!" It soon became our family ritual.'

'That could be our home too,' Niki smiled, 'except it'd be tea and pakoras.'

'I do that too; onion pakora, cauliflower pakora, methi pakora…' Juanita sat up on the sofa, legs crossed, and sipped her tea. On the wall behind her was a poster of glazed purple eggplants and ripe green avocados spilling out of a cane basket. Seeing Niki's surprise, she said, 'My father was with the British Army in Hong Kong when he first heard about California. The sun, people said, was bright as brass, the air dry as a crone, and the soil just like in Punjab. So, in 1917, he arrived in California and started work on a farm,' Juanita laughed. 'It was on one of those farms that Mamā met Andreas.'

'Andreas?'

'Mi Papā. He spoke some English but no Spanish. When he said "Inder Singh", the Mexican farmhands heard "Andreas". So, Andreas he became. He left his landlocked village, rode the seas, lived on islands and what it taught him was that he was like a bamboo – he could bend with the wind.'

'Which is why he married a Mexican woman?'

'No, no! Punjabi immigrants were aliens and were not allowed to bring wives back from India. So they married the Mexican women who worked on the same farms. Miscegenation was illegal but only if it involved white skin. Mexicans and Punjabis were both brown and could intermarry, even though they came from opposite ends of the earth. Ha! And I guess it was the food that brought them together as well. My father said he had spent enough time with the English to learn that their food was like them – bleached of colour and flavour. I owe my existence to chilli-onion-garlic and yes, corn.'

'Wow,' Niki shook her head in appreciation. 'That's some story!'

'Got a big catering job today,' Juanita said as she bustled to the kitchen. 'I'm paid by the dish, not time. When I was growing up, people called us half-and-half. Now, half-and-half, fusion, is fashionable, eh? Like chicken curry enchiladas, mi Mamā's signature dish, which we all ate without realizing its novelty. Mamā took a food her husband loved, learnt how to cook it from him and put it into a Mexican staple. Fusion food was normal for us, and now it's my livelihood!'

Niki saw her plucking leaves off a bunch of fresh fenugreek. She had an entire basket of it to go through, and it would shrivel to a handful when cooked. Jyot, who had been sitting silent throughout, said, 'Bring it here,' indicating the table where they sat. 'We can do it together.'

Juanita deposited the colander on the centre table and settled on the sofa beside Jyot. Soon, the women were busy plucking fenugreek leaves. 'Ah,' Juanita sighed, 'this reminds me of home. Jyot, where in Punjab did you say you came from?'

Jyot continued to pluck the tiny leaves with dexterity and said, 'Folks like their food fused, not blood.'

She had sidestepped Juanita's question with a leading remark. The twin tragedies of Jyot's life had to do with the question of purity that obsessed India, which had given rise to one nation of the pure, Pakistan, and almost birthed another, Khalistan. Before Niki could say something appropriate to draw her out, Juanita, lacking the specific subcontinental context, clucked.

'Obama got elected because he was seen as fusion. But when he finally became president, he became black.'

Niki sat facing the front door, which was ajar. Now, it swung open and a woman filled it, her painted face aglow from the phone she frowned at. Despite the cold, she was dressed in a red bodice, a leather jacket with tassels and torn jeans. 'Hola,' she said in an offhand manner.

Across from Niki, Juanita's head jerked up and swivelled towards the door as she addressed the woman in brisk Spanish. The woman shrugged and replied, the rapid exchange sounding like the spit and hiss of firecrackers. Juanita swung herself off the couch as she made to stand when a man loomed up behind the woman in the doorway. With a strangled scream, Juanita sped to the kitchen from where she grabbed something and charged at the door. The woman in the doorway howled, ducked, and Juanita's plump, short forearm landed with force on the man behind. He clutched his head, spitting and swearing loudly.

From the corner of her eye, Niki realized Mehar had come to the living room and was watching the scene wide-eyed. She stood up, covered the distance quickly and wrapped her arms around her daughter.

Behind them, the man banged a fist repeatedly on the door, spewing rapid-fire Spanish. The elaborately made-up woman bawled in the doorway. Jabbing the air in Juanita's direction, the man disappeared down the passageway. Niki squeezed Mehar. Jyot's hands hovered above the colander. The woman, her face now smudged, jerked her head into Juanita's face, hissed, then clattered away on her heels.

Juanita stood arms akimbo, blocking her doorway with her short, rotund self, glaring at the passageway. 'Son of a whore, I will cook your balls the next time you dare come here!' She shook her right fist, and something clanged in her hand.

The drama ended with the same alacrity with which it had begun. Niki gulped, massaged Mehar's forearms and suggested she return to playing with Asha.

Juanita's eyes, which usually disappeared with mirth into the hillocks of her cheeks, were hard as she rejoined them. 'The whore! She dared to bring that devil back into my house.' But as Juanita settled on the sofa, she appeared to deflate. 'Madre de Dios,' she said in a voice several notches lower. 'It is my fault that my daughter está jodido.' Then she explained.

The dolled-up woman was her daughter, Mercedes, Asha's mother. The man was her pimp. After Jyot took Asha to SAYA, Mercedes had promised never to let her boyfriend near the apartment. And yet, there he was! So, Juanita grabbed the first item she could from the kitchen – a molinillo – which, bless its rings, had torn the cabron's eyelid! Juanita released the wooden whisk onto the table.

But the excitement had taken its toll. She shook her head and retreated to the kitchen to get ingredients ready for the evening. Jyot and Niki resumed working their way through the bunches of fenugreek stalks.

The sudden silence needed a rupture and Niki waded in. 'Jyotji, did you know Mr Malik was a soldier, a sepoy in the Second World War? Did he ever talk about it? Apparently, upon his return, he set Lahore on fire.'

Jyot narrowed her eyes. 'How do you know?'

Niki told Jyot about her father's manuscript, his interviews with Mr Malik over several years and what she had learnt of his role in the sectarian riots as independence had approached.

Jyot sat in her chair, stiff, upright. 'Why are you telling me all this?'

Niki shrugged. She felt like a nervous tween. She licked her lips. 'Papa wrote to you as well, via Mr Malik. Did you, uh, get his letters?'

'I never opened any letters from India. Threw them straight into the dustbin.'

'Oh!'

Niki felt a tingling in her face, like she had been slapped. She bent her head and tried to focus her eyes, glazed over with sudden tears, on the colander of fenugreek. Excited voices floated from the room where Mehar and Asha played, unaffected by the drama that had erupted at the doorstep. A chink and clang filtered from Juanita's exertions in the kitchen. Niki was aware of each sound as she attempted to regain calm. If Jyot had never read Papa's letters, did she even recall the connection between the Nalwa family and her? Dadima's decision to place Jyot in a foster home had distressed Papa and her greatly after '84. But Jyot showed no familiarity—

'More tea?'

Juanita popped her head through the kitchen entrance. When Jyot didn't respond, Niki thanked her and declined on their behalf. 'You don't speak much, Jyot,' Juanita commented and returned to her kitchen.

Niki decided to plough on. 'As a sepoy,' she began again, 'in '47, Mr Malik facilitated terrible riots in Lahore. At some point, though, he realized his folly and tried to make amends.' She looked up from snipping the fenugreek leaves to find Jyot studying her. 'Perhaps that is the reason he abandoned his religion and became Sufi—'

'To save his soul?' Jyot offered.

'I don't know, but he did a lot to help others through SAYA.'

'Mr Malik told me once that we were all trying to make amends – for the wrongs done to us and for the wrongs we had done. That the thing to remember was that the people who opened shelters to help others might not be doing it out of a noble spirit, but because something gnawed at them daily.' She raked the heap of leaves in a practiced manner, her fingertips green.

A familiar gesture, it took Niki back to the Chandigarh kitchen where Nooran chopped vegetables and hummed as Niki sat on the counter.

'Jyotji,' Niki said softly, 'did you feel he was a kindred spirit?'

'What Mr Malik did was good for others and saved his soul. He made an easy bargain. But what if there are no easy bargains to be made?'

Jyot locked eyes with Niki and held her gaze. Niki felt as if she was on a trapeze and had to be absolutely still, not even breathe, or the air would shift and she would plummet to her death. The world stopped spinning. Was that moisture in Jyot's eyes? A lid snapped shut. Juanita packed jalapeños in an airtight container. The moment broke. Jyot withdrew, gathered the colander in her hands and got to her feet.

'Jyotji,' Niki extended her arm to prevent her from leaving, 'tell me your story.'

'What story? One like Mr Malik's?' Her mouth curled in dismissal. 'With redemption at the end?'

53
(2014)

A FEW DAYS LATER, Niki was rushing out of SAYA when Jyot handed her a folded sheet of paper. It was the text of a speech Mr Malik had given when he had been felicitated by the New York Punjabi Sabha a year before he passed away. 'You will find it useful,' she said.

Thanking her, Niki sped towards the subway – Mehar had texted to say that she had a fever. She had been sniffling in the morning but had eaten a good breakfast. Since it was Christmas break and she had no homework, Niki had felt okay leaving her at home. Seated on the 7 train, brow furrowed, she read Mr Malik's speech as the subway swayed towards Manhattan.

During the British Raj, the Punjabi signed up for the Queen's army and returned from the trenches, damaged in parts, his curiosity about the world whetted on the battlefields of Tripoli and Italy, Burma and Baghdad. Hearing those stories, other Punjabis wanted to travel too. So they went across the world, skilled as they were in bringing to life both barren fields and broken machines.

But wherever this new home is made – Australia, Malaya, England, California, Canada, New York – it is filled with pining for the old, which manifests itself in sentimental songs, basement bhangra, curry eateries, pirated DVDs, Indian grocery stores and neighbourhoods like Jackson Heights!

I have kept you from the samosas and butter chicken too long already, but I hope you will bear with me as I tell you a story I once heard from an Indian scholar. It comes from the Upanishads, which, as you know, contain the philosophy of Hinduism, and were composed seven hundred years before Christ. This story is about a young man, Svetaketu, who returns home after a twelve-year period of instruction with his guru.

'What have you learnt?' his father asks.

The son puffs his chest and rattles off the names of the subjects: astronomy, algebra, geometry and so on. But the father is not impressed. 'What else have you learnt – beyond all this?'

The son is puzzled and asks his father for clarification.

'Have you learnt what is real and what is unreal?'

Now the son is truly befuddled.

'No problem,' the father says. He tells him to fetch a tumbler of water, pour some salt in it and let it sit overnight. In the morning, father and son approach the tumbler. 'Take a sip,' the father instructs. 'What does it taste like?'

'Salty,' the boy says.

'Drain half the water and sip again. Now?'

'It's salty.'

'All right, drain most of the tumbler and drink from close to the bottom.'

'It's still salty,' the boy insists.

'What does that tell you?' the father asks.

The boy shrugs. He doesn't know.

Then the father explains to young Svetaketu that just as there is no border between the salt and water, there is no border between a man and the essence that pervades the world. Man, atman, and his creator, Brahman, are woven seamlessly into each other. When that is the case, how can there be any difference between one man and another? In which case, what follows logically is that there can be no 'us' and 'them' – that, indeed, there is no 'other'.

Our forefathers of the Indus Valley created what we can consider the Bronze Age Manhattan, the city of Mohenjo-Daro. And today, we find ourselves in one of the world's great cities, Manhattan. Yet, one lesson that our forefathers distilled all those years back is relevant to this day: tat tvam asi. There is no other.

I have spent a lifetime and am creaking like an old earthen vessel now. If there is one true lesson I have learnt, it is this: there is no other.

The train pulled into 81st Street station and Niki hopped out. Emerging onto Central Park West at the giant steps leading up to the American Museum of Natural History, she passed by the statute of Theodore Roosevelt on horseback, flanked by a black man and an Indian on foot. She tossed her chin at the equestrian Teddy daubed with ice, the white man in charge of and atop the primitives. Across the road sat the snowy Central Park with its fairy-tale sculptures of Alice, Mother Goose and Juliet, but no real historical women. It seemed that only men had contributed to the world and were to be commemorated in busts and statues: Beethoven, Columbus, Hamilton, Jagiello.

Mr Malik's speech did not mention that in the Punjab he lauded, there had always been an 'other': its women. Like Heer.

Amrita Pritam, the beloved poet and Dadima's acquaintance from Lahore, had evoked Heer during Partition, wondering why the plight of countless Punjabi women, traumatized by violence, had not roused Heer's composer Waris Shah from his grave? Was Heer so publicly resonant with the private stories of thousands of Heers folded into the epic, that she embodied the Punjabi way of expiating guilt? A beautiful, wealthy, high-class woman who railed against family, society and clergy, ultimately sacrificing her life for love, Heer was a rebel and a martyr, both traits of the Punjabi hyper-masculine self-image. In life, she had inconvenienced patriarchy; in death, they had appropriated her even as Punjabis continued to murder infant daughters as casually as they had once disposed Heer.

At home, Niki found Mehar in bed while Arjun took her temperature.

'Appa came home early!'

Arjun had been travelling on work and looked none too pleased with his return.

'Hello!' Niki said. He ignored her, and handed Mehar two pills and a glass of water. Thereafter, he tucked her in and walked out.

Niki followed. 'What's wrong?'

Arjun spun around. 'What's *wrong*?' he hissed. 'Why would you take our daughter to a whore's home?'

Niki stopped, stung. Mehar and Asha had caught the drama at Juanita's home from the bedroom and Niki had explained what had happened as best as she could during the train ride home. 'It is not a whore's home!'

'The woman's daughter is a whore, right?'

'Yes, but that doesn't make Juanita—'

'Spare me the nuance. Point is, it is not the right place to take our daughter.' He glanced in the direction of Mehar's room, its door ajar. 'What with her sullen behaviour and falling grades … seriously, Niki!' Shaking his head, he stalked off.

In the bathroom, Niki ran the tap and washed her hands.

Tat tvam asi. Yeah, right. For all your philosophy, Mr Malik, there is always an other.

54
(2014)

❋

'YOU KNOW TRISTAN, right?' Mehar asked as she shook jalapeño pretzel pieces into a bowl, a snack for Leyla and herself as they did their homework in Mehar's room. 'He calls us the Curry Girls. What does curry even mean?'

Ah! Niki was surprised it hadn't come up before – a racial epithet. But then, Mehar's school was rather international with students from Latin America, Asia, Europe and, the US, of course.

'Curry,' Niki said, 'is the English attempt to describe Indian food. Which makes Tristan the curry boy, really.'

'Tell me more.'

'Well, the English came to India and discovered spices, rather the peculiar alchemy of spices in dishes that varied as much as the topography of India. Tamarind and jaggery in the south, onion and tomato in the north, mustard in the east, sweet yogurt in the west and endless permutations of gravy from Peshawar to Periyar. The English, nostrils leaking, tongues aflame, discombobulated by the perpetual heat, roiling over the polysyllabic names, did what they could with the multiplicity of India: they reduced it to a single constant. Hence, curry.'

'Dis-com-*what*?'

'Discombobulate. To confuse.'

'Hmm. Curry sounds like tari, no?' Mehar said, referring to the gravy dishes of their meals.

'Yes. It could be a corruption of that as well.'

Leyla had walked up and was listening to them. Niki saw her look around the living room, her eyes resting on the centrepiece: Nooran's bagh embroidery framed and hung on the wall. She popped a Snyder piece into her mouth and nodded. 'Oh my god, Tristan is *such* an ass. Call him Tristan tikka masala.'

'Why?' Niki asked.

'Tristan is so behind on his slurs,' Leyla said. 'He might think he's being clever, but he probably wolfs down chicken tikka masala every night – that too from the corner takeaway!' She'd grown up in England; she would know.

'Tristan tikka masala!' Mehar shrieked with laughter.

'So, what did you do at school today?' Niki asked.

'Oh, the usual.' Mehar shrugged.

'Tell me about one thing, please.'

'Well, in social studies, we read about Little Boy.'

'Little boy?'

'Uh-huh. And Fat Man.' She watched her mother intently.

'Ah! The atom bombs over Hiroshima and Nagasaki.'

'Real slow, Amma – admit it!' Mehar teased.

'Perhaps. But do you know who is called the father of the atom bomb?'

Mehar twisted her mouth. 'He has a long name, and yes,' she snapped her fingers, 'it was called the Manhattan Project.' She angled her head: score.

'Right. J. Robert Oppenheimer. That the name you were looking for?'

The girls nodded.

'And do you know,' Niki asked as she retrieved the pressure pan, 'what Oppenheimer had to say when he stood in a control room and saw the explosion of the first atom bomb they tested in a desert in New Mexico?'

'Pumped his fist, I guess?' Leyla said.

'Perhaps,' Niki said, 'though I think the scientists were rather overawed by what they saw.'

'Why?' Mehar asked, popping a pretzel piece in her mouth.

'This was the atom bomb, remember. It destroyed entire cities and ended the Second World War. Apparently, Oppenheimer was so struck by the blinding light that he quoted from the Bhagavad Gita, recalling the radiance of a thousand suns, the splendour of the mighty one.'

'Hmmm…' Mehar said, chewing slowly. 'Mighty one?'

'From the scene where Krishna shows Arjuna his godly form, the destroyer of time, the one who shattered entire worlds?'

Mehar nodded. 'Seeing which Arjuna said "Roger that!" and rejoined the battle.'

'Something like that,' Niki laughed. The girls went back to Mehar's room, and she got busy with preparations for dinner: soaking black lentils in a pan with minced ginger, garlic and half a teaspoon each of red chilli powder, ground turmeric and salt. The book was her Manhattan Project: she was in a race against time and Jyot's story was the critical fissile material needed for delivery.

At dinner, Mehar pointed to the framed bagh embroidery. 'It *does* look ugly, you know.'

Niki was stung but she held her tongue and glared instead.

'Well, Leyla is right – it looks unfinished…'

'Do *you* find it ugly?'

Mehar studied her dinner.

'You know the story behind Nooran's bagh.' When Mehar didn't answer, Niki said in a quiet voice, 'Words can hurt, mean words especially so.'

Niki's cheeks were freezing, even as her jaw seemed to have locked itself. The rainwater in the puddles from yesterday had become the black ice of today as she jogged in Central Park. Pin oak leaves were impaled on a fence by the wind and an austere artistry had replaced the profusion of summer. A tree of twigs, bare and brown, dotted with wondrously red cherries. A squirrel, scooting up a tree trunk. A swirling eddy of dry leaves like a curtain of confetti she must part to go through.

How could she make Mehar connect with her past? Their relocation could not become a dislocation, her roots upended and flailing in the exposed air. She thought of her friend Aruna, who had come to the US after getting married. Aruna was sanguine: 'Home is where our feet take us,' she always said. It reminded Niki of Dadima's mang tikka, the pendant framed for posterity on Roop's forehead as a bride.

The ornament had journeyed from Peshawar to Lahore to Amritsar to Mumbai, to Hong Kong, and now it was in Manhattan. If it could tell its story, where would it say its home was? In the cradle of the north-western frontier of Pakistan, infamous now as the site of the US war on terror, where three mountain ranges – the Himalayas, Hindukush and Karakoram – had come together to birth its precious stones? In the by-lanes of Lahore, where it first came to rest on the graceful forehead of the first woman to possess it? In the bag in which it was ensconced during the inky flight across Ravi? In the two-room brick house in Amritsar, where it was guarded fiercely against the temptation to pawn it for cash? In the locker of a steel almirah in a quiet bungalow in leafy Chandigarh, where it nestled with other jewels that were collected for a granddaughter's trousseau? In the peripatetic bag of the itinerant expat woman, who had taken it to most of the financial centres of the world? Eventually with Mehar, whose home would be god alone knew where. Wherever her feet took her…

From the corner of her eye, Niki saw a child gather pine cones and pour them into a woman's gloved hands, which reminded Niki of gathering jamun with Nooran every monsoon of her childhood. Once, while returning from the neighbourhood park, they had met a tall man with whom Nooran had chatted for a bit. Something about the exchange had made Niki jealous.

When they had been back in the kitchen, she had asked, 'Who was that man?'

'My man,' Nooran had answered.

'His name?'

'Allah Ditta.'

'God given? You mean God gave him to you?'

'No, I gave him to myself,' Nooran had laughed. 'That's his name.'

Niki had frowned. 'What kind of name is that?'

Nooran had grinned. 'His mother didn't want to announce in public that having given birth, she felt like a God. That is why she called him Allah Ditta, when we all know *who* gave him to the world.' Nooran snorted. 'A woman only has to say the most incredible things with a straight face, and the world swallows it wholesale.'

Niki had laughed, not sure if she got it entirely though. 'If you had a child, Nooran, you'd call it Nooran Ditta?'

'If I had a child,' Nooran had said, rolling the pin as she flattened a ball of dough, 'I would call it Niki, so I could spank it any time.' She slapped the disc of dough in her palms and plonked it on the griddle.

From behind her, Niki had clasped her arms around Nooran. The satin of her kameez was scratchy, she had smelled of sweat and flour, and Niki had been happy to rest against Nooran's ample behind. Twin treats had followed: a hot dish of choori and a dessert of pulpy jamun.

As she reached her apartment, Niki shook herself out of her memory. Once inside, she sank on the low chair by the door, her chest heaving with quiet sobs. Tears rolled down her cheeks. She saw one fall to the wooden floor, staining it. Head in her hands, Niki felt both under- and overwhelmed. A black figure blurred into view. It stepped closer before sitting on its haunches right beneath her line of vision, emerald green eyes studying her intently. With one hand

Niki stroked Jade, with the other, she wiped her face. As Nooran and Old Man Bullah would have said, 'People say their lentils won't soften, and I have seen stones dissolve often.'

'*Am-ma!*' Mehar stopped as she caught Niki wiping her eyes. 'What happened?'

'Nothing.'

'No, tell me,' Mehar crouched beside Jade, looking up at her.

'I … was remembering Nooran.'

Mehar crossed her legs, took Jade in her lap and sat down. 'What about Nooran?'

'Oh, nothing.'

'Go on, you have so many stories about Nooran – tell us one.'

Niki recounted how she would go with Nooran to the park each monsoon to look for juicy jamuns scattered at the base of the jamun tree, pick the good ones, pile them in the dupatta that Nooran would spread out like a net, rinse them at home, sprinkle them with salt and pop into her mouth one by delicious one, the tangy taste yielding to sweetness and a tongue dyed deep purple. 'Jamun is better than any strawberry, blackberry or other berry,' Niki concluded.

'And what about mangoes?' Mehar asked, aware of her mother's fondness for it.

'After mangoes, jamuns are the finest fruit of the Indian summer.'

'And Nooran's dupatta?'

'Dadima gave her a fresh one when jamun season ended, and the stained dupatta became a head wrap for when Nooran dusted the house!'

Niki paused. Nooran was Niki's mother as much as Dadima was. When a mewling motherless infant was delivered to Jinder Nalwa, Nooran had swaddled the baby in soft mulmul as Dadima had dipped her finger in honey and touched the infant's tongue. She had suckled on Dadima's finger as Nooran's capable hands cradled her. How did Niki know this? It was her favourite story of the trove of stories they had nurtured her on. The umbilical cord that Nooran had always talked about pulsed not only with oxygen-carrying blood but life-giving stories also. Everything that Niki knew had come from the conversations that filled her home.

Even on the day that Niki had lost Nooran, she knew she could always find her way back to her for they were intimately connected through that umbilical cord. Like dust motes that become apparent in the air in the chink of light breaking through a parted curtain, Nooran's stories would remain in the ether of her life, to be plucked and re-plucked when needed. What could sum up the woman whom she had always called by her first name, who had cared for her as a mother but treated her as a friend-sister-daughter, whose laugh was heartier than any man's, who was truer than the blazing sun, whose snort could cut through her bullshit, who would cradle her to her bosom and cure all her heartaches?

'What, Amma? What are you thinking?'

'Nooran,' Niki smiled.

'What about Nooran?'

'That she had the radiance of a thousand suns.'

'Little Boy or Fat Man?'

'Her Own Woman. Nooran was her own woman,' and Niki reached out and embraced her daughter. As long as there were stories to tell, there was a way to connect.

=

In yoga class, Niki stretched her torso in the warrior pose, her arms extended upwards. Across from her, Oonagh made an effortless yogi as she arched backwards gracefully with her palms together. Over the instructor's rhythmic 'In-hale, ex-hale,' a story about another mythical warrior popped up in Niki's mind.

In the Mahabharata, the war at Kurukshetra had raged for eighteen days. For the first nine days, the two sides were evenly matched. With the body count mounting, the Pandavas asked their adviser Krishna for a way out. Krishna knew that with Bhishma the grandsire leading the Kauravas, victory was elusive if not impossible. Bhishma had been blessed by the gods that he could choose the time of his death. In which case, he had to be tricked into lowering his weapons – but how? Krishna had then invited upon his chariot Shikhandi, who looked like a woman but was a man. Or was she a woman with a man's organs? The debate raged on over what Shikhandi was exactly, and the only agreement they could reach was that Shikhandi, being neither man nor woman, was an anomaly. But Krishna, being the God that he was, knew it was the midpoint of the battle and the right time to introduce Shikhandi into the battlefield. Bhishma would never fight a woman.

'Inhale deeply into your belly and chest.'

The old order changeth, yielding place to new, and God fulfils himself in many ways... Perhaps Tennyson had read the Mahabharata. As Krishna foresaw, the introduction of Shikhandi ended the seesaw of battle, giving it a decisive direction.

'Feel your body expanding.'

A decisive new direction was exactly what Niki needed in her interaction with Jyot. If her reading was correct, Jyot wanted to shatter her silence and yet, something held her back. Was it something Jyot had done? Something that had left her with a lifetime's guilt? Tiny Uncle's father killed a Muslim during the madness of '47 and was haunted by that man's ghost all his life. When her neighbours were killed, Veervati stole the trousseau of their daughter and used it for her marriage; she blamed it for her sterile womb. Kulwant Singh had gathered the women of his family and shot them with his rifle to save them from defilement. When Papa interviewed him, he remained adamant that he had done the right thing. That was all he would say, refusing to talk in any detail about that time. It was war, he asserted, and in war people did things they wouldn't in normal times. Did the mighty Bheema eat entrails for dinner daily? No – only in battle.

What battles had Jyot fought?

Nahm-as-tay.

With six months to deadline and the book missing its spine, Niki needed her own Shikhandi. Someone to break the seesaw. Lately, Nooran had been on her mind and, Nooran was an anomaly: a woman in a man's world. Perhaps Nooran would help breach Jyot's defences?

XVII
(2015)
Jyot

55
(2015)

AS PEOPLE SPED by, fleeing the chilly darkness, I marched stiffly down Roosevelt Avenue. A new year had started, the 'happy holidays' were over and people were back to their harried selves. A snowstorm had piled up fresh snow on the sidewalks. Where the old ice peeped through, it was ashen – evidence of a relentless winter. A man cut into my path.

He looked back, his eyes sweeping over me before turning ahead, his jeans-clad legs matching pace with me. He wore shoes with thick soles and lofty uppers that swallowed the ankles as if attempting to drown him. His leather jacket was an open challenge to feeble folks who were zippered up and scurrying indoors, their heads bent against the wind that smacked dry leaves and wastepaper into them. The man's left hand moved to his waistband to tug his jeans up, during which his jacket lifted to reveal a metallic object sticking out of the back. In a city where people operated from within self-contained bubbles, this man was attempting to be noticed. Again, he turned to look back. Again, he locked eyes with me. Then he slowed down, falling in step beside me, studying me.

Why this interest?

In Jackson Heights, which was like the bus terminal of the world, he could be from anywhere with his dark skin and dark eyes. Casually, the man took the metallic object from his back and cradled it in his hand, showing the gun to me like an offering.

Abruptly, in my mind, the evening turned to night, in the manner of a Delhi winter, unleashing the predators who picked off prey. There were usually small fires by the roadside, outside a hovel, beside a taxi stand, and it was a common way to stay warm as people huddled over the flames in their woollens. What was unusual was to see one of those huddled men become tinder. But the unusual became usual in '84, when men gathered the turbaned, bearded ones within them to feed the communal fire, a sacrificial fire last seen in '47.

The stranger kept studying me, cradling the gun, walking alongside. What did he want?

At the entrance to the subway, a woman joined him, looping her arm into his, nuzzling his neck. They descended the steps into the subway together, beside me. There was a pressure to my right that jabbed through my puffer jacket. The man locked eyes with me. The woman bent forward and showed me her middle finger. I recognized her then. Beneath the stiff curls and that face paint were Juanita's apple cheeks and high forehead. Smirking at me, she aligned two horizontal fingers that cocked up. Beside her, the man gave a lazy wink.

I'd been slow. The man was Mercedes' pimp. And he was trying to scare me. If he could see what I had seen and never stopped seeing since – women dragged by their hair and stripped in public, as husbands watched with vacant eyes, as police watched with impunity, as men feasted on flesh to the disgust of vultures that feed on corpses – would he shoot me or would he sprint?

I was not afraid, I had no fear to show. So I gave the pimp a stiff smile.

He recoiled as if I had struck him. 'Puta,' he swore thickly, spat and swivelled to ascend, as if fleeing a ghost. Juanita's daughter, startled, scrambled after him in her high-heeled boots.

Inside me, acid rose as images from the past collided in my blood and hammered my brain. This was not good. All my life, violence had trailed me. At each stage, it had snatched what was valuable to me from me, but spared me. Now, violence had shown its ugly face again. And in the pit of my stomach, dread pooled. Now that I had something of value in my life again, violence was stalking me again, to rob me once again.

I pushed the acid down my throat and consumed it. After so many years, she had come back into my life, and I must steer violence away from Niki.

XVIII
(2015)
Karma and Dharma

As Duryodhana lies dying on the battlefield, he mocks Yudhishthira about the kingdom he will now inherit, ravaged by war and cursed by the dead. Yudhishthira, ankle-deep in the blood of the slain, hangs his head as wails of women rent the air. The grief-stricken Draupadi is lying prone on the ground. Gandhari, having lost all hundred sons, picks her way through the corpses. Thus, the Great War ends, and Vyasa reaches the end of his non-stop narration that will give the world its longest poem: the Mahabharata. It is a gargantuan task and Vyasa can rest now. But a thought niggles him. What if succeeding generations confuse the moral of the battle for dharma and, seduced by cascading arrows, whirring weapons, flying chariots and the headlong rush of adrenaline, choose battle over Dharma? And the Mahabharata repeats over and over, the past forever intruding into the present?

56
(2015)

✦

IN THE SAYA office, Niki sat across the table from Jyot. The heating in the building was distinctly uneven – it was boiling that day, and Niki had even shed her cardigan. Jyot, though, still wore her pullover with the dupatta-like-scarf looped over one shoulder, as still as a Buddha. Niki realized that analogy was false as soon as it formed in her mind: the Buddha was synonymous with renunciation, a voluntary forsaking, while Jyot was a simulacrum of loss, perpetually bereft.

'Anything else you can tell me about Mr Malik?'

There was again a long lapse between answers. Niki's progress on the note on SAYA's founder mimicked that on her book. Papa's manuscript had revealed a great deal about Sepoy Malik but much less about Mr Malik.

'I need you to speak up, Jyotji, or we'll never get this done,' a note of exasperation made her voice shrill. To compose herself, she surveyed her surroundings. A plastic Christmas tree festooned with cards made by SAYA children stood in one corner, attempting cheer past its expiry date.

Niki straightened. 'Why don't I tell you a story instead?' She began talking about Nooran, the nine-year-old girl who had sought refuge in the Nalwa home and ended up becoming the star at the centre of that universe instead. Jyot looked up and listened. At some point, she leaned in, hands entwined, elbows on the table between them, until Niki reached the point where every story must end.

'How did she die?'

The tapping of Ms Dixit's keyboard provided a staccato beat to their staccato exchange.

'How?' Niki repeated the word, adjusted the collar of her shirt and started to talk about the bus ride from long ago. When she finished, her left hand was pressed to her mouth, physically keeping the tremors at bay.

'Silence is not so bad, you see?'

'Huh?' Niki was puzzled and hurt that Jyot looked so unemotional, so, so … unmoved.

'Nooran should have stayed quiet. Better still, you should have kept your mouth shut. A little grope would not have killed you. Instead, Nooran would have lived to see you get married, see your daughter, spend time with her.'

Niki couldn't believe her eyes or ears. Jyot spoke with a complete lack of passion, but bitterness oozed from the wrinkled face, radiating out of hard eyes. Why, oh why, was she trying to get familiar with this woman who was so cruel, so joyless, so unkind she didn't deserve to hear even a scrap of Nooran's story?

Niki's chest rose and fell as she breathed with effort. Her throat clogged. She rose and hurried to the washroom as the pit of her stomach hollowed, before it pooled with grief. Jyot had scratched a wound that she worked hard to keep scabbed over. She had always blamed herself for Nooran's death, despite the protestations of Papa and Dadima and her own rational self. For her heart insisted that on the bus that day, there was a way to be which would've kept Nooran alive. Instead, Niki had behaved in such a way that Nooran had died, her brain bleeding on the tarmac as the sun rose higher, the police dithered, people gawked and flies gathered.

57
(2015)

✳

THEREAFTER, THE DAY had the quality of a Punjabi sky overcast with an approaching dust storm, the eyes blinking due to unseen grit, time turned ponderous as the pall thickened. Niki worked alone, trying to compose a wholesome piece on Mr Malik from the dribbles she'd gathered from the SAYA staff. She was looking to leave early when Ms Dixit asked her to join a meeting with a representative of an NGO, South Asian Legal Defence. They discussed her write-up of Mr Singh, the taxi driver's case, and their plans to bundle such cases together to leverage the mayor for action. It was interesting work, but Niki's mind was mushy with memories of Nooran piling up on collision with guilt. As the meeting dragged on, she texted Mehar to eat her snack and start homework, and that she would be home soonest.

By the time Niki was at the subway station, the evening sky was as dark as a winter night. The 7 train was running late because of 'train traffic ahead'. Commuters fermented on platforms, huddles burgeoning in the warmth of the underground as minutes ticked until they started to coalesce into one mass. When the train arrived, they poured into it en masse. At the 42nd Street station, Niki waited forever to change to the 1 train, too confused to think of options. When she glanced at her watch – 7.30 p.m.! – she wove her way outside to catch a cab.

A freezing rain – was this what they called sleet? – made her edge along the storefronts, seeking spotty shelter under short awnings as she kept an eye out for a yellow cab. The other folks milling around Times Square had the same idea too, as necks craned out of hoodies, umbrellas or awnings and swung as if viewing a tennis match. The spot was no good. Niki slithered up. A sign on a glass door caught her eye: 'Flamenco! Want to learn? Join our open class – it's for everyone! At $20, what you gotta lose? Except your inhibitions!'

A woman in a red silk dress leapt out of the poster, her right arm flung to the sky, her left clutching a train, her neck poised like a peacock's – the statuesque, sexy pose could well have been Nooran's. The woman in the poster – Clarabella Barrio – was a peacock as well. Both oozed the same comfort with their bodies. And Niki wanted that. Since the first time she had seen a flamenco performance at the Hong Kong Arts Festival, she knew she wanted to strut and stomp and be sensuous like a flamenco dancer. In Hong Kong, it was a routine struggle for Niki to find clothes to fit her because, in comparison with petite Chinese women, she was an XXL size. What joy it was then to behold a dance meant for women with womanly butts and bosoms. Right now, she wanted to shed her torpor, stomp her feet, fling her arms, twirl her body, let go. Let go.

The class was starting and, why yes, they had a couple of spots for a trial, you lucky thing! 'No worries if you haven't done it before, darling,' the Shikhandi-like androgynous person at the counter assured her. 'You'll be swell!' There was no need for a dress; her short boots and loose pants would work great! Her phone was at five per cent battery. Niki messaged Mehar that she was running late, switched the phone to low-power mode, deposited her bag, swelled up and strode out to the dance floor.

Twenty-odd women in flowing skirts and polka dot dresses, frilly tops, arched feet over barres and extended bodies like seasoned yogis were strewn across the floor like confetti – was she the only novice? There were a couple of younger women in pants, so she might have beginner company. But there was no time for second thoughts, as the instructor swept in and put them through a brisk warm-up routine. Then she showed them la postura, the flamenco pose: back straight, shoulders level, chest high, stomach in. Nooran's pose, and Niki smiled as she copied it. Next came arm work: braceo. 'Make your arms into eagles, powerful yet graceful,' the instructor urged. Undulating limbs danced towards the ceiling. In her mind, Niki was a soaring eagle when the instructor glided by, 'Don't flutter like a butterfly! Use more energy!'

She stole a look around and tried imitating a woman in a frilly dress a few places ahead, whose arms were exquisite, no doubt from the kind of vigorous exertions flamenco demanded. Niki's biceps were protesting when footwork demonstration began. *Stamp, stamp, heel.* Thunder shook the room as assorted women stomped in unison. *Ball, heel, heel, ball.* Skirts shimmied, trains swung, backsides heaved, Niki panted. Clearly, jogging in Central Park was no match for robust flamenco.

'Ladies, show me that gypsy!' the instructor shouted. 'You ain't ballerinas, don't go soft on me!' Hands and feet moving in unison, she stomped, spun, twirled and a roomful of women followed.

Niki couldn't get her heels and balls and arms and fingers to coordinate. She had to stop moving to get the eagle arms going, which she followed with heel, ball – or was it ball, heel? As she floundered, she came into the path of a dancer stomping beside her. She barely escaped getting jabbed in the eye when she stumbled on her train, a ripping sounded, the woman spun away, the floor came up and Niki's bum bounced onto the floor.

Ouch! Niki registered the pain, but the humiliation was greater as women continued dancing around her, avoiding her; meanwhile, her fingers splayed on the floor would get chopped any minute by some hard heel.

'Hear the rhythm, catch the rhythm!'

Niki was glad for the continued frenzy as she picked herself up and threaded her way out. As she clambered up the steps with her bag, the mirror reflected a woman with crazy hair, red nose, glittering eyes. The antipode to a regal self-possessed peacock.

$$=$$

At home, Niki opened the door to Arjun frowning at his phone. 'I was about to call 911! Where *were* you?' Anxiety and anger fought for dominance on his face.

Flamenco dancing. A beginner class on a freezing January night. After a hurried message sent home. If she blurted that out, Arjun might just call 911 – his wife needed therapy.

'Why weren't you answering your phone?'

Niki dug out her iPhone. 'Dead,' she said.

'What's up, Niki?' Arjun waved a hand, then brought it to rest on his forehead. It was a dramatic gesture, but he was clearly agitated. 'Look, I don't know what's up, but you need to get a handle on this. You need to be around your daughter...'

As Niki frowned, he continued, 'Mehar has an Instagram account. Did you know about that? I returned early and saw her Instagramming instead of finishing her homework. When I asked to be shown her account, she resisted greatly. You know she uses the hashtag "Cumberbitch" to describe herself?'

What fresh hell was this? 'Okay, okay, calm down. Since when has our daughter become my sole responsibility?'

'You are the one at home, right?'

'And if I was working at a corporate job?'

'Then we would rethink things. But you need to get this right.' A jolly tune sang its way into their argument. Arjun studied his phone, his brow knitted. Rearranging his face, he answered the phone, 'Hi

Steve, yeah, tell me,' and walked to the guest room, which doubled up as his study.

Why was Arjun being so unfair? Niki peeled off her wet boots and left them to dry in the laundry closet. As she hung her wet jacket, it slipped off the hanger. She gathered it up and fumbled with the hanger, her mind on Mehar's Instagram page. Since when had Mehar stopped sharing things with her? Mehar was not a secretive child; the jacket pooled on the floor. Niki retrieved it and as her hands moved towards the hanger, she scrunched up the jacket, crumpling it with force until it balled up such that her fingers hurt. She then flung it aside and stormed out.

At Mehar's ajar door, she paused. Mehar lay on one side, back to the door. For a child who slept on her back, it was a sign of sullen protest. Likely to be awake, it was still not 10 p.m., she had heard her parents arguing. Niki sighed. Jade's green eyes glowed from the perch beside the bed.

She padded to the bathroom. Turning the tap full on, she looked at herself in the mirror. 'I can't get a thing right,' she said to her image. 'Indeed, a complete loser: at odds with my book, not earning an income, not being a good mother, a poor wife, a negligent grandchild, so, so gauche at flamenco...'

Niki snorted as the vision of herself tripping on the woman's train surfaced in her un-peacock self. The snigger became a laugh, which became a hysterical sob. And Niki broke down, bawling into the sink. The water carried her tears and drivel down the drain.

58
(2015)

✳

NIKI WAS A puddle on the bathroom floor. And yet, the puddle woke up in the morning, drank the tea Arjun made before leaving for office, made Mehar breakfast, walked her to school and started jogging in Central Park until a pregnant woman overtook it. Then the puddle gave up. The tundra of the park offered little consolation.

Despondent, back in bed, Niki opened Facebook on her laptop. As she scanned the feed, a link caught her eye. She clicked.

'Women's breasts are very, very powerful.' The article referred to a topless march in summer. It was freezing outside and Niki couldn't imagine going anywhere without ten layers of clothing, but she read on. A few dozen women had decided to illustrate an existing state law: the right of all women to go bare-chested if they so chose. Apparently, it drew leering loafers with cameras, who filmed frantically as the few topless women marched for their right to do so, a privilege men took casually.

Niki shut her MacBook, angled her chin in a hand and started thinking. In India, it was not uncommon for men to go bare-chested and bare-legged, their cotton loincloths folded upwards from the knee

300

and tucked in at the waist. After her wedding, she had visited a South Indian temple and had been shocked at the level of male nudity on display. It was something to do with purity rituals and humidity levels, they said. Still. And yet, women didn't have a choice in the matter. First world or third world, women had to put up with shit everywhere.

If Heer was alive, in Manhattan, she would have been one of those topless women.

The building outside her window was smoking. The Upper West Side spouted steam like it were an assembly of kettles. It was the pre-war buildings, she was told. The heating was via a central boiler and the excess steam was allowed no escape. Along with ancient-looking water towers that topped buildings like rockets that had failed to launch, these were quintessential Upper West Side features. And the eyes that watched. The stone figures carved on building facades included Assyrian heads, winged lions, angels and hunchbacks holding up balconies. In downtown Manhattan, new constructions were booming but in the historic district of the Upper West Side, the past was valued and valuable.

Unlike the world she came from. Papa's manuscript was the result of twenty-plus years of work as he recorded the individual stories of Vand and Chaurasi, Punjabi shorthand for Partition of '47 and the pogrom of '84, lost in the swathe of an ahistorical yet ancient land. A land where mythology supplanted history, where mythic gods were worshipped and real men sacrificed, where hoary epics were refreshed and recent narrations redacted. A land of the world's oldest continuous civilization. Could it then be blamed for one infirmity: amnesia? The Internet had given record-keepers access to survivors outside of India. Yet, the work remained akin to gathering an ocean with a teacup. Niki had seen Papa despondent, but he had never given up. Nor did Dadima. Dedicated to their work, practising detachment from its result, they were karma yogis.

Meanwhile, Niki was struggling with everything. Every interaction with Jyot was hopeless, yet she needed to unearth Jyot's story to complete Papa's book, which reminded her daily of her loss.

The relocation was proving tougher than she had thought: housework never seemed to end, Mehar was in constant rebellion and Arjun had too much work on his hands. Dadima was so far, she was homesick, and Nooran was on her mind all the time ... Niki sniffled.

What would Nooran do?

Be a puddle or try being a karma yogi like the rest of her family?

Tossing the blanket aside, Niki marched to the laundry closet. As she began vacuuming, she ran through the list of things she needed to get on top of.

———

She started with her daughter. As Mehar ate her after-school snack, Niki drew a chair and sat down at the dining table. 'We need to talk.'

Mehar's eyes narrowed. 'I've got homework to finish.'

'Sure, but this comes first.'

'This what?' Mehar made to get up.

'Sit down, young lady!'

'Don't "young lady" me!' Mehar folded her arms.

'You are a young lady and I *am* your mother, and you *don't* get to talk to me like that. I expect you to show me the same courtesy and respect you show your teachers. Sit down.'

If it was a comic book, Mehar would have had puffs of breath shooting out of her nostrils.

'First, your grades. They've slipped – badly. We got you the cat because you said you needed a pet, and you promised you'd be responsible. Well, time to keep your end of the bargain. Shore up your grades. Two, the cat. As you well know, your father's allergy is acting up. We need to manage the cat—'

'She has a name,' Mehar harrumphed.

'—such that we keep our home as clean and dander-free as possible,' Niki ploughed on. 'Which means that you have to keep your room tidy, stop the cat from climbing the living room sofas and tables, including,' she tapped the dining table, 'this one—'

'She's a cat! Didn't I tell you they can't be trained?'

Niki paused and regarded her daughter. 'In which case, the choice is between your father and the cat – one has to go. And since Appa is the breadwinner of this family, Jade it will be.'

Mehar's chest rose from beneath crossed arms. 'I don't need him to be the breadwinner.'

'Oh you do, believe me, you do, to be fed and clothed and schooled. Or, you could attend the public school across the street from yours? Cheaper, more affordable.'

The chin wobbled. Mutiny was difficult from a chair.

'So, find a way to manage the cat such that we can live together as a family. Appa was aware of the allergy before we brought Jade home. Yet, he agreed to bring her home. Our turn now to help him manage his allergy.' Niki paused. Mehar had deflated, the arms by her side now.

'The HEPA filter is up and running. Aruna Aunty is getting me an herbal medicine from India that helps fight allergy.' Niki extended her hands, which her daughter refused to take. 'We are in this together as a family. And we *gotta* look out for each other.' She rose and helped Mehar out of the chair. Draping her arm around her back, she said, 'Let's train Jade, shall we?'

Later, Niki called the landlord and updated him on the harassment she was facing from an unknown building resident about mothballs. Mr Levy promised to look into it at once. Then, she called Dadima, whom she hadn't spoken to for some days.

Afterwards, she opened a bottle of Malbec, poured herself a glass and started to cook Arjun's favourite dinner. Karma and dharma had so bedevilled Arjuna in the battlefield that Krishna had to declare a time out and teach him how to act in accordance with his duty. And this was the essence of the Bhagavad Gita: to be a karma yogi. Or how not to be a puddle.

59
(2015)

✽

IT WAS SPRING break – despite the ankle-deep snow – and Mehar was at home, chatting with a friend on her laptop. After the Instagram incident, the new rule was that all electronic devices were to be used only in the living room. Niki was spending more time at home with Mehar, the challenges of relocation were never-ending. She sat down to write. Continuing with her karma yogi approach, she focused on Nooran's story, which she was interweaving with Papa's narrative.

Mehar's phone pinged. Niki looked up. Her daughter ignored the phone and continued the conversation on her laptop. Outside, the city's winter palette was minimalist, as if inspired by New York Fashion Week: a sweep of white contrasted with the brown of bare branches and brownstones.

The phone pinged again. And again. '*Me-har*, answer it!'

'Okay, okay!'

Her train of thought broken, Niki decided to run a load in the washing machine.

Mehar was frowning at her phone.

'What's up?'

Mehar shook her head. 'Kia,' she said.

'What about Kia?' Niki asked as she loaded clothes into the washer.

'She's acting up.'

'Acting up? How?'

Mehar sighed. 'Her parents are getting a divorce and she's gone all weird. She wants attention all the time from *all* her friends. And then she complains that Ally or Carlotta or someone is being mean to her – she's so needy.'

'Hmmm...' Niki shut the door of the machine and started the wash cycle. 'Seems like she's acting out in response to what's happening at her home. It's called projecting. You feel bad about one thing and you attribute it to a convenient target.'

Mehar lifted one brow. 'You mean, her parents are getting a divorce, and she feels bad, obviously. So she thinks badly about them but that makes her uncomfortable, so she pushes those bad feelings onto her friends? Wow, that's complicated!'

'The heart is deeper than an ocean. Who can fathom its mysteries?'

With a knowing look, Mehar asked, 'Nooran?'

Niki nodded. 'Another of her Sufi quotes. Useful. The Sufi poets were acquainted with Freudian analysis well before Freud knew it himself.'

The phone pinged again. As Mehar read the new message, Niki recalled how Jyot had criticized Nooran and her and their actions on the bus – hang on ... Niki stood frozen in place, a hand against her mouth. Had Jyot done what Kia was doing? When she had held Niki responsible for Nooran's death, who was she accusing really? And for what action?

60
(2015)

✳

'VANDANA SAID THE note needs my help,' Jyot said as Niki entered SAYA.

Jyot walked like women who carried weight on their heads – basket, water pitcher, firewood – and yet, not quite. There was a deliberateness to her gait as opposed to the swinging ease of those other women, as if she were keenly aware of each step she took.

So now she wanted to work together? That was perfect because Niki had a plan. 'Of course,' she said with a smile, depositing her bag at the volunteer table.

Jyot pulled up a chair and sat down to read the note, an index finger tapping along the text as she mouthed the words.

'Jyotji,' Niki started, 'that day when I shared Nooran's story and you ... uh ... blamed me? You weren't really blaming me, were you?'

Jyot raised her eyes. A screeching sounded outside as an ambulance threaded its way through traffic. Niki licked her lips. 'Y-you were blaming yourself. You did something for which you can't ... you haven't ... forgiven yourself.'

Jyot's expression did not change. 'How would you know?' Her voice was hoarse.

'Because I blamed myself for Nooran's death. If only I had stayed quiet, Nooran would be alive. But then the men were caught. Someone in the bus identified them and their village. I was a minor. Papa asked if I would identify the men. He told me how it would unfold. A case would be filed, and I would be called to testify as a witness, which would mean missing school, sitting in a grimy hot corridor for hours awaiting my turn at the stand. It could even mean pressure from the families of the accused men. It would be messy, laboured, entirely unpleasant, he assured me.'

Niki paused. Memories crowded her mind, like the passengers packing the bus that day. She could smell sweat, carried on a cool breeze, the scratch and slide of Nooran's polyester kameez, the hard, probing fingers at her groin, the flutter in her heart, the pee trickling down her thigh ... She shook her head, inhaled deeply.

Jyot watched her intently.

Niki had wanted to take Nooran's fly swatter and squash the men to bloody entrails. 'I nodded yes, but I was scared. In my nightmares, I was caught in a crowded bus and Nooran left and I could never squeeze my way out of the thicket of men pressing in... Surely my voice would fail in court.'

Abruptly, the heating unit roared before settling into its low rumble. A phone rang to the tune of a popular Hindi film song, but Jyot sat still. Niki breathed as if at the end of a jog.

'W-when the day came for me to go to court with Papa, my palms wouldn't stop sweating. I couldn't see people. All I saw was eyes, eyes boring into me, picking apart my body parts.' She licked her lips. 'As we waited my turn in the musty courtroom with lizards listening on the walls, Nooran stood in front of me. Tall, assured, bright as a peacock. "Niki," she said, "look the world in the eye, puttar!" The case took three years and two men were sent to jail.'

Niki studied her hands, willing herself not to cry. 'You see,' she said without raising her head, 'if I had kept quiet in the bus, I would have betrayed Nooran. She never raised me to be quiet.'

Jyot did not speak for some time. The two women looked at each other. The clattering of keyboards filled the quiet around them.

Her eyes were brown, indeed the brown of a moist gunny sack, and she had a mole on her chin like a beauty spot. A slim nose, a generous mouth with the rise and dip of the Shivalik Hills – Jyot must have been a beauty before those wrinkles had claimed her.

'Yuno,' Jyot spoke, her voice grating. 'I am glad you think Nooran's story is to be celebrated.' She cleared her throat. 'Mine is a cautionary tale.'

'Let me decide that, Jyotji—'

'I have looked the world in the eye, and it killed me.'

'No, you are alive.'

A shrug. 'This is a husk of Jyot. A marjiwara.' One of the living dead, with none of the tropes or thrills of TV zombies.

In a soft voice, Niki urged, 'Tell me your story, Jyotji. I promise only to listen, and not to judge or even discuss it if you don't want to. *Please.*'

'You don't understand. I *have* no story. Only shards, which course through my veins.' Jyot gazed at her forever.

When she spoke, her voice seemed suffocated. 'I have a black tongue, Niki. What I say comes true. But only the bad things, never the good. For your sake, you should stay away from me.'

61
(2015)

✳

NIKI WAS HEADING to buy coffee to carry to SAYA. She was thinking about a YouTube video Mehar had shown her. In it, a Sikh boy in a top knot was riding a school bus when some children heckled him, saying, 'Terrorist! Terrorist!' He tried to ignore them. As cries of 'Afghan terrorist' and 'Go back!' became an incantation, the boy jauntily tossed back, 'Who cares?'

The boy was Mehar's age, and the video was being discussed in her critical thinking class, and she appeared blasé. Still. If Mehar had been a boy wearing a top knot...

As she crossed Roosevelt Avenue, she saw Jyot a few paces ahead. 'Jyotji!' she called. Jyot halted and Niki jogged up to her. 'Shall I treat you to coffee?' she hooked a thumb in the direction of the coffee shop.

'So many years in Amreeka, but I have never taken to coffee, yuno.'

'No problem,' Niki shrugged. 'Tea in the office then.'

A woman arranged gold necklaces in the display window of Sona Jewels of Jaipur, two painted caparisoned camels bookending the name on the board. The hiss of steam and crisp, buttery batter

309

wafted over them as they passed Dosa Delight. They were washed in
soy and garlic as Ming Wok Free Delivery bustled to the clanging
of ladles. Manhattan might like black or white, but Jackson Heights
was as colourful as an Indian saree shop. Niki had been coming to
SAYA for months now, yet the astonishing diversity of people in
the area continued to surprise her. Away from the tourist trap of
Times Square, this was the one place in New York that was truly the
crossroads of the world. From the corner of her eye, Niki glanced at
her companion, who marched in silence.

'Jaikishan Heights,' Niki snorted.

'What?'

'Isn't that what the desis call this neighbourhood?' As Jyot
frowned, Niki swept her right palm, capturing the array of spice, silk
and sweet shops all around. 'I know someone who drives in from
Manhattan to get his nightly paan!'

Jyot shrugged lightly. 'I don't notice these things.'

Niki was pondering how a psychedelic market could be blocked
out from a person's mind when a man fell in step with them. He
loped along Niki's right, weaving around other pedestrians. He was
Hispanic most likely. Niki looked ahead.

'Hola,' the man said.

She had been mistaken for Latina before, but the man was
attempting a familiarity she didn't like. She ignored him and
kept walking. Before Niki realized anything was amiss, Jyot, with
surprising alacrity, had moved to Niki's right.

The man continued to keep pace with them and, leaning forward,
spoke directly with Niki. 'This woman,' he indicated Jyot with his
right hand, 'your friend?'

They ignored him. The man jumped in front of them. They stalled.
Jyot's arm shot up, like a barrier between Niki and him.

'Tell your friend,' the man hissed, head lowered into them, 'to
stay away from Asha. Not her business, you know.' He pulled back
like a snake retracting. A gash extended upwards from his right
brow. 'Otherwise,' he shrugged elaborately, thumbs hooked in the

loops of his waistband, 'people die in New York every day, no?' His hooded eyes bored into Jyot's and, at that moment, Niki was back in a crowded bus where a sea of men crashed against Nooran and her. She was perspiring, the air cool against her suddenly moist face, her hands clammy within the leather gloves. With a thunder, the 7 train rattled above their heads, drowning all other sounds. The man turned around and coalesced into the crowd.

Niki's breath came rapidly. 'Was that the same man Juanita had chased off that day?'

Jyot nodded stiffly, clutched Niki's upper arm and started to march, propelling her onwards. By the time they reached SAYA, Niki had recovered enough to insist they inform Ms Dixit about the encounter.

'Why worry her more?'

'Worry more?'

'She thinks I am going to jump from one of the office windows or walk into a bus anyway. That's why she asked you to spend time with me, no?'

Niki registered Jyot's sudden willingness to talk, but she shook her head in protest. 'No, I,' she licked her lips, 'am spending time with you to find out more about Mr Malik, you see, for the anniversary write-up on SAYA's founder, which is coming soon … and …'

'You are not very good at lying. You never were,' Jyot said with a tremulous smile.

'And to know your story,' Niki blurted out.

Her fingers brushed Niki's cheek lightly. 'Come, let's make tea.'

'But … but … that man threatened you!'

'Did he?'

Jyot was either being strangely cocky or characteristically wooden.

'I am not afraid of him,' she said in her straightforward manner. 'You live in Manhattan, and you've been in the city for less than six months. Jackson Heights is a khichri of the world, and I have lived here for thirty years. I have seen men like that – they know to talk.'

Niki was unconvinced. She glanced in the direction of Ms Dixit's office, which was vacant, and resolved to catch her later as Jyot marched stiffly in the direction of the pantry.

She put a pan with water to boil. Was she overreacting? Jyot's unruffled demeanour was calming. If she didn't bludgeon her with demands to hear her story, would Jyot perhaps share something of her life? As Oonagh had said during one of their coffee conversations, 'Maybe you're approaching it the wrong way, Niki?'

'What do you mean?' Niki had frowned.

'Maybe,' Oonagh swirled the leaf pattern atop her cortado, 'your father was interested in Jyot's story in order to get to know the person behind that story, to learn the trajectory of her life since the day their lives forked in different directions.'

As Jyot watched the pan, Niki pounded a couple of green cardamom seeds to add to it.

'Jyotji, you said these people talk much. Right after 9/11, with the violence against South Asians, what did people say?' The YouTube video was on Niki's mind. It was worrisome that a decade and a half later, a teacher in an international private school in New York, admittedly the most UN of all world cities, felt the need to discuss it in class. And Mehar said that a boy occasionally called out 'Osama!' to Leyla.

'Against those who wear a turban. Like Mr Singh, the terrorist?'

'What was SAYA's response?'

'Mr Malik said it was lack of awareness which was behind the discrimination. He made a presentation to share with schools, community centres, so on. But the hate crimes did not stop. People started to say that SAYA and Mr Malik, needed to help spread awareness about Sikhs and how Sikhs were different from Muslims. But...' She added tea leaves to the boiling water and lowered the flame. 'Mr Malik was unconvinced. He felt that would be equal to saying that attacks against Muslims were okay.'

Niki listened, her brow furrowed. The encounter with the pimp seemed to have lifted the gate of some dam in Jyot...

'Sikh men put stickers of the US flag on their turbans, but they were still targeted by those who thought a turban meant Taliban. The leaders of the Sikh community said that the ignorance had to be tackled head on and that Mr Malik's Sufi response wasn't the answer.'

'What did you think?'

'Go home, terrorist!'

Niki practically jumped.

'If your daughter hears this at school, what would you do?'

'Uh … I don't know. Take up the matter with school authorities, I guess.'

'Would you tell them that the "terrorist" has no home to go back to?'

'Huh?'

'Say you are a white Amreekan and I am a brown man with a turban, a terrorist to you. But this terrorist left his home because he was told there was no place for him there. Where does this man find a home? Where he can live without being the "other" who is always suspect? What if you had spent all your life being shunted out of homes because what you called home kept changing its conditions for residency?'

Jyot added milk to the brew, enquiring, 'Strong tea, okay?', her capable hands equipped with the routine task. This expressive woman was so removed from the reticent stiff person she had come to know. Niki nodded wordlessly and took two mugs from the rack: 'I heart NY' emblazoned on one, the quintessential Statue of Liberty on the other. 'Jyotji, is that why you left home and came here, to America?'

Jyot stirred the brew with a spoon and replaced the lid on the pan. 'Technically, I left home twice. In '47 and after '84. At the ages of six and forty-four. The first time was because of Partition riots, and the second time because of the anti-Sikh riots. The first time I left my home in Lahore, the second time in Delhi. I was too young to remember the first time, and the second I can never forget.'

She spoke in a steady, emotionless voice. Two cataclysmic events, recounted with telegraphic precision. Niki shivered, as if she had stepped out into the chill. The tea came to a boil and Jyot lowered the flame to simmer.

'Is America home now, Jyotji?'

'It is where I live.'

'Were you,' Niki licked her lips, 'ever attacked here?'

'Yes.' Jyot busied herself with the tea, plucking a strainer dangling from a shelf ahead. 'In Central Park. A boy put a gun to my head. It turned out to be a toy.'

Niki gasped.

'Mr Malik faced abuse too. But he thought like a Sufi, and focused on what is common to all of us, not the differences.' The tea had simmered enough. She turned off the stove, allowed the brew a minute to settle before straining the tea into the cups.

Niki moved the pan and strainer to the sink, and started to clean them. Turning to Jyot, she asked, 'And you? Are you a Sufi too?'

Jyot was sipping her tea already. She must like it piping hot. Niki placed the utensils on a drying rack and wiped her hands on a towel. 'Wait,' she said, 'I have some munchies to go with the tea.' From her purse, she extricated a Ziploc bag of murukku, a crisp batter-fried South Indian snack, and offered it to Jyot. 'My mother-in-law sent it.' Jyot took one. They walked to a row of chairs that lined the wall and sat down, the bag of savouries between them.

Niki started to sip her tea, with alternate bites of a murukku. 'Like it?'

Jyot looked puzzled. Niki indicated the crisp in her hand. 'Tastes like sawdust. Wait, that came out wrong. What I mean is that my tongue can't separate salty from sweet, it's all porridge. I … I've lost that sense of taste. Juanita,' she snorted, 'has wasted so much food on me.'

Jyot's world appeared as bleak as Oliver Twist's gruel, which Niki had first encountered on a winter's day in Chandigarh when the kitchen had been redolent with the fragrance of red carrots caramelized in ghee, simmering in sweetened milk which Nooran had stirred every now and then as she chopped mustard greens for lunch. The world of the starving Oliver had been entirely alien then, but as Niki grew, she learnt that the riotous meals Nooran cooked were soul warming too. When the world was too much for her, Nooran's hands kneaded and stirred, sewed and embroidered, washed and ironed it back to life. Why had Jyot forsaken the respite that cooking could provide?

Niki attempted to resume the pre-murukku thread of their conversation, 'You were saying that Mr Malik was a Sufi.'

'And I am not,' Jyot said. 'To love everyone, you first have to be able to love yourself.' She had finished her tea and was cradling her cup in both hands, sitting upright, looking straight ahead.

'It was a spring day in the park. As I walked, I saw leaves on the mounds of ice on the sidewalks. But the trees were bare as a baby's bottom between a nappy change. Where had the leaves come from? Further ahead, there was a soggy clump. Then it hit me! The melting snow was yielding its autumn harvest. Winter was over, and the earth was rebirthing itself. Every birth is a fresh creation, but it comes from the past, never from a void. If the gun had not been plastic, the winter of my life would have ended. And I would have gone, gladly. Because unlike the park, my past was a void, a cipher, there were no leaves to show. I had neither family nor faith left … you need at least one to live.'

The soliloquy stunned Niki into silence.

Abruptly, Jyot stood up. 'The snack was nice. I'll go finish my work now.' Her hand rested on Niki's head for a brief moment as she whispered something and then walked away.

Too many things had happened too fast, and Niki felt she was in a parallel universe where strange men accosted her and Jyot was protective and fierce, chatty and affectionate, intimate even. She could still feel her fleshy, maternal hand on her cheeks, the way she had parted with that commonplace Punjabi gesture of the elderly, the blessing to 'keep living'.

Niki knew the broad contours of Jyot's story, and yet her work with trauma patients suggested that what burdened Jyot was more than survivor's guilt. But what *was* Jyot's secret that made her one of the living dead?

62
(2015)

✳

THERE WERE THREE knocks on the door. Mehar's signature. Niki opened the door to her daughter and kissed her on the forehead. 'How was school?'

'The usual.' Mehar slid her backpack on the floor and scooped up Jade from the Mandarin chair. The cat registered her protest with variously-pitched meows.

'How was fashion design?' Niki heated the griddle to make dosa as she waited to hear about the extracurricular class Mehar had begged to join.

'Interesting,' she beamed.

The exhaust on full throttle drowned out the HEPA filter purring in one corner and made conversation difficult. Mehar went to freshen up and Niki tested the griddle's readiness by dropping some batter onto it. A sizzle and puff, and it was just right.

After Mehar had finished eating, she cleared the table and rinsed her plate. 'Amma,' she approached the bagh embroidery mounted on the wall, 'can I add my motif to this?'

Niki's eyes opened with undisguised pleasure. 'What did you have in mind?'

Mehar gave a small smile.

'I think Nooran would like that very much.'

Mehar nodded as she retrieved her laptop from the backpack. Jade jumped on the sofa and was stretching out when Mehar crept up on her and growled. The cat emitted an aggrieved meow and jumped away. With a superior look, Mehar explained to her mother, 'When Jade sees me as an alpha cat, she defers to me.'

'I'm impressed,' Niki grinned. Her phone rang. It was Mr Levy.

'Yes, I had a word with the building manager,' he informed Niki. 'Apparently, the matter is already with the board because this particular resident has made other complaints about other residents earlier. A case of a sensitive nose,' he grunted. 'The board believes the nose is her concern, not the building's.'

'Right,' Niki said, feeling a weight lift off her.

'I think you should just ignore her.'

'I will, Mr Levy, as long as my husband and I are not harassed with more emails.'

'As I said, the manager has confirmed they will handle the matter. Really, if the problem is with that resident's nose, then she needs to deal with it instead of complaining about others. I like spicy food, you know, but some people can't manage it – it's their problem entirely.'

Niki's ears pricked up. 'So she *has* complained about food?'

'No, but between us, what *is* a mothball smell? But don't worry, just ignore her.'

'And you'll take care of it?'

'Oh yes.'

'Excellent, thank you, Mr Levy. Have a good day!'

Just ignore her.

She got busy with preparations for dinner. Soaking a ball of tamarind in water, adding turmeric and slit green chilli, she set the pan to boil. Mehar came back to tap on her shoulder.

'See,' Mehar held up a square of black cloth on which a large golden sun was embroidered in long stitches, the rays emanating over a quarter of the circumference. 'I made it in my fashion design class. Ms Salvatore said we will try embroidery over the next few lessons.'

'*Niiice*,' Niki nodded, as she washed rice under running water and glanced at the cloth.

'It's a *mo-teef*.' Mehar watched her mother.

Niki placed the pan of rice in the pressure cooker. 'Of what?'

'What do you think?' Mehar stepped back and displayed the cloth.

Niki stood with her palms on her waist and studied the pattern. 'It's a sun, a grand sun, going by its size,' she grinned. 'And it's a work-in-progress.'

'And?' Mehar prodded.

As Niki scrunched her mouth, Mehar pointed with her eyes to the mounted bagh embroidery. 'This is a practice run. I thought I would add a similar motif to Nooran's bagh. The light of a grand sun. Or an atom bomb! You did say Nooran had the radiance of a thousand suns.'

Niki glanced from her daughter to the embroidered cloth, scanning the different motifs woven in over the decades. When Nooran was once embroidering in her room and Niki had been sitting there doing her homework, they had talked about a neighbour who was pregnant again, striving for a son. Nooran said she never understood why men were the ones from whom the family line supposedly descended. If one were to track it, then all mankind would trace its way back to that first mother. Imagine: each person linked by their umbilical cord to their mother who linked back to her mother. The umbilical cord would terminate with each male offspring, continuing only with each female offspring. A woman, therefore, carried within her the memory of all mothers before her.

Niki reached for the air around her daughter with both hands, curling them as she tucked them to the sides of her head.

63
(2015)

✳

IT WAS A bracing, radiant morning, the blue sky annealed with
sunshine. The ice was thawing, exposing clumps of dried London
plane leaves, perfectly preserved, crisp even. And shoots in the park!
Tender greens, spiralling tree trunks, neon spindles decorating shrubs,
tight-fisted brown buds, purple crocuses, pink cherry blossoms – such
joy! At Strawberry Fields, Niki saw a man walk down the pathway,
arms outstretched, a humungous smile on his face, as if greeting an
old friend. She knew that look; of people reacquainting themselves
with once-familiar greenery that had disappeared from their lives
in the developing world, bulldozed to make way for glass and
chrome high-rises, their surroundings shrouded with dust that had
sedimented upon the leaves of the few remaining trees, concocting
a new colour: dust-green. Tourists flocked to Central Park as if to
reunite with a lost love.

She was approaching Bethesda Terrace when her phone rang.
Hopping on spot she retrieved it – it was Ms Dixit – and answered.
As she heard the SAYA director speak, Niki's blood ran backwards.
Her whole body was coalescing into the pit of her stomach, which

was descending, descending, as if there was no bottom. She heard herself mumble something, the caller signed off, her hand was clammy and the pond ahead swam up to her—

'Are you all right?' An anxious face peered at her. 'You better sit down.' A hand grabbed her elbow, guiding her to a bench. Niki sank down, eyes glued to the tarmac where a child's mitten lay. The legs of the nearby benches were freshly painted – when had that happened?

'Are you okay?' A kindly creased face appeared. 'Water?' it asked.

Niki waved a reassuring hand, 'I'm fine.' The man hesitated, nodded, then resumed his jog in the direction of Bethesda. But Niki was on a highway, cradling Nooran's head in her lap, a pool of blood radiating outwards. Ms Dixit's voice replayed in her mind. 'Jyot is in the hospital. She was attacked with a knife last night. She's lost a lot of blood, and suffered severe trauma. It looks grim. She's at Elmhurst Hospital, Queens.'

=

Ms Dixit rubbed her forehead with her right thumb and forefinger repeatedly, as if easing out some throbbing pain. Anxiety shrouded her slim frame like a heavy overcoat. 'The doctor,' she pursed her mouth, 'is not very hopeful. Massive internal bleeding, you see. She called your name several times. So, we thought that perhaps you might like to sit by her side in case she regains consciousness.'

Niki reached out to touch her hand and the next instant, the two women were embracing each other and there were tears running down Niki's cheeks.

Sheila walked down the corridor with a plastic bag. 'I brought some food. You need to eat,' she said to Ms Dixit, who had been at the hospital since midnight. A 911 call had been placed around 10 p.m. last night, and Jyot was wheeled into the hospital soon after. A terrified Asha had accompanied her. What Ms Dixit had been able to glean from the girl was that she had been at home with her mother when the mother's boyfriend had arrived and asked her to get dressed. Her grandmother was away catering a party in New Jersey. A scared Asha had snuck out to Jyot's apartment to seek refuge. It was then that the pimp had caught up. He had reached the door before Jyot could bolt it, brandishing a knife at her to get out of the way since Asha was hiding behind her. Jyot had refused, threatened him. The man had been drunk and lunged at her, stabbing her abdomen. As Jyot had fallen bleeding to the ground, the man had fled with Asha's mother. Meanwhile, Asha's hysterical screaming had alerted their other neighbours, one of whom had dialled 911.

Jyot was a ghost, white as the sheet on which she lay, the hospital's vivid green gown an affront almost. Tubes sprung out of her, an IV bag dripped some colourless liquid into her, but the body, out of which radiated the pipes, was creased like a walnut, frail as a seed without a casing. Niki knew not to think or feel as she dredged up the old memory of how to conduct herself as a robot, first in a courtroom and now in a hospital. Arjun was travelling, so she texted Aruna to see if she was free. Niki wanted to stay beside Jyot for as long as possible.

A nurse walked in, adjusted valves and dials on the tubes, plucked up a clipboard from the raised table to Jyot's left, wrote, nodded at Niki – 'Let me know when she wakes up' – and left the room.

Niki's phone lit up. Aruna was in a presentation. She then messaged Oonagh. A low thrum pervaded the room, perhaps from all those machines approximating bodily functions for the patient who lay still as silence. The chemical smell of hospitals, astringent, antiseptic, laced her nostrils and throat. Outside the room, hospital staff dressed variously in white, sea green and pink were a steady stream, disrupted occasionally by a flurry of feet and the trundle of a trolley.

Jyot had had a laparotomy within minutes of arrival at the hospital. But the doctor had said it was a 'penetrating trauma' to her abdomen, which the surgeon operated immediately to stem the bleeding.

Niki's phone lit up. Oonagh could check on Mehar and stay with her till Niki reached home. 'No worries. Smiley emoticon.' Niki messaged back her thanks. The door opened and Sheila beckoned her wordlessly. Niki stepped out. An NYPD cop introduced himself and confirmed that Niki was with Jyot the morning she had been threatened. Then he showed her a photograph to corroborate if that was indeed Mercedes' pimp. Niki nodded. Asha had earlier confirmed that the man who stabbed Jyot was the same person.

'He has fled, but we will find him,' the cop asserted. 'Ma'am,' he nodded and excused himself.

Sheila and Niki stepped back into the room. Jyot's eyes were open. Sheila hurried to the bed. 'Jyotji,' she whispered, 'Jyotji!'

Her eyeballs were static and, to Niki, Jyot appeared to be in a distant place. Sheila, meanwhile, was almost draped over the hospital bed.

'Jyotji, Niki is here. Niki – you were asking for her. Niki's here.'

Jyot's eyes came alive. Sheila grabbed Niki's arm and tugged her forward. Jyot's mouth pulsed soundlessly like a fish. 'Yes,' Sheila urged, 'we are listening.' Again, Jyot opened her mouth; again, she mouthed something inaudible.

The person lying prone in bed was even more ancient and distant than the one Niki had found in the frigid apartment some months ago. This was parchment over bones; the woman Jyot had vanished.

'S-say something, Niki,' Sheila urged.

'Jyotji,' the words came unstuck. Niki's hand was at Jyot's face, feeling the dried-up skin. As she caressed it, she felt Jyot press her face into the cup of her palm. She breathed her name. Niki bent her head down. 'Yes,' she nodded, 'I am here.'

Jyot raised her right hand and rested its quivering fingers on Niki's shoulder, lighter than a fall leaf. Sheila watched from the other side of the bed, her mouth grim. Jyot whispered again, an index finger pointed to herself.

'Say something? You want to say something,' Sheila said.

Jyot's gaze fixed on Niki.

Sheila glanced from Jyot to Niki. 'You want to tell Niki,' her manner like that of an adult articulating a child's telegraphic bits. She retreated to a chair near the door.

Niki sat on the edge of the bed and held Jyot's hand. Amidst the thrum of the hospital equipment, Jyot started to speak softly. Niki leaned in to listen.

XIX
(1984)
Jyot

64
(1984)

THE MOB WOULD arrive at my doorstep. Satwant, my neighbour, said the attackers knew which houses belonged to Sikhs. They had been supplied with electoral rolls to guide them through the colony.

I barricaded the doors, did not switch on any lights, pretended like no one was at home. But the mob knew I had no man to protect the house. The news of Jeet's murder had flashed through the block like the strident emergency lights of an approaching ambulance. To that were added stories of other murders, each more macabre than the other. In Block 32, the mob had burnt an infant on a stovetop. In the market, they had lined up Sikhs, doused them in white powder and watched them crackle like Diwali sizzlers. So many men shaved their beards and top knots, the drains clogged with hair. Frantic folks ventured to the police station, only to discover the policemen had vanished. It was each man to himself.

Was that how Father had felt? I didn't remember him, but I could picture him: a tall, bearded, turbaned Sikh. Had he looked out on to a night such as this? The sky obscured by a pall of smoke? The air hissing with hatred? Had his hand faltered as he had handed out the opium pellets to his daughters? And when he lopped off the heads of his family? He could as easily have killed himself and gone to his death. Why not?

As I debated what to do, I remembered a story Bapuji would tell us after his evening prayers. When the tenth guru was battling the mighty Mughal army from inside the Anandpur Fort, his eldest son asked to be excused so he could drink some water before entering the battlefield. The guru denied his request; duty before everything else, he said. The son never returned from the battlefield.

Did the guru think of him when he was alone in Machhiwara? Did he think about how he could have let his son drink water, and perhaps he would have survived? Water could save lives. I taught oral rehydration to young illiterate mothers. In the harsh summer months when heat rose from the road and birds died on branches and children suffered diarrhoea, water saved lives. Six teaspoons of sugar, half a teaspoon of salt, one litre of boiled and cooled water.

A dense crackle filled the air. My spine stiffened. Raucous shouts floated through. I tried to listen. Shots rang out. The police! Yes, they had finally arrived. Late as always, as all Hindi movies showed us, the police arriving when the hero had sorted out the villain. Shouts rang out. 'Khoon ka badla khoon! Blood for blood! Sikhs are traitors! Kill the traitors!' No, the police had failed even the Hindi film test. It was the mob, bloodthirsty and unstoppable.

When all else failed, it was right to resist. In the woods of Machhiwara, even as he addressed his beloved friend, the guru knew that. Alone, having lost his family and his army, he wrote a letter to the mighty Mughal emperor Aurangzeb. Zafarnama, he called it: the epistle of victory. Down but not out. When I heard the story, I understood why Father had not killed himself with the rest of our family. He was a Sikh, a follower of the guru, and it was his duty to resist wrongdoing.

I made up my mind.

Dinner was early. I made choori. Thick wholewheat rotis, which I tore into bites, with a mound of clarified butter and generous amounts of jaggery and mixed it all together in a steel bowl. With my right hand, I kneaded and massaged the mixture, threading the ghee and sugar into the roti's texture, the aroma taking me back to when my children were babies. When he sulked because he didn't like the food; when she shook her head because she wasn't hungry; when she sought refuge in my lap; when he stamped his foot in anger – choori was the magic that never failed. I would take Niki in my lap, feeding my firstborn with my hand, watching the tiny mouth work the sweet morsels, her lips glistening with ghee. Now Niki was twelve, a woman almost, with dimpled cheeks and skin like butter. My stomach flooded with acid. Almost a woman. To the mob, she would be meat, flesh to be ravaged. My mouth disappeared in a firm line.

Then, I fed them all by hand. Laali was the only one who was happy, oblivious to the smoke pervading the air, the shrieks that rent it periodically, the heaviness in our hearts. Niki knew. Niki saw it in my eyes as I fed her, lingering to caress her hair and cheek. I suggested the children get some sleep. Veer wanted to stay up with me and guard our home. Soni asked if they could watch some TV with the volume very low? Niki, her mouth quivering, took Laali from my arms and cradled him to sleep. The others followed her to bed. In time, they slumped over. I arranged their bodies, smoothed down their clothes, patted their hair, kissed each one of them in turn.

'Khoon ka badla khoon se leynge!' The cries were getting closer. My children lay quietly. Undisturbed, I worked in the yard. It is said that after witnessing the unending horror of Partition, the rivers of Punjab said, 'Enough!' They swelled up and offloaded all that had been dumped within them on the scarred plains, washing away the bloodstained soil, the rotting carcasses, the burnt dwellings, the dried fields, the detritus of inhumanity. Water was a force that the divided people on both sides hadn't reckoned with.

A slashing sounded so close, I could feel the air ring. Any minute now. I looped Jeet's turban around my neck several times. I gazed at my children. It had been an hour now since they lay down reluctantly. I swallowed a fat white capsule. Four of those I had powdered into the choori for the children's dinner. Five minutes. After that it would be too late.

Wood ripped close by. I mounted the steps to the first floor, which we had just finished constructing – one bedroom, an attached bathroom, a balcony. The plan was to give it to Niki, who needed time and space to study. Soni could share it with her. The girls' floor, Niki had beamed.

At the balcony, I opened the door a sliver. Sure enough, my neighbours were burning. Fires ringed their block like the whole community was the demon Raavan who had to be burnt down. A thunderous noise erupted below. The wood door splintered. Like some viscous liquid, the mob poured into the courtyard, bodies packed tight like at a free performance. Eyes scanned our two-storeyed house, envious, hate-filled, lusty. *Steel glinted off the light of flame torches as cries resounded. 'Come out, come out, we know you are inside! We will rape your daughters, kill your men and avenge the death of our leader!'* The mass surged towards the ground floor door. Now!

I threw the doors open, grabbed the pail of water from the balcony floor and flung it out onto the courtyard. A few faces turned up at the sight, others still surging forward, while some shuffled their feet awkwardly, their faces puzzled. Murder on their minds, they were mindless to the reality on ground. As the first drops from the shower of cascading rain from the bucket splattered to the ground, a hissing arose. It became a steam cloud, trapping the horde in its stinging vapours. The smell of rotten eggs filled the air, overcoming the thick odour of smoke outside. The cries of the horde turned into shrieks as the men hopped, thrashed and attempted to escape the courtyard which they had minutes before eagerly occupied. I shut the door.

I walked down the stairs and approached the bed. Outside, the contents of Tiwari's delivery van lay on the courtyard floor like a second sheet. Colourless, odourless, until … my hospital rubber gloves, rubber apron and rubber shoes had been handy. The hospital cleaning agent was essential while cleaning utensils and equipment. It was powerful enough to get rid of all possible germs and infections.

One had to be careful with it though; under the right conditions, it could be worse than fire. Such was its nature that the hospital staff very cautiously added acid to a large quantity of water, whereas I had added a bucket of water to four large canisters of sulphuric acid. It was only ten per cent concentration, but it would suffice. Water was a force. The mob need not rot in hell – it could burn in my yard.

I climbed into bed, easing myself between my four children, two on each side. Slipping the yellow turban from around my neck, I shook it out before draping it across all of them. Then I stretched my arms out, right upper arm snug with Laali, the left embracing Soni, while my fingers curled around and held Niki and Veer. The aroma of my children filled me: Laali's ghee-smeared mouth, Niki's Nivea-creamed face, Soni's jaggery-sweet breath, Veer's mustard-oiled hair. My skin enveloped them.

I fanned out and drew them in, embracing them tightly. One by one, I poured my babies back into me.

Epilogue
(2015)

JYOT HAD FINALLY divulged her secret, but her body had betrayed it to Niki the day a fire had broken out in the building adjacent to SAYA. Niki realized she was sobbing. When she wiped her face, it was wet, like she had dunked it in a bucket of water. At some point, Jyot's voice became whispery. Niki put her ear so close to Jyot's mouth that she heard every breath. It reminded her of when Mehar was a baby and Niki would place an index finger below her nose as she slept to confirm that she was breathing. Niki's lower back ached from bending over. When she became a mother, all the lifting, bending, twisting to get Mehar into her crib, out of her stroller, because she demanded to be carried, had strained her lower back. 'Welcome to the physical toll of motherhood,' her doctor had stated matter-of-factly and recommended yoga.

Then Jyot was quiet for a long time as she studied the ceiling. Niki got off the bed to pace the floor as she kneaded her back. Jyot's breathing became slow and irregular. Sheila called the nurse. She read the clipboard, monitored Jyot's vitals and said, 'I'll call the doctor' as she left the room. Sheila caught up with her at the door.

331

With a glance back, the nurse said, 'I don't think there's much time now.'

From the other side of the bed, Sheila exchanged a look with Niki. Jyot's body was forgetting to either inhale or exhale, an intermittent puff signalling the breath. Her eyelids started to sink.

'Sheeeila!' Niki screamed.

'Jyotji!' Sheila cupped her face, stroking it.

As the elderly woman's eyes closed, she murmured. Sheila hurried out of the room yelling for a doctor, nurse – for help, for them to hurry.

A gasp. The hand Niki cradled was limp. She strained for that erratic puff. Nothing but silence. *Finished*. And in her mind were Jyot's last words.

'*Keep living*.'

=

Niki was in a state of dazed fatigue as she left the hospital. The emotional upheavals of the day, coupled with her physical exertions, had left her in a strange limbo. In the subway station and on the train ride home, she was hyper aware of her surroundings – the yorkie with a pink clip, the man asleep with his mouth open, the breast augmentation ad with a 'This oppresses women!' sticker slapped on it – but she processed everything as if from within a bubble. She felt like a spectator to her own life, observing Niki go through the motions of exiting the turnstile at 86th Street, emerging onto Central Park West, waiting for the White Man to blaze to cross Columbus Avenue. All the while, Jyot's story played on a loop like a recurring nightmare. As the traffic light looked set to change, she stepped onto the road and a hurricane whizzed by. Niki gasped and stiffened as the cyclist flew down the avenue. A second longer and she would have ended up in a hospital again. In her apartment building, she exited the elevator to the left to a dead end. She stared at the wall awhile before recalling where her apartment was located on the floor.

The trauma of Jyot's story was still with Niki as she let herself in at home. Oonagh came hurrying from the walkway and enveloped her in a fierce hug. Mehar was finishing her homework at the dining table and waved to her. Oonagh offered to make her a cup of tea and talk. Or a shot of whisky?

'Thanks, but no,' Niki sighed. 'I need to get Jyot's story down before I forget. It's in bits and fragments and all scrambled up. You've had a long day. Get some rest and we'll get coffee soon. Or get drunk. Or both.'

Oonagh eyed Niki intently. 'You're sure you're fine?'

Niki nodded. Shrugged.

'Arjun back tomorrow?' Work had taken Arjun to the London office for a week. 'Promise you'll call me if anything, hmm, whatever, comes up?' When Niki promised, she whispered, 'Wash 'em eyes,' in her ear and left.

'Bathroom,' Niki shouted in Mehar's direction and hurried down the hallway. Once inside, she perched on the edge of the bathtub.

Her mouth trembled, her eyes filled and she exhaled and bit her lower lip. The tears started afresh. Jyot was dead, but the physical death had only followed her spiritual death from long ago. Underneath the sorrow was a trace of exhilaration. Nine months after pursuing her, after being alternately rebuffed and embraced, after unending uncertainty over whether she would finish Papa's book, she had finally won Jyot's trust. And Jyot was finally free, Papa would be glad to know that. Jyot had ended her silence and Niki could tell her story.

Later, she splashed cold water on her face and eyes. Her head swimming with images, Niki walked to the sideboard on which sat the wooden temple with its images of Guru Nanak and Guru Gobind, Durga and a Ganesha idol. She lit a fresh lamp and prayed softly. Then she walked to Mehar with a smile and kissed her forehead. 'Need a snack?'

'I had chips, after strawberries,' her daughter grinned.

In the window facing westward, dusk laced the sky pink and ochre as Niki sat down at her desk and started to write. Her head brimmed with images, her tongue swelled with Jyot's words, but Niki couldn't write. The cursor winked on and on and on. Until Niki browsed to YouTube, put on a rendition of 'Bulleh Shah' by Abida Parveen and poured herself a double shot of Laphroaig.

The next thing Niki knew was that Mehar was switching on the overhead lamp. Night. As she typed, she was vaguely aware of her daughter feeding the cat, helping herself to her favourite dinner, speaking in the background. 'Amma!'

'What?' Niki's head jerked up.

'Dinner – don't you want any?'

'Later. I need to get this done first.'

A plate appeared on her left, and the fragrance of steaming dal filled her nostrils as her daughter's arm slid over her back. 'Amma, you should eat.'

Niki glanced at the computer and looked back at her daughter. 'Do you want me to feed you?' Mehar asked. Niki smiled and dug her face into her daughter's belly.

'I'll eat, and, oh heavens! It's 11 p.m. – you need to be in bed!'

'Yes, yes, I'll read in bed, and before you ask, I have brushed already!'

Niki rolled a roti in her left hand and continued typing with one hand. She spooned dal into her mouth every now and then. By midnight, she was done. Her shoulders were stiff. She stood up, inhaled deeply, stood on her toes, then slowly slumped, letting her arms hang loose, her stomach deflated.

She tiptoed to her daughter's room. A half-moon hung outside the window, lighting up the bed. Niki extricated the Percy Jackson book from Mehar's hands, straightened her head and tucked the duvet around her. Plucking Eddy the elephant from the floor, she arranged the soft toys around the bed. There were vague aches in her body from hunching over through the day, her eyes felt dry, and her mouth had the raw, acidic feel of having thrown up. She watched

Mehar's chest rise and fall gently as she breathed, and it filled her with gratitude. Then she slipped into bed, aligning her body with her daughter's, cradling her with an arm. She had not pulled the blind, and watched their soft shadows on the wall across as she breathed in her daughter and slept.

⸻

Ten days after Jyot died, it was Mother's Day. The manufactured enthusiasm around it had begun building right after Easter, the proximate Labour Day being good for plain vanilla deals only, without the toppings of celebratory love. It was also Jyot's Day. The end of the ten-day period of mourning, time to bid her a final farewell at her bhog ceremony. Niki couldn't help reflecting on the irony.

An unsung mother being seen off the earth on the one day when mothers were being seen by their offspring on mandate. A Spartan life was being commemorated on a day when everything – furniture, apparel, cars, restaurant meals, the entire retail machinery – was spitting deals at guilt-ridden offspring.

At the 86th Street subway station, Niki stood away from the platform edge, the display informing her of the C train's arrival in two minutes. What a life Jyot Kaur had led: bookended by violence, which spared no one in her life but her; shrouded in silence, which consumed her with each breath. The Mahabharata said that the greatest wonder of all was that death struck daily and people continued to live as if they were immortal. Yet Jyot Kaur, after returning from the dead, baited death every day without success. Another great wonder, Vyasa would concede.

Violence begets violence was a homily, but Jyot's life had been a seven-decade illustration. She had broken that cycle by sacrificing her life for another child. Perhaps that was what kept her alive despite her attempts to take her life? That she had a price to pay for one terrible decision? Which might not have been hers to make, conditioned as it was by the spiral of violence in which she was just another unwitting player? The hand that fed Jyot's children the choori – was it hers or her father's? Or was it the guru's? In which case, how far back did it go?

The train boomed in the distance as it barrelled its way through the tunnel. Niki hoisted her bag on her shoulder and stood in line. In life, Jyot Kaur had been silent. In death, she had spoken. And thus, she lived on – in the life she had given Asha and the story she had entrusted Niki to tell.

At the gurdwara, the priest sang, 'Mittar pyaare nu, haal mureedan da kehna'. Niki had suggested that particular hymn. 'To my beloved friend, of my plight do tell.' It held a resonance for Jyot as she had learnt from her story. Jyot had sought refuge in it, and like the guru, she had sacrificed her life for a greater good. 'May she find the peace she was due,' Niki prayed with closed eyes as she remembered Jyot's four children: Niki, the eldest; Veer, the second; Soni, the third; Laali, the youngest. If there truly was a heaven, Jyot would finally be with her children.

At the end of the ceremony, they distributed karah parshad, sweet roasted semolina pudding blessed by prayers. Niki took it in her cupped hands and sat down cross-legged on the carpeted floor with the SAYA staff. Its saccharine smell, warmth in her palms, buttery descent down her throat, filled her with fond memories of previous gurdwara visits with Dadima and Papa, Nooran refraining from any such exertions. Afterwards, Niki went around the holy book, then requested an extra helping of the parshad for Mehar.

Juanita hugged her and told her that with SAYA's help, she had initiated proceedings to legally adopt Asha – and applied to change her name to Asha Jyot Singh.

True to her name, Jyot had passed the light on.

Later, as Niki exited the subway station near her home, a man on the sidewalk swung his arms and proclaimed, 'Hell's freezing over! Did ya hear me, hell's freezing over! We're headed straight for winter, no spring, no summer for the sinners! Hell's freezing over!' He had a sense of rhythm, both in words and body, as he lilted and tilted synchronously. Some people passing him acknowledged his glum prediction with a thumbs up or by nodding.

With the heavy unseasonal rain and the grey sunless day, it did appear as if summer had decided to take a break. The winter had been long and hard, and was in danger of becoming a bad habit. An Indian summer – that was what Niki needed. Not the balmy heat the ignorant British swooned about, no. A summer when perspiration dripped more consistently from pores than dry taps. That summer meant the lightest of muslin, sweetest of mangoes, blinds of bamboo, bare feet, cool floors, siestas and stories…

At home, Niki deposited the parshad in the fridge, rubbed the cat's chin, washed her hands and walked to her desk. She had placed Jyot Kaur's story in the top drawer, along with her writerly toolkit of ruled and plain notepads, coloured pencils, clips and ball pens. She pulled the blind down.

She sat down, opened her laptop and started to write.

<hr />

There was a sharp smell of fennel. Her eyes opened a slit. She could see emerald. Her eyes felt heavy-lidded, but she forced them open. Jade crouched on the edge of the table, studying her. Next to Jade, partially obscured by her black fur, glinted a wooden peacock in splendid colours of purple, red, gold. Above the cat, a steaming cup of tea hovered in the air. 'The way to begin is to begin' read the inscription on the cup. Mehar's gift for Niki from her Boston school trip, picked from Eleanor and Franklin D. Roosevelt's family home in Hyde Park in upstate New York. The rising vapours obscured a grinning visage.

'Good morning, Sleeping Beauty!'

Niki smiled. The blind's edges showed that the sun was up. How much up though? She had slept late, but at what time exactly she didn't know. At some point, she ran out of words and stumbled to Mehar's bed where, shoving the tiger, lion and elephant aside, she had reached for her daughter and snuggled in. She could feel a crick in her neck, the result of heavy sleep in a body that had lain like a sack. Tea would be perfect. She slid up, back against the cushion and the headrest, and reached for the teacup with both hands.

'What time did you sleep?' Mehar asked.

Niki shrugged and took a sip of the sweet, strong, fragrant tea. Perfect.

Mehar walked to the window. 'Stay,' she said as she made for the blind.

'You talking to me or the cat?'

The blind rolled up. A golden orb—

'Look!' Mehar's arms were extended in a dramatic fashion, beckoning her gaze to the exhibit.

A dazzling sun glinted off black cloth. Mehar's craft project mounted on a frame sat on the window sill. Niki smiled, and Mehar grinned in the manner of children who, when revealing something unexpected to their parents, will do so in the manner of innovators.

'It's gorgeous,' Niki said.

'Would Nooran like it?' Mehar asked.

'She would tell me to learn from you!'

A click sounded, and the front door opened. Mehar whirled around and scrambled down the hallway.

'Appa! You're home early!'

Niki's smile grew. She heard Arjun tell their excited daughter that he was able to catch an earlier flight. The sounds of bags being deposited, shoes being taken off, Mehar's chatter filtered through. Niki gazed at the cat who looked solemnly back, emerald eyes in a coal-black body. The next instant, Arjun and Mehar were in bed with her, Arjun's chin bristly as he kissed her. 'No tea for me?' he mock complained to Mehar, who had launched into the stories of her exploits of the week. Niki passed him the teacup. She nestled against her husband, inhaling his familiar smell, and watched her daughter's hands fly in an excited retelling.

She would complete Papa's book, the father-daughter collaboration that he always wanted. She had found her story. Rather, the story had found her. The story that had been waiting to be born, Mehar's twin, twelve years in the making. No, it was many years in the making – decades, aeons – for the narrative thread stretched all the way back to that feisty woman of the Mahabharata whom Niki had always felt she'd known. Now she knew why. She was connected to Draupadi and to Heer as she was to Dadima and Nooran and Roop and Mehar, and to Jyot and to all the women who came before and who would come after, the umbilical cord never ever severed.

In her mind, a page turned, revealing the dedication of the book she now knew she could write.

For Nooran, the radiance of a thousand suns.

Acknowledgements

SOMETIMES, TO GRAPPLE with the present, we have to engage with the past. I don't mean a rehash. What I have in mind is a close scrutiny of tradition, an exploration of homilies, a deep dive into myths so we can parse the narrative for *our* stories and question the status quo.

Why, for instance, after seventy plus years of Partition, have we not been able to lay the ghosts to rest? In 1947, when women's bodies became the battlefield, did that template of sexual violence derive from our foundational epic? Does the fact that women bore the brunt of that violence echo in this time of #metoo?

In India, the past is forever intruding upon the present. So why not reckon with that past, I asked myself, and invited the dead to populate my novel. The history of independent India has literally been 'his' story. This novel attempts to reconstruct the (hi)story and add to it the missing, suppressed, and absent stories of women.

I have wrestled with this novel for many many years. To rephrase that famous dialogue from the film *Damini*, 'Draft pe draft, draft pe draft, draft pe draft likhti gayi, par manuscript nahin mila.' Until it finally did. Phew! There are so many people and writers and books to thank that I will inevitably fall short. All of them have a special place in my heart, even as space constraint allows me to name only a few.

I am so lucky to be part of the writing community at The City College of New York, where the faculty and students have given me a second home. Thanks to my brilliant professors: Emily Raboteau, Mikhal Dekel and Michelle Valladares. To Misti Duvall and Minoshka Narayan, for painstaking reading, valuable feedback, and friendship. To Ashis Nandy, whose books I devour for their psychological acuity. To Vyasa, for the original; and to the many other fine writers for their retellings of the Mahabharata. To Guru Gobind Singh, for the rousing Zafarnama and a life that was its very illustration. To the Sufi poets of Punjab, and Urdu shayars of the subcontinent, who nourish me daily.

I am grateful to the entire team at HarperCollins India and my editors, especially Prema Govindan and Udayan Mitra, for shepherding this book. My gratitude and much affection to Gulzar Saab. His lyrics, films and poetry have inspired me since I first encountered them while watching a late-night show of *Mausam* at the age of eight. (Not age appropriate, perhaps, but it enabled me to read and see beyond my years – some gift!)

I grew up amidst women who made me realize that Draupadi was alive and living amongst us. For a girl child in Punjab, there couldn't have been better role models. My parents have always been my inspiration and this book is dedicated to them. As it is to my feline assistant who brings her best game to the writing job daily: purrs, nibbles and naps on the laptop. My husband Prasanna is the first reader of all my books. (If you are married to a writer, you will appreciate how volatile the terrain is at feedback time.) Twenty-eight years and seven books later, I concur with Bullah: '*Tere ishq nachaya...*' To my daughter, Malvika, who frequently suffers grouch-mode-Mama struggling with writing, I offer all my jubilation! And the wisdom that we are the ones who shape our narrative. The power of the story lies in the hands of the storyteller.

Dig them out, dust them off, dress them up ... imagine them, grow them, tell them.

Our stories.